AGEL∃SS

AGELƎSS

A NOVEL

PAUL INMAN

INKSHARES

This is a work of fiction. Names, characters, organizations, places, events, and incidents are either products of the author's imagination or are used fictitiously.

Published by Inkshares, Inc., San Francisco, California
www.inkshares.com

Edited and designed by Girl Friday Productions
www.girlfridayproductions.com

Cover design by Marc Cohen
Cover photograph © Brykulskyi/Shutterstock

ISBN: 9781941758618
e-ISBN: 9781941758625
Library of Congress Control Number: 2015944041

First edition

Printed in the United States of America

For Kim and Parker,
who let me play with my imaginary friends

2020s
Threat Shuts Down Franklin Institute
First Manned Mission to Mars
Final Government Records Digitalized
Sesame Place Theme Park Closes Due to Deaths
2010s
Meltdown of the Fukushima Nuclear Power Plant
Coast2Coast WiFi - Free For All
Affordable Healthcare Act
Electronic Assistants Emerge
2000s
Barack Obama Becomes America's First Black President
9/11 Attacks on the USA
Y2K
iPod/iPhone/iPad Are Introduced
1990s
World Wide Web Creates True Global Culture
Waco Cult Compound Raided
Columbine Massacre
Oklahoma City Bombing
1980s
CIA Investigates Friendship, SC
Mount St. Helens Erupts
Exxon Valdez Oil Spill
Berlin Wall Falls
Chernobyl Nuclear Disaster

1930s
Great Depression
Hindenburg Disaster
Birth of A. Sartori
War of the Worlds Radio Broadcast Causes Panic
1940s
Pearl Harbor Attacked
Anne Frank Goes into Hiding
Hiroshima and Nagasaki Bombed
Italian/German Eugenics Lab Destroyed
1950s
Segregation Ruled Illegal in U.S.
Castro Becomes Dictator of Cuba
First Modern Credit Card Introduced
Elvis Gyrates on Ed Sullivan's Show
1960s
First Man on the Moon
Woodstock Music Festival
Beatles Become Popular in the U.S.
Martin Luther King Jr. Assassinated
Charles Manson and His "Family" Kill
1970s
Jonestown Massacre
Tangshan Earthquake
Terra-Cotta Army Discovered in China
First Test-Tube Baby Born

"All we have to decide is what to do with the time that is given to us."
–Gandalf the Grey, J. R. R. Tolkien, *The Fellowship of the Ring*

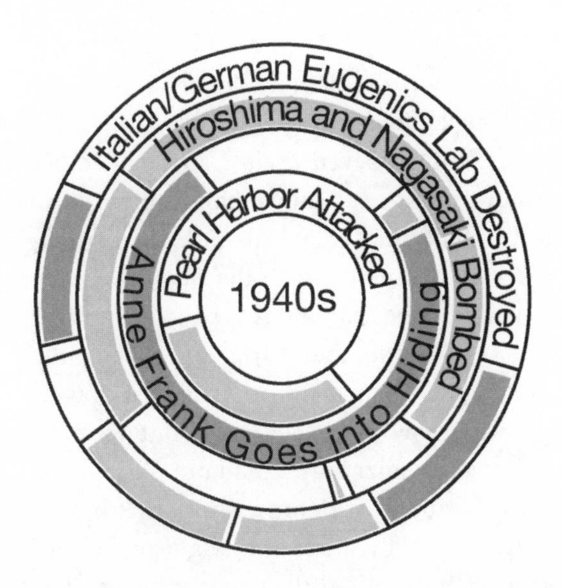

5:23 P.M.

ITALY, 1943

One of the doll's eyes wasn't closing anymore. It hadn't worked properly since the last time it was thrown to the ground. The doll was very plain. Only a small dress covered the grungy body. At one time, the dress would have shown a wonderfully bright-white flower, a cartoonish daisy with a silly smile across the short yellow disk florets, which had probably been a big selling point for the doll. The tattered arm of this relic dangled from the small pale hand of the young girl who was caring for it.

The girl was about nine but could have easily passed for six or seven. She looked disheveled, much like her inanimate counterpart. Her gaunt features showed signs of malnutrition. She had shoulder-length light-blonde hair. At the moment, as with most moments, her hair was a bird's nest of tangles, and it looked as if it hadn't been washed in more than a week. The knotted hair flowed into her face, covering the smoky blue-green eyes, which still had the innocence of youth and the curiosity of a puppy. She wore a teal hospital gown. It wasn't tied in the rear, but the girl paid no mind to this trivial fact. She was too preoccupied with covering her ears with her tiny hands.

The girl was lying on the floor, cradled in the fetal position, screaming a hoarse, panicked shriek to drown out the bleating of the emergency alert sirens. Her attempts proved useless and ineffective. The sirens blared their piercing sounds for more than a minute. All the doctor-men, as her mother had once called them, looked frightened and began packing several documents from the many file cabinets that lined the corridor into garbage bins and tote bags. The young girl didn't understand what was going on, and it frightened her more when the doctor-men began to ignite the paperwork that was savagely shoved into the garbage bins. She tried to keep her wits about her, even through the piercing sirens, but she realized she could not understand the words the doctor-men were using. Not because she wasn't intelligent—she was—but the fact was, she only spoke one language, the language of her mother and her mother's mother. The doctor-men were no longer speaking that language. Now the words they used seemed hard, dirty, and thick. The sirens continued to screech out their unyielding whine, resonating in the deepest cavities of the girl's chest, causing her discomfort that occasionally took her breath away. Each time the girl drew in a lungful of air between her shrieks, it intensified the pain in her chest. During one of these breaths, between the guttural, harsh sounds coming from the men, a familiar word drew the girl's attention.

"Dr. Vogel, das ist alles! Was nun mit der Alessandra? Das Mädchen, das Mädchen! Was mit dem Mädchen?" one of the doctor-men bellowed over the sirens.

Even through the nasty, difficult language, with its heavy accent, she instantly recognized her own name. The man had said "Alessandra." They were speaking about her, perhaps deciding whether or not to help calm her as they had done in the past.

Dr. Vogel made eye contact with Alessandra, who was still in a crumpled mess on the floor. He had only three words for his fellow scientist.

"Nein, verlass' sie."

Even through the language barrier and the earsplitting sirens, Alessandra knew what those words meant. The cold, uncaring deadness of Dr. Vogel's eyes gave it all away. They were going to leave her here to whatever fate came with those sirens. She closed her eyes, began to cry, and, through the sirens, listened to the footsteps of the doctor-men as they stepped over her. She clutched the doll with its grungy dress between her arms and breastbone and wept.

The concerned doctor-man looked down on the small child and considered scooping her limp body into his arms and following his superior into the unknown. She was, after all, the last and best chance that the men had—everything they had worked for during the last four years.

"Los jetzt!" Dr. Vogel barked definitively, snapping the man back into focus. He never looked at Alessandra again.

She lay cradling the ragged doll, which she simply called Bambolina, as the men stepped around and over her small frame. They moved quickly toward the large steel door. Alessandra watched through blurry tears as the last man in the small group paused, throwing one last fleeting glance back at the crying child. After a beat of indecision, he, too, left her alone.

Time stretched as she lay there listening to the sirens wind down into nothingness. The silence was a ghost lingering in the shadows, waiting to break her sanity. In reality, mere seconds had passed.

Alessandra felt a wave of relief sweep over her as she heard a new commotion come from the outer hallway. Maybe the man had stood up to Dr. Vogel and decided to come back for her! In the hallway outside the door, she heard men begin shouting at her former caretakers. This was, yet again, a language that Alessandra couldn't understand. Although similar to the doctor-men's language, it was different enough to tell the two languages apart from each other. Very shortly after, the shooting began. Alessandra heard no more voices from either language. She had decided that if she wanted to live to see her next birthday, she should find somewhere else to be, somewhere safe. She squeezed her eyes shut tightly and drew a slow, calming breath like the doctor-men had taught her to do in order to relax her mind. She exhaled and stood up and scanned the hallway, still shaking but determined to survive.

Alessandra only knew of one safe place here. A place that even the doctor-men didn't know about. And why would they? So many different doctor-men had come and gone in the years since Alessandra had been brought to this small set of underground laboratories. She thought that she was five when she'd first come, but it was hard to remember.

I could have been four, maybe even younger—it was so long ago. I remember they took my parents away. They told me that if I was good, then they could come to visit. I guess I haven't been a good girl.

Alessandra pushed the thought back down to wherever it had come from as she ran lightly down the corridor between what the doctor-men had called Lab A and Lab B. She knew them as the "playroom" and the "yucky room." In the yucky room, the doctor-men used a lot of needles and different masks that scared her. Fortunately, she was going to the playroom. In this room, the doctor-men gave her lots of things to play with, and she could do whatever she liked with these toys. The doctor-men didn't come into this room often, and when they did, they would wear strange suits that covered their entire bodies. It always made Alessandra laugh at how silly they looked. Sometimes, the playroom would light up with funny colors while she was playing, and the toys would melt like ice cream, as if they had been put too close to a hot fire. Alessandra didn't mind too much about that; the doctor-men would always replace the toys soon enough.

It was in the playroom that Alessandra had discovered a loose bolt in a floor panel behind the almost life-size dollhouse. It took her a lot of effort in the beginning to work the bolt loose, but when she succeeded, she found she was able to move the floor panel just enough for her to slide down inside. It was a cozy little retreat. The only issue was all the wires in the crawl space. But Alessandra had spent enough time in this place to carefully move the wires out of the way, creating a little nesting area. She mostly came here at night. Some part of her understood the doctor-men were probably watching her constantly, but she didn't care. She needed her own place, her own space away from the needles, the scary masks, and the other children. It was here that she crept now, feeling more alone and afraid than she ever had with the doctor-men. It wasn't great living here, but they were nice most of the time. She had made a few true friends as the other children trickled in and out of her life, but they were all gone now. As she settled into the small dark space, she began to cry again, making sure to weep silently, until sleep overtook her like darkness takes the day.

9:34 A.M.

WASHINGTON, DC, 2022

The tablet lay on the desk. The file labeled "Case Number It110102" had been open for the last hour. Truth be told, he had been looking through this file for the last thirty-six years. Back then it was a thick folder that was once stored in an authentic filing cabinet. Now, it was nothing more than digital disk space. There were witness reports; photos dating back more than eighty years; and several incident reports, the most recent from about fifteen years ago. He had written that one himself. This was a cold case if there ever was one. The scanned photos in the file—the ones taken before the digital camera age—were grainy, out-of-focus gems. He liked looking at them; they reminded him of his mother, God rest her soul.

He had been with the agency for over forty years, well beyond the years of service recommended for retirement. It was the case, number It110102, that kept him here day in and day out. He had begun his career when he was fresh out of high school, a cool eighteen years old. His uncle had worked for the agency and had talked someone into putting him in the mail room. As a mail boy, he didn't get much in the way of action, so he pursued moving out of the mail room. It took him five long years to pass the battery of examinations that would give him his own desk with a nameplate like his uncle. Today, the new recruits had to have college degrees and participate in a professional trainee program, just to put their lives on the line and earn a nameplate. He was staring at the back of one of those nameplates now, letting his mind wander. Engraved on the front of the plate were two words in large, bold print: "MARK RICHARDS."

Richards had an assignment today, one that the younger brats might call a "diplomatic" assignment. With his advancing age, it seemed to be the only type of assignment he was given anymore. He had to drive to the airport, pick up a package, and hand deliver it to a scuzz. This particular scuzz had been undercover for the better part of the last three years. The scuzz's assignment was to smoke out a ring of foreign weapons smugglers that were in the country and doing very well at their jobs.

As Richards drove to the airport, he went over his mental checklist of items from case It110102, as he did every day. He thought about the eyewitness reports from a young man and a young woman. Richards combed his memory of the past events and relived all of them. A driver behind him honked the car horn. *Oops, green light. Maybe I should leave off the reminiscing,* he thought.

At the airport, Richards quickly signed for the package and then sped away to meet the scuzz at the drop zone. He tried to keep his mind clear and focused on the task at hand, but his total consumption with It110102 had, as his ex-wife would have testified, ruined his ability to fully commit to anything or anyone else. He replayed the events of the day documented in the case file. The girl had walked out first, Chapman behind her. She was smiling—*smiling, for God's sake.* Richards shook his head and fell deeper into the memory. He could still see her light-blonde hair blowing across her youthful features.

Lost in thought, he didn't notice a car pull up behind him a few blocks from where he parked in the terminal's short-term lot. It was a nondescript vehicle, about six to ten years old, maroon in color, with no distinguishing marks.

The pursuer followed at a safe distance behind the company car that Richards drove. His car was an early hybrid. The agency had bought a bunch of them a few presidents back as a cost-cutting measure. Richards thought of this as a diplomatic move, a way for the president to show that he was environmentally conscious, and to sink some money into the, once again, struggling American car companies. Of course, the agency's hybrids had a few upgrades that were more than just your standard leather seats and power windows. They had bigger engines, which could accelerate faster, and also better steering and turning radii for more accurate handling, just to name a few.

Richards was getting close to the drop point. He reached up to his Bluetooth earpiece and tapped it once. There was an answer after the first ring.

"Hi," Richards said in a cheerful voice. "I was wondering if I could get some directions to your shop, please."

"This isn't a shop, bud," the voice on the other end said. "I think you got the wrong number."

"Really?" Richards asked. "This isn't Phil's Greenhouse of Flowers? I ported the number right from the web."

"Flowers?" the voice said. "Nope, sorry. Good luck."

There was a short series of digital beeps in the earpiece as the man disconnected the call. Richards had said the code words to the letter, as he'd been taught. Basically, the conversation had been code for "I am almost to the drop, come alone."

As Richards sat in the light morning traffic, he tried to recall the name of the undercover agent who'd answered the phone. He was fairly certain it was Lucas. He didn't envy the guy; Lucas had spent his whole career undercover. That made it hard to have a normal life. Lucas probably had no immediate family. No wife or kids to come home to at the end of a long day. *Seems like we have more in common than I initially realized,* Richards thought. Right now, Lucas was probably telling the other guys about how he was out of smokes and was just going to take a quick walk to the corner store to grab a pack. There were always inventive ways to get some time to yourself.

The cars ahead of Mark began to move through a blinking red light. He turned left and immediately saw an open spot up the street.

Richards parked across from a small alley on Twenty-First and Pine. He hopped out of the vehicle and grabbed the package, which contained more bugging equipment. The bugs were for phone taps as well as room taps. It was increasingly difficult to tap phones, with technology seeming to change daily. Landlines were all but extinct, and there were apps made just for sniffing out bugs available in all app stores and markets. Luckily, the government had had the foresight to regulate these types of apps in the late 2010s. Room taps were more accessible and yet more difficult because of the amount of information that had to be processed. Computer programs singled out key words, but ultimately a technician had to listen to large amounts of data that could range from what the targets had ordered for lunch to dirty talk with webcam ladies.

As Richards started to cross the street, the man who'd been tailing him pressed his own Bluetooth earpiece, spoke one phrase, and then tapped to hang up.

"Dead or alive?" the man had asked.

The voice on the other end had replied, "Dead."

Richards hurried across the four lanes of traffic, narrowly missing getting smashed by a sports car, and cursed the driver for being an idiot. As he stepped onto the sidewalk on the opposite side of the street, he felt the strange sensation of being watched. Richards paused and bent down, pretending to retie his shoe so that he could scan the immediate area for anyone who looked to be following him. This wasn't his first day on the job, but he had been in la-la land for a lot of his drive. He untied and retied his shoe twice, giving himself plenty of time to look for suspicious activity from the people who were around him. He saw nothing that struck him as out of the ordinary. He thought, *I guess I'm getting spooked. It may be time to really think about retiring.* But he always told himself that, sometimes more than once a day. He scooped up the package under his right arm, feeling it bump the holstered weapon hidden under his jacket, and walked toward the small alleyway. Richards wasn't more than ten feet into the alley when he heard a voice speak up.

"Hold up right there, old man," Lucas demanded. "I was wondering if you had the time."

Without hesitation, Richards replied, "Oh, I've got plenty of time."

More code. Lucas and Richards had never met each other, but they both knew how these things worked. Usually, the dropper was always different, and the drop zone was never the same, so the code words helped determine where and when drops would happen. Mark had read that the last drop Lucas had picked up was right out in front of everyone, on Main Street in the middle of a parade. This one, in a hidden alley in the scummy part of town, should be cake by comparison. But sometimes, cakes weren't very good.

"Place the package on the ground right there," Lucas said, pointing to a spot a few feet to the left of where Richards was standing, "and take your 'plenty of time' back out of my alley."

Oh great, another idiot kid who thinks this is all fun and games, Richards thought as he placed the box on the ground. Before he turned to leave the alley, he asked, "Anything I should tell your parents?" which was more code to ask if there was anything to report to the bosses downtown.

Lucas turned his eyes down to the package that contained the bugs, thought for a second, and shook his head. That second was all the man who'd been trailing Richards needed to step into the alleyway, draw his gun, and fire.

Richards would be fifty-nine years old this year, over forty of those years working as part of the agency. It was safe to say that his instincts were what had kept him alive all this time. Today was no different. As Lucas looked at the package, Richards had noticed—no, *felt* is more accurate—that something was moving quickly and close behind him. Without thinking, Richards jumped to his right behind a small Dumpster, crashing his shoulder into the plaster-covered cinder-block wall. The momentum that carried Richards did a full reversal, and he bounced off the wall and crashed to the ground.

The assassin was spry. He leveled his gun, took a deep breath, and exhaled as he squeezed the trigger.

The firing pin in the handheld weapon shot forward. The point of the pin struck the primer, causing instantaneous ignition, which, in turn, caused the cordite in the bullet casing to ignite from the heat of the primer. The pressure built up behind the projectile and forced it down the bore of the gun, exploding from the barrel in a fiery and deafening eruption of sound and light. Lucas didn't have time to draw a last breath before the first bullet struck him in the chest, ripping through his heart and stopping the eternal thump midpump.

Richards saw these events unfold before his eyes in a fraction of a second. He watched as the assassin changed his shooting stance to fire again while Lucas attempted to pull the gun free of his ankle holster. He saw Lucas take another powerful shot to the chest, his back exploding out from the inertia of the projectile.

Richards had drawn his own gun just after the man had fired the first shot. The assassin watched as Lucas dropped violently down to the ground. *He never had a chance,* Mark thought. The assassin turned and ran out of the alleyway. Richards gave chase but knew that he was outmatched, due to the obvious age difference—the assassin was most likely in his midthirties like Lucas. So he turned and ran toward the company hybrid. This proved to be a good choice. The assassin also ran for his car, which was parked on the alleyway side of the street. Richards saw out of his peripheral vision that the assassin jumped into his car, cranked it to life with a roar, and peeled away from the curb. Three seconds later, Richards did the same.

Agent Richards had his hybrid pushed to the max, weaving in and out of cars, trying to keep up with the assassin's gas-eating combustion-mobile. The chase continued for several minutes, moving up and down different avenues and blocks of the city. Richards had driven these streets for what seemed like—and was damn near close to—fifty years. Hopefully this gave him some sort of advantage over the assassin. Richards's first duty when the foot chase had turned into a car chase was to radio in an ambulance for Lucas (he didn't think the kid would recover, but, whatever, give it a shot, right?), immediately followed by radioing the local fuzz to see if they could corner this evil and stop any collateral damage that might occur, or at least prevent *any more* from occurring.

The assassin drove like he was in an open-world video game, driving on both sides of the street and causing major accidents on almost every road that the rubber of his tires touched. He was also up on sidewalks when he couldn't get into clear lanes and hitting pedestrians whenever possible—and it was possible a lot on the busy lunchtime sidewalks. Richards didn't know it yet, but there would be several people in critical condition and more than one hundred injuries from this incident. There would also be two fatalities: Lucas would not survive, and an old man would have a heart attack while trying to jump out of the way of the two runaway automobiles.

At that moment there was a hiss from the radio. A voice came crackling through. "Agent Richa . . . his is Sergeant Michaels of the . . . olice department. See if you can pus . . . nto Hyatt Street and Moore. We ha . . . up some barricades and we hope . . . orner him there, copy?"

Filled with adrenaline, he grabbed the receiver and shouted, "Yeah, I got it. Look for us in two minutes, at most!"

He jerked the wheel to the left, letting the forgotten receiver bounce down onto the bucket seat beside him. Richards knew that if they didn't end this soon, it would only escalate. He took advantage of the crowded area they were in and began to nudge the assassin's car, driving him closer to the blockade that was set up by Michaels and his police force. The two cars were still more than a few blocks away from the barricades, but if luck were on his side—

Just then, the assassin yanked his car to the left down a one-way street, going the wrong way, of course, and began to plow into the parked cars that lined the side of the one-way.

Richards wasn't worried; he took the next road, knowing it would come out onto the same street as the assassin's car, but would be quicker without parked cars to drive through. He used this to his advantage by pulling out ahead of the man and cutting off the number of streets for the assassin to choose from. Richards stopped in front of the assassin, leaving only one way for him to go. That turn was one step closer to the blockade. The assassin's old gas-only car had taken a beating during this chase; the one-way street was the worst, involving head-on collisions with other cars and, in effect, destroying the front of the man's car and some of the engine. The assassin was still trying to flee, but the car was beginning to betray him. Richards was pushing him closer to the police blockade with every turn. They were one block away now—just one more correct turn. Richards was guiding the assassin right to that turn when the gas-guzzler's engine died.

"Shit!" bellowed Richards, as he watched the car rolling toward a curb. Before the car stopped all the way, the assassin jumped out, and this became a foot chase all over again. Richards grabbed the receiver out of the bucket seat.

"Suspect is on foot, repeat, on foot, Hyatt Street and Juniper. I'm pursuing!"

He jumped out of the hybrid, pulled his gun, and began shooting as he ran after the assassin. Richards wasn't shooting directly at the man running fifty yards ahead of him; he was shooting wide left. This caused the assassin to streak to his right down an open alley toward the blockade the police had set up. If they were smart, and sometimes they were, they would have left enough men to cover the blockade. That was, after all, why he'd radioed his position to them.

As the assassin got to the next street, he at once saw what he had gotten himself into, drew his gun with a blazing speed that the police had not expected, and began firing. He was very accurate, clipping an officer with his first shot and shattering a window into the face of another with his second. He jumped behind a parked car for cover and looked back in the direction of the alley, waiting for Richards to appear. Instinct once again guided Richards. This time it led him to hang back in the shadows of the alley to wait for what was surely going to result in an old-fashioned standoff or, if everyone were unlucky, a gunfight.

The assassin sat with his back against the car, sweat dripping into his eyes as he tried to steady his breathing and think of some way out of this nightmare. He'd had a simple job: kill the mole and fade into the crowd, and then show up when the heat was off and collect the other half of the payment. Now he was surrounded by cops and had nothing to show for it. If his count were correct, he had ten or twelve more shots left in his clip before he was out of ammunition.

Why did I only bring one clip? he asked himself, annoyed. He knew why—it didn't take more than a bullet or two to finish the job, so why would he want to carry extra? Why, indeed.

Richards, Sergeant Michaels, and the police were in a time crunch, the situation rapidly declining with every second wasted. Even more frustrating, Richards could only somewhat see the assassin but couldn't communicate with anyone. He was in danger of getting shot by the police if he came out of the alley, guns blazing like a madman, in an attempt to get a clear shot. They were going to have to wait for Mr. It's My Job to Kill People to make a move first. It turned out they didn't have to wait more than thirty seconds.

As the assassin sat with his back against the car, it must have occurred to him that there wasn't a way out of the situation. If he were taken in, someone loyal on the inside would kill him to prevent him from talking. Richards watched as the man suddenly leapt to his feet, probably coming to a hasty decision that he would kill as many as he could and be at peace when he was taken out himself. He'd fired two shots before his spinal cord was severed with a bullet in his neck and he lost all motor function. Due to the injury, he couldn't have felt any of the other bullets that raced through his body. The killer fell to the ground, gasping to breathe through the hole in his neck. He was unconscious twenty seconds later, and another minute after that, he had bled out.

Forensics reports later stated that the first bullet, the killing blow, had come from Richards's gun. The autopsy showed the bullet had entered at the back of the neck and exited the front, disintegrating two of the assassin's cervical vertebrae and the entire Adam's apple. That was the only bullet of his to hit the assassin, the only one fired from his gun during the standoff. The rest of the injuries came from the onslaught of policemen firing on the man.

Richards was old. His body felt it too. His legs were screaming with the pain of having to give chase on foot—not once, but twice—during this hellish "diplomatic" mission. He felt tired. After the last twenty-five to thirty minutes of nonstop adrenaline, his body had just about given up on him. He felt like he could sleep the next three days away. He lay down on one of the empty ambulance stretchers and did sleep. No one bothered him—no one but Sartori, the golden-haired girl in his unpleasant dreams. That and his guilt.

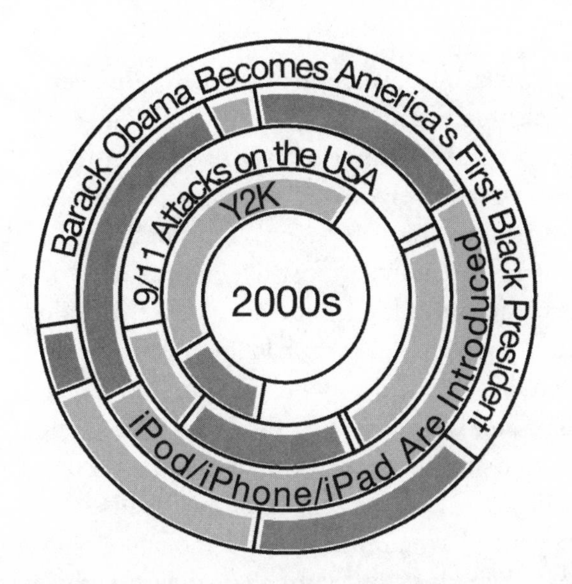

8:19 P.M.

FLORIDA, 2005

OK, boys and girls, we need this loot!" said Magis_Ka, energized. "More importantly, we need to take down this boss. It's the fifth one. That means only three more. When we get to the clearing, you all know the drill. If you don't, now is the time to speak up. The last raid worked wonderfully, but this boss is a bitch. DD's come across whatever open side there is. I would prefer you get around to the back if at all possible."

There was an excited clamoring of agreement.

The band of virtual misfits then proceeded to a clearing in the virtual forest, which, according to an updated map pack, was called the Path of the Cimmerian. There were tall trees that looked like great oak trees, possibly hundreds of years old, on the edge of the clearing. Several large and small stones outlined the southwest area. It would prove to be a natural fortification that the team would find useful in the showdown. The wild grass that was depicted in the clearing swayed from side to side, showing there was some process in the software that simulated wind as well. The graphics of the game were outstanding and unbelievably realistic. TakeMeGnomeTonight's HDTV really showed the amazing work that the animation design team had put into this game over its two and half years of development. Once the players were in the clearing, the real game began.

Suddenly, the fifth monstrosity emerged. According to the lore of the game, this monster was called Hadroc, the keeper of the key. The monster dwarfed the on-screen characters. In its most basic form, it was reminiscent of a four-legged animal, most like a large deer or moose. The key difference came above the front legs, where the body bent upward, creating an L-shaped creature that had jointed arms that ended in furry, four-fingered hands. There was a tuft of thick dark hair that ran up the sternum. The face of Hadroc was the feature that kept pulling the mind's eye back to being a moose. If the seven people controlling the avatars in this field had time to reflect, or even pause the game for a better look, they may have noticed the resemblance to an old cartoon moose named Bullwinkle. Atop Hadroc's head was a magnificent set of antlers—magical antlers, apparently. It took no time for the team to notice this fact, as they were instantly attacked.

"Damn!" a surprised PunkZappa said. "I'm already down to half life. Gnome, hit me up! I'm rolling right."

TakeMeGnomeTonight was far from the days of being a noob. He had already begun casting healing spells toward the damage dealer known as PunkZappa.

"OK, I got left!" said XinXin.

TakeMeGnomeTonight and BearISA_fo_MunDIE took their places behind the stone formation, with Merlin's_Neck_Beard far behind them. Tactically, this was the safest place for the healer, the long-distance damager, and the cloth-armored mage. FDO's Right-Hand Man bounced to the left behind XinXin. Magis_Ka, the Tank, went headlong up the gut, looking for trouble.

It's difficult to say exactly where Hadroc was, as he seemed to be everywhere at once. The magical bursts that flew from the antlers of the beast covered a 360-degree radius. XinXin went straight for the top of the screen to cover the left flank and was instantly obliterated by three magical zaps from the head of Hadroc.

"I see you. I'm already casting," TakeMeGnomeTonight bellowed into his microphone headset as he began sending healing spells XinXin's way.

"Holy shit, whatcha doing, Tank? You haven't been touched yet!" PunkZappa moaned. "Get out there and give us some breathing room, or this will be over before it starts."

"What do you think I'm trying to do? Blow-dry my hair?" said Magis_Ka, de facto leader of this band of online misfits. "I can't get in front of him; he's, like, hopping around all over the damn place."

With XinXin, the paladin blood elf, out for the count until healed, FDO's Right-Hand Man moved his warrior human avatar into attacking position. He charged toward Hadroc's back and began a melee attack. The monstrosity, who had taken a small amount of damage, kicked out with his hind legs and sent FDO flying. Immediately, TakeMeGnomeTonight was doing his job casting healing spells. It should be noted that, so far, TakeMeGnomeTonight had brought his A game to tonight's raid.

"I HAVE HIM!" Magis_Ka suddenly exclaimed. "ATTACK! ATTACK! ATTACK!"

Everyone began attacking. XinXin, PunkZappa, and FDO's Right-Hand Man began a brutal onslaught on the left, right, and rear of the monstrosity. The night elf, BearISA_fo_MunDIE, began firing arrows toward Hadroc's head and torso, while TakeMeGnomeTonight and Merlin's_Neck_Beard cast high-damaging spells directly toward him. Collectively, the group was functioning better since their disheveled introduction to Hadroc. However, the moose/deer beast wasn't going to be taken down so easily. It was, after all, the fifth of eight programmed game bosses.

Hadroc reared back onto its hind legs, made what could only be called a battle cry, and slammed his front legs down onto the fantasy earth of the Path of the Cimmerian with such force that every member of the opposing brood was knocked to the ground and stunned. The attack from the team had not taken Hadroc down below three-quarters of its life, and now, as the entire group lay stunned on the ground, the meter representing his life began to replenish.

"Son of a bitch!" TakeMeGnomeTonight exclaimed, knowing that his avatar would be the first to rise from this dazed state. "We have been grinding for a while; clearly our attack method isn't the best solution. Let's try something different. We need to take out his weapons, the antlers."

"I'm all ears," Magis_Ka stated.

"The antlers use magic . . . so, what if magic could neutralize 'em? Maybe they also function as a power source," TakeMeGnomeTonight proposed. "We all have some magical ability; let's focus it toward the antlers, all at once. Kinda like crossing the streams." There were some chuckles as all except the youngest member of the group picked up his reference.

"Sounds good to me," said XinXin. "My sword isn't doing shit. It's like I'm hacking away at a concrete block."

"Yeah, my arrows are causing zero damage," BearISA agreed.

"Here's what I think, let's go back to the same attacking positions and alternate between physical attacks and spell casting," Magis_Ka advised.

"You're the boss," replied TakeMeGnomeTonight, which was concurred by the others.

The lot moved their virtual counterparts back into their original attack positions while taking a beating from the magic-casting antlers, all the while being healed by spells cast from TakeMeGnomeTonight. The group continued the onslaught against the monstrosity.

The physical attack proved useless. Every tactic that involved trying to muscle Hadroc into submission was failing. The casting of spells was also not going well. The group was struggling to find a flow with their casting pattern. They had succeeded in destroying one of the antler tines, but there were still both entire beams to worry about. After destroying one of the tines, the crew noticed that Hadroc could no longer send blasts 360 degrees, but it was still close enough. The mage with the clever name of Merlin's_Neck_Beard was playing things too safely. Beard was hiding behind others for protection and throwing out weak spells.

"Merlin, what are you *doing*? Dude, freeze this guy and hit him with some high-powered, face-melting shit!" said PunkZappa. "Stop being a loser."

"Come on, stop the negativity. Let's focus on getting the job done!" said an annoyed Magis_Ka.

"I'm doing what I can," said a timid Merlin's_Neck_Beard. "Comparatively speaking, I'm still pretty new at this."

Merlin's_Neck_Beard had the birth name of Jimmy. Jimmy had started to consider himself a gamer just within the last few weeks. He had been on a few raids with this group in the past, but he was always relegated the light duties. Just as Jimmy started feeling performance anxiety, Magis_Ka sent TakeMeGnomeTonight a private message.

We gotta boost his ego. It seems he has gotta be the one to take out this damn thing. After this raid, we may need to look for a new mage.

TakeMeGnomeTonight frowned and typed out a response to the private message.

He will do what he needs to do. Have faith. I have a plan.

Magis_Ka shook her head and then began another full frontal assault on Hadroc. "Let's get this done, boys and girls," she said. "Give me some options."

"We flank all sides after Merlin freezes him," TakeMeGnomeTonight said in a commanding voice. "Then, we attack with everything, casting spells and physical assaults. This should open you up, Merlin, to hit him with one of your most powerful spells. But you'll need to refreeze him, because your biggest damage dealer is not instant. Go for the antlers. Got it?"

"Yeah, I got it," he said hesitantly.

Magis_Ka jumped in, "Good, let's do it!"

The team rallied once again, bent on defeating Hadroc once and for all. XinXin and FDO's Right-Hand Man flanked left, high on the playing screen. PunkZappa and BearISA_fo_MunDIE flanked right, with Magis_Ka going headlong into the face of the monster. Merlin's_Neck_Beard fired off a spell that froze the gargantuan deer/moose, buying everyone some time to attack the creature.

"Now, Merlin, NOW!" cried TakeMeGnomeTonight.

Merlin's_Neck_Beard cast his most powerful spell, and it struck dead-on. The group cried a thunderous roar, although it was a little tinny through their headphones. The band of misfits weren't out of the woods yet, so to speak. The spell wasn't instantaneous. Even during the small celebration, Magis_Ka was pushing them forward.

"Nice job, Merlin! We haven't crested the peak yet, so keep o—"

Connection lost.

The words blinked on and off on TakeMeGnomeTonight's screen. They seemed to be laughing at him.

"You've got to be kidding me!" TakeMeGnomeTonight gasped.

Twenty minutes went by while the young man attempted to figure out the connection issue. He tried everything, starting logically enough by just checking to see if he was still receiving a signal from the wireless router. Check. Next, he went to the router and rebooted. Check. Everything seemed to be in proper working order. After that, he rebooted his system. The PC powered back into life and opened his game. The icon still showed the tiny PC with a big red *X* over it. He knew, by now, anyway, that his friends had either defeated Hadroc without him or they'd been destroyed. Feeling despair set in, he knew he only had one option left. He didn't like it, but he reached into his pocket for his cell.

He could hear the humming rings as they progressed from two, to three, to four. *I guess I may not get an answer. I wonder if they are in bed,* he thought. Just as the young man thought he would have to leave a voice mail, there was an answer.

"Well, well," the voice on the other end said, doing without the formalities.

He sighed.

"Hey, Ma, how's it going?" he asked rhetorically. She answered anyway.

"It's going OK, I guess," she said, with a hint of a guilt trip. "Your father's hip is acting up again, and I am on a new diet. I have been following that TV show where they have those obese people—"

"Yeah, I know the one," he interrupted. "Listen, I can't talk long . . . minutes, you know. I wanted to know if you got the cable bill. Something's going on with my Internet."

Now she sighed.

"Yes, I was wondering when you would call." She hesitated. "We didn't pay it. In fact, we dropped it over a week ago."

"What?" he almost shouted. "Why would you drop the Internet? I use it every day."

"To be honest, we feel you need to be paying for these things on your own. You are almost twenty-five years old, and the only thing you pay for is rent. Half of the time you ask us to help you with that. We have paid your utilities, all of them, mind you; we've paid them and your cell-phone bill for the last three years while you've floated around from job to job, doing nothing more than riding our coattails. It's time to trim the fat. Your father and I aren't going to be working forever to pay your bills *and* ours. Twenty-five years is more than we signed on for. You are old enough to figure it out or suffer through the rough times like the rest of us."

He sat in stunned silence, letting all these new revelations sink in. His mother didn't step on his reflective silence. Finally, he spoke.

"OK, then. Well, thanks for answering my question. I think I am gonna go."

"Honey," she said with sadness, and then called him by his real name. "Grey, we love you. You need to learn to do for yourself."

"I'll call you soon," he said, irritated.

"We love you!" Grey's mom said quickly into the receiver.

There was silence. Grey was gone.

He stared at the HD screen and slumped deep into his oversize pleather desk chair. His mind wandered briefly back to the game—to his friends, virtual or not. He shook his head in disgust at his own actions. His mother was right, but he could never tell her that. He looked down at the phone in his hand and realized why it had taken his mom so long to answer. It was after 1:30 a.m. *Were we really grinding against that thing for that long?* he questioned. *No wonder Mom didn't answer right away. Man, I gotta sleep.*

• • •

The cell phone rang as it sat atop the nightstand by the small bed. The buzz of the vibrate feature was the only sound being made, but it was enough to do its job. A sleepy hand reached out from under the blankets and flipped open the phone.

"Hello . . ." said a groggy voice into the receiver, followed by a short pause. "Oh my God, what time is it!?"

The no-longer-sleeping Grey Chapman threw the phone down onto the bed as he violently kicked the covers away. The call was from his friend; the same friend who had gotten him the job at the computer repair store; the same friend whose neck was on the line for recommending him. She had called to find out where Grey was and why he was late for his first day on the job.

Grey wasted no time by showering; instead, he threw on his shirt and tie and grabbed his black slacks. After pulling them over his legs, he slid into a pair of loafers and then ran out the door of his apartment toward his car. Grey put the pedal to the metal and fought his way through the morning traffic.

God, how could I be so stupid to forget the alarm on my first day? He slammed his fist on the steering wheel as he thought, *Idiot! After everything Kelly did for me, getting the interview, helping me out, what a friend I am. Idiot!*

After a twenty-minute commute, he pulled into a parking garage downtown. He took his parking voucher from the lady in the booth—he hadn't yet bothered to get a pass, even though he had known about having the job for more than a week—and looked for a space. After parking, he ran out of the garage and hung a left. He was almost in a full sprint, running down the sidewalk, trying to cover the block and a half as fast as humanly possible. A mother yanked her small boy out of the way right as Grey was crossing his path. Grey jumped and contorted his body, like some strange ritual dance, trying to avoid stepping on the child and tripping himself. As he did, a young woman shot out of an alley to Grey's right and slammed into him, which was just as well since he would have probably fallen from overcompensating to dodge the boy, anyway. The two people went down hard, slamming themselves into a homeless man who had chosen his daily begging spot poorly.

The side of Grey's head slammed into the face of the homeless man, shattering the man's nose and making Grey brown out. The female's legs entangled with Grey's as she fell face-first toward the sidewalk slab. At the last second, she turned her shoulder and rolled through the fall, still slamming hard onto the concrete. The people that were passing by gasped as they heard the sickening, smashing sound of the bodies crumpling. Many people continued on their way, hurrying to their jobs or appointments, or just running away from the responsibility of helping people in need. By this point, Grey sat up and felt blood on his cheek. For a terrifying second he was sure that he had broken his cheekbone or jawbone, but then he noticed, through his double vision, how the homeless man was writhing in pain and holding his exploded nose. The lady who had clipped him seemed to be no worse for wear, except for a torn shirt. Underneath the tear, Grey thought he noticed some sort of scrape that had scabbed over recently. The female brought herself into a sitting position.

"What are you running for?" she screamed. "Are you crazy?"

"What are you running for?" Grey said. "Are you OK? You look OK."

"I'm fine." She stood, rotating her shoulder. "I've got to get going; I'm late . . . for work." She was clearly lying.

"Wait, you aren't even going to stick around to make sure this guy is OK?" Grey said, standing as well. "I mean, it's obvious that his nose is broken. We need to get him some help." Grey looked to the man, who was still rolling on the ground, and noticed the handwritten sign next to him with the words "NEED $$" scribbled on a piece of cardboard. There were splatters of blood splashed across the dirty old sign.

She looked at the man on the ground and made an annoyed face about the situation that was keeping her from whatever she had going on that was more important. She reached down to pick up her bag that had fallen during their literal run-in and hastily retrieved some items that had scattered when she fell. As she dug around in the bag, she took a quick, concerned glance back down the alley she'd come from, and then finally produced a wad of rolled cash. She pulled off the first five bills, reached down, and stuffed them into one of the homeless man's hands.

"Happy?" she said. Then she turned on her heel and ran off in the opposite direction. Grey stood dumbfounded as she disappeared into the crowd. After about twenty seconds he shook his head and turned back to the man, who was sitting up and looking at the now blood-streaked money in his right hand.

"You OK, mister?" Grey asked the homeless man.

"Yeah," he said with a pinched nose, "and my nose isn't broken, it just bleeds really easily."

"Well, that's good. I guess. Should we call somebody just in case?"

"No, it has mostly stopped. Another minute of holding it, and it will be fine. I have had tons of bloody noses in my life; this isn't even the worst one."

"At least let me give you some money for your trouble. I don't think she left you much; I'll double it." Grey reached for his wallet.

"Son, I don't think you can afford this. She left me five hundo, but if you can match it, I'll gladly take it," the man said with a smirk.

Grey barely heard what the man had said. He was digging into his pockets and spinning around, looking on the ground for his missing billfold.

"I think . . . I think she took my wallet," Grey said to the man. *Did I even bring my wallet?* he thought. *I was in such a hurry I don't even remember.*

Grey looked down at the man, who was covered in blood and pinching his nose. For the second time that day, Grey felt inadequate in every way, and it wasn't yet ten o'clock.

Grey helped the homeless man to his feet, looked over his shoulder toward his new office as a computer repairman, and decided he had already lost the job. He was now more than an hour late on his first day, with a flimsy excuse. He looked back in the direction he had come, not noticing the homeless man wander away to where the mysterious crazy lady had run off to.

What is going on? The universe has it in for me: parents cut me off, no Internet, I sleep in, I'm going to lose my job (probably), then I get knocked out by a beautiful woman who is psychotic (probably, again), but wow! I sank into those bluish-green eyes instantly.

He sighed and began walking back in the direction of the parking garage.

If I am not going to work, then I am going back to sleep. This whole staying up all night and getting up at the butt crack of dawn is not for me! I need to find a job that is more like two until eight rather than nine to five.

As Grey lost himself in thought walking down the sidewalk, Alessandra watched him from the shadows of the small alley she'd disappeared down. She was rummaging through his old brown leather wallet. The bifold was worn and conformed to his body from where it lived in his back pocket. His Florida-issued driver's license said his name was Jason Chapman and that he was born in 1980. Tucked into one of the bill pockets was a dingy ten-dollar bill creased and folded in half. She left the bill in the pocket and went back to the driver's license. She stared at the picture of the young man for a few seconds before turning her gaze back to the living version across the street. There was something about him that appealed to her. It couldn't have been his looks, as he was average looking at best. Still, she saw something in those eyes.

Alessandra felt a twinge of guilt for having the wallet. It wasn't like she'd taken it on purpose; she didn't need to steal his money or identity. She must have picked it up accidentally when she was gathering the things that had fallen out of her bag. She folded the wallet, dropped it back into her bag, stepped out of the alleyway, and began following Grey. She kept her distance but made no effort to conceal herself from him. In fact, she almost willed him to turn and see her, and there were a few times he almost did. As they reached the parking garage, Alessandra called out to him.

"Hey! Hey you!" she said, no longer with the accent of her "youth."

Grey turned and looked for the person the voice belonged to, momentarily getting lost in the reverberated echo that bounced off the parking garage's concrete. Then he locked eyes with her.

"Yeah?" he asked. "Oh, it's you. What . . . did you feel bad and want to give me some money too? I mean, I *was* on my way to my new job, but I can't show up on my first day looking like this." He gestured to the homeless man's blood on his shirt, quickly convincing himself that the blood was the real reason that he was returning home.

"I'm sorry about bumping into you," Alessandra said as she reached deep into the bag slung across her body. She pulled out the wallet. "I accidentally picked this up with my own stuff, sorry." She held it out to Grey. "I wanted to get it back to you, because obviously it's important."

He took the wallet from her. "Thanks," he began. "Sorry about the guilt trip just then. Today's not my day, I guess. Anyway, thanks again." He started to turn away.

"Wait," Alessandra began on a whim, "let me make it up to you. Do you like pancakes?" *What am I doing?* she thought. But she wanted to know more about the young man, and breakfast was a good place to start.

Grey was dumbfounded. Was he being asked out to breakfast? This sort of thing didn't happen to him. Sure, he had dated some people, but very few of those girls had approached him.

Alessandra continued. "You have to drive, though. I don't have a car." Then she smiled sweetly. Grey was lost in the beauty of that face.

Finally, after ten seconds or more had passed, he said, "OK, come on." He watched her approach, almost studying her, trying to read her body language but coming up short.

She reached out her right hand. "My name is Alessandra"—she hesitated because she slipped up and used her real name, but she went with it—"but you can call me Aless, with two *S*'s." Grey shook the outstretched hand.

"Grey, sort of like the color, but not really." He didn't know why he said it that way. *Trying too hard to be funny*, he thought. Instead, he came off sounding silly. She flashed her brilliant smile once again.

"My car is up a few floors. So you decided not to go to work today either?" Grey asked slyly.

Now Aless favored him with a mischievous smirk. "I wasn't on my way to work," she admitted. "I'm sorry for the way I treated you. I . . . it's complicated."

Grey nodded his head. He didn't want to pry into Alessandra's life; after all, they'd just met. They walked in silence. After a minute or so, the young man and his new friend reached his car.

"So, where are we headed?" he asked. "I prefer little mom-and-pop-type places over the big chains, but you're buying, so I won't be picky." He opened her door for her and gestured for her to get in. Then he noticed the garbage from fast-food restaurants littering the floorboard of his car and grimaced.

"Oh, sorry about the mess. I wasn't expecting company."

She wrinkled her nose, smiled, and waved her hand in dismissal. "You take me to your favorite place; I want to see what *you* consider the best."

"OK. There is this great little diner-type place a few miles from here. It shouldn't take long to get there." Grey entered the driver's side of the car and cranked the engine. After paying the fee to park, they drove south toward a mom-and-pop restaurant that was famous for their chocolate-chip pancakes.

Once inside, Alessandra sat across from Grey in a small booth. The faux-leather seats had worn through from years of use, exposing the cushion underneath. The small family-owned and -operated restaurant was open six days a week for breakfast hours only. Grey had only ever eaten here after a long night of hanging out, mostly with his online friends, but the occasional face-to-face social interaction brought him here as well. The dining room, if it could be called a dining room, was small. So small it felt more like being in a home kitchen with three too many tables. The walls were lined with a few small two-person booths, and in the middle of the room were three four-seaters. The small room's decor was cozy. There was impressionist music by Debussy or perhaps Ravel coming from a small boom box in one corner of the room. The music gave the whole place an unexpected, and unnoticed until now, romantic feel. The kitchen was undoubtedly just behind the door directly across from their table. With each swing of the door, a wonderful mixture of all the mouthwatering breakfast items that could be imagined wafted unimpeded to Grey's and Alessandra's nostrils. A smile ran across Alessandra's face every time the door opened.

The conversation over breakfast was light and casual. Grey managed to ask all the right questions, and Alessandra managed to dodge all the difficult ones. The two began, innocent as it always was, learning about one another.

Grey was born in a small suburb of Detroit, but his family moved to Florida to escape the terrible winters of the northern United States. He had a typical childhood from the '80s, filled with video games, fast food, and too much television. At one point, he could name all the Saturday-morning cartoons from the three major networks. As he entered into young adulthood, he found himself increasingly more awkward. Other young people were doing things such as going to the mall, the movies, bowling, or various other social activities. Grey, on the other hand, stayed indoors and indulged himself in the various forms of electronic entertainment. He soon found himself to be a bit of an outcast—a social misfit. This did not bother him in the least. In fact, Grey embraced the lifestyle that he had fallen into. He began letting his imagination stretch its legs and take him into other worlds. It was around this point that Grey began keeping a journal and collecting all of his ideas and thoughts. When he was a high-school freshman, his English teacher had assigned a writing task to his class. They were to write in the journal every day, at least once, throughout the course of one week. Grey found that once he started writing, the words didn't stop. The first day he wrote more than one page in the journal, but by the time the week finished out, he was writing an average of five full pages a day. These writings—Grey referred to them as the "early writings"—were little more than jumbled thoughts and ideas that were not fleshed out enough to be more than a few confusing stories and diary entries. But still he wrote. That assignment awakened something inside of him, and he knew that he would be writing about today's turn of events before the things could slip out of his mind like water down the drain. Aless was a unique person, and Grey was falling fast.

Grey filled Alessandra in on the few years of college that he'd managed to get through. He had tried to pursue an English degree but found that it was extremely difficult to choose a career in anything other than teaching. He did *not* see himself as a teacher. Grey explained that even with his love of writing, he mostly wrote about the things that happened to him and he was mediocre at best. So that ruled out writing as a career, but he'd been working odd jobs here and there to make ends meet. Also, there was the gaming, which he played up as more than a hobby. He said he wanted to learn as much as he could so that he could create them in the future. He managed to leave out the part about how his parents had been supporting him financially for the past three years. He figured that would not make the greatest first impression. And he wanted to make a good first impression; she was beautiful, maybe the most beautiful woman Grey had ever seen.

Alessandra had the most amazingly haunting blue-green eyes. They were rare like a precious stone buried deep in the earth. The color was that of the Caribbean Sea. Her hair was pulled back into a messy ponytail. The hair was sandy blonde, and several strands dangled in front of her face, dropping all the way down to the side of her chin. It also appeared to be long, perhaps stopping just below the curve of her breasts. Her smile was infectious, with deep dimples framing both sides of her lips. She had a perfect smile, the kind you might see in a toothpaste commercial. Alessandra's skin was fair, lighter than most, but a decent amount of freckles outlined her forehead and the bridge of her nose. Grey could see there were also freckles on her shoulder, where her shirt had torn when they collided. Something was wrong with that shoulder, but Grey couldn't immediately put his finger on what was different. He felt wrong about looking at her bare skin and looked away, but he stole another glance when she was briefly talking with the waiter.

Wasn't there a large scab on her shoulder? he asked himself. *I feel pretty certain I saw one there after we ran into each other.*

"Where were you going?" Grey asked abruptly.

She turned her gaze back to him, confused by his question.

"This morning, I mean. What were you running from?"

Aless breathed in as if to speak, but she couldn't find the words.

Grey broke the silence. "*Who* were you running from? It's about that giant roll of cash that you have, isn't it? If you stole money, I don't think—"

"I didn't steal it," Aless interrupted. "It's my money, no one else's." She paused and looked down at her hands, which had begun to sweat, and then continued. "I was running from a man; a very bad man. I think he wants to kill me."

Grey listened as Aless gave the quick-and-dirty version of the story. Of course he didn't realize it, but she left out a lot of details that might have led him to more pointed questions. She rushed through, barely taking a breath, and finished in less than minute.

"I came out of the alley, and from there you know what happened," Alessandra said.

Grey shifted in his chair. "Who is this guy?" he asked, adopting a New York Mafia–like accent.

She smiled wearily, shook her head, and whispered, "I don't know, not really. I wish I did."

Grey reached his hands across the small table and cupped hers inside of his. They were not much larger than hers, but his hands still covered hers. He noticed that they were freezing. He could tell that the emotions were carrying over from the memory of the incident; she was reliving it. She was probably still scared for her life; from the sound of it, she should be. God knows he would have been. He wanted to comfort her, but he couldn't find the words. Instead he just sat, waiting patiently for her to continue. After a moment of silence, Aless spoke with difficulty.

"There are a lot of things about me that are"—she searched for the right word—"confusing. I can't really explain it all, not yet anyway."

"Don't worry, you don't need to." He squeezed her hands. "I am sure that when you're ready, you'll tell me, and you may never be ready. I'm OK with that. I know we just met, but I feel a bond with you that I haven't felt with anyone in a long time." She squeezed his hands in return while he continued. "Like I said, I haven't had a lot of experience with people, but there's something about you, that's, I don't know . . . different."

She smiled with an authentic look of thanks. That smile blew him away. The waiter came by the table with the refill Aless had requested and asked if they would like anything else. They both smiled and declined.

"Just the check would be fine," Alessandra said. The waiter smiled cordially and dropped the check between the two people in the small booth.

"I know you didn't ask for my opinion, but if you want it, I'll give it."

"Sure, apparently I need all the help I can get."

"Well, the way I see it, this guy can't know where you are now, and that buys us some time. Time we can use to our advantage. I think we may need to leave town."

Aless sighed as her face crumpled. "I've been running for a long time. These people have been after me forever. I'm so sick of run—" She stopped abruptly, apparently having said more than she wanted to.

Grey nodded slowly and thought about what she could have done to be on the run. He came up with wild scenarios, ranging from a broken marriage and crazy husband all the way to being a baby killer, and everything in between.

"Then you're an old pro at this, and I don't want to drag you down. This is a pretty large city; you should be OK for today. Plus, I am sure he thinks you already rolled out after the chase. Do you have anywhere to stay?"

She drew in a deep breath, let it out slowly, and spoke.

"I should be—"

"You can stay with me," Grey interrupted, knowing how she was going to finish, "if you want to. It will at least give you some time to plan your next move. I have the Internet at my apartment, and we can use it to find a good place to lay low."

"Thanks for being so kind, Grey." She picked up the check and assessed the damage. Grey was right about this little place: it was a wonderful little mom and pop. She had dined at many over the years and found this one could hang with the best of them.

Alessandra paid the check at the small cashier's stand. They left and headed toward his apartment. It was a twenty-minute drive to Grey's modest one bedroom on the other side of town. It wasn't the best neighborhood, but it wasn't the worst either. They drove in silence for the first few minutes. Grey was giving Aless the space she wanted, even though he had a plethora of questions racing through his mind: Why was she running? Who was following her? Then there was the question of how long she had been running: a week, a month, years? He tried to shake these nagging questions, but until he had a few answers, he knew it was going to be an arduous task.

Aless was in her own little world. She was thinking about Lela, and thinking about trust. Could she trust Grey? Did she need to trust anyone? After so many years hidden, what mistakes had she made to draw them back to her? Could she be sure that she didn't know the man chasing her through the streets this morning? If she decided to trust Grey, like she had trusted Lela, how would she justify lying to him? Would she chalk it up to being careful? She imagined that Grey was thinking about everything she hadn't told him. She didn't want to lie to him, but she wasn't ready to divulge the past. So she chose option C: omission (with some white lies, for good measure). She had kept her past brief and vague. She'd only told him variations of the truth, that she was adopted by a woman named Lela and she hadn't seen her biological parents for many years. She'd told Grey the money was from a trust fund left by Lela when she'd passed away, and that was mostly true. What she left out was that she was forced to divide the money into many different overseas banks under many different names. She did this to ensure that she had a contingency plan in case one of the accounts was compromised. It was not cheap being on the run, especially with the inflation of the last twenty years or so. Next to her, Grey sighed and reached down to turn on the radio.

"How 'bout some music? What do you like?" Grey asked.

"I'm easy; anything is fine with me," Aless responded, clearly lost in her thoughts just as Grey had been.

"I just need a distraction. The weight of all this is . . ." He shook his head.

Alessandra gave him a shy, sideways smile and thought, *You don't know the half of it.*

When they got to his apartment, Grey parked and led Aless to the door. He slipped the key into the door of the apartment. He unlocked the dead bolt and motioned for Aless to enter.

"I need to make a phone call. Please, make yourself at home. I'll just be a minute."

She thanked him and glanced around the apartment; Grey remained outside and fished for his cell phone deep in his pocket. He removed his phone, which was the latest model on the newly merged Sprint/Nextel network. He flipped the phone open and began to dial.

"Mom," he said, "listen, I sort of have a problem."

"Oh, so you can call when there's a problem."

"Come on, Ma, get off my back! This is serious!" he said, exasperated. "I met this girl—"

"Really, a girl?" she said quizzically, interrupting him. "I knew this day would come someday, I will admit, although I thought it wouldn't be for a few more years."

"MOM!" Grey yelled into the phone. "Shut up and listen to me for a minute!"

Grey waited for the silence to erupt into screaming, but it didn't. He drew in a large breath, exhaled, and then continued.

"I met a girl. She needs some help. I can't really explain it, but I feel I have to help her." He paused with reluctance, then closed his eyes and continued. "I need some money."

"And there it is; I knew this wasn't about a girl. I guess you didn't go to your new job today, did you? I told you before that your father and I can no longer support you."

"It's not like that, truly. There *is* a girl; her name is Aless. She needs real help."

"Then let the real helpers help her. Let her go to the police if she is in that much trouble."

Grey sighed. "You know what, this was a mistake. I am sorry I called and asked for money. I will manage. Oh, and I am going out of town for a while. I will call you if I can."

"Wait," she said. "This is serious, isn't it? Are you OK, Grey?"

"Like I said, I will manage. Bye." He closed the flip phone, disconnecting the call, and tapped the device against his hand.

Grey shook his head and sighed. Why did everything have to be so difficult for him? He stuffed the phone back into his pocket and entered his apartment. He scanned the main room.

"Aless? Where you at?" he called.

Alessandra cleared her throat. "I'm in here," she called from the restroom. "Too much water with breakfast! I'll be out in a second."

Grey grabbed his laptop and then sat on the couch. He opened his browser, typed in a URL address, and realized that the Internet was still out. With all the excitement he'd forgotten that it was currently disconnected. In frustration he slammed the lid closed, tossed the computer onto the couch to his left, and slumped back into the cushions with a sigh.

In the bathroom, Aless sat on the lid of the toilet, crying silently. She was physically, emotionally, and mentally spent. "It will never stop," she murmured to herself. "I will never feel safe and secure, no matter how many months or years go by." She dropped her head onto her lap and bit her arm to keep the sobs from being heard. Two minutes later she had dried her tears and begun to compose herself. Aless washed her hands out of habit more than anything else and looked at her reflection in the mirror. Her eyes stood out, not just the bloodshot whites but the irises too. She'd had quite a long time to look at those eyes, many days, months, and years, but had never noticed what she did in this moment. The color was wrong somehow. The blue-green seemed to have faded to more of a grayish color. As she stared, she wondered if this were one of the signs she had been looking for—the beginning of the end.

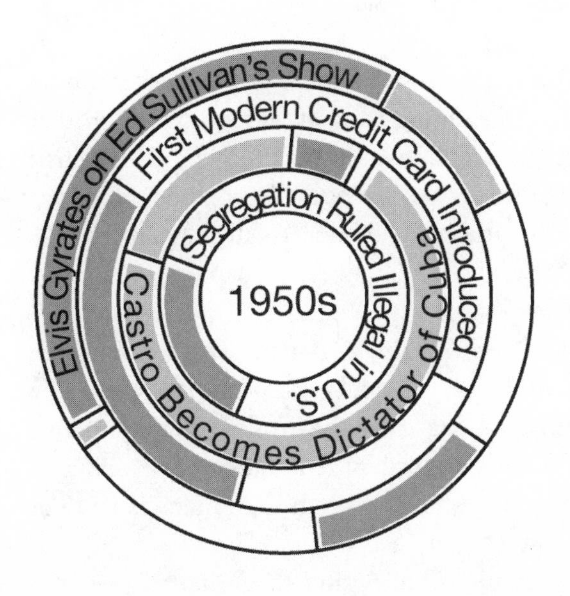

7:49 P.M.

KANSAS, 1951

The night sky was amazing. The waning moon, and the stars that showed the light from thousands of years ago, gave the cosmic void a majestic grace. Alessandra lay on her back in the soft grass, dozing in and out of consciousness. Her mind filled with images of the past few days, months, and years. The air was crisp, exhilarating against her flesh, but not cold. She'd become accustomed to the cooler air produced in the labs of her "younger" days, so she paid little attention to the gooseflesh that had appeared. It had been eight years since she had slipped into the cozy crawl space in the floor of the playroom. As she lay with her eyes closed, thinking about that final day and the madness that erupted around her, she heard a voice in the distance.

"Alessandra?" the voice said. "Come in, dear, you will catch a frightful cold out in this weather. Plus, it's almost time."

A cold—she had always wanted a cold. She could not remember ever being sick, unless you counted how she felt in the yucky room. Somehow, Alessandra knew that feeling was different. She felt ill in her stomach, sometimes her bones, even, but she was always feeling better within a few hours, a day, at the most. She could not recall having any illness that wasn't induced in that room. Not fever, chills, a running bottom, or even so much as a running nose. It was strange, now that she thought of it; almost every doctor-man that came and went had been sick occasionally. That wasn't the strangest thing, though.

"Alessandra? Do you hear me, girl?" the voice called again.

"Sì, ti sento." Alessandra replied.

"Ah, *in inglese, per favore*."

Alessandra struggled. ". . . Jes . . . I hear . . . jou." *Y*'s were not quite working out for her yet. Still, she was picking up the language very easily. She had only been studying with the woman for about five weeks, and she had a vocabulary equivalent to a four- or five-year-old. Pronunciation notwithstanding, she was progressing far faster than most could at any age, much less her age.

As she sat up, a noise drew her attention to the far edge of the clearing. She peered into the near darkness and made out the shape of what looked like a large brown rabbit chewing on the petals of a daisy. Alessandra gasped with surprise, startling the creature back into the woods. She then got to her feet, gave one last fleeting look toward the brilliant sky above her head, and walked toward the little house. Once inside, the woman, who had asked to be called Lela, motioned for Alessandra to sit. She sat on the couch as Lela walked over to the other side of the den toward the bulky box sitting on a built-in speaker system and its own support legs. She picked up the pronged plug and pushed it into the outlet on the wall. Lela tuned the dial as the tubes warmed up; magically a picture appeared on the nineteen-inch screen. They had only had the television a few months; it was a black-and-white Zenith, but the paper had said color was in the works and should be available soon. A brand-new show on CBS was being talked up by the media. The show featured a young married man and woman and the high jinks the new housewife found herself in from week to week. Lela and Alessandra had watched the first few episodes together. This week's was supposed to be about the husband trying to murder the wife, but this was a comedy, so there was sure to be plenty of fun times and probably very little murder. Sometimes Alessandra had a hard time following the show. It wasn't her English skills that hindered her as much as the accents that the characters had. The woman did this thing where she would be very whiny and silly, and the man had a thick Latino accent that vaguely sounded like her own when she spoke English. Alessandra tuned out the television set and let her mind wander. After the show, Alessandra and Lela retired for the evening.

• • •

The darkness of night masked the clouds that rolled in while the world slumbered. All, that is, except the ten-year-old with the memories of a seventeen-year-old. Alessandra was lying awake in her bed with the covers thrown onto the floor, letting her nightmare slip away into nothingness. She had been having this reoccurring dream for as long as she could remember. The good news was that the dream always left as quickly as it came. But the bad news was that she only retained bits and pieces, fragments of a greater whole, of which she couldn't make much sense. There was a hallway, but that didn't seem right; maybe it was an alleyway. It was day sometimes, night others. It seemed like ghosts were floating around in the dream, but even these small details wouldn't congeal into anything worthwhile. One thing was constant: she always woke up crying, with the feeling of death.

Alessandra tried to get comfortable, her eyes still wet and her pulse still quick from the agitation of the nightmare. As she tossed, her mind drifted, for the second time, to the events of the past eight years. She closed her puffy eyes as she remembered getting off the first plane so long ago. It was just after she'd been rescued from the labs. They had flown her to the mainland of Italy in hopes of returning her to her family. That was before they knew what she was. If only her family had come forward to claim her, she may have never had to come to America and been lost for so long. Alessandra wondered if her family even bothered: Had they stayed up countless nights wondering where she was—if she were even alive—or did they drop her off because they didn't want her? Did they leave her to the experiments with the doctor-men because they couldn't care less? She shifted in the bed, pushing the ugly feelings back down into the blackness. She then switched her thoughts to newer memories, beginning with the floods that ravaged the local town, farms, houses, and everything in between. She had just arrived in Kansas right before the natural disaster had struck. She thought about how Lela had invited her into her home just days before the torrential rains. At that time, the only English she spoke was no more than a few simple phrases and the swear words all kids learned.

Alessandra had sought out Lela. About five months ago, she had been traveling across the country when she randomly came across a flyer that caught her eye. She couldn't read the flyer, but she recognized the word "Italian," so she took the flyer with her. As she walked around the town, she showed the flyer to the folks she came across. Once the townsfolk realized she didn't speak English, they were kind enough to point Alessandra in the right direction.

Her mind wandered in a different direction as she started to fall asleep again; the memories of the Allies discovering what she was pulled up from the depths of her semiconsciousness. It was pure chance and bad luck. Some of the documents and files that the Germans were trying to smuggle and burn had survived, of course, but Aless was sure they were fragmented and confusing. She had taken her seat belt off on the plane ride from Rome to London, which might have been OK if she weren't flying on a military aircraft. The plane flew through a small but powerful rain band that caused sudden major turbulence, kicking her out of the jump seat that she was supposed to be locked down to. Alessandra had fallen hard, face-first into the folded seat beside her, splitting her scalp in the process. The private assigned to babysit her was quick to his feet; he'd grabbed the first-aid kit and picked her up off the floor within seconds. He flipped her around to assess the damage and watched with confusion at what he later described as an impossible miracle—her wound had completely healed right in front of his eyes. After wiping away the leftover blood, which there was a lot of, he strapped her back into the seat and went to the cockpit. Once on the ground she was taken by more doctors, who assured her that they were not going to hurt her—not like the others had. But they had proceeded to test her anyway—for a few weeks, at least, until she was flown to America and was able to slip away from them at the airport.

As she lay struggling with these memories, the tears began trickling down her cheeks and she willed herself to think about something happier: the day she was found underneath the panel in the playroom lab. These memories were clear, unlike her fleeting nightmare. She rolled onto her side, flipping her pillow over. The cool side of the pillow always made her feel good; she didn't know why and didn't care. Alessandra continued to think about that day as she closed her eyes and drifted away.

• • •

When Alessandra opened her eyes, it was dark, and she instantly knew this was a dream. She heard the sounds of footfalls and voices above her. She was disoriented in the darkness, and panic immediately took over. She hurriedly tried to sit up but smashed her forehead into the panel above her, causing a loud banging sound. Alessandra knew that the men speaking the awkward language, which she would later come to know as English, would not overlook her noise. Her heart simultaneously raced and sank in her small chest. Seconds later the floor panel was ripped from its position behind the playhouse.

"Oh my God," the private murmured. Then, speaking to someone else in his strange language, he said, "Sir, there's a little kid over here."

Alessandra's subconscious reproduced these events with stunning lucidity. The man's hands gently helped her out of the hole in the floor. The hands were tender when moving her, but they were dirty, rough, and calloused. The hands had shown the hard work that they had seen over the twenty-two years of his life. He smelled of body odor and cigarettes. She had never forgotten his pungent, but somehow sweet aroma, and she would remember the man every time she smelled a similar mixture. His eyes were brown but dark enough that they could be mistaken for black. His hair was short, but she could still make out the drab, coffee-colored follicles. His uniform was a dingy green-colored thing that looked about as stylish as a dead fish. His face was lean. There was stubble growing through the smudges of dirt and grime. To Alessandra he was the most beautiful person she had ever seen.

Another man came running over to them, carrying a blanket.

"Are you hurt, little girl?" the new man asked.

Alessandra stared back with confusion in her eyes.

The new man, realizing his error, repeated his question in her tongue. *"Sei ferita, bambina?"* The grammar was not quite correct, but it was close enough. Alessandra shook her head, which should have had a knot from where she hit it on the panel but was smooth as glass.

She would later learn that the man who had pulled her from the hole, wrapped the blanket around her, and took her from the playroom was named Saunders. He carried her back down the corridor that she had run through to get to her private place. The large hallway now looked more like hell than a connecting pathway. There were entire sections of wall missing, where Alessandra could see the earth mixed with solid rock. Bullet holes decorated the remaining walls, creating an unusual, almost artistic, pattern. They swirled in large and small arcs, crisscrossing each other in a dance of death and destruction.

Saunders continued to carry Alessandra to the main stairwell. She had never been allowed to wander to this part of the facility. Normally, a large locked door would have stopped Alessandra, and all the other children, from entering. But some type of explosive, probably a grenade, had mostly destroyed the door. The man carried her up the slightly damaged stairs. There were at least four flights of stairs, perhaps more; Alessandra couldn't have known with any certainty. The shock from the ordeal, as well as never having been on the stairs before, intensified her confusion. When they crested the last step, Alessandra was treated to something she had not seen for more than half of her short life.

Her jaw slackened as she beheld the beauty of the sky and the afternoon sun burning across her face. The warmth that her body felt from the yellow ball amazed her. She breathed the pure air deep into her lungs, noticing how it did not have the metallic blandness of the recycled air from her home of the last several years. The green from the trees, grass, and plant life filled her amazed eyes. She saw the snowcapped mountains in the distance, shooting out of the earth thousands of feet into the air, and wondered how long they had lived, pushing their way up from the ground into the blueness of the heavens. Suddenly, she was overcome by the impulse to run. She desired to have her bare feet unite with the soil of the earth, to roll from her back to her stomach and embrace nature with her every living cell. She had been locked away inside of the labs for the majority of her life and had few memories of the outside world. To Alessandra, it was as if she had landed on the face of a new planet, and was discovering all the enchanting, unimaginable treasures that a place could hide. Sadly, she could not run; she could not move from the arms of the man, Saunders.

He carried her to a nearby tent. It was very large and made of a creamy-colored canvas. There were tables and beds inside the tent. People were being treated for major and minor injuries. She did not recognize anyone. They all wore similar clothes to the man, Saunders, who had brought her here. He placed Alessandra on a cot and knelt.

"Stay here, I will find you some food and water," he said.

Even though she did not understand him, his tone was full of kindness. As he walked away, she clutched her Bambolina and felt safe.

◆ ◆ ◆

The sun shined through the open curtains at Lela's house, dancing on the face of the girl. She had thrown the covers off during the night, and they lay crumpled on the floor in a pile. Her hair was a mess, tangled and scattered across the pillow. As her eyes fluttered into the waking world, Alessandra remembered her dream. It wasn't her usual nightmare, but she had dreamed about the day she'd begun her new life, the day she had left the underground labs eight years ago. She stretched herself across the bed diagonally and relaxed, thinking about how beautiful the day was going to be.

Alessandra stared out of the window and noticed it had rained during the night. She imagined the wonderful smell that came after it rained, the fresh, clean air that accompanies nature's shower. With this in mind, she decided to open the window and no longer only imagine. Even after eight years, the beauty of the world around her was something she had never taken for granted. As Alessandra sat and took in the morning, her stomach spoke up and said it was time for something with a little more substance.

She left her small room and went into the kitchen, where Lela was already cooking breakfast. The aroma of the bacon was overwhelming. It filled Alessandra's nostrils and made her stomach speak even louder than before.

"Good morning, sleepy!" Lela exclaimed. Apparently, it was late morning. Alessandra smiled.

"Alessandra, no words for me this morning?" she asked.

Alessandra sighed and said, "Good morning, Lela. I hope jou sleep well."

"Very good, you are doing great!" said Lela. "Today, we are going into town. I need to go to the market to get some things. How do you want your eggs? Scrambled?"

Alessandra didn't like to go into town. She was very private, and for good reason. She was, after all, a seventeen-year-old trapped in the body of a ten-year-old, and she had no idea how or why.

I haven't been out in a while, so . . . I guess I can stretch my legs and spend some time with Lela, Alessandra was thinking as Lela said, "Eggs, do you want them or what?"

Alessandra smiled. "Jes, scrambled es good."

Lela smiled at her, a deep, loving smile, and said, "Go set the table, kiddo. Breakfast will be ready in a minute."

As they ate the bacon and eggs, it occurred to Alessandra that she had never thought to inquire about Lela's age; it seemed an inappropriate question to ask a lady. Aless did know that Lela had been married when she was still very young to the young man that she had been dating for all four years of high school. He was a member of the track team and had been one of the more popular boys in their small Kansas school. What she didn't know was that they were not married long before he'd begun to stay out until all hours of the early mornings. He had always claimed to be with his guy friends, that they were out late bowling, or drinking, or fishing, or any other pastimes that could be labeled as guy activities. But in her heart, Lela had known that these stories were just that—stories. They were fabrications to keep him out of the doghouse. Lela's father-in-law was a notorious ladies' man. The problem with small towns is everyone knows everything about everyone else, and, like his father, Lela's husband just couldn't be content with his lovely housewife.

Lela had grounds for divorce (Stacy, Mary, Valerie, Diane), and the proceedings went quickly. She was awarded alimony from the judge, who was well aware that she had grown accustomed to the lifestyle she had been living. This income, coupled with the fact that she had started giving Italian lessons around town, provided Lela with plenty of money to make ends meet and have some left over to do the shopping. But ultimately she was alone and longed for a more normal life. Divorced women were looked on as second class, even during this modern age, and Alessandra helped balance out the longings. Alessandra didn't yet realize it, but Lela needed her as much as she needed Lela.

The two ladies cleaned the kitchen and dishes after they finished their breakfast and small talk. Every bit of English practice was helpful to Alessandra, especially casual talk about nothing important. For Lela it was a chance to get to know the young girl a little bit better. Alessandra had told Lela so little about herself, and most of the story so far had been fabricated. The truth was too difficult to share with anyone, and frankly, Alessandra didn't know if the trust was strong enough.

"Thanks for the help. Go change and we'll go shopping for a bit," Lela said to Alessandra.

It didn't take long for the girl to get ready.

Lela drove a 1949 Chevy pickup, with white-walled tires and a coat of forest-green paint. Most people in this part of the country drove a pickup, as it made farm life easier. There were a lot of farms around the little town where Lela and Alessandra went to do the shopping.

Shopping was what Lela called all activities that had to do with going into the town—unless it was getting her hair done—and today Alessandra and Lela were doing more than just picking up some fresh vegetables at the farmers' market. They went to the local family-owned stores to window-shop for clothing and buy something they fancied. Alessandra also was badly in need of a new pair of shoes. She still wore the same shoes she had when she came to town five months prior. Even at that point, the shoes had been worn down. After they had purchased new shoes, the two of them stocked up at the meat market, buying pork, ground chuck, chicken, and bacon to replace this morning's fare, as well as some high-dollar steaks. Some type of meat was a staple for almost every meal that touched the table in their household.

The butcher was having a special on some new beef jerky, and it caught Alessandra's eye. She asked Lela if she could get a sample, and

Lela gave her sixty cents to spend, but only if Alessandra could go over to the post and get fifteen cents' worth of stamps. With forty-five cents she bought herself two ounces of jerky.

She carried the jerky around in a small paper bag the butcher had given her. She gnawed on a small piece as she crossed the four-way intersection in the center of town on her way to the post office. As Aless walked, she half sang, half hummed the tune of a song that was stuck in her head from the car ride into town. She didn't know all the words, because they were in English, but she thought it went something like—

"Heh, good looking, what do jou has cooking? How is about cooking something's up wit me?"

A pickup drove past her as she crossed to the opposite side of the street, still humming and singing. She waved to the driver and smiled, per the customs of this small town, and disappeared into the post office. She stood in the short line of people waiting to mail letters or packages to loved ones, undoubtedly for early, or late, birthday presents.

Heh, good looking . . .

She was humming now and looking around the office with curiosity.

What do jou has cooking?

Alessandra couldn't recall ever coming into the post office before today.

How is about cooking . . .

She had the urge to turn and look behind her. She had an overwhelming sensation of being watched, but Alessandra really didn't think anyone could be watching her, at least not with any intention other than normal people watching. She casually turned as she hummed.

Something's up wit me?

The breath that had been entering and exiting Alessandra's body as normal as you please suddenly froze and tried to crawl back deep into her lungs, just as a child tries to escape the monster under the bed. Staring right back into Alessandra's frightened face was her name. It was posted on a board with several other names. Her comprehension of written English was still too elementary to read most of the words that accompanied her name, but after struggling she finally made out the words "Missing Persons" and knew that things were no longer OK for her here. Her mind flooded with recollections of the past eight years, the incredibly grueling eight years, most of which were spent on the streets, eating from trash cans and sleeping under bridges or on benches in parks. Even the occasional helpful hand only lasted a day before she ran again, mostly because some of them tried to turn her over to authorities and orphanages. Even through the language barrier, Alessandra knew this was the worst thing that could happen. Lela had been the first to really open her home to the child. She didn't want to fix Aless by shipping her off; she wanted to hold Aless, she wanted to love her and be her family. Alessandra had grown to love Lela too, and that's why she had stayed. But she knew that Lela could be in danger now.

Her emotions had begun to betray her and tears formed. She had thought the running was over, that the stress of looking over her shoulder was dissipating. It seemed that the floodwaters would never run dry. Alessandra absently wiped away the briny tears. She walked toward the posting on the board, her eyes never leaving her name, and continued out of the post office into the street, forgetting all about the stamps.

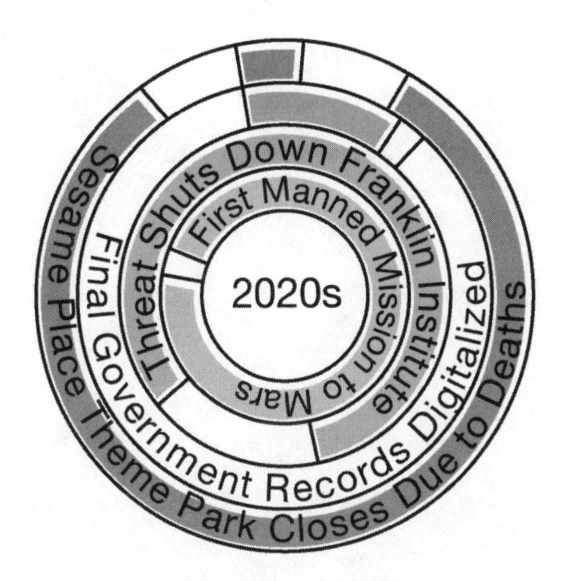

2:53 P.M.

PENNSYLVANIA, 2024

She didn't think; she just reacted.

Alessandra felt her shoulder exploding in white-hot pain as the first bullet ripped through her. She ignored the pain and kept moving forward like Roland of Gilead on his quest for the Tower. The second shot came immediately after the first, striking lower and sending a fresh burning agony up her already bloody right arm. Aless raised her hands just before the third shot reverberated in the small hallway, but it wasn't a defensive gesture.

The shot exploded less than a foot from Alessandra's outstretched hands. She felt the weight of the world sink into her chest as the last bullet struck. She lunged forward, drawing in a struggling breath. Her hands fastened around the shooter's neck. Aless sucked in a small breath between her gritted teeth as she pressed all the force she could muster into her talon-like digits. Something inside her mind snapped.

I am done with this! I'm sick of you people chasing me! she thought. *I'm so tired of running!*

To her right, seemingly a million miles away, Grey was getting back to his feet after being violently shoved to the ground.

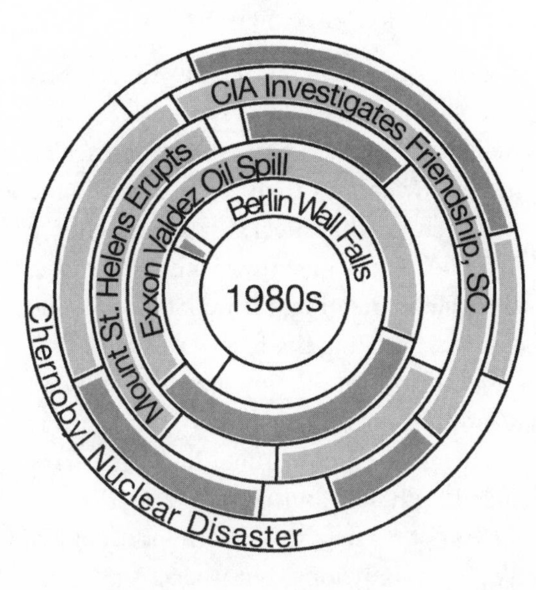

12:15 P.M.

WASHINGTON, DC, 1986

Tony Richards had taken his nephew to the best sandwich shop in the district to celebrate the guy finally moving up out of the mail room. They ordered their food, and Tony ordered a few bottles of beer, they weren't getting drunk on the job, just partaking in some celebratory brews. The men grabbed a seat in a booth in the back area of the small shop.

"You're gonna love this place, kid; I eat here twice a week. They got a Reuben that might as well be the last sandwich you ever eat!" Tony exclaimed. "So, tell me how good it feels to get out of that mail room once and for all."

Mark smirked and thought about his first day in the mail room five years prior. Strangely, he remembered the smell of the small room first. Perhaps it was because he went there every day until today, but he thought maybe it was because the smell was as much home to him as his actual apartment.

"I'm gonna miss the place, Uncle Tony," Mark said after a moment. "It's all I have known since I left high school."

"Well, kid, now you are gonna know this Reuben!" Tony said with wide eyes as the waitress brought their lunch over to the table. The waitress divvied out their orders; Tony winked at her. Then, Tony grabbed half of his massive sandwich and drew in a large sniff.

"Aw, man, doesn't that smell like heaven?" Tony asked rhetorically.

The older man bit into his sandwich and then let out an audible sigh, presumably to show how much joy that meat, kraut, and cheese could bring to a man's life. Most likely it was just how Uncle Tony was. Mark wondered how Tony stayed slender eating this junk twice a week and then quickly decided that it was smoking the rest of the week that kept him this way. The man was easily one of those people who smoked a pack a day. Mark knew that estimate was conservative; the man was probably a three packer. His hair, once upon a time, had been dark brown, but now it was sprinkled with salt and pepper, a stark contrast to his reddish mustache. He kept his hair styled with lots of blow-drying and hairspray. It wasn't particularly long, but it wasn't as short as most guys at the office.

Tony had never married; he was too keen on the ladies. He reminded his nephew, somewhat, of a real living James Bond when it came to women. As an agent, he met women all over the world, and Tony enjoyed his time with all of them; the physical time, that is, not the emotional time. When it came to women, Tony was an emotional grapefruit. He was thin-skinned and just sour enough to make most women pucker up. The truth is, he purposely shut down when a woman did more than look pretty. It was in his nature; his DNA was coded that way. He came to this dumpy sandwich shop for the eye candy more than the real candy. The waitress that served him twice a week also *served* him twice a week, and she was OK with that. So was he.

After lunch, the two men returned to the office in the company car. The car wasn't exactly the style either of the men was accustomed to, but it was what the government had recently acquired for the agency. They pulled into the parking garage in the black Lincoln Mark VII LSC. Tony had already given it an appropriate nickname—the Brooklyn Menace—because it reminded him of a gangster's getaway car. The new engine purred with the fine-tuning that could only be heard during the car's first month off the assembly line. They circled around the first and second floors, searching for an empty spot. Finally, Mark pointed a finger to an area ahead on the right.

"There's an open one, Uncle Tony," he said.

The car squeezed in between two boat-size cars. The one to the right looked like a Chevy Caprice, while the one on the left was definitely a Chevy Impala. After Tony killed the engine, Mark stepped out onto the concrete ocean that was the third floor.

"You ready for your first big day with the CIA?" Tony asked. He lit the leftover half of his after-lunch cigarette as he walked around the back of the Lincoln.

"Uncle Tony, I have already worked here, in this building, for the last five years. Besides, the day's half over."

"You know what I mean, kid," Tony said, smiling. The two of them continued across the third floor of the garage toward the doors to the building. "I still can't believe they let me teach you the ropes; my own blood working right alongside of me."

"Yeah, filing paperwork; I get the feeling it will be strangely reminiscent of the mail room," Mark said, with some playful ribbing. His uncle responded with a mildly annoyed look.

"I hope you realize you aren't going to be shooting at people every day. In fact, there is a lot more of this paperwork stuff than chasing bad guys," Tony lectured as he flipped away the butt of a cigarette.

"I know. Can't a guy make a joke around here? Loosen your tie a bit; let your hair down—God knows it could use a break from all the products you put into it."

"OH!" Tony exclaimed, examining his hair in the reflective window with an exaggerated look of pain on his face. "Let's hope you still have hair when you're my age."

The men entered the building and took the elevator up to the fifth floor. The offices on the fifth floor were dedicated to the Directorate of Operations (DO), later known as the National Clandestine Services (NCS). The DO's main purpose was covert operations, and this particular branch was housed in a nondescript building in the downtown area of the city, far from the main headquarters.

Tony Richards had been around the world several times on numerous covert missions and had just as many missions stateside. The general public would never know that Tony Richards was a hero many times over. Sometimes it was better that way. Mark Richards, however, did know. To Mark, his uncle was the biggest hero in his life. He looked up to Tony with a child's eyes looking at a parent. In fact, Mark's father was killed during the war, and it was Tony who had stepped up to help raise the boy. Mark's mother did all she could to make sure that Mark had everything he needed in his life. She worked two jobs most of the time to make ends meet. Being from the free-love generation, Mark's parents had never married; they were too liberal for such things (hence Mark took on his mother's name instead of his father's). After Mark's father was drafted, they considered marrying but decided against it, which meant that their family received no death benefits after he was killed in action. Living in a big city did not come cheap. Tony helped his sister financially whenever he could and hung around the fatherless boy in his limited downtime. He told Mark fantastical stories from his missions overseas and here in America. He embellished virtually every detail while keeping the gruesome stuff to a minimum. These stories were what inspired Mark to seek a job with the agency after he finished high school. Mark loved Tony with all of his heart and soul; nothing would ever replace his father, but Tony was sure close. Tony would die before Mark could tell him this.

The elevator opened onto the fifth floor, spilling out both Richards men into a traditional office space. There weren't cubicles, because the bosses wanted an open office floor plan, which included several dual workstations where two desks butted up against each other. From one side of the room came the sound of a radio, softly playing "King of Pain" from *Synchronicity* by The Police. The Police were a pop/rock/new wave band from the late '70s that had seen their popularity sky-rocket in the first half of the '80s. They were still riding high and supposedly working on a new album. Mark hummed along as the men strolled past the radio, heading for the two adjoining desks on the far side of the room.

The desks were surprisingly tidy. They both had a personal computer, and incoming box, and an outgoing box. Mark's desk was newly assigned and completely devoid of any actual work. Tony's in- and out-boxes, on the other hand, were full of files and paperwork that needed to be processed. Tony grabbed a file, told Mark to bring the chair around to his side, and then opened it. Inside the file was the usual:

paperwork that needed processing, like food and hotel receipts, among many other trivial things. Things that people outside of the agency never thought that the DO bothered with, but these things were just as important as completing any mission. Apparently, the bookkeepers kept a close eye on the expenses used by each division of government.

Mark and Tony sat at the pair of desks for the next several hours, doing what Tony affectionately referred to as "tedious tie-ups," as in tying up any loose ends. Tony instructed Mark how to write reports, how to sign off on other people's accounts, who's incoming box to drop the outgoings into, and pretty much how to dot all the i's and cross the t's. As the day was winding down, they reached the bottom of the pile of folders, where the last folder stood out in stark contrast from the rest. The final folder was red, where the rest had all been some shade of tan or gray. Mark picked it up and read the large bold words: "TOP SECRET."

"Uncle Tony, what's this one?"

"Nothing gets done with that one; it's still ongoing," Tony said, with a mater-of-fact tone.

Mark's eyes widened by the sudden change in Tony's usual easy-going demeanor.

"OK. I'll just put it back," the younger Richards started, "but of course all the mystery has me more than curious."

Tony sighed, a deep, breathy sound from the bottom of his lungs. "It's quitting time," Tony said. "Let's go get a drink."

As Mark was putting the folder back in the incoming box, he read the small label under the large bold words: "Case It110102."

On the elevator ride down from the fifth floor, Tony didn't speak to his nephew, which was surprising because there were lots of times that it was near impossible to get a syllable in when Tony was on a roll. Mark watched the man through his peripheral vision and saw that he seemed to be deep in thought. Mark did not speak either, feeling that if his uncle wanted to talk about it, he would soon enough, and if not, he could take a look through the file some other time when his uncle was off on assignment somewhere saving the world . . . *again.* Although, that was unlikely, given he had been reassigned because of his advancing age.

When the elevator doors opened, Mark and Tony reentered the parking garage, but this time walked in the opposite direction of the Brooklyn Menace, toward Tony's personal car. Tony had been working in this business a long time. So long, in fact, that he was close to retirement; for all Mark knew, he was past retirement. Tony had been earning a lot of money for the past dozen years or more. Working for the DO could be a dangerous job, and the agents that had longevity were paid accordingly. Tony's car showed this fact. He drove a 1981 DMC-12 DeLorean, one of the very first off the assembly line. It was a stainless-steel monster, with the engine in the rear of the car, where the trunk normally would be located. Mark walked toward the passenger door and opened it. The doors swung in an upward arc, which gave it the look of having wings—and the clever name of gull-wing doors. Mark positioned himself into the passenger seat and noticed that Tony had popped open the trunk, which was located where the engine would be on a standard American car. The trunk pivoted at the nose of the vehicle and opened to a roomy space. Mark stared out of the front window with a perplexed look on his face.

"You don't think we can talk about top-secret shit at O'Malley's, do ya?" Tony said quizzically. "Really, kid, you got a lot to learn about this whole for-the-good-of-the-country thing."

Tony reached into the trunk of the DeLorean, produced a three-quarter-filled bottle of malt whiskey, and said, "Never leave home without it! Let's go back in and get a soda from the vending machine, and I will tell you everything I can about case It110102."

"You know that vending machine is terrible, right? Nothing is ever cold," Mark said as they reentered the building.

Inside the office Tony produced some paper cups from one of his desk drawers and popped the tab on the warm soda the men had purchased from the machine down the hall. He poured the malt whiskey first, followed by the soda. The fizz from the soda spilled over the sides of the waxy paper cups. Tony reached across the desk and retrieved the top-secret file. Mark noticed, for the first time, that the file was very thick. He neglected to notice this when he'd first held it, assuming it was like the other dozens they had processed that day. Tony downed half of his drink, three-to-one whiskey, in one gulp, then picked a tattered pack of cigarettes out of his shirt pocket. He threw the file down in front of him, opened it, and spoke.

"Top secret," he said as he took his first drag, "case file number It110102. Alessandra Sartori"—he exhaled smoke into the air—"born in 1934 outside of a small town in Naples, Italy." He hesitated and then looked down, reflectively, at the black-and-white photo of a young girl. "I have been looking at this file for something like thirty years. Almost every day I am reminded of this case." He stopped again.

"Why I have never heard about this? I mean, obviously it's top secret, but not one mention . . . ever?" Mark asked.

"This is a cold case, kid. I have more urgent cases, as you could see from all that paperwork." He pointed toward the finished pile. "Cold cases need a lead to make them hot again. So, in the meanwhile, they sit and wait, while I go off and save the world." Tony chuckled at his sarcastic wit.

"Uncle Tony, we don't have to—" Mark began but was waved off by cigarette-filled fingers.

"Yes, we do. In case you have to keep working on this after I retire, you need to hear it." Tony breathed deep and sighed.

"I guess the beginning is the best place to start, but I only know secondhand from the file before it came to me," he said as he tapped the pages. "Sometime in the thirties the Italians and the Germans began thinking about how they could manipulate the future of the human race. Apparently, there was a lot of money put into improving our species through genetics, though I don't have the details, and frankly, I don't give a shit. Of course, the Germans thought the only way to do it at that time was to actually do human experimentation. The Allied intelligence had some information about the human genetic experiments, but most of it was outrageous rumors, like crossbreeding human and animals—ridiculous, right? I'm sure you have heard a tale or two about how the Germans were trying to perfect the Aryan race with blond-haired, blue-eyed super humans."

He took another long drag of his cigarette and then swallowed the rest of his drink. "The crazy thing is, hair and eye color had very little to do with any of it. The super-human part, that's where they focused the resources, that was the ultimate goal. I bet you are thinking about comic books, where they having flying men and giant green monsters that can jump across miles of wilderness, but that shit is all fiction. From what I can gather, the changes were not supposed to yield results like that. According to the paperwork"—Tony tapped the papers as he spoke—"the purpose was to improve the functions the body already did. You know, like healing, just in fast-forward. A soldier could get his face burned off and be back out in the field in a day or two, or at least that was the idea."

Tony strategically paused. He grabbed the bottle of whiskey from the bottom drawer, where he'd stashed it after pouring the first drink (just in case someone came in), filled his cup halfway, and held the bottle out to Mark, who waved it away. Mark hadn't even touched his first drink. He was too engaged in the conversation. This time Tony skipped the soda. After returning the bottle to the drawer, he tipped up the paper cup, and then continued. "You're a smart kid, Mark; why would our government not want the Italians and Germans to be successful?"

Mark did not need to think; he knew the reason why. "Because, we would want that . . . technology first." Mark struggled to find a better word than "technology," but unfortunately, that was what it was, technology. Tony took the last drag of his cigarette, exhaled, and touched his left-hand pointer finger to his nose. He snuffed the butt inside of his empty paper cup.

"Like I said: smart kid. Think about it this way: What might have happened if Hitler couldn't be killed? Or, something closer to home, what if Castro had some way to guarantee that he would never get sick, or old? Do you think the Cuban Missile Crisis would have ended so easily?"

Mark shook his head slowly as he realized the trouble those scenarios could cause.

"So, the Allies conspire to find this so-called human experimentation. We sent spies all over Germany to gather information, but the only intel that we got is that there wasn't anything going on in Germany, other than some children disappearing, but that wasn't even a red flag until later. As it turns out, the main base of the whole operation was located in Italy, not Germany, where we'd been scouting. Our troops came on the place almost by accident. Long story short—I know, too late—after the dust settled, there was one little girl alive."

"Alessandra."

"Yep, Alessandra," Tony agreed. "At that point she was about nine years old. She was detained by the government, shipped to the United States, and then she somehow vanished without a trace. She was totally off the grid for something like thirteen or fourteen years; I was assigned the case during that time, and one day we got a lead. It was random and came out of nowhere. There was a letter addressed directly to me and it was from her, Alessandra," he said, pointing at the old black-and-white photo.

"At least it said it was from her. The letter gave a detailed time and place where she wanted to meet to talk about her options. Of course, she had no options from us, but we'll get to that. It was the fall of '56, or maybe it was '57, well, it's in the reports; I you want to read 'em. At any rate, it was fall, and the letter said to meet at this middle-of-nowhere town in South Carolina. Friendship was the name of it. I think about Friendship a lot, and how she set us up. Alessandra made us all look like fools; she never showed up. I guess she got cold feet when it came to turning herself in."

Tony shook his head as the feelings came rushing back, like the events had taken place only minutes ago instead of years ago.

"Do we know . . ." Mark began but hesitated. "Does she have some sort of ability?"

Tony half shrugged his shoulders. "We don't have anything solid," he replied. "The best we've got says that she doesn't age, not normally anyway. Some of the oldest documents vaguely allude to the fact that she may have some healing abilities, but it isn't clear."

He closed the folder, leaving his hand on top of it, and then slowly slid it across his desk onto Mark's. "You are going to take lead on this case from now on. I want it to be the first case you work on. Don't worry; I will work it with you. Honestly, it's been cold for a lot of years. I think it's a good jumping-off point for you. My old, tired eyes may be rolling over something your eyes instantly see." He threw his hands in the air as if to say, *I don't know.*

"I will tell you one thing, though. In the early seventies we had a really promising lead; an old Nazi scientist who defected to the US had apparently known Alessandra. He claimed he was one of the people who worked directly with the girl, dosing her with radiation. He disappeared before we could debrief him. One phone call is all we ever had; he wanted money, and would have gotten it, too, if his intel were correct." Tony stared at the folder now on Mark's desk. "It's all in the file."

Mark opened the file and stared at the old black-and-white photo. "Uncle Tony, do we have any kind of recent intel?"

Tony rolled out his neck, stretching the muscles and popping tendons. "My best guess is she would look anywhere between late teens and early thirties, and that's assuming there hasn't been any life-threatening side effects. As for intel, there are always whispers of a girl who doesn't age, but most of it's crap. They are all documented in the file. Look it over, study it, and memorize it. Starting tomorrow," Tony concluded, "'cause right now we're getting the hell out of here."

And that is just what the two Richards men did.

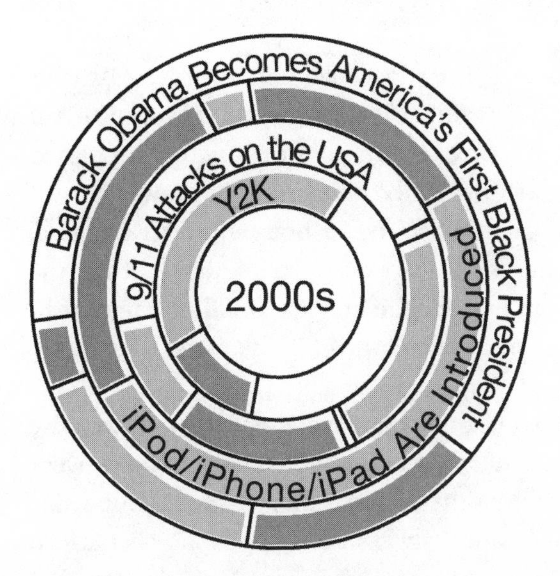

8:17 A.M.

FLORIDA, 2005

Mark Richards glanced down at the digital display of the cheap watch. The display read 8:17:13 a.m.

The seconds crept by: *fourteen . . . fifteen . . . sixteen . . . seventeen . . . eighteen . . .*

He waited. He had been waiting for twenty years. He would wait as long as it took. Richards had been close before, but not quite this close, not since the incident at the farm; he could actually see the girl with his own two eyes. He wasn't looking at a grainy photograph or surveillance-camera footage. He was seeing flesh and blood, skin and bone. He saw the wind blow her sandy-blonde hair into her face and saw her sweep it away with one smooth jerk of her head and fluid motion of her hand. Then she flashed that ridiculous manipulating smile to a man passing her on the street. Richards had no doubt she was trying to find someone she could use as her pawn, someone to sacrifice when things went down. A touch of a smile floated across Richards's own lips because he knew things would go down very soon.

Richards sat across the four-lane road on a public bench. The bench might have been a bus stop long ago, but the route had been changed at some point, dropping this particular stop. Now, the bench was used mainly as a billboard. The advertisement that currently covered the back of the bench was for director Quentin Tarantino's *Kill Bill: Volume 1* and *Volume 2* box set. The entire bench was painted bright yellow with the back showing The Bride in her yellow jumpsuit and her katana sword angled away from her body in her right hand. If anyone had known Richards's history and plans for the future, the irony of him sitting on an ad for revenge movies would not have been lost on them. Richards had not noticed, nor had he cared to ever see the set of movies.

He'd been working to track Alessandra ever since he was given the top-secret folder that contained case number It110102. There were dry spells of months, and sometimes more than a year, without a single sighting. Eventually, she would always turn up. Cash was hard to have all the time, especially in the world of plastic. Most people used credit or debit cards for nearly every transaction that took place. These things were easy to trace. Alessandra was smart; she stayed away from these kinds of blatantly ridiculous ways of being caught. After all, she had been running a long time; she knew to stay away from anything that could be traced. It was the things she could not avoid that usually gave her away. Things like traffic cameras; and just about every modern business that anyone went into had a security-system camera. She did the best she could to stay out of those places, but everyone had need of the basic necessities, even Alessandra. Food, shelter, and clothing were where the largest clues had come from over the years. In the end, it was dumb luck.

Alessandra had been a regular on the missing-persons posters long before Mark was working in the mail room of the CIA, but it wasn't until after the incident with Uncle Tony that Mark had her added to the most-wanted posters as well. The poster only had to be seen by the right person once. That person was a kid who made coffee for a living, and he was the reason Richards was staring at Sartori now.

The story Richards had gotten was that the barista had been at the post office shipping a vintage set of Marvel tin lunchboxes to the highest bidder of his online auction when he recognized the grainy digitally enhanced photograph of a daily customer. She was wearing sunglasses and a hat in the photo, but the resemblance was unmistakable. He said he had been serving her the same iced latte for the last two weeks, while trying to build up the nerve to ask her for her number. As he waited in the line at the post, a moral battle raged inside of his head. Somehow, he was sure that she should not be on that poster, the one with the most-wanted people in the country, the same poster with Osama bin Laden taking up the top third. He'd fixated on the picture of the young woman and willed it to change. He had the power to alter her life: by asking her out or by turning her in. The barista's mind pleaded with the picture to swap one detail, begged the nose to be wrong, wished for a cleft in the chin. Not one of those things happened, and as the line moved closer to the poster, he grew certain it was the blonde girl with the radiant smile. It was then that he'd decided he would call the hotline.

The capability of technology meant that within seconds of the barista's phone call Mark Richards was alerted. He'd called his superiors and was on a plane within an hour. After a short layover in the Charlotte Douglas International Airport, his connecting flight had touched down in the early evening at a small airport in southern Florida. That was last night, less than twenty-four hours before. Richards had not had a lead in the last seven months, and the last one was only a small amount of footage from a fast-food joint outside of Niagara Falls, New York. He guessed she was probably out of the country for the duration of the last seven months. But now here he was sitting across the street from the coffee shop Alessandra had been frequenting for the past few weeks, and there she was, right on time.

Mark watched as she entered the shop. As soon as the door closed behind her, Richards hopped off the bench and darted through the four lanes of heavy, slow-moving traffic. Just twenty seconds after the door closed behind Alessandra, Richards was stepping up on the curb in front of the shop. He walked over and leaned against the wall outside the entrance. On the outside, he was calm and collected, and seemed like any other person out for a morning stroll. The casual passerby would not have consciously remembered him from anyone else on that street, which is precisely what Richards wanted. Inside Richards's mind, he thought of how this event could play out. She'd never seen him up close, so he had no reason to hide—and he wouldn't have hidden even if she had. He was confronting the woman for the first time. He wanted to see her and wanted to be seen. The only thing that posed any problem was the location. This place was bad, if she caused a scene, if she screamed and ran, he would have to chase, and he would have to use force. That would not look good, especially in plain clothes. Richards would do what he had to do.

Inside the shop, Alessandra moved forward in the short line. There were not very many people working in the coffee shop today, but they were efficient enough. The barista who had reported seeing Alessandra had conveniently called in sick that day. Alessandra stepped up to the counter and ordered her usual iced latte. The skeleton crew on duty had it ready for her in under a minute; she thanked them and turned for the door.

She walked out into the brilliant sunlight and paused as it warmed up her skin. She breathed in deeply, held it for a moment, and thought how the day was going to turn out to be beautiful. She hung a right and walked down the sidewalk, passing so close to Richards that she pardoned herself.

Mark Richards nodded, smiled, and turned to follow her after she was a few steps ahead of him. He had decided to shadow her to a less populated area of the city. Luckily, there were many travelers walking in the same direction.

Probably off to work or somewhere to make money, Richards thought, *or maybe they are trailing someone like I am; maybe they're trailing me while I do some trailing of my own.*

He smiled as this thought came to him and then looked over his shoulder, just to be safe. They walked down the sidewalk for more than five minutes, taking frequent rights and lefts. Richards was beginning to think that she was onto him when she stopped at a small magazine stand on a corner.

Instead of stopping, Richards kept walking and crossed the street at the crosswalk. He backed out of the way of the flowing traffic and waited until Alessandra began to move again. She bent, picked up a paper, and stood there looking at it for no longer than ten seconds. She put down the paper just as the crosswalk changed to "Walk," and she started down the street opposite him in much more of a hurry than she had been before she'd stopped at the stand.

Richards recognized this instantly. He had been spotted, and now she was running. He mentally kicked himself for making a rookie mistake. He had been too close to outright stop at the magazine stand when she did, so he'd been left with no choice but to keep walking. He picked up his pace, but he could barely see her up ahead through the crowd. Richards wasn't overly tall at six foot one, but he could see over most of the people. Alessandra had a good jump on Richards—plus there was the fact that they were still on opposite sides of the road. At any point she could shake Richards just by finding an alleyway that went through to the next street, and he knew it.

Frustration overcame Mark Richards's normally professional demeanor, and he screamed out with fury as he jumped into the street and bolted toward Alessandra. An SUV swerved to miss him while another car slammed on the brakes. Alessandra spun around at the sound of the squealing tires and saw the man clearly. She turned back around and broke into a full-out sprint, pushing pedestrians out of her way. She was fast and nimble as she banked right and turned down another street. Richards was at least fifty yards behind her, pushing his way through the crowded sidewalks. He mapped her moves as she made them so he could make up some of the lost ground between them. She was so quick and light on her feet that somehow she was actually breaking away. The gap widened to seventy-five yards, almost a full block. Ahead of Alessandra the crowd was dispersing at a four-way intersection; she saw the thinning of the crowd was at its most uncongested toward the right side, and she pushed her burning tight thigh muscles in that direction. Richards also saw the crowd thinning out and realized this was the break he needed.

He barreled through the people in front of him, bellowing for Alessandra to stop. She didn't even turn for a quick look over her shoulder. She bolted past the remaining pedestrians, staying on the clearer inside area of the sidewalk, and darted through the intersection, hesitating just long enough to make sure she would be safe. She reached the opposite sidewalk just as the sign changed from "Walk" to "Don't Walk."

Richards, still running full bore, busted through the crowd (knocking one person into the gutter) and right into oncoming traffic. The squelch of rubber tires fighting against the asphalt was immediate and deafening at this close range. He was on the ground before he realized what had happened. Blue-gray smoke and the stench of burned rubber filled the air around him. There was a white-hot pain in his left hand and forearm. Eyewitnesses would say that the man who pushed through the crowd was hit by the first car that passed. Luckily, it was a small compact car and it had only clipped him as he was jumping to try to clear the hood of the small automobile. The eyewitnesses would go on to say the man was then flipped through the air and came down onto his left arm.

Richards knew that the arm was broken, and probably parts of the hand too. He'd had broken bones before and was aware of the awkward, painful sensation that accompanied the injury. As he lay on the ground looking up into the blue sky with the fluffy whites, he realized that he had lost—the first genuine opportunity to catch Alessandra in many years. How could he have been so careless?

Alessandra heard the sound of the tires skidding on the road behind her. She did not stop to look back. She did not even slow. She came to a narrow alley and scrambled down the long corridor. As she burst out the opposite side, she ran head-on into the person she would later know as Grey.

• • •

The hospital had that musty, queer smell that most hospitals seemed to have. To Mark Richards, it was like no matter how many times you had the linens washed and pressed, the smell of death just lingered around the corner. He suspected that she was now out of the city and on the run again. She had slipped through his fingers easier than water flowing through a sieve. Richards would never let himself be so careless again.

He sat in a padded chair near the sliding-door entrance to the ER. On his right was a woman who had come in with severe abdominal pain. The pain was most likely caused by something she had eaten earlier in the day. She had spent the better part of the last half hour telling him about all the things that she ate and was slowly narrowing it down to a few so she could tell the doctor when he asked. The woman was probably in her midforties, and she stank of nicotine. Richards wouldn't be surprised if she had some sort of large tumor in her gut squeezing the shit out of the rest of her oxygen-depleted organs. God knew he would be ecstatic if her name was called next to be moved to a room and wait on the doctor. The young man to his left wasn't much better. He had a nail—no, that wasn't quite right—he had a spike sticking out of his shin. The brief few words that Mark and the young man spoke were about the incident with his leg. Apparently, the young man had been using the spike to break up some large rocks he had been paid to move off a vacant lot. The sledge had hit the spike at an awkward angle and had caused the hunk of metal to be driven deep into his muscle tissue. Richards watched it twitch every time the boy readjusted in his seat. This trick might have been neat on *Ripley's Believe It or Not!*, but here and now, it was turning Richards's stomach into knots.

His arm ached, throbbing with each pulse of his heart. The EMTs had splinted the facture as well as they could in the field, but the break was still loose. The fractured ends of the bones rubbed together like sandpaper, grinding and grating, leaving shards of bone floating in his arm. The meds the EMT guys had given him dulled the pain but not the sensations. The combination of the spiked leg, the suffocating nicotine, and the rubbing bones was becoming a real threat to his breakfast. He could feel his stomach doing cartwheels when the nurse called his name.

"Mark Richards?" He stood. "Hi, sir, how are you?" she said, smiling as he approached.

"My arm is broken, my suspect is gone, and I have been sitting next to a talking ashtray for the last two hours; how do you think I am?" he responded bitterly as he brushed by the nurse and headed toward the hall labeled "Radiology." The nurse sighed, and turned to show him to the imaging room.

After the nurse finished his bone pictures, Richards had to wait another twenty minutes for the doctor to come in and inspect his splinted arm. The nametag pinned to his white coat said "Dr. Gathers."

He had the X-rays of Richards's arm with him. Obviously, he was a man of little time, as he didn't bother to introduce himself. Dr. Gathers produced the X-rays, and together the two men assessed the damage inside of Richards's swollen arm.

"You see this area here," Gathers said, pointing to the larger of the two bones, "the fractured area of ulna is what we call a greenstick fracture. You can see that the bone bent and cracked but didn't break all the way. Kind of like a tree branch might—hence greenstick. I would say a few weeks in a short arm cast will take care of it." He paused and stared at Richards.

"From what I hear, you were lucky that you didn't get killed running out into traffic like that."

Richards said nothing in response. He just glared back at Gathers with a look that said, *I don't need your stinking lecture, Dr. Too Busy for Names.*

"Anyway, the nurse will be along shortly to get your cast taken care of. Here's a script to keep the pain manageable." Gathers scratched something illegible onto a pad and tore it off for the man. "And take a nonsteroidal anti-inflammatory twice a day to keep the swelling at bay until you feel comfortable."

Richards took the prescription and thanked the man with a silent, dismissive nod, to which Gathers responded by turning tail and hurrying away. He lay back on the table covered with paper. He closed his eyes and once again saw the girl running down the street; he saw his greatest chance slipping away, over and over, and his lips thinned with frustration into little more than white lines. *This could have all ended with Friendship. Should have . . . but I dropped the ball then,* he thought, *and now I've dropped it again. We'll finish it, Uncle Tony, I promise. No matter what it takes, we'll finish it.*

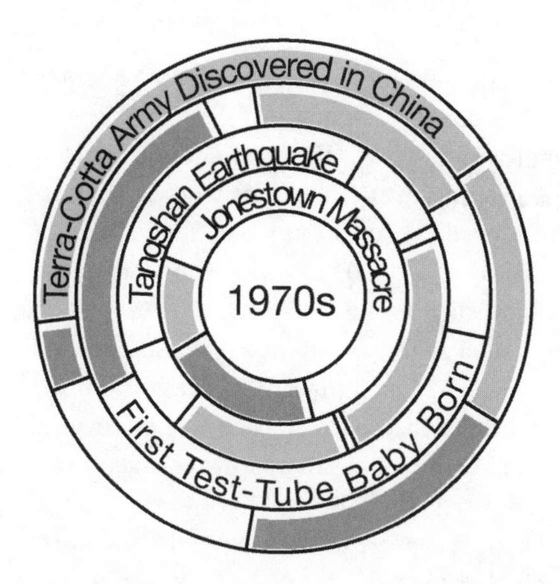

2:44 P.M.

OREGON, 1974

"You have reached the residence of Lela Jenkins. I am not home right now, but please leave me a message on my brand-new answering machine"—then, under her breath—"now, which button stops the reco—" *Beep.*

A voice came through the scratchy reel to reel.

"This is a courtesy call from Mountain View Hospital. We are calling to inform the next of kin to Lela Jenkins that she has suffered a heart attack. She is currently in critical condition in our ICU ward. Please come to the hospital as soon as possible; I am sorry to be the bearer of bad news. Good-bye."

With a click Alessandra stopped the machine. She wound the reel back and played the message again. Both times she'd listened to the message, she'd stood dumbfounded with her mouth open, waiting on her neurons to work out its meaning. She wound the reel back and played the message a third time.

Hospital . . . Lela . . . heart . . . critical . . . come as soon as possible . . .

Alessandra's eyes stung as the tears came hot and fast, spilling over her lashes and cutting channels into her face, and she began to finally accept what she had heard. She grabbed her car key from the counter and ran from the house in silence.

Mountain View Hospital was at least a thirty-minute drive from the Jenkins residence in the foothills of the Cascades west of Madras, Oregon. Lela had purchased a used Datsun 1200 sedan for Alessandra last spring at the bargain price of $1,300. It was the first car that Alessandra had legally driven during her life.

She was very much mentally capable of driving, and had been for decades, but only recently had she peaked physically. Alessandra had long golden hair that flowed down her narrow back to her curving hips, and her face had a pimply complexion like most teenagers. Her body was nearing the end of puberty; over the past five or six years she had experienced what most people experience over the course of a year or two. Alessandra grew six inches to the height of five feet four inches. Her breasts had begun poking outward and continued changing and growing until they filled a C-cup bra. Alessandra had known these changes would be coming and was mentally prepared for everything; time was the only variable.

She was currently pushing the speed of the small foreign auto as fast as she felt safe. The speedometer's top speed appeared to be ninety miles per hour, although the needle hadn't worked since before Lela had purchased the car. Alessandra could only guess that she was driving faster than she ever had. The long country road that led to the small town of Madras was deserted as usual. Lela and Alessandra had moved to this remote area for that very reason. The isolated region was the perfect place to live a normal life without attracting attention. Lela had done some research in the local library for low-population areas after Alessandra had told her about seeing her photo on a missing-person poster in the post office that day in 1951.

Alessandra had panicked that day and ran back to Lela's house. She went into her room and hid beneath the bed. She lay there sheepishly sobbing and wondering how she would explain this to Lela. She contemplated leaving Lela behind, grabbing what she could carry and walking out the door never to return. But she couldn't do that—not to Lela or herself. Lela was her mother, at least the closest thing she'd ever had to a mother. So, she waited.

Lela came back to the house after an hour or so. She had not been overly concerned that Alessandra hadn't found her in town after going to the post office; after all, the child was very independent. She had come to this town alone, looking for help after her parents had died while they were here visiting America. A tragic story if she had ever heard one. A young girl half a world away from home, her parents killed in a fire—or was it a car accident? . . . maybe it was a car that caught on fire?—Alessandra was never too clear on the details, and who could blame her. After wandering the streets in a strange country where you could not speak the language, she was sure it would be hard to trust anyone, especially with something as personal as death. Lela had been more than willing to take her in and help her learn to speak English. She needed a friend herself, so it was a perfect symbiotic relationship.

Lela had assumed that Alessandra had got caught up with spending her fifty cents in town and that she would find her way back to the house before dark. The drive was short, less than two miles, and it could easily be walked in about twenty-five to thirty minutes. As day began to spill into night, though, Lela did begin to worry. She called into town, knowing that the shops were closed but feeling the need to try anyway. After she asked the operator to transfer her half a dozen times, she finally gave up. Then a thought emerged: maybe Alessandra had come home *before* she did. Lela walked into her small room and looked for any sign that she had been there. A note maybe, or a change of clothes dirtying up the floor, but nothing seemed out of the ordinary. As she turned to leave the room, she noticed a shoe sticking out from under the bed; one that was instantly recognizable as Alessandra's worn-out shoe, even though she had just bought her new ones. She bent down, pulling up the cover to peek under, and found Alessandra sound asleep.

Lela reached under the bed and shook the young girl awake.

"Hey, sleepy," the woman said, "most people choose to sleep on top of the bed, not under it." She winked at Aless and produced a genuine smile. Aless began to return the gesture, but her face crumpled and melted into a sob.

"Aless," Lela began, concerned, "what is it, child?" She gently took the girl by the arm and helped her from under the bed.

Aless spoke the first few sentences in a weepy Italian. As she settled down, she reflexively switched to English.

"I has lied to jou. I'm sorry, Lela," she choked out.

"Lied about what, sweetie?"

"Almost everything." She paused to sort out her thoughts and smooth out the English. "My parents did not die here. I do not know if they are alive or not. I has not seen them in *dodici anni.*"

Lela stared in stunned silence for a few seconds, and then she shook her head slightly. "Twelve years? That can't be right. I thought you were only ten at most. Maybe eleven . . ."

"I has seventeen years," Alessandra interjected.

"Wha . . . seven . . . *diciassette anni*? It's impossible. You haven't gone through puberty."

"Puberty?"

"Umm . . . never mind. This just can't be," Lela said, astounded.

"It is true. I has seventeen and four mouths," Alessandra said gravely.

Lela cracked a sideways smile.

"What?"

"It's *months* not *mouths*, sweetie. We eat with our mouths," Lela said with a small chuckle.

"Sorry, I . . ." Her face fell apart once again, bringing fresh salty tears.

"No, no, don't be sorry." Lela leaned in and hugged the little girl, squeezing her tight. She rocked her while she cried and stroked her hair in an attempt to soothe the child. "It's OK, little one. Just let it out. We will figure all this out together."

"There's something wrong with me," Alessandra squelched out in between hitching breaths.

"Oh, honey, there is nothing wrong with you. You miss your parents, and that's OK, it's normal. I miss my folks too."

Aless leaned up from the embrace and faced Lela. "No, Lela. I not come here for holiday. I am brought here by military. I escape. Lived on my own for about eight years. Hiding. Waiting for someone to find me. Hoping they cannot."

Lela looked deep into the blue-green irises and the bloodshot whites of the young girl's eyes. "You really believe this, huh? And you want me to believe it too?"

Aless nodded slightly, feeling embarrassed. "I can show you," she said.

The young girl sat up the rest of the way, held out her right forearm, and dragged the nails of her left hand quickly and forcefully across her arm.

"Alessandra!" Lela gasped. Miniscule blood droplets formed almost instantly in the fresh wounds.

"Watch," Aless said. Almost before she could finish the word, the four tiny gashes began closing.

Lela, mouth agape, stared in fascination. "Oh my . . ." she half whispered.

"I think this"—she held out her now healed arm—"also keeps me small. I not know, though."

Lela looked hard at the arm where the torn flesh had been only seconds ago. She reached out and pulled Alessandra back into a loving motherly embrace. She rocked the girl for a minute longer before she decided to talk. "Tell me everything. I want to know everything."

Aless longed to trust someone and let go of the stress that had built over the years. So, when she opened up, she poured her heart out and relief took the place of sorrow. She explained the incident at the post office and also opened up about how she felt like she was being hunted like an animal. She had no hard evidence of this, but she had feelings of being watched. The older woman was very compassionate and caring toward the young girl. Within a week they were on a plane to their new life.

That was twenty-three years ago. Now, Alessandra was on the verge of losing Lela, losing the woman who cared when she could have turned away, losing her mom.

Her tears had turned into sobs as she came into Madras and drove down the avenues toward the Mountain View Hospital. Every minute of the drive had stretched her nerves exponentially more than the minute before. All she could think was Lela would be dead before she could get to the damned hospital. When she finally parked and ran inside, she was all but yelling through her sobs at the attendant behind the information desk.

"Ma'am, please, *please*, tell me where ICU is. My . . . my mom is dying; I have to see her!" Alessandra squeaked through a closed throat.

"Young lady," the attendant spoke calmly, obviously having dealt with similar situations before, "the ICU is on the next floor, but you will need to prepare yourself, the doctors may not allow visitors at this time. Really it all depends on the state your mother is in."

Alessandra did not pay much attention to the end of the attendant's sentence; she'd already begun rushing toward the stairwell. As she ran up the stairs, she could feel more tears streaming from ducts that should have no tears left. Her eyes were burning in their sockets, bloodshot almost beyond recognition. She had to wipe them twice as she came out of the stairwell so she could read the signs pointing the way to the ICU's cardiac ward. Finally, she deciphered that it was to the left, near the end of the hall. She tried to compose herself some as she approached the nurses' station.

"Excuse me, I am looking for Lela Jenkins. I'm her daughter, Alessandra . . . Jenkins," she said through a closing throat, her chin quivering.

The nurse, who was seated at the desk, rose and extended her hands but not to shake hands. She took both of Alessandra's and held them firmly. Alessandra took a fleeting glance at the woman's nametag. Stamped into the plastic was the name "Jackie." She was calm and caring when she spoke.

"Ms. Jenkins, your mother, has suffered a severe cardiac arrest and several mild arrests since she arrived here. She has been in and out of consciousness and sometimes incoherent. The major cardiac arrest stopped her heart for a short period of time. The paramedics arrived in time to revive her; however, there is large chance that she suffered from a lack of oxygen to the brain, causing brain damage. The severity of the damage is unknown at this point."

"Oh my God!" Alessandra exclaimed as she pulled her hands free and dropped her face into them. She repeated the phrase several times, shaking her head. She felt numbness spread across her entire body, slowly enveloping every inch of her. Her legs felt as if they were made of gelatin, and she waited for them to collapse under her. They did not.

"Young lady, I wouldn't tell you this if I didn't think we were very close to the end. I am truly sorry. If you would like to spend some time with her, I like to think that she's waited for you."

Alessandra slowly nodded.

The nurse grabbed Alessandra's hands again and took her across the ward. During the walk to the last curtain in the hall, Alessandra decided that she hated this place; it was nothing more than a place of death to her. Lela, her mother, was dying behind the curtain ten feet in front of her. As she walked, she cursed her own existence, lamented the fact that she would have to watch many people die because she was different than they were. She would have to suffer while others moved on. She wanted to die like everyone else; that's what you were supposed to do. You lived, and then you died. She wanted to be normal, not a freak of nature.

"She may not be awake, but you are welcome to sit in with her and wait," Nurse Jackie said. "If you need anything, I am right out here." Jackie turned and walked away.

Alessandra stared at the light-green curtain for what felt like years. Her eyes burned from all the crying, yet there were no tears coming now. She wasn't ready to see Lela lying there unresponsive. She wasn't ready to face brain damage and incoherent conversations that might be no more than phrases pasted together like kindergarten magazine collages. Most of all, she wasn't ready to let go. Lela was her only parental figure, her only friend, the only person she could confide in. With this, the tears came again. In reality, no more than thirty seconds went by. Nurse Jackie had just returned to the desk down the hall when Alessandra ducked under the curtain.

The room was dark and made her stomach twist into knots. She could see a figure on the bed, but she couldn't make out the features. The beeps from the heart-monitor machine filled the small room with a monotonous, frightening pulse that instantly made Alessandra want to withdraw back to the safety of the hallway. She fought the urge to flee and pressed forward, the tears coming harder now. It only took a handful of steps to be within arm's reach of the bed and the all-too-mortal body under the pale sheet.

"Lela?" Alessandra whispered hoarsely through her trembling lips. "It's me, Aless."

She drew in a large breath and exhaled, hoping that some of the nerves would go with the spent air.

"Lela? Can you hear me?"

There was labored breathing, accompanied by a moment of sheer panic and terror that Alessandra was watching her breathe for the last time, but then Lela spoke.

"Aless, my child," she said in a whisper that was barely audible.

"Don't talk, Lela, just rest; I just want you to know I'm here," she said, wiping away tears.

"No." Lela slowly and minutely shook her head. "No, I'm dying. There is something you must know. Something I have never told you," Lela said through much-labored breaths.

"Whatever it is, it can wait until we get you back in good health."

"Child, I *am* dying. It has taken all my will . . . please listen, Alessandra."

Her strength was fading fast.

"OK." Alessandra pulled a chair to the edge of the bed and sat. She gently lifted Lela's hand into her own.

"Before you came to me, a man told me you were coming. He told me that I was to look after you. He paid me, paid me a lot of money, and I needed it. I told you the money was alimony, but it was more than that."

"Wh-what? I don't understand."

Lela motioned for Alessandra to give her time to explain.

"Aless, you are special. I am sorry for what I have done."

"What are you talking—"

"You must go see the man. He knows all about you—everything . . . from when you were a child. He has answers."

Lela's breathing was now quite sporadic, and the pulse from the heart monitor was becoming irregular.

"Lela, relax."

"NO!" Lela spat. She was breathing so hard that her body seemed as if it were convulsing. "You must hear me! He is in Portland."

The heart monitor began making a screeching sound that must have been an alarm of some sort.

"NO, dammit!" Lela cried as she struggled to huff in the precious oxygen that she needed. "AHH!"

Lela clutched her chest, and her eyes began rolling into her head. Alessandra stood and hovered over her, not knowing what to do. At that moment, the nurses tore the curtain open.

"LELA! NO! MOM! MOM! Please help! Help her!" Alessandra moaned.

"Aless!" Lela hissed through dry blue lips. She held her hand out and pulled Alessandra so close that the two women's faces were touching and drew a shallow, wheezing gasp.

"Felix . . ." slid out in a gargled rasp. Alessandra looked into the dying woman's eyes as her own began to fill once again with tears that would soon be mourning sobs and watched her lips soundlessly pronounce the last name.

Miller.

Immediately, Lela Jenkins exhaled for the last time on this earth, and as her muscles slackened, Alessandra's tears overflowed, creating tiny streams of sorrow. Nurse Jackie took her by the shoulders and moved her away from the bed.

"Would you like us to try to resuscitate, sweetie?" Jackie asked kindly.

Alessandra looked past Jackie over to the bed where her mother for the past twenty-three years lay dead and shook her head slowly.

"I am sorry for your loss," Jackie said, placing her arm around Alessandra. "Your mother has gone home, honey."

"No, no, no, no!" She shook and wept with each word.

• • •

The next week was all a blur for Alessandra. The hospital took care of the funeral arrangements for Lela, presumably because Alessandra was still in the body of a minor. She didn't mind; the grieving was making most everyday tasks impossible enough. The funeral was closed casket, and some of the locals from around Madras attended. Lela was buried in a small cemetery near the home the two women shared for more than two decades. Alessandra was in a position that she hadn't been in since the early '50s. She was alone, again, and it hurt her to lose her surrogate mother; it hurt to be alone. She had never lost anyone close to her. There had never been anyone to lose, not after the labs. She had been a drifter, and chances were she would drift again. Things would be difficult. She remembered having to eat garbage, remembered having to sleep in the rain, remembered having to steal clothes to keep warm. Most of all, she remembered that she had looked like a child, and was always treated like one. There were always adults trying to do what was "best" for her. It may not be as bad this time since she was an adolescent, but she wasn't looking forward to finding out. The biggest difference this time around was that she had a purpose. Felix Miller.

The reading of her last will and testament came a few days after the funeral service. Alessandra was the only one in attendance other than the lawyer who was acting as the executor. The will was brief; it had some burial information that must have been passed on to the hospital or funeral directors before the arrangements were made. Then the executor read aloud the part concerning Alessandra.

"For Alessandra, my surrogate child, I leave all of my estate, all of my physical possessions, and all of my monetary assets. When combined through liquidation they equal a sum of two point five million dollars. The monetary assets currently (as of December 1972) equal two point three-five million and are stored in several different certificates of deposit with a renewing three-month interval. Alessandra may stop the renewal anytime the three-month period ends and withdraw the money. I ask that upon my death one certificate of deposit will be immediately withdrawn and the penalty paid outright, to be used for funeral and living expenses until the next three-month period comes to an end, at which time the choice will be hers to remove the money or leave it."

Alessandra stared at the man in shock and requested, "Can you explain that to me?"

"Sure, I can," the executor said. "Basically, you've been left everything; the house, the cars, the land, the money. There's a *lot* of money. The will goes on to explain all the accounts you have access to and gives the specific instructions for the account to withdraw from for the funeral and for your living expenses. Before the funeral it contained fifty thousand dollars. There is still a considerable amount of that left. I would say you are in good shape for the rest of your life, kid."

Alessandra sat back in her chair and began to cry. The tears slowly turned into chuckles as she realized she would be OK. Even if she had to drift, she did not have to sleep on the streets and eat garbage anymore.

"Thank you, Lela, thank you, Mom!" she whispered. She wept as she looked toward the ceiling, hoping somewhere Lela could hear her gratitude.

• • •

Thunder shook the cheap glass in its wooden frame as the light rain thrummed on the window and rolled downward in unpredictable patterns. The clouds hung dark and dangerous in the distance but still allowed for the lightning to color the sky with white-hot flashes of electricity. Behind the curtain, Alessandra's brow furrowed in thought.

He's just so old! Alessandra concluded. *How does he know who I am?* There was a brief tingle of recognition that blew away in the same instant it formed in her mind. She wondered if he would recognize her more than she recognized him.

Alessandra had rented a motel room across the street from a small rundown clinic south of Portland. She had paid a private detective to track down the whereabouts of the man named Felix Miller. He was said to frequent this clinic at least once a week, but more often than not, he came several days in a row. Alessandra stared out the window across the street at the haggard fossil of a man. She surveyed his gaunt frame, locking in as many details as she could from this distance. His skin hung loose around his face and neck. This reminded Alessandra of that flabby piece of a turkey's neck, and she smiled. His hair was silver white in color, and it was nonexistent from the top of his ear up. She noticed he wasn't extremely tall, although his looks could be deceiving her because he had a hunched back. He walked with the help of a cane in his left hand. The cane was very plain and cheap looking from this distance. She also saw he had what appeared to be a handbag or satchel slung across his frame.

Whatcha got in the bag, grandpa? she mused. *Secrets seem to be your thing, huh? Why are you here at this shithole clinic? I can't believe you're so old!*

She watched him hobble up the few steps and disappear into the building, and then she pulled the curtains closed.

◆ ◆ ◆

The alleyway was dark, musty, and wet from a fresh rain. Alessandra could see pulsating light as cars passed by the far opening of the alley. The cars hovered above the ground several feet and seemed to have legs contorting from their thin, top-heavy bodies. As Aless moved closer, she realized that these automobiles did not truly exist. Her mind was fabricating this strange dream world. She began to see reflections on hard surfaces that were nonreflective. Visions floated along the walls and ceilings of what seemed to be an alleyway, but now felt like an empty room with black walls. She did not see herself in these reflections as one would imagine, but she saw things that she did not understand. There was a man whom she did not recognize, a building she had never seen, and electrical devices that she could not comprehend among the more recognizable things. Still other images were more abstract. There were digital numbers floating and moving out of sequence on her right; above her she saw what she could only describe as a doe—no, a cartoon doe with arms. When she turned to her left, she saw what was most disturbing about this whole place:

She was back in the lab with the doctor-men—Lab B, the yucky room. Only this was a distorted, black version, making the room much more ominous than Aless remembered.

Aless watched as the men hovered over the small body of a young boy. They had stripped him naked and sedated him to unconsciousness. She saw that he wasn't strapped to the table, and the doctor-men were handling him as if he were a rag doll; they were flipping him violently over from his stomach to his back repeatedly as if looking for something. Seemingly satisfied with this, the doctor-men abruptly stopped, and all of them at once turned toward Aless, who was frozen with fear. The doctor-man who had been examining the boy pointed to a monitor behind the men, signaling for Aless to watch. On the monitor she could see the back of the boy's head and neck. The doctor-man picked something up that Aless could not see. He then checked to see if Aless was still looking.

She was.

He moved the object in his left hand into the view of the monitor, where Aless could see the ethereal gleam. The light reflected from an oversize scalpel, and Aless knew what was to come.

The man quickly and precisely inserted the cold surgical steel into the epidermis at the base of the boy's skull. He rapidly made a deep but short incision perpendicular to the boy's hairline. Aless wanted to scream but was too horrified to do more than take shallow breaths. A different doctor-man used forceps to hold open the bleeding wound, while a third tilted the head forward to reveal space between the vertebrae of the neck. Aless's eyes began to water with tears.

In the monitor she could see inside of the boy's opening, into the neck, beyond the stretched muscles and to the ligaments between the vertebrae. The head doctor-man looked up once more to be sure Aless was still observing. Once satisfied that she was, he opened a drawer and removed a syringe and a bottle. The liquid inside the bottle was a putrid green, and it had the consistency of infected mucus. The doctor-man filled the syringe and moved it into view of the monitor, amplifying the size of the needle to a monstrous proportion. Next, the doctor-man inserted the needle into the ligaments and cartilage between the first and second vertebrae—this distorted memory was the reason Aless still often awoke with a feeling of death. The sound made was a wet pop that was accompanied by a scream of pain so violent that it shattered the dream world into oblivion.

• • •

Thunder erupted outside of the small motel room, ripping Aless from the same nightmare she had been having for most of her life. Instantly and simultaneously she was filled with dread and hope; then everything was gone as quickly as it had come. All that was left was the darkness of the room, the sound of the rain, and the headlights of the traffic outside. She sat up and switched on the lamp bordering the bed. The light chased away the remaining bad feelings. Aless sighed and reached for a glass of water that was not there; instead she touched a sheet of paper. The paper had the clinic's address written in a scratchy print that was barely legible. The private detective had given her the address over the telephone; she had scribbled it down and immediately started packing. That was this past Wednesday; three days ago. It had taken her a day to get all her affairs in order before she'd headed for Portland. Yesterday, the old fart had not shown up at the clinic.

Must've been having a "good" day, Aless thought.

Today had brought bad weather but good fortune on Aless. She'd finally seen the man with all the answers hobbling from the cab up the stairs and disappearing behind the double glass doors. Tomorrow, if the weather broke, she would be waiting for him, but now sleep was what she needed. She replaced the paper from its home on the nightstand and returned the room to darkness.

Aless slept dreamlessly.

When Aless awoke in the morning, the rain had cleared away, showing a cloudless blue canopy above. She'd decided that the best way to handle her situation was to "convince" Miller to return to her hotel room. She awoke early, showered, and ate a banana. Aless then decided to put her mind to work. This man knew who she was and most likely would recognize her if she walked right up to him. She would need something to disguise herself. After a few minutes, she settled on a large pair of sunglasses.

Hey, if that super guy in the tights can hide behind some glasses . . . she thought. They weren't conspicuous to others around her, and, if she stayed out of his direct sight, at least in the beginning, she could keep her identity secret. *OK, one problem solved, but how do I lure him away from his intended destination?* Forcibly, of course, was the only way. Aless had learned from the private detective that Miller was a creature of habit, and that meant he would be at the clinic, if he came today, no later than 4:30 p.m.

Aless was seated on the bench next to the steps by 4:15. She wore a light jacket, which was more than she needed for this late-summer day, to conceal her weapon. While rummaging through some of Lela's boxes in the garage, looking for information about Felix Miller to give to the detective, Aless had found a Browning Sportsman folding knife in an old leather casing. It was nothing spectacular, it had a four-inch blade and a little more than four inches of dark wooden handle bookended with brass bolsters. She fingered the casing of the weapon in her jacket pocket as she waited for the cab to drop Miller. She popped the button flap of the leather casing open and shut dozens of times with nervous reflexes, letting out pent-up energy. Aless had no idea how much time had passed when, finally, she saw a yellow cab approaching. She hastily pulled the sunglasses down over her eyes. Next, she reached into her pocket and fumbled with the Browning in its case. For a horrifying moment she didn't think the knife was going to slide out from the worn leather. Then, as the taxi was slowing to a stop, the knife finally slipped free from the grip of the case, and she snapped the blade open, catching it briefly on her pocket lining. By this point Miller had swung the door open and was paying the cab driver. Aless would have to time everything perfectly so the cab would not still be around and Miller would not be too close to entering the clinic. Being a creature of habit, he no doubt had an appointment and was expected. Fortunately, for both of them, everything went smoothly.

Miller exited the cab, using his cane to help steady his frail frame. From this close vantage point, Aless could see he was in even more delicate shape than she recognized from the motel. She could also distinguish that the satchel across his frame was for oxygen. She saw the plastic tubes going into his nostrils, supplying him with life. After he closed the cab door and had taken two steps up the sidewalk, the vehicle swiftly pulled out and spun back toward Portland. There were no other people on the sidewalk, just Aless on the bench and Miller slowly heading for the steps to her left. She would not let him make it to the first of the nine steps for fear that someone inside the clinic would see him coming. Aless stood instantly and flanked his rear. She placed the point of the blade, still in her pocket, directly into the small of his back and whispered commandingly into his right ear.

"I will push this blade all the way through you if you make a sound. Turn slowly toward the road and walk across the street. No questions, no funny movements, unless you want to see what your insides look like spilled in the street. Keep your mouth closed and your feet moving."

She pushed the knife harder, puncturing her jacket, his clothing, and his paper-thin skin, bringing a small trickle of warm blood. He drew in air through clenched teeth but did not talk, and he began to move in the direction of the motel across the street. The old man was in no physical shape to protest. He moved slowly but steadily, and with the aid of his cane he put one foot in front of the other. It was less than two minutes before they were in the Johnson Inn parking lot. If anyone had been watching the two people cross the street, they would have found nothing very unusual about the pair. From most vantage points it looked as if Aless were helping the old man cross the road. The gesture seemed noble.

Once in the parking lot, Aless whispered again with the same commanding tone into Miller's right ear.

"Number seven; it's unlocked, you open it. Don't talk. I won't hesitate to spill your guts outside or inside on the carpet, so don't do anything stupid."

Miller followed the orders to the letter. Aless threw her sunglasses on the bed, hoping her eyes would adjust quickly. The curtains were already drawn, and there were no lights on in the room. Once all the way inside with the door shut and locked, Aless forced the man to sit in an old wooden armchair, then she tied his arms to the chair arms with the motel pillowcases. She turned on the bedside lamp and walked into Miller's full view for the first time. Their eyes met, and Aless saw that Miller was not surprised; he seemed to be smirking.

"I assume by the look on your face, you are not surprised to be here," she said. "You know who I am, don't you?"

Miller wheezed in a shallow breath and responded to her question with a single nod of his bald head.

He added, "Alessandra, it's remarkable. I have not seen you in many years, but you've only aged slightly, or so it seems."

"Neither of us leaves here until I know how and why," Aless responded pertly.

The next thing that Miller said was unexpected.

"I have cancer," Miller said with a small touch of a German accent. "Stage four. Ironically, a genetic defect; I am dying. Unbound my hands; I am not going anywhere. You have your blade, and as you have seen, I can hardly stand without the use of that damned cane or other help."

Aless shook her head as she moved the cane away from the man. "Nope, sorry."

"Then reach into my shirt pocket and remove the items," Miller responded with a sigh.

Aless moved forward, pointing the now unhidden knife toward Miller's face, and reached into the man's shirt pocket. She removed a pack of matches and one hand-rolled cigarette, filter-free.

"Can you light it and put it in my mouth?" Miller requested.

She looked at him in shocked disbelief and made a show of glaring at the small bag holding an oxygen tank in his lap.

"Don't worry about that. It's been dry for a few days. I was hoping to get it refilled today," he said in a matter-of-fact tone. "Take it if you'd like. But please, light the cigarette and let me enjoy it."

"For crying out loud," Aless said, exasperated. She placed the matches and cigarette in his left hand and reached down to untie the pillowcase, leaving the right hand still bound. "Do it yourself. For someone who has stage four cancer, you should learn when to quit."

Miller placed the cig between his lips and shook his head. "You have it wrong; this is my final vice. I have a feeling I am not leaving this room alive, so I will smoke and have some joy for my final hour." He struck the match against his thumbnail. Aless watched the phosphorus sulfide explode into flame. The light danced around wildly and showed the deep lines in Miller's face. He inhaled deeply and held the toxic smoke in his lungs as long as he could. Then he let it out in a burst of choking hacks. She closed the blade but kept it in sight.

"Ahh! How I have missed this," he mused. "Thank you, Alessandra."

She glared at him for using her name. "How do you know me?" she began, and then added, "I want to know everything that you can tell me."

"Well, everything I can tell you may not be everything that you want to know, or want to hear," he said genuinely. "I can start by telling you what you already undoubtedly know. You, among others, were part of an experiment."

"Why?"

"There is no why. Not that I was ever made aware of. Why is the sky blue, the grass green? These things are unimportant. 'Why' is not the right question, I think. Let's back up a little more. My name is not Miller, or was not before. My name is Müller. Felix Müller. I was born outside of Munich seventy years ago." He took another drag from his cigarette and exhaled while he reflected. "But my life matters little to you until our paths crossed in 1938."

"I was four," Aless murmured as she slowly sank into the second wooden armchair.

"You were. Your parents . . . do you remember your parents, Alessandra?"

She glared at him with hatred, but he continued before she could answer.

"It matters not, your parents, they were lied to. They were told that you were to be taken from Italy to North America where the war had not yet leaked its black death. I never had contact with them. In reality, you were then property of the Third Reich, pioneers in furthering human evolution," Müller continued soberly.

"So you were one of the doctors at the lab?" Alessandra inquired. "You did . . . things to us?"

"There is no easy answer," he said, pulling another drag from his cancer stick. "I did what I was ordered to do, but that doesn't make it right, I guess. I was only an assistant. The actual doctors had us doing terrible things to children, and even some adults."

"What kinds of things?"

"That's the right question. We were looking for any kind of anomalies, brought on by a multitude of tests. Stress testing, physical endurance testing, chemical testing, radiation testing; we really didn't know how or what we were doing. We looked at ourselves as explorers."

Aless coldly interrupted, "What type of anomalies?"

"Well, let me ask you, do you remember ever being sick? Hmm? A cold or a broken bone; anything like that?"

Alessandra thought and slowly began to shake her head. She knew for certain that she'd never had a broken bone or, for that matter, had any type of illness.

"Your anomaly, as you undoubtedly already know, is that your body heals at an incredible rate. Let's take a cut for example. Have you had a cut recently?" Müller asked.

She stared speechless for a moment, then shook her head. He knew she could heal, but what else did he know?

"OK, no problem. Uh, let's say you scraped your hand and I scraped my hand falling when we were crossing the road outside. Yeah? My healing period, or cicatrization, as it's technically called, would be about fifteen to forty days. You see, all of us have a natural built-in healing ability, but for you it is supercharged. Your cicatrization could be anywhere—"

Suddenly, Aless flipped the Browning open and moved rapidly toward Müller. He instinctively flinched backward, shielding his face with the hand that held the smoldering cigarette, and almost knocked himself over. Instead of stabbing the man, she pushed her hand in front of his face and violently sliced it open. He watched the crimson blood run down her palm onto her forearm. The wound itself looked as if it were moving in reverse. Müller's eyes widened with fascination as the gash went from bone deep to a flesh wound, then a scrape, and finally to nothing—not even a scar.

"Do you think I don't *know* how it works by now?" Aless said through gritted teeth. She was breathing heavily; sweat had formed on her forehead. The pain was still real and went all the way to her core. She bent and picked up the pillowcase she'd used to shackle the old man to the chair and began wiping the blood from her hand and arm onto the cotton. She finished by wiping the blade and threw the cloth to the ground. Müller's eyes flicked to the case and back to Aless as she returned the knife to her pocket.

"That was incredible," Müller said with unfeigned awe. "I was saying that it might take several hours to a few days, depending on the injury, but I was wrong . . . it was almost instantaneous and could stay that way, if you have changed."

Alessandra frowned. "Changed? Changed how? What does that mean?"

"Well, we introduced several . . . outside factors into everyone's genetic makeup to see what was promising. You responded the best out of all the other subjects to—"

"Children!"

"Oh yes, children, sorry. You responded best to all the treatments because of your unique genetic skill."

"*Treatments?* I was a human guinea pig!" Alessandra roared. "My life has been a nightmare because of you!"

"Not liking the answers to your questions does not change the fact that these *are* the answers!" Müller spat back, as if he weren't tied to the chair. "If you did not want to know, you shouldn't have kidnapped me and asked! Your nightmare is not because of me, Alessandra! I did not do these things to you!"

"But you didn't stop them either," she said coldly.

"I suppose I didn't," Müller said. "But I wanted out when the children stared dying. The changes you asked about manifested in different ways. They were physical, mental, genetic, all across the spectrum. You should be aware that these things may still happen to you. There is no way of knowing the full extent of the changes there may have been, but the majority of the subj—*children* died, within a year. I couldn't watch that happen any longer, so I requested a transfer, thinking that I would be denied or killed. But to my surprise, they granted it. Almost immediately after I was reassigned, the war efforts began to implode for the Third Reich. My unit was captured, and I traded information for my life. It was seeing the children being discarded like garbage that made it easier to betray my country. My information led the Americans to the facility where you were found. I offered my unique knowledge of the program and they took me on as a consultant."

"Well, weren't you the lucky one," Alessandra sarcastically shot back.

"Yes, I was. Just like you. Your body wasn't piled into an incinerator, burned to char, and then scooped out and used as filler in someone's garden. You should remember how lucky you are," Müller replied.

The two sat in silence for a moment, letting the pungent words linger in the air. Müller puffed his cigarette down to the last quarter and looked past Aless until she broke the silence.

"Why do I age the way I do? My body moves so slowly, but my mind knows the time that has passed; why?" she asked.

A trail of white smoke floated off the lips of the old German before he finally spoke.

"I don't know. Whatever they did to make you this way likely happened after I was reassigned. I can only speculate that it has something to do with your unique anomaly. Maybe they isolated an aging gene and manipulated it to work the same way as your other gift. It's plausible. Or maybe your anomaly includes age deceleration. From the observations that Ms. Jenkins made, I would say this is most likely the case."

"You leave Lela out of this," she said with a trembling voice that was still full of pain.

"Ah yes. I was sorry to hear about Ms. Jenkins," he said.

"You have *no* right—"

"The rabbit hole grows ever deeper, dear," he began, cutting the girl off. "I am afraid that Ms. Jenkins wasn't who you thought, at least not in the beginning."

Aless's face contorted into a look of painful confusion and disbelief. Müller continued.

"Ms. Jenkins was selected to be your shadow. She was picked because of her ability to communicate with you, and because she had nothing in her life to tie her down. She had just come through a nasty divorce and needed the money that the United States government was willing to pay her. She was told to give you a fake story about where the money came from, but be assured that it wasn't alimony."

This information dump was becoming too much for Aless, even though she already had a vague idea of these things. She placed her head into her hands and rubbed her eyes with a desperate intensity. Explosions of white light filled the blackness behind her darkened lids.

"She knew . . ." Aless said to herself more than to Müller. "She knew, and she lied."

"No, she didn't know until you told her back in Kansas," Müller said. "She only knew that she was making more money than she could spend to keep an eye on you, and keep you in one spot."

"Stop," Aless said, deflated. "I don't want to hear anymore."

But Müller went on.

"I was Lela Jenkins's contact. She relayed all important happenings directly to me."

"But I was on the run; I had escaped them," Aless interjected.

"*Mädchen*, there is no running; you were but a child. Your leaving the airport was but a minor setback. Within a month you had been tracked. We decided to give you the illusion of freedom so we could study you from afar. We followed you as you wandered the countryside not settling anywhere for more than a few days. Several times we helped you survive by sending someone to give you food or offer you shelter. One thing that we didn't expect was your age progression." He dragged hard on the remaining stump of his cigarette. "Eight years passed and you barely changed. We needed to study you in a more controlled environment with someone you could trust. By the time you reached Kansas, everything had been set up. Lela was placed in the nearest town along with posters advertising Italian, to catch your eye."

"You bastard!" Alessandra commented. "My entire life has been a lie."

Müller chortled at this, and then began hacking once again.

"Aless, you are simply wrong. Ms. Jenkins initially worked with us for the monetary gain. Guilt began to consume her, and eventually she grew to love you as her own child. She stopped taking the money several years ago, and if she saved right, she probably had a large chunk. Our meetings became sporadic until they dwindled into nothing. Like I said, I haven't seen you in a long time. Lela Jenkins did what you could not; she escaped."

Aless was shocked by this final statement. Lela had risked everything for her. Just like a mother would risk everything for her child. *Her* mother had been willing to throw it all away.

"Who did you work for? Are they the same people who are trying to find me now?" Aless asked.

"I don't know who you are referring to," Müller said. "And they don't exactly keep me in the loop now that I am dying, my dear. Besides, they will find you when they need you."

"Who is 'they'?" she asked.

"An organization funded by the US government."

"Like the FBI or something?"

The old man shook his head as a small coughing fit came and went. "It's complex. Let's just say it doesn't have an acronym and leave it at that."

"What do they want from me?" she asked.

"They want your gift. It's as simple as that. We all want to live forever."

Alessandra didn't like the answer. "Well, they can have it," she spat. "Tell me everything about these people."

"There isn't much to tell. I know very little," he said. "I've been somewhat retired since my illness. Besides, they are only observing."

Aless was frustrated. "So, Mr. Miller, or Müller, or whatever, where does this leave me now? Some lone freak survivor from a forgotten Nazi experiment running from some government 'organization' for the next one hundred years; it sounds like a terrible B movie."

Müller shook his head as the smoky lamplight caught his eyes. "There is another—a boy."

11:56 A.M.

SOUTH CAROLINA, 1957

Tony Richards's first field assignment was down south in a small town named Friendship. "Town" might be overselling Friendship; it was actually designated as an unincorporated community. Friendship was a small place that did not make it onto the larger maps of South Carolina. One would have to buy a regional map of the coastal plain to even put one's finger over the dot. Friendship's only claims to fame were the smallish train station that could carry passengers out to the big cities like Columbia, Charleston, or Charlotte and the small dairy farm, known as Livin' the Cream, on the edge of the community. The train station sat square off Main Street; the tracks paralleled the asphalt all the way out of the small community. The layout was not complex; Main Street cut through the center of the town, and it also functioned as the northern and southern divides of the community. Perpendicular to Main Street ran eight avenues split evenly with First through Fourth on the west side of the community and Fifth through Eighth on the east. Running parallel with Main Street were the "plant" roads of Hibiscus, Daisy, and Peace Lily to the north, with Fern and Rose to the south. If you took Rose west until it dead-ended, you would run smack into Livin' the

Cream dairy farm. Near the west end of Daisy and First Avenue was an elementary school, which was little more than an old small house that was converted into a three-room school. On the opposite side of town, on the corner of Seventh and Fern, stood the only place of worship: the Friendship Baptist Community Church and Activity Center.

The church was easily the newest building in the community. The residents had been pouring money into the infrastructure of the church over the last decade for modernization. The original church was built in the late 1860s and had been held together with glue and rat droppings since the early '40s. The new church had had its groundbreaking ceremony about four years before and was completed that past spring. It had all of the newest toys of most large churches, including a brand-new pipe organ that sat squarely in the center of the choir loft and had more settings than Janet Reins, the town piano teacher and part-time organist, could or would ever use. There was a state-of-the-art four-channel PA system installed so that every person could hear the word of God no matter where they sat in the congregation. That crazy rock-and-roll music the kids were beginning to listen to (and learning to play) drove the cost of the PA systems down, and the FBCCAC was able to afford a quality system for a fraction of the cost that was quoted a decade before when all of this was in the planning stages.

Just off Main and Fifth was a small sheriff's office that stood next to an even smaller post office–bank combination. There were shops sprinkled throughout Main Street; one could find any knickknack that was totally worthless and useless. Most of the shops were little mom and pops, like Gina's Consignment or the Gordon Diner. The diner was just a hop, skip, and a jump from the train station, deliberately situated for any passengers who might need a bite to eat in their twenty-five minute layover. The train ambled through Friendship three times daily. The first stop was in the early morning, and the train filled with commuters heading for out-of-town work. The train made another stop during the midday, but it came from the opposite direction and usually brought supplies in once a week to support the community. The final stop of the evening came around 6:00 p.m. and carried all the townsfolk back home after a grueling workday.

There were roughly six hundred residents in or around Friendship. The name fit well enough, it seemed; all of the local yokels were friendly. Most of these people commuted to work in the neighboring cities of Florence, to the northwest, or Conway, to the southeast. The local breadwinners found work where they could, mostly in manufacturing jobs, or tourism jobs closer to the coast. People were generally happy in their little community.

Tony Richards had arrived in the small community four days before the date Sartori had indicated she'd surrender herself. He spent his time talking to the local law enforcement and in the mom and pops perusing local delectables, and he was developing a wonderful rapport with the one of the rookie deputies, Jack Wilson. He was even invited over for supper on the first night of his visit by Jack's wife, Virginia. The couple lived two houses west of the corner of Third and Fern. Their house was not extravagant or flashy, but it gave one the feeling of being home. It was an off-white bungalow that stood less than twenty feet from the pavement lining Fern Street. The grass was thick but short and well maintained. On the left side of the home was a small one-car garage ornamented with beautiful hinges that swung the doors outward instead of upward. Stretched across the front of the home was a wooden porch that led into the red oak front door; to the left of the entrance were two small white rocking chairs that were probably used by the Wilsons on cool evenings like the one that would be landing in Friendship on this night.

Virginia Wilson was a lovely young woman who made a fantastic home-cooked Southern meal. She had long reddish hair, carefully curled into fat locks that draped around her smooth face, accenting her deep-blue eyes and ivory skin. She wore a beautiful light-blue evening dress that fell slightly lower than her knees. The shoulders of the dress were sleeveless simple straight lines, and a crinoline slip caused the dress to pouf out slightly. It was very elegant dinner wear indeed. Mrs. Wilson served them the entrée of the meal, which was a whole roasted chicken, basted with a honey glaze. It was delicious.

I might get married one day, if I ever find a woman who cooked and looked like this, Tony thought. He cracked a sideways smirk, shook the silly thought out of his brain, and continued eating.

"Jack tells me that you are from Washington, DC, Mr. Richards," Virginia began with polite conversation. "How did you manage to find your way down here to little Friendship?"

"Well, Mrs. Wilson—"

"Ginny, please. Mrs. Wilson makes me feel like a grandmother."

"Well, Ginny, I am fairly new in my line of work, still a little wet behind the ears, you might say, and this is my first assignment on my own. I guess they wanted to start me small so I wouldn't ruin anything."

She offered him the bowl of smashed potatoes, and he graciously helped himself to a heaping second helping. Ginny had seen her husband eat as much before, but Tony Richards was almost ravenous. He was a bear having his fill for the first time in months, or maybe, Ginny decided, he spent most of his evenings eating those dreadful TV dinners. Any home-cooked slop would fare better than TV dinners.

"Thanks again for the invitation to dinner, Jack," Tony choked through a mouthful of corn on the cob fresh from the market in Conway. Ginny had scooted down just this morning for some fresh vegetables. Friendship had its share of home gardens, but most fresh produce had to be acquired from out of town. Sometimes the shops off Main carried seasonal produce, and you would not be hard-pressed to find everything you needed for a nice meal, but during this time of year most produce was out of season.

"Not a problem, Mr. Richards," Jack Wilson responded.

"Please, if your wife insists that I call her Ginny, then I think you will do well with Tony," Tony said as he slid himself from the table, tossing his kerchief down on his unfinished plate. "I guess my eyes must have been bigger than my stomach. It was a lovely meal, Ginny, and I look forward to many more."

"Oh? Will you be here in town for a while?" she questioned. "I would love to make up something a little better than this thrown-together last-minute supper."

Tony retorted, "Are you kidding me? That was amazing; my own mother couldn't have thrown that together on her best day in the kitchen!"

Ginny laughed a schoolgirl's polite giggle as she blushed a little at the compliment.

"I will be in town for a few days. I am here to investigate a possible lead on a cold case, which is to say a case that hasn't been active in fifteen years or more." Tony deliberated. "I don't think I can get into more details than that. Not without having to kill you afterward."

Tony waited for a response to his dark humor, but the Wilsons only stared in his direction with a perplexed look. This look made Tony laugh nervously and speak quickly.

"I guess that one is a bit of an inside joke for us company men. Well, anyway, Jack, care to join me outside?"

The two men cleared their respective dishes and then began to head to the door. Jack stopped briefly to deliver a small, tender kiss on his wife's left check. Tony also noticed he lightly gripped her left hand in his right. During that exchange Tony may have, for the first time, seen true love. When Tony was a growing boy in the suburbs of DC, his parents' love had faded to toleration. Over the years they had grown complacent in their love for one another. His parents rarely showed any signs of affection toward each other. Mostly Tony's parents seemed to be more roommates than lovers, and in the end that had turned out to be more true than not. He felt a strange longing for the affection that he was witnessing between his new friends, Jack and Ginny. If the two of them had seen Tony's expression as they shared the moment, they would have noticed how lost and alone Tony had been. But the fleeting moment was over as quickly as it had manifested itself, and Tony turned for the screened door that stood between him and the freedom of the outdoors. He retreated to the front porch with the vision of the two hands touching burned into his mind.

"What's on your mind, Tony?" Jack said as he pushed the screen door open onto the cool of the evening air.

Tony removed the pack of Lucky Strike cigarettes from his breast pocket, tamped the package, and offered Jack a smoke. Jack, usually a nonsmoker, took one of the unfiltered sticks as a social gesture.

"Lucky Strike means fine tobacco," Jack quoted as he watched Tony pull his Zippo from the left pocket of his slacks, then proceed to light Jack's cigarette as well as his own. The two men stood silently inhaling and exhaling blue-gray smoke for what seemed like an eternity, but in reality it was no longer than forty-five seconds. Jack was a patient man—in his line of work it paid to be patient—and he was willing to wait while Tony settled into his thoughts. Tony looked at the wooden porch under his feet, puffed out thick smoke from his nostrils, and finally spoke.

"Jack, I may be in over my head here," Tony began. Jack puffed lightly on his Lucky Strike, beginning to feel a queasy convulsion stirring in his insides. He swallowed hard and held the cigarette down by his thigh to give his lungs a chance to fill with something closer to oxygen.

"I don't know," Tony continued. "I asked for this assignment because I have been pushing paper for a few years, and I wanted to stretch my legs, I guess. Not too many people have even heard about it. Aw hell, you don't even know what I'm talking about."

He sucked down the last quarter inch of his Lucky Strike and tossed the butt across the yard. Then gave Jack a remorseful look as he realized that this was not DC, and the person who would clean the gutter was standing five feet across from him.

"Shit, sorry, Jack, I'll pick it up on my way out," he said sincerely, and with a look of concentration he redoubled his effort to explain his dilemma. "To put it as simply as I can, there is a missing kid from Italy that the CIA has been looking for, and she's . . . *unique*. Apparently, we had her once, but she got away. So, skip over a dozen or so years, with few to no leads, and add in some paper pusher who is longing to get out from behind a desk, and a letter shows up, saying I'm the kid you've been looking for and I want to turn myself in. That was two months ago, Jack. The date on the letter is this coming Thursday and the place is here in Friendship. Right now, I am here to see if there is any truth to this letter. No one seems to think it's legitimate, but so few people even know of this cold case that the guys upstairs are at least entertaining the idea."

While Tony was talking, Jack had dropped his Lucky Strike onto the wooden plank under his foot and stamped it out, concentrating on what Tony was telling him. He stared at Tony, letting the words form visions inside of his brain. Jack Wilson had always been a visual learner, and sometimes he needed time to process the sounds into mental pictures.

"Jack, I'm afraid . . . insecure, really. I would like you to be there with me when the surrender is supposed to take place on Thursday. I mean, I know it's just a kid, but—"

"Not anymore," Jack interjected. "This 'kid' must have grown a dozen or more years since the case went cold. That would make her at least as old as you are, if not older."

"Right," Tony said, letting his voice fall faintly.

"Listen, Tony, I will be there if you need me; my duty is to the town, and if this"—he hesitated—"this person is going to cause a problem in my town, you better believe I am going to do what's necessary for the good of Friendship."

Tony stared off into the darkening dusk and slowly began to nod.

"Thanks, Jack. Tell Ginny that dinner was amazing for me."

He then turned on his heels, shook Jack Wilson's hand, spun again, and hustled down the two small steps of the Wilson's porch. Jack watched as the young man reached the edge of the yard and picked his smoldering butt off the ground, not turning to look back as he did so. Deputy Jack Wilson continued to watch Special Agent Anthony Richards until he was little more than a silhouette.

During his walk back the night had crept out of hiding to become full dark; the new moon did not help. Tony had time to think about the situation that Jack was being thrown into. It was not fair of him to withhold so much information about It110102, but he had given Jack enough to be ready if something went bad. Tony reached the doorstep to the sometimes bed-and-breakfast over Gina's Consignment about ten minutes after he parted ways with the Wilsons.

Tony climbed the stairs to the small two-room apartment that Gina Henderson had rented to him earlier that morning. The CIA had given him money and instructions on where to stay, which was fine by him, since it meant less work to do when he arrived. Tony entered the apartment for the second time that day and scanned the room. His dull-brown leather suitcase was resting near the foot of the twin bed, which appeared to be older than he was, judging by the headboard and sheets. The bed was positioned against the back wall of the small room. A few feet to the right of the bed was a small writing desk arranged near the room's only window; it held a picturesque view of Main Street.

The only other furniture in the room was a small table to the left of the bed; it held a reading lamp that served as the only illumination for the room.

Richards walked over to the window and momentarily gazed down at the street, then drew the curtains closed. He turned to face the far side of the room, peering halfway into the diminutive washroom. From here he could see the basin and toilet that constituted three-quarters of the space available. He moved to the opposite side of the bed, switching on the lamp as he went. He sat on the edge nearest the suitcase and popped the two latches to open the container. There were no internal pockets or hidden areas in the piece of luggage. Richards had brought enough clothing for a week and had packed his shaving kit, but he was interested in the file inside the large envelope lying on top of his personal items. The file was a plain red, scuffed, worn, and felt old—not *physically* felt, as in the way you touch an old person's skin and it feels like tissue paper, but felt as in the emotional meaning of the word, like an old friend.

When he first began sitting behind a desk every day, he was given case It110102 to restructure and reorganize. His familiarity with the file was partially why he was chosen to come to Middle-of-Nowhere, South Carolina. He had seen every picture in the file dozens of times over, had studied each report thoroughly. It110102 had become somewhat of a hobby for him after the restructure. On several occasions Tony had asked his superiors if he could study the cold case to see if he could glean any new information that others may have missed. Another reason he'd been sent to Friendship was that he'd been asking for over a year to exchange the office environment for fieldwork. He was never officially assigned case It110102 until two months ago.

Richards opened the beige envelope and removed the folder. He tossed the envelope aside, moved to the old desk, and placed the faded red folder down. For a long moment Tony Richards stared at the folder as if waiting for it to come to life and share its secrets like two old friends catching up after many years apart. Tony, apparently, decided that this would not be the case tonight; he sat in the creaky wooden chair and opened the folder. On the top of the pile was the latest addition to the photos and reports, a letter that had gotten Tony Richards finally assigned to the case; the case that had slowly changed from his pastime to an obsession. He carefully picked up the plastic-encased document and began to read the words that were scrawled in what seemed like a child's script.

CIA,

I know you are looking for me. For a long time I have been running, but I am ready to stop the running. I need help. I want to turn myself over to you. Friendship, South Carolina, on October 24 behind the largest building of the dairy farm, in the a.m. I was held captive in Italy during the war. You know who I am.

-Invisible

Richards didn't need to read the letter; he'd memorized it over the last seven and a half weeks that it had been in the possession of the CIA. The letter hadn't had a physical return address when it had arrived at the agency. The PO box that was penned across the envelope was traced to a rural post office in Kentucky, where the owner had only used the box on the one occasion. Richards flipped over the letter and scanned the blank back for what must have been the hundredth time.

A few more days and I can get the answers that you hide . . . hopefully, he thought. He removed the crumpled cigarette pack from his breast pocket and lipped another filter-free, lighting it with the same Zippo he'd lit Jack Wilson's cigarette with earlier that evening.

The letter went through the usual transit that all mail in the large agency underwent. It began by delivery from the postal service, along with hundreds of other weekly letters. From there, it was sent to the mail room for sorting, and because of its ambiguity, it sat in an uncategorized section of the mail room for an undisclosed amount of time—in hindsight it was possibly no longer than a week. The truth was, when a letter shows up addressed to the "CIA" and no one in particular, it was low priority, at least until the contents of the package were revealed.

The envelope had contained the letter Tony was currently pondering and a portion of a map of Italy. The section of map highlighted the island of Sardinia with a circle around the central mountainous area. Once the letter had been read and it was decided that it wasn't a hoax, the information had been passed on to Tony Richards, who was then officially assigned his first field assignment. Tony immediately recognized the circled section of the map as the area where German scientists had held Alessandra Sartori, among others, captive. The initial army reports indicated that she was a young girl approximately six to nine years of age, in shock and malnourished. The report also stated that the area of Sardinia was desolate, its population was sparse, and that it was the perfect place for an underground research facility. Research for what, he wasn't sure. Richards deduced from It110102 that the primary objective was almost certainly eugenics. Unfortunately, the entire place was "accidentally" destroyed by the Italian government, so a field trip was out of the question.

Richards returned the letter to the folder, took a final drag on his cigarette, and snuffed it out. He held the smoke deep in his lungs while his mind raced. His thoughts spread like wildfire, dancing from one detail to the next. He had a feeling of slight dread building in his stomach.

"The hell with it," Richards said out loud as he finally exhaled. He dragged his hands across his tired face; his eyes were stinging and the lids were heavy. It had been a draining day, between traveling through the night by train and meeting up with the local police—even if he had begun a friendship in Friendship!—and Tony was tired! He gave the file another fleeting glace as he got up from the desk and began his evening rituals. Three minutes after Tony went down, he went out.

• • •

The next few days went by quickly for Tony Richards. He spent a lot of time with Deputy Wilson, both on and off duty. The two men were hitting it off professionally as well as personally. Tony still could not bring himself to give many more details about the fugitive, other than that she would possibly not be alone and that she wasn't thought to be dangerous—but one could not be too careful.

Tony toured the dairy farm, Livin' the Cream, on two separate occasions. The first time was a quick tour of the grounds focused on the largest barn, as per the letter, that would most likely be the point of contact. This was decided by its proximity to the woods. Where most of the dairy farm was too open for someone to not be seen from a great distance, the one lone barn would afford Alessandra a bit of cover. There was another barn near the same size, but it was far too exposed to be the contact zone. Just to be safe, Wilson would be stationed at the other barn. He first visited the morning after he arrived; it was where Jack Wilson and Tony Richards had made their acquaintance. Tony was sleep deprived thanks to more than twelve hours' hopping from train to train from DC to Friendship. He had pulled into the station on the first train of the day, bright and early. His second visit afforded him slightly more time to look around.

Livin' the Cream dairy farm was situated at the end of Rose Road. It was no more than three miles from the main area of town. There were days when the wind was just right that the townsfolk could smell the fresh milk on the breeze, as if they had milked it themselves. The farm had begun as a small family affair in the early 1930s, serving Friendship and the surrounding areas. The current owner was a man named Jefferson Fillmore. Mr. Fillmore had been running the farm since his father had passed away of respiratory failure due to pneumonia in the winter of '49. Fillmore wasn't a great dairy farmer or even an outdoorsman. He was, however, a fantastic businessman.

Livin' the Cream had prospered mightily in the eight years that Jefferson had taken over the leadership duties. He had personally projected short-term profit growth by spreading the business from the towns in the county to a regional affair. It had all run very smoothly. The profits outweighed the overhead cost in the long term, even though it wasn't by much. The small expansion opened the doors to the second step of Fillmore's lifetime goals. During the past twelve months the company had been slowly gearing up for further expansion to statewide distribution, though none of the locals or workers knew about the long-term plans. An additional delivery truck had been purchased eight months ago, followed by the purchase of six more milk cows, two of them ready for insemination. About three months ago Fillmore had toyed with the idea of hiring more staff to keep the production high as he introduced new areas of distribution. Ultimately, he decided to hold off, so he could keep his overhead low as they moved into the new quarter. Besides, the eight he had on staff were more than sufficient for the milking. Fillmore still had his crew milking by hand, even though the practice was dated. He had some sort of superstitious silliness when it came to purchasing vacuum buckets for the cows. His dad had always told him that a human should get to know his animal, forming trust with the creature and earning a mutual respect. So, that's what Jefferson Fillmore continued doing. Besides, those damned things cut into his profit, even if it were an investment for the future.

Fillmore was willing to accommodate Deputy Jack Wilson and Agent Tony Richards in any way he could. The two men had been out to visit the farm for the first time on Monday morning. Fillmore had met Richards and personally given both the men a tractor-driven tour of the grounds. He stopped briefly at the large barn near the woods, pointing out that the barn was only used for storing the hay. They circled back around to the dirt parking area, and the two visiting men had thanked Fillmore for being willing to help with the surrender. Fillmore liked the idea of being part of a real-life investigation, even if he were a little scared that this person had chosen his farm for their surrender.

On Tuesday afternoon Wilson and Richards pulled up into the dirt driveway again and were greeted by a toothy Jefferson Fillmore.

"So, when and where can I expect this person to show up? Do I need to bring out my rifle; for my protection, of course?" Fillmore had asked Wilson as he was stepping out of the police cruiser.

"Jefferson, relax." Wilson sighed. "The farm will be closed on Thursday. Tell your employees not to come in and make sure that Doug understands that he can't tear off on a drunk Wednesday and show up to work two hours late on Thursday."

Fillmore blushed. Yes, sometimes Douglas Carter took to the drink, but he was a hard worker, hungover or not.

"Fine, fine . . . I'll tell 'em. Don't you worry 'bout that now," he declared in his light drawl. "So, where do you need me to be stationed during this . . . standoff or whatever?"

"The farm will be closed, Mr. Fillmore, so I assume that you will be stationed at your house," Tony said dryly.

Fillmore winced, as if he had been slapped.

"Now, now, wait just a minute, Mr. FBI, or whatever, this is my farm; private property. This ain't s-s-s-s-some ka-ka-ka-kinda, kinda . . . sh-sh-sh-shot-gunned . . ." Jefferson Fillmore began stuttering wildly, which didn't happen to the man often. Luckily, Jack Wilson interrupted, defusing the situation before it could build any further.

"Listen, Jefferson, this isn't local business; you know there's enough time for this man to make a couple of calls; the government will likely send out a warrant in a hurry and this will happen anyway. Why not just stay home with Charlene and have a nice picnic lunch, and see if one thing can lead to another."

"Jack, this is my farm," Fillmore repeated, but he was already losing the intensity that he'd previously had. "What about the cows? They will need to be milked, we do it twice a day, mornin' and late afternoon."

"Their teats aren't gonna bust over twenty-four hours; don't you give your boys Christmas off? You and I both know they will be OK for one day. Hell, chances are good that you'll be able to come back to the farm that afternoon."

Tony waited while the stout man with thinning hair played out his internal conflict. He watched as the man's face changed from disbelief and horror to reluctant acceptance.

"Fine," Fillmore said shortly. "Do your tour, then get outta here so I can make some money today at least."

That was when Jefferson Fillmore knew he wasn't going to be appointed an honorary deputy.

Wilson and Richards walked the small farm, alone this time, assessing as much of the terrain as possible as they headed to the barn by the edge of the woods. The two men nodded a greeting as they passed some of the workers, one being Mr. Douglas Carter. When they reached the barn, they walked the perimeter twice looking for places that Alessandra might be able to hide. Wilson and Richards also walked into the woods a short distance, looking for a campsite or a trail that she might be able to travel and not be seen. They found neither of these, instead finding only some scattered litter.

Wilson circled around to the entrance of the barn and opened the heavy doors. Richards fell in behind him. Inside the barn they found exactly what they'd expected to find, hay bales tightly packed into every nook and cranny.

"I'm going to set up here and I'd like you to station yourself at the other large barn over there," Richards told Wilson, pointing to the barn across the way.

Wilson nodded in agreement.

"What are we dealing with here, Tony? This is my town; it's my job to protect it."

"Hopefully," Richards replied, "just a kid who wants to surrender."

Jack Wilson looked at his new ally sideways. "I need more than that, Tony."

"I can't give you more, Jack. If I could, I would. Just know I'm going to do everything I can to keep your town safe."

Jack sighed heavily. "I guess I'm going to have to trust you, huh?"

"I guess so."

The two men left the barn and headed back to the squad car they'd arrived in not an hour before. Richards was satisfied with his second inspection of the farm; he had a better layout of both barns, and, more importantly, he knew that Jack Wilson was going to stick through this with him, knowledge or no knowledge.

As they were driving back to town, Jack mentioned that Ginny wanted Tony Richards to come over for supper on Wednesday, and she wouldn't take no for an answer, not like tonight, in which Tony had already declined her offer. Tony smiled as Jack Wilson explained that he was going to come over or else Ginny would come to his place and drag him the few blocks by the ear. Richards actually laughed out loud when Wilson remarked that he had seen it done on one occasion, and it wasn't a pretty sight. So, Tony accepted to offer cordially, and asked if he could bring anything, as any houseguest should. Jack left it to him to decide.

• • •

At 6:15 the next day, Richards rang the doorbell to the quaint house on Fern Street. In one hand he held a nice sauvignon wine that he had stumbled across in town, in the other a cigarette burned down to his fingertips. He took one final drag, and snuffed what remained on the sole of his Cole Haan Shell Cordovan Wingtips, and pocketed the butt. Ginny opened the door with the brightest, most elegant smile Tony had ever seen. He took in the moment like a sunset over the ocean. She was radiant, positively glowing. He smiled back, a silly sideways smile that cracked his handsome face into distorted features.

"Well, Mr. Richards, please come in, and try not to make the lady wait," Ginny winked.

In that moment he could have loved her, except she wouldn't have returned his love. Jack came from nowhere, showering his wife with affection in the form of a beautifully choreographed spin into a sensual dip that ended with a resonant gaze deep into her soul and a light kiss on the mouth. Ginny forgot the world around her, closed her eyes, and drew air deep into her lungs, breathing in pure love. She held it there for a beat and then exhaled, feeling emotions race through her entire body, causing tingling to erupt from her toes to her nose. She felt as if the world spun only for her. In that moment, it did.

"I envy you," Tony said, breaking the silence.

"Come in, buddy!" Jack welcomed his friend and took the bottle of wine and his jacket.

That night's meal was, once again, amazing. Tony Richards ate until he could hardly breathe, having seconds of everything and thirds of the wonderful asparagus that Ginny had prepared. The trio retired into the den after the meal, bringing their wineglasses with them and the half-finished bottle of sauvignon.

"How about a game while we finish this bottle?" Jack suggested.

"Oh yes! Can we play the new game, hon?" Ginny said with obvious excitement. "I have been waiting until we had someone over, and this is perfect!"

"Sure, sweetheart. Why don't you go get it from the other room?" Jack asked with a wink.

"You like games, Tony?"

"Sure. Who doesn't?"

"We sure love 'em around here. We must have a dozen different board games; seems like we can't even play them all. Ah, here we are"—Jack set his glass down and reached out to take the box from

Ginny—"this is the newest edition to our little game family. Have you ever played it?" Jack asked, as he held the box up for Tony to read.

The box contained a game by Milton Bradley called Name That Tune. On the cover of the box was the face of George DeWitt.

"Oh yeah, well, no, I haven't played the game before but I have seen it on television," Richards said with recognition. "It looks like great fun."

"It's a little different than the television show, more like Bingo, but it's sure to be good for a laugh," Ginny said with a broad smile.

She passed the playing cards around until the three of them each held one; next came the space markers. It seemed that the game was quite a lot like Bingo. The object was to fill a vertical, horizontal, or diagonal line on your card. Song titles were randomly placed in each space, and no two cards were alike.

Jack took the record that accompanied the game from its sleeve and headed to the RCA High Fidelity record player. Tony recognized it because he owned a sister model, although his came with an AM/FM receiver. He watched as Jack removed the few pictures from the top of the player's cabinet, opened the lid, and set the record onto the turntable.

"Are you guys ready?" Jack grinned as eagerly as his wife.

For the next hour the three people listened to the short snippets of popular songs and standards while covering their game boards to the best of their ability. Amazingly, each person won the game at least once with hurrahs and cheers all around. The half-finished bottle of wine quickly diminished to empty as the night settled into darkness. Ginny had been right, there was much laughter.

"Ladies and gentlemen," Richards proclaimed as he rubbed his now sore cheeks, "now that I have finally won a round, I believe I will leave on a high note!"

"Aww, not yet, Tony! Let's have one more round," Ginny huffed.

"Baby, the man's right, there's no better way to go out than on top, and, Tony, you aren't getting any higher tonight." Jack chortled.

He smiled. "We've got a big day tomorrow too; it'll be good to be rested."

Jack's smile faded. "Yes, sir, you couldn't be more right. Let me walk you out." The two men stood.

"Ginny, again, thank you for the amazing evening, I wouldn't have believed you had time to cook all of that wonderful food, but somehow you did, and my stomach thanks you extra." He smiled graciously.

"Tony Richards, you are quite welcome anytime."

Her eyes glowed a stunning deep blue, and Tony, once again, felt the tweak of envy for what he was sure to never have. His smiled lost a bit of its brilliance, but he was able to recover before anyone noticed. Jack clasped him on the back with Tony's coat in hand, and the two men walked out the front door. Tony immediately went for his smokes, offering one to Jack, who refused with a polite wave of the hand.

"Tomorrow morning," Tony began as he lit his Lucky Strike, "pick me up at Gina's at six forty-five. I want us to be in position by seven." He inhaled. "We may have long day ahead of us, so make sure you have some food."

White pillars of smoke flowed from his nostrils. "Also, do you guys have any handheld two-way radios?"

"We have the ones in the cruiser . . ."

"Never mind, I have two handhelds that I brought along," Richards said, remembering the devices were packed under his clothes in his only bag.

Tony turned and let his wingtips click down the wooden stairs.

"Try to get some sleep, Jack," he called over his shoulder and once again disappeared into the night.

Fifteen minutes later, Tony Richards was lying in bed staring at the cracked plaster on the ceiling of his room above Gina's Consignment. Eventually he closed his eyes; he did not sleep, not even a little.

• • •

"Test. Test, Jack, can you hear my voice?" All Richards heard was static.

"It works just like the radio in the car, Jack. Press the button on the side and speak when I'm not," Richards instructed.

"Yeah, Tony, I understand how to do it. I'm sorry. I just got spooked a little; I thought I heard something," Jack's tinny voice spoke through the tiny speaker on the two-way.

"Do you see anything?" Richards asked anxiously. The palpitations of his heart came in increasingly hurried bursts. "Jack, do you see anything, anything at all?"

White noise came quietly from the speaker.

"JACK?" he bellowed.

"Negative, Tony, it's all clear as far as I can see."

"Dammit." Richards sighed under his breath and wiped the back of his hand across his face.

The two men had arrived at Livin' the Cream dairy farm at ten minutes before seven and had done a preliminary sweep of the entire area. Together they'd made sure that there were no workers on-site, as well as checked for any signs that Alessandra might have been squatting nearby. Of course, they came up empty. By the time the two men were ready to split up, it was shortly past 7:30 a.m.

Tony had asked Jack to keep the radio chatter to a minimum to conserve the batteries in case the radios were needed later in the day. After a few hours, Jack couldn't help himself; he liked technology, and his customary patience was beginning to thin.

"Tony, how will we know what we're looking for?" Jack inquired through the static. "I mean, all you have told me so far is that it is a girl."

"How well do you know the people of Friendship, Jack?" Tony responded.

"Pretty well, I think."

"Then, if you see a female you don't know, chances are it will be her." Tony smirked at his sardonic response, then continued. "She's blonde, between five feet and five feet five inches"—he hesitated, trying to word this next part perfectly—"and here's the hard pill to swallow, she may be teenaged, or younger."

Jack Wilson stared at his radio as if it were growing legs. He frowned as confusion washed over him. A quick burst of static pulsed over the transceivers.

"I thought you said this bird has been missing since the war. That would mean she was barely born when she went missing. How is that even possible? Was she kidnapped?"

"Something like that," Richards squelched in response. He was surprisingly finding it easier to dance around any truths that might pop up. "It'll be a great story to talk about someday after this is all over."

He smiled, and that was when he heard it.

• • •

Tony Richards had grown tired of pacing around the barn; it had been more than four straight hours. He decided to take a break, and he sat with his back against the side of the oversize hay hideaway with his eyes toward the woods. The woods were no more than one hundred and fifty feet away, and Richards had a clear view of almost the entire tree line. Ten minutes, no more, no less, then he would get back up and do it all over again. Almost as soon as he sat down, Jack broke the long radio silence with questions about the Sartori girl. It was a welcome conversation for Tony. It helped him to keep his mind off the seconds that were anvils being dragged by a sickly mule. Tony and Jack were becoming very close, really a lot closer than some of the people he considered close back in DC. He hoped that they would continue to have a relationship after this case was over. Maybe he would come down whenever he had some time off.

"Someday after this is all over," he heard himself saying. He smiled and took a breath to continue ribbing Jack when he heard movement in the woods directly in front of him.

Tony threw the radio on the ground as Jack was asking another question; he scrambled to his feet. Instinctively, Tony put his hand on the butt of his gun, but he did not draw the firearm. It was just past noon, the sun was a blazing mass in the center of the puffy-clouded sky, causing just enough shade to be spilled into the wooded area so that Tony could only make out the basic shape of a person moving slowly closer. He raised his free hand over his brow and squinted in a futile attempt to improve his vision.

"I see you in there," Richards called in a surprisingly calm voice. His heart was pounding out a march in his eardrums, but one would have never known.

"I'm Special Agent Anthony Richards of the Central Intelligence Agency. Keep on coming out into the light where I can see you better."

Richards waited. Then he realized that his hand was still on the butt of his gun inside his jacket. He slowly removed his hand, putting both his palms forward in a gesture that said, *see, nothing up my sleeves.* Tony saw the shadow begin to move again toward the clearing; it became increasingly more apparent that the figure was using a cane, and he realized, *This is not Alessandra.*

"I sent that letter to the CIA because I thought you could get it to *them.* They don't have an address like the CIA," the shadow said with a light British accent as he slowly advanced.

Tony skipped the cordialities. "I don't know who *they* are, buddy, or what you're talking about, but are you Invisible?"

A chuckle. "You can see me, can't you, Special Agent Anthony Richards?" The young man continued moving with the assistance of the cane. As he crossed the imaginary threshold from the woods to the clearing, Tony could see that he was indeed a *he.* A he who was dark skinned yet somehow incredibly pale; he had beaded sweat running down through his thick, tangled hair into his face and wetting the front of his shirt. It seemed that just walking was a very difficult task for him. He was favoring the cane—a lot.

"I suppose I can," Richards said, lowering his hands. "Why are you here? And do you need medical attention, I mean, are you hurt?"

"I'm here because I am *Invisible,*" he said, emphasizing the last word. "I'm here to surrender, as I said in the letter."

Tony stared at the young man with a hard poker face, giving him room to fill the silence, as he had been trained to do. The man stopped short, leaving a wide berth between them. He wore faded blue jeans that were loosely cuffed at the bottom. His worn red T-shirt was mostly covered by his denim jacket. He dressed like a teenager but was clearly a bit older, possibly in his late twenties.

"I assume you received the letter, and that it's why you're here, Special Agent Anthony Richards," he finally said sarcastically.

"Let's just make it Tony, and to be honest, I was expecting someone else."

The man's smirk instantaneously changed to confusion.

"How . . . who else could have written that letter?"

Now it was Tony's turn to smirk.

"Well, I guess that's something I can't really talk about," Richards said, trying to get a read on the young man. "Classified information, you know how it is." He paused, stepping to his left. "But"—his smile was now full blown—"let's play twenty questions, you know the game?"

"Of course I know it. Animal, vegetable, or mineral . . . wait, animal, as in a human."

"Very good . . . what's your name, buddy?" Richards asked, stopping and stuffing his hands into his pockets.

"Why don't you just call me *Friend*, as in Friendship?"

"We need to build some trust, Friend. A name can't hurt."

"A name is just a word, like trust is an illusion."

"OK . . . Friend it is," Richards took out his smokes, put a cigarette between his lips, and lit the Zippo. "Smoke?"

"That shit will kill you. I've seen enough death."

"Really"—he inhaled deeply, held and then exhaled the smoke through his nostrils—"care to elaborate?"

"The island, you know the one," he began.

"Sardinia, the one on the map you sent. That's where you saw the death, huh?" Richards guessed.

"Not just death; dead children, at least a half dozen. That's why I ran. I ran to live."

Tony thought he could see the pain in the man's distant eyes. He puffed again, then waited.

"I couldn't save them . . . there isn't a lot that a kid can do." He looked up at Tony with tears overfilling his eyes. "So I ran, and I didn't stop." Tony's Friend wiped at his eyes with the heel of his free hand.

Richards hesitated, then questioned, "Are you alone? Is there anyone else with you?"

The Friend sighed. "That's not how twenty questions works, Tony. I'm supposed to ask the questions. How about, would I be here if I weren't alone?"

"This is where I answer yes or no, right . . . I'm gonna go with no."

"Ding, ding, ding!" the Friend said, tapping his nose and pointing toward Richards.

At that moment that radio crackled and Jack Wilson began talking. "Tony, are you there? Did you go take a piss or something?"

The two men turned toward the sound. Tony looked back at his new Friend.

"I have to respond, you know? If I don't, he'll come running," Richards said. "I assume you're ready to surrender peacefully."

"Sorry, not until I know who you were expecting," the man stated.

Tony's lips thinned into nothingness. He nodded.

"What the hell does it matter anyway?" he said more to himself than his Friend. "Her name is Alessandra and she was in the facility on Sardinia also."

The Friend's face lit up in surprise and astonishment.

"She's alive? Alessandra is alive?"

"Yes, as far as we can tell, and she is very important to the United States government. Do you know anything about her whereabouts?"

He shook his head slowly, still in awe.

"How did she escape?" asked the man while leaning on the cane.

"She was rescued; the army beat down the door to the place and found her inside."

"She's special you know . . . different." The Friend began to get excited and speak quickly. "She never got sick from all the tests, not like the others. Not like me. I mean, I have my thing, and she must have something too."

"Slow down, Friend, what thing?" Richards stepped backward, away from the man.

"What does she have, what can she do? Tell me, Tony!" he said hysterically. "Damn you! TELL ME!"

He immediately began closing the gap between the two men in an awkward, limping run. Tony reflexively dropped his cigarette, reached into his jacket, placed one hand upon the butt of his standard-issue firearm, and threw the opposite hand up in a stopping gesture.

"Hold on, Friend! Let's keep this surrender peaceful!" Richards barked.

The man stopped dead in his tracks; he stood up, raised his arms straight out, inhaled sharply, and then began to shimmer like he was light reflected off a glass door. Then everything changed.

• • •

The radio static refocused Tony Richards.

"I thought you said this bird was missing since the war. That would mean she was barely born when she went missing. How is that even possible? Was she kidnapped?"

"Something like that," Richards squelched in response. He was surprisingly finding it easier to dance around any truths that might pop up. "It'll be a great story to talk about someday after this is all over." He smiled, hesitated with an overwhelming feeling of déjà vu, then his smile changed into a muddled frown.

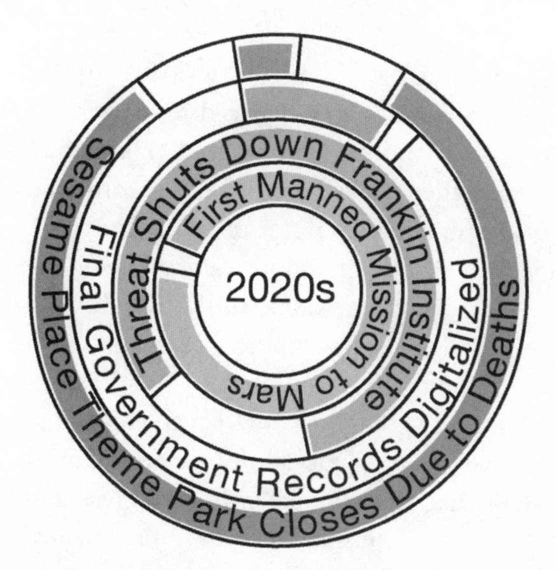

4:17 A.M.

WASHINGTON, DC, 2023

"GET DOWN ON THE GROUND!" Mark Richards screamed into the night.

His eyes flew open in startled surprise as he sat up into the darkness. It took him several seconds to get his bearings. Cold sweat ran down his face and shirtless chest through the tangled gray hairs pooling in his belly button. His breath was coming in gulping waves, and his heart was beating like fluttering hummingbird wings. The dreams were relentless; they'd been breaking into his mind night after night for the last thirty-five years. They just kept coming, harsh and daunting, even when they faded away as quickly as this one.

Richards's apartment was semidark with the orange glow of the streetlights seeping around the shades of the only tiny window. He threw his legs over the side of his bed and gingerly hopped down from the four-foot height. He grabbed the edge of the Murphy bed and folded it up into the wall, securing it in place with three separate latches. On the underside of the bed—now the wall—was a touch screen that he brought to life by tapping the upper right-hand corner. It showed the time as 4:19 a.m. He tapped the opposite corner, and a display popped up, showing the weather radar for the surrounding areas. Across the bottom of the screen was a video news ticker spouting off incidents from the previous evening. He placed his fingers on the screen and pinched to push out to his home screen. He tapped the icon labeled "YouTube+" and then clicked on the local sports icon. The screen flashed to life with snippets of a range of DC-area sports. They were categorized into a video cloud, the most watched being the largest. Richards had never changed the settings, so the video cloud always came up in randomly designed patterns; this time the video cloud made a picture that represented the continental United States. He stared at the video cloud, knowing that he would never get used to seeing the changed shape of the US, even though it had been almost five years since the new states had been voted in by Congress and signed off by the POTUS. It reminded him of when the International Astronomical Union had revoked Pluto's planet status and reassigned it as a dwarf planet.

Bastards, he thought. *It's still a planet to me.*

Disgusted with the video cloud, he double tapped the top right corner of the screen and shut the whole thing down.

It's all about money with these people.

His apartment was a miniscule studio of barely two hundred square feet. The only full dividing wall was the one that sectioned off the bathroom. The floor plan was as open as it could be in such a small space. The living/sleeping area opened up into a kitchenette with no more than a sink and a tiny range squashed into a corner. The refrigerator was on the opposite end and was one of those three-foot jobs that fit under the counter. It didn't matter; it was basically empty anyway. Richards was not much of a materialist—at least not since the divorce, which had forced him into his current living conditions. The room held some small but comfortable furnishings. An oversize chair that could hold two people sat in the corner adjacent to the fold-up small single mattress. He had a short bookshelf with some collector bindings that he had kept the majority of his life, even though he had read most only once; since e-readers had come along in the early part of the century, most reading had changed over to the digital realm. And why not? E-readers could hold more books than most people could read in their lifetimes. Positioned directly underneath the fold-out single was one of the only things that he'd received from the so-called settlement. It was a solid oak desk with a dark stain finish and intricate ornamentations. The desk had a total of eight drawers, three on the left, four on the right, and one large one centered above the chair. The desk was an antique. It was hand crafted in the 1940s, and it had belonged to his uncle, Tony Richards.

Mark looked down at the clutter that had accumulated on the top of the old desk. Most of it was Mark's own ramblings and theories about It110102. He pulled the chair back and sat wearily. One sheet of paper had a drawing of a section of crossroads and intersections. They meant nothing; they were only Mark's way of trying to piece together information that did not have any discernible connection to anything else. He cleared away some of the papers and saw his tablet lying on the finished edge of the desk. His picked it up and stared through the glass down onto the pile of papers and slivers of caramel wood peeking through. He still found technology amazing sometimes. During his career he had watched the rise of the personal computer and saw many companies fail for not taking the PC seriously. The computer made way for programmers to make games and eventually gaming systems, which seemed to drive the technological feats, as each company vied for control of the market. Richards had witnessed the birth of the Internet and the public embrace making a small world after all. He watched it change from modems with dial-up and loading speeds of hours to entire web pages with video and complex programming load at 99.7 percent the speed of light. Fiber-optic cables could still be found on the floors of every ocean, even though that method was beginning to become dated. He saw the PC become mobile with laptops and long-life batteries, which led to cellular devices changing from a communication tool to a pocket-size computer. When the tablet revolution began in the early part of the century, he was awed that the same science fiction he watched on television as a boy was becoming reality.

Mark waved his hand behind the tablet, and then drew his pattern code on the glass to wake the tablet. It was bioencoded just like all tablets issued by the agency. He was a bit of a dinosaur compared to the young guys in the office. He used a Bluetooth earpiece for phone conversations, which was acceptable, if not slightly old-fashioned. He just could not wrap his head around the biohacking that some of these agents were getting into. A few of the guys had recently implanted variations of earbuds directly into their ear canals along with miniature microphone in their throats. They could even listen to music without anyone knowing, until they started singing out loud. McMillian had LED implants in his forearm that monitored his bodily function since his heart attack he had last June. The damned things lit up and showed his BP, heart rate, everything, even his blood sugar! Transhumanism had been around since the end of the twentieth century when some college student put an RFID transmitter under his own skin. Richards also remembered some guy put magnets inside of his arm to hold his MP3 player in place. These body mods were getting a little extreme, with some underground markets replacing or modifying entire bodily systems, calling the process "getting Mann'd," whatever that meant.

The screen on his tablet went from completely transparent to a deep black with the company logo in the background.

"Hello, Special Agent Markus Richards. Case It110102 loading . . ." The tablet spoke in a decidedly computerized female voice as the words popped up on the screen. It freaked him out to think about the amount of rapid changes in technology over the last forty years. He went from having to walk across the room to change one of your thirteen channels to being able to watch anything you could think of just by asking your device to do a simple search. He felt like a man out of time playing catch-up.

"File found, would you like a specific location, Agent Richards?" the nonfemale inquired.

"Random," Mark mumbled, realizing this was the first time he had spoken since he'd awoken. The sound was loud inside his head.

Richards knew all the information in the file. He'd seen all the pictures countless times. When he was feeling particularly low, and the dreams always put him here, he did a random search through the file and studied whatever the demon lady in the software thought was of importance. Tonight's random search hit a little too close to home.

"I found this for you," said the nonfemale.

It was a grainy picture with a digital blurb posted over the left-hand side. The picture was of a man in his midfifties, with dark skin and more gray than he should have had at that age. He wore khaki slacks and a green polo shirt. The coloring was approximate, because the original was black and white. But none of these things was his defining feature; in fact most of his features had been destroyed beyond recognition, but luckily the video guys pulled this image from a surveillance camera. What did define him was his wheelchair. Mark read the blurb.

Man in a wheelchair. SC 1986
Connection to A. Sartori: Unknown; possible leverage
Status: Deceased
Source: Video Surveillance Camera

Mark forced his eyes closed, rubbed his brow, and pushed the memories away. He had already relived that day enough in his strained mind. It was too much right now. Hell, it was *always* too much.

"Close; good-bye." Richards spoke the commands to shut down the tablet.

"Good-bye, Agent Richards." The nonfemale fell silent.

Richards placed the tablet on top of the papers on the desk and sat back in his chair, with the memories flooding, despite his efforts to suppress them. He placed his hands over his face and rubbed the salt-and-pepper scruff that had formed overnight. When he removed them from his line of sight, Mark's eyes fell upon the top right-hand drawer of the desk. He reached out lazily and grasped the tarnished brass handle, opening the drawer about six inches. Mark could not see inside the drawer but knew what he was reaching for. Once he'd grabbed the object, he closed his eyes again and let his sense of touch take over. He felt cold against his flesh. The metal was smooth and worn, a chromed steel he knew well. Initials that had been carved into the casing of the object were now all but worn away due to overhandling or, more than likely, overuse. The initials belonged to his uncle, Anthony James Richards.

Mark opened his eyes and looked at the Zippo lighter in the palm of his hand. He instinctively flipped the lid and turned the wheel. Nothing but a spark came from the practically spent flint. Mark didn't expect any different. He had not fueled the lighter in ten years or more.

The rope wick was all but nonexistent as well. He turned the wheel again and watched the quick shower of sparks.

• • •

The sparks turned to fire, then lit the Lucky Strike hanging from Tony's mouth just under his Magnum, P.I. mustache. He snapped the lid closed with a trained flip of the wrist.

"We know she's in the area. There are multiple eyewitnesses that confirm seeing her in the past hour," Tony Richards explained to his nephew as they drove to the airport. He exhaled white smoke out of the driver's-side window. "Today is gonna be the day, kid. You ready?"

• • •

Mark closed the Zippo and his eyes, squeezing them tight with distress. The memory had a physical pain to it. Emotions were hard on the body; not even mods could change that. The sun was peeking through the slits in the blinds. Another day was beginning.

When he got to the office, Mark Richards sat his steaming coffee cup down on his desk, along with his tablet, and opened the center drawer. He always kept some pain relievers here for mornings like this one. His lack of sleep and stressful dreams did a number on his head. This morning the pain was turning from pesky to red hot in a hurry. He shook out three of the generic painkillers, paused briefly, and then decided that one more was in order. He bounced the chemical quartet off the back of his throat and drank just enough coffee to float them downstream, burning his mouth slightly while doing so.

His desk mate was a young woman named Myers; most of the asshole group called her Oscar, though she didn't seem to mind. Mark preferred her real name to her childish nickname. Emily, or Em to Mark, was particularly young, at twenty-five, to be an agent. Although, working his way from up the mail room, and with a little help from his uncle, he'd had his own desk by age twenty-three . . . or twenty-four; he couldn't remember anymore. Em had two separate degrees, accumulated hundreds of hours training through dozens of programs, and was a natural when it came to seeing all possible outcomes. She was also a lot better to stare at than the other idiots around the office. Not that she was a supermodel or anything, but she did have a nice feminine quality behind her analytical exterior. She was not too tall, five four, perhaps, and slender with an athletic build. Her hair was a natural dark chocolate and her eyes were a vivid green. She wore it up most days, in either a bun or a ponytail. Today she wore it down, and it framed her modest face perfectly.

"Morning, Mark! You look like hell . . . again," Em said, smiling.

He nodded and responded with a single word: "Em." That's how it went with the two of them sometimes. Saying little was saying just enough.

Mark began his day, like most days, by skimming his inbox for anything important. It was always the same—some stuff from the superiors and lots of damn junk mail. This morning Mark shook his head and wondered why the government of the United Freaking States of America couldn't keep spam from his professional inbox. A few e-mails were deemed semi-important, but he had nothing for the *only* case that mattered. Mark spent the first hour of the morning cleaning his spammy mailbox and thinking about Alessandra Sartori. The trail had been cold for so long that Richards didn't want to check his calendar app to see when he'd gotten his last lead. He knew he could do it quickly on his tablet, but he decided he might have some sort of breakdown if he found it had been years. It had been.

"Hey, Richards," Em said, bringing Mark back to reality.

"Yeah?" It was all he could muster.

"We have been sitting across from each other for almost a year now."

My God, had it been that long? Em must be twenty-six by now! Richards thought in a haze.

"Things are slowing down for me for the next few weeks," she continued. "I wanted to ask you if I could take a look at that cold case you're always obse—well, you know."

He did know; the case *was* his obsession.

"You'll have to get the proper OKs, but I don't mind," Richards said untruthfully. The case belonged to him, and he wasn't about to lose it to Emily "Oscar" Myers. He sighed. Those feelings were nothing but jealousy, because logic told him that a new pair of eyes might see something that he could not. Finding Alessandra was the greater good here, not pride.

"Great!" Em exclaimed. She picked up her own tablet and clicked the Skype icon. "Call ASAC."

The gall of this woman to call Spary right here in front of me, Richards thought with a scoff.

"Yes, Myers, what do you need?" Spary answered the video call quickly.

"Hey, Chief—"

"Don't call me that, Myers."

"Sorry, right." She tapped her head in mock frustration. "I wanted to work on that cold case with Richards, you know the one. I just finalized everything for the Pender investigation, and I wanted to run this by you," Em said with the cool confidence of a seasoned agent.

Spary drew in a breath and raised his brow in thought. "I don't see why not. Maybe he could use the help. Good idea, Myers."

"Sir?" Richards almost bellowed across the two desks.

"Thanks, Chief—sir, sorry." Em smiled brightly as she tapped the "End Call" button on the tablet. "OK, where do we begin?"

Mark Richards stared in disbelief with his mouth agape. *Great,* he thought, *now I get to babysit.* He watched as she shut down her tablet and waited for it to reboot, which was standard procedure when getting access to new records—and then an idea occurred to him.

Richards tapped the Bluetooth tucked into his ear. "Records."

An older woman answered.

"This is the records department, Julie speaking, how can I help you?" she asked.

"Hi, Julie, this is Agent Mark Richards with the CIA. My ID number is alpha eight zero five sierra one niner eight zero. I would like to come down and see a file you have in storage. The number is India Tango one one zero one zero two."

Julie typed the numbers into the computer touch screen on her desk to pull up the information about the file.

"Our records show that you have digital access to this file from your issued tablet and any government desktop, Agent Richards."

"That's correct; however, I would like to come inspect some of the documents in person." He swiveled his chair to face away from Em. "Does Agent Emily Myers also have access to the file?" Richards lowered his voice, suspecting she did.

"According to our records, yes, sir, she does." He slumped slightly at the news, but what could he expect? The information highway seemingly traveled at the speed of light. "Will she be accompanying you to see the file?" Julie inquired.

Mark turned and stared across the desk at Em for a brief second. The tablet had rebooted, and she was attempting to sync it so she could access It110102.

"Possibly, is thirty minutes OK? It'll take us that long to drive over with traffic," Richards responded.

"Perfect, I'll make sure you have a clean room available," said Julie. "Thank you, sir."

"Yep, thanks." He tapped his earpiece and ended the call.

"Come on, Em. Let's take a ride." He stood, put his sport coat on, and grabbed his tablet.

Em followed suit without question.

When the two agents entered the parking garage, Em took out her personal car keys and Richards waved her off. They were going to drive his government-issued hybrid. This was a case, after all; business was on the company's dime. He noticed she had put on her augmented-reality glasses. She wasn't into transhumanism, that he was aware of, but she liked those stupid glasses. He had to admit, though, they were useful, and he had considered buying into the hype before his divorce had sent him into slight financial ruin. So, maybe he was bitter about the AR glasses. The two agents got into the vehicle without a word. This same vehicle had chased down Lucas Henley's killer eleven months prior. It had spent about a week in the shop after that chase getting the full work up—systems checks, engine checks—and everything had come out clean. The boys in the shop had to repair some body damage from playing bumper cars, but that was all.

The black hybrid pulled out from the cover of the parking garage into the rainy afternoon. The storm clouds had darkened the sky during the early morning but held their payload until just after lunch. Richards flicked the switch for the wipers. The agents drove with only the swish-swash sound for a while until Em broke the silence.

"Mark, I know why this case is important to you. All of us do," she began. "Your uncle was a great agent, and his death—"

"Let's just listen to the radio," he said, cutting her short and switching on the satellite radio. The station was tuned to NPR, where they were talking about the latest North Korean hostilities. The reporter said that the government had refused to let the UN enter to search for nuclear weapons on the basis that North Korea had already demonstrated that the weapons were there when they sent a small test nuke into the Sea of Japan two hundred miles from the island of Sado. The tension was growing thick between the UN and North Korea. The reporter turned the conversation over to an analyst, who opinioned that there could be an imminent future war. Luckily, Richards and Myers only caught the tail end of that report before NPR moved on to lighter stories.

Mark took the time to let his mind wander back to his uncle. He looked at the road ahead of him, saw the traffic that lay between him and the records building, and remembered when his uncle taught him to drive. Uncle Tony had had a '75 Chevy Malibu, and it was in great shape. Richards remembered that the car was as long as a boat, with white-walled tires, and a trunk you could live in. He smiled. That first day, Tony had taken him to an old overgrown parking lot of some store that had gone out of business long before. Mark had swung that monster of a car all over that weedy lot for a good hour or more. Then Tony said he was ready for the highway, and directed him out into the street. Fortunately, it wasn't a busy street, because Mark drove the boat across the lines in the road while Tony sat back and course corrected. The happy memory turned cold as Mark felt the pain of loss all over again.

He reached forward, switched off the radio, and let the silence grow long and uncomfortable. Em reached up, adjusted her AR glasses, and swiped through the menu screens. She stopped on record video. The functions on the AR glasses could also be controlled with voice commands, but she knew that that would ruin the stale, lingering silence. Besides, she wasn't sure she wanted him to know she was recording.

"Look," Mark eventually began, as Em reached up and tapped the swipe bar on the side of the AR glasses to begin video recording, "my uncle began this investigation a long time ago, and then he passed it down to me as my first assignment. I don't know what you think you know, but I watched him die . . . die trying to capture this fugitive. He wasn't even supposed to be there. I hesitated, and he paid the price for my insecurities . . . I was"—he swallowed hard with an audible clicking of his larynx—"scared to go alone. Since then, I've wanted to finish this for him and get some closure." The guilt was eating him like a cancer from the inside out.

Em inconspicuously reached up and tapped the bar to stop the recording.

"I'm sorry," was all she could manage to say. Seven silent minutes later they were parking at the records building.

"If you don't mind, I'd like to do the talking," Em Myers said as the two agents moved under the awning out of the light drizzle.

Richards grasped the handle and said, "I do mind," then pulled the door open for Em.

She shook her head in disbelief and marched through the door with Richards following behind her, grinning.

The cream-colored interior of the records building was dull and drab. There were very few pictures on any of the walls, and most of those were of landscapes. The space was not as open as Em had imagined it to be; in fact it was the opposite. She was thinking it would be a large lobby with big cushy chairs to wait in, but instead they came through the front doors into a small hallway. At the far end was a window reminiscent of a bank-teller window, with a small opening for documents to be fed through. A few different women in the small office behind the glass were sorting files or working on data entry. The woman closest to the window was somewhere in her mid-to-late fifties. She wore a name badge that showed a picture that was at least a half a dozen years old with the name "Julie Davies" underneath.

"May I help you?" Julie smiled.

"Hello, Julie, I'm Agent Mark Richards," he said, pressing his thumb on the scanner below the opening in the glass, "and this is Agent Emily Myers. I spoke to you a little while ago about taking a look at a file."

Julie took a long glance at the information that appeared on her computer screen, then gestured toward Em. "Your turn, honey."

Em placed her right thumb on the scanner, then waited and watched as her thumbprint was scanned.

"Thank you," Julie said. "You both seem to be who you say you are and have the proper clearance. Come on back."

Julie placed her hand under the counter and pressed a hidden button that released the electromagnet that held the large door to their right in place. Mark pushed it open with some effort and held it for Em to come through. Julie guided them down a long hallway with similar doors on each side about every five or six feet. Mark had been here before, but this was Myers's first encounter with the records department. Of course she wasn't naive enough to believe that all of the CIA's records were stored here, but apparently there were some heavy hitters like It110102.

The three people stopped at a room near the end of the corridor labeled with a single letter: "R."

"Sorry, sweetie," Julie stated. "Those AR glasses are going to have to stay with me. Also, any recording device that you may have—phones, tablets, cameras—they all have to be left with me."

Em was visibly annoyed but complied without complaint, handing over her glasses and her cell phone. Richards took the Bluetooth device from his ear and removed the dinosaur-age cell from his inner jacket pocket.

"Wow, I'm surprised that antique even has Bluetooth," Em said. "You know what? I had that phone when I was twelve! Small world . . ."

Mark just stared at her and waited for her to finish. "Can we go in now, or do you want to discuss any other electronic deficiencies that I may or may not have?"

Em threw her hands up, feigning frustration while smiling a bit. Julie took out a large set of key cards and shuffled through them until she found the one labeled "R." She scanned the card, and then placed her thumb on the pad. The door unlocked with a clank. She pushed it open.

"Lights," Julie said, cueing the lights. "The file is already in the room; take as much time as you need," she explained. "Oh, and I'll have your personal items up front; when you are finished, pick up the receiver"—she pointed to a phone on the wall—"and we'll come let you out."

Julie Davies shut the door behind her as she left; the door hissed as it locked the agents in the room. The room, Mark noticed, looked much like an interrogation room that one might see in a movie or television show but without the one-way mirror. There was a large table centered in the room, empty except for the red case file It110102. Other than that, there were only two chairs for the agents to sit in and a phone hanging on the wall. Mark moved to the table, sat down, and turned the file toward him. Em moved across the table to the other chair, sat, and then leaned eagerly forward.

"So this is it, huh?" she asked.

"Yep, It110102, my first real case—my uncle's too."

Mark opened the red folder. His uncle had taught him to organize the folder with the most recent and important information on the top. In the case of It110102, the best, most recent picture of Alessandra Sartori was front and center, followed by a physical description and her last known whereabouts. The last time Mark had seen this folder was just before he'd seen Alessandra about fifteen years ago. The agency had begun digitalizing all documentation sometime around '04 or '05. The top-secret files were some of the first to move to the digital world. Richards was assigned a tablet shortly after so he could continue working this case, as well as others. Apparently, there were many governmental files and folder to digitalize; the projected finish date wasn't until 2027. He spun the folder in Em's direction and tapped the picture.

"This is the face I can't get out of my head," he said. "You need to learn this face. It shouldn't have changed much, even though this picture's fifteen years old."

"So, that would make her around forty now?" Em asked.

Mark looked up from the photo. He knew every detail of the contents of It110102, and it was strange sharing them with someone else after so many years.

"There are some fundamental things that we have to discuss about this girl. I take 'em for granted because I have lived with 'em for so long," Mark said and thumbed through the middle of the folder until he found another picture. He placed it beside the most recent photo of Alessandra. It had a distinct grainy video quality to, it but Em had no doubt it was the same girl.

"OK." Em began to study the pictures. "What am I looking at here, Richards?"

Mark Richards tapped the upper left-hand corner of each picture where some identifying markers had been placed by Mark himself long ago.

The most recent photograph showed:

A. Sartori: VA 2006
Current Whereabouts: Unknown
Status: Missing; presumed alive
Source: Cellular phone

The grainy photograph pulled from the middle of the file showed:

A. Sartori: SC 1986
Current Whereabouts: Unknown
Status: Missing; presumed alive
Source: Video surveillance camera

Em read the information several times in an attempt to process what she was seeing. The pictures were definitely taken at different times and pulled from different sources, but . . .

"These pictures are stamped twenty years apart. There must be a mistake; this girl hasn't aged a year if she's aged a day!" she said, goofing up the idiom.

"I was there, on both days. I assure you that it isn't wrong or doctored in any way," Mark responded. "There's something unique about her; for some reason, she doesn't age, not like you or me, at least. All we know is in that file. Go ahead, read it."

Emily Myers had already started to read the file. She tore through each page, trying to grasp what was going on. She started by combing through some of the recovered documents from Sardinia. Most of these documents were almost a century old, and they were in sealed plastic bags for preservation. The records were all in German, but each had an English translation attached to the outside of the bag. One with information about the transfer of the child to the custody of the Third Reich caught her eye. She read the English translation.

> *The subject has an extremely high probability of manifestation. According to her parents, she will be turning five years old in the spring. Physically, the subject appears to be no more than two or possibly three years old. The parents were told that she would live a happy full life in America. They have struggled with the loss of the twin brother and feel she is too much of a burden to bear. They say all they see is the boy when they look at her. If their story is to be believed, he died from some sort of osteoporosis, which is more commonly found in the older population, specifically women. We let them say good-bye to the girl, and we had them removed after they left the facility. We have told the girl that if she is good, her parents may come back for her . . .*

"This is crazy!" Myers said to herself.

"It's hard to believe that human beings can be so cruel to children, isn't it?" Richards interjected.

"To anyone . . ."

She continued to flip through the pages; her head spun. At times she stopped and asked a question or two, but mostly she read. It didn't take her nearly as long as Richards thought it would. She focused on the hard facts and most important information, knowing that she would be able to dig through it all with a fine-tooth comb on her tablet anytime she wanted once the damned thing synced.

After nearly half of an hour, Em looked up in a daze. She sighed loudly and told Mark that she may need to talk to Spary and get more than a few weeks for this project before moving on to her next case. He smiled a humorless smirk as he leaned against the wall on the far side of the room. She returned her attention to the file.

"So we keep tabs on Chapman," Em said.

"Not anymore; after five years with no apparent contact, we cut our losses."

"That wasn't a question, Mark." She looked up at him strangely. "You must be slipping in your old age; right here you have phone records from this year."

"What?" he said in disbelief. "Right where?" He walked over to the table and craned his neck to see the records.

"Right here at the back of the file," she responded.

"Horse shit! Give me that!"

Em slid the folder toward him, opened to the phone records that she spoke of. His eyes darted back and forth as he skimmed the records. Then he lifted his head and stared off toward the opposite wall.

"I didn't add this," he whispered, more to himself than Em Myers.

The phone caught his gaze; an idea formulated in his head. He walked to the receiver and scooped it from its cradle into his slightly wrinkled hand. There were no numbers to press, but it didn't matter—the phone began ringing before it had made it to his lobe. Julie answered on the third ring.

"Are you two all finished? I'll come let you out," she said.

"No," Mark quickly said. "No, we aren't ready. I have a question; how often do you update the digital versions of the files?"

"We update them when new information is brought to us, usually within five business days," Julie replied. Mark hung up the phone then turned toward Em, a look of concentration on his face. Then his eyes darted to the corners of the room.

"Mark, what—"

He held up one finger, cutting her off midthought. Then he quickly walked to the table and looked at the phone records that had been compiled over the last six months or so. He contemplated pocketing the records, but he knew they weighed each file before and after viewing, and if the weight was off even a few ounces, then the two agents would not get to leave the building, much less continue the investigation. He bent, scanning the records again, looking desperately for some sort of pattern. All of a sudden it jumped out at him like a snake hiding in the brush, waiting on its next meal. He stood upright again and moved to the phone.

"Mark!"

Again he held up one finger. He picked up the phone, waited for an answer, and said, "Julie we *are* ready, come get us."

"What the hell is going on, Mark? And if you hush me one more time—"

That is exactly what Mark Richards did.

At once, he could hear the hissing lock loosening outside the door and knew that Julie would be waiting with her bright smile on the other side. Mark willed Em to relax, hoping she would get the hint. Julie informed the two agents that procedure dictated that the file be checked for integrity before they could be allowed to leave; policies were policies, after all. Mark smiled and stood in the corridor with Em glaring at him while Julie took the file into a room near the front. The entire procedure did not take long at all. Julie came out of the small room, informed the agents that everything was shipshape, and reminded them not to forget their belongings on the way out.

"Thank you for all your help, Julie," Mark said, smiling widely. The two agents gathered their belongings and quickly walked to the hybrid. Mark fell into the driver seat while Em walked to the opposite side.

Mark sat behind the wheel of the hybrid, waiting for Em to get in. When she did, she slammed the door hard and took in a controlled breath.

"Listen, I may have overreacted a little bit back there, but I don't deserve to be treated poorly." Her newfound calm was disintegrating. "Your finger in my face was totally unprofessional and unnecessary." She sighed heavily, rubbing her face. "What is your deal?"

"I didn't add those phone records," he said.

"So?"

"So," he stated, "I'm the only person officially on this case for the last *thirty-five* years. Who the hell added to the file? More importantly, why?"

Her frustration was instantly gone, replaced by curiosity. "Some other person or people are trying to find her too . . . maybe." It was a stretch, but it was the best she could come up with.

"I guess so," he speculated, "and they're keeping it from me. Julie said they update all new information digitally within five days. Those phone records went back at least six months. We need to see Chapman, today."

Em put her AR glasses back on her face, then tapped the touch bar on the side, which brought the glasses to life, and moved to the heads-up display.

"Find Grey Chapman, Philadelphia, Pennsylvania." Em's voice commands changed to text inside of her field of vision. After proofreading, she said, "Go." The display in her field of vision was equivalent to looking at a translucent 8K UHD fifty-inch monitor from about eight feet away. The word "Searching" was flashing on the display at the moment. Technically, the image was being projected directly into her right retina, making the floating display more of an optical allusion.

"I got him," Em said, smiling. "Plan route."

"I don't have a GPS," Mark said, slightly embarrassed.

Em glanced at Mark. "Not you, I was talking to the glasses."

Mark was impressed; maybe he would have to rethink augmenting reality with more than just alcohol.

Em continued, "He lives northeast of Philly in a place called Levittown. We can be there in two hours and forty-five minutes."

"Perfect."

• • •

Outside of Baltimore they merged onto Interstate 95, still discussing the possibility of someone tampering with the file in the records building and why. Em wanted to take the time to review It110102 more closely. Her tablet, however, had other ideas. She tried to sync the tablet for the next hour of the trip with no luck. She'd used her AR glasses to look up solutions, but she couldn't seem to find a problem that needed solving. She didn't understand what was going on; there was plenty of signal coming from 5G and Coast2Coast Wi-Fi. C2C Wi-Fi had been officially given the green light in the last quarter of 2016. Within a year, all areas of the continental United States (except the newest additions) were set up for free government-funded Wi-Fi. In mid 2018, all areas of the country were fully capable of supporting all devices. Samsung had been developing their 5G, or fifth-generation wireless system, since early 2013. It was buggy, though, and in comparison to C2C Wi-Fi, 5G was still in its infancy, but it was a whole lot faster at data transference.

Em went to the tablet's settings and ticked the box for 5G. The signal indicator burst into life, showing that the 5G signal was being received as strongly as possible. She opened a web browser—no problems with that. She opened her app store; yep, working too. Finally she clicked the CIA icon, entered her ID and password biometrically, and clicked the "Sync All" tab. A loading screen opened just like normal and gave a percentage indicator. And, just like every attempt she'd made today, the indicator remained at 0%.

"Damn," she said, shaking her head. "I don't know why this isn't working."

Mark glanced her way but said nothing.

"Do you think you could pull the file up on your tablet and let me have a look?" Em asked. She shut down her own tablet manually.

He looked at her questioningly. "You know as well as I do that the tablets are bioencoded to each agent. Even if I opened the file and handed you the tablet, it would shut down the second your hand touched the screen."

"I know." She sighed. "I'm just frustrated with this. I guess you're going to have to fill me in. I've got all the basics, like Germans and eugenics and crazy ageless Italian girls. I wanna dive into the details. I skimmed across the name Lela Jenkins; who's that?"

"As far as we could tell, she was an accomplice; it's likely she acted as a foster parent. Sartori's slow progression of aging would've made her look like a teenager at best during the time she was with Ms. Jenkins," Mark speculated, "but that's just my guess. Medical records show Jenkins died in Oregon in the mid-1970s; heart failure. We don't have any hard evidence of Alessandra through the entire decade of the sixties, but during the early fifties she was identified as being in a rural part of Kansas."

"OK . . . ?" Em said, unsure of where he was going.

"It was the same town where Lela Jenkins spent most of her life before uprooting suddenly." He raised his eyebrows and threw her a sideways look. "My uncle talked with some of the people from that area and discovered there was a young girl living with her who fit the description of Alessandra."

"What led him there?"

"The nurse at the hospital was calling around, looking for next of kin, and she discovered that Jenkins wasn't from the area and called back to her hometown," he paused, squinting to read a road sign.

"No, we don't exit here. Stay on I-95, no tolls this way, look for Exit 40 in about twenty miles," Em said, consulting her AR glasses.

"Whoever she spoke to there," he continued, "told her about the kid that should have been with her, and how, according to the papers in the post office long ago, she was probably a wanted girl. One call led to another, and my uncle was on the next plane to Oregon."

"Wow."

"Yeah, the only other thing the nurse remembered was Jenkins told Alessandra a name before she died; she couldn't remember it, though. Said it might've been Alex."

They sat in silence, looking at the city of Philadelphia building up around them. As they drove farther north, the rain had changed to light snow. Em Myers stared out of the passenger-side window, taking in the landscape and the information on the display of her AR glasses. The translucent window showed that the name of the river outside of the car window was the Delaware, although she didn't need the glasses to tell her that. The display also showed that the Pennsylvania-Jersey state line was situated in the middle of the Delaware River. When she turned her head back to I-95, the planned route reappeared in the window with the next turn highlighted.

Em was no stranger to cities, working in and around DC most of her adult life, but she tried to avoid looking toward Philly with her AR glasses on; the amount of information would be too distracting for her, so she turned her concentration back to the case.

"So, what do we say when we get there?" she asked Mark.

"We'll see. I'd like to play it by ear. Any luck syncing your tablet?" he asked.

Em hadn't touched her tablet since shutting it down. Now, she picked up the device and used the voice-activation feature to restart it. She went through the process of signing in and retried the sync. The digital wheel turned around and around.

"Still no luck," Em stated.

"I've been thinking about that," he started. "I've got a bad feeling that the file will never sync to your tablet."

"You think someone has tampered with it?" she asked.

"I think it is becoming more likely." He stared ahead, looking for Exit 40. Then, after a moment, said, "Julie said they update whenever something new is brought in, which means that those phone records had to be updated."

"Unless they were paid off," she interjected.

"Yeah, maybe, but paying off all the people; the data entry people, supervisory people, second, and maybe a third shift's worth too? It seems unlikely."

Em closed her eyes and let her mind run some different scenarios. She thought things through more rationally if she were given time to process all the information. The agents drove along in silence for a moment while she thought.

Finally she spoke. "It seems logical that someone might be hacking into the system and tampering with our ability to sync and update remotely. It would also make sense for whomever it is to keep up the illusion that the record keepers are doing their jobs, in order to store the new info. Otherwise, Julie or someone else would have noticed that documents were added when they did the file check."

"True."

"Which leaves the questions of who and why," she finished. "The exit is coming up in about a mile."

He put his indicator on and moved the hybrid into the right-hand lane.

"Why's the easy one," he said. "Who wouldn't want to live forever? Or better, who wouldn't want to *make money* by controlling who lives forever?"

Em nodded.

"Hell, the people who held that power would be the top of the totem pole, don't you think?"

Em nodded again, adding, "Yeah, you're right. Here." She pointed to his off-ramp as he pulled the car to the right, exiting I-95.

Em Myers had been to this part of the country once before when she was a little girl. Both of her parents were teachers, and the family took a vacation to a new destination every summer. When she was nine, they'd traveled to northern Philadelphia so little Emily could see Sesame Place. It once was an amusement theme park that glorified the old television show *Sesame Street.* Even though the show left the air after fifty years of entertaining and teaching, the park still thrived until a fatal accident left several adults and children dead, and many more injured.

The investigation found that the daily preopening inspection of a small rollercoaster called Grover's Vapor Trail was made in haste, due to the employee being late for work that morning. It was speculated that the twenty-year-old had been at a party drinking all night. During the first packed run of the day, the first few cars jumped the track at the beginning of the first turn, a 540-degree upward helix, yanking the remaining six cars off the track along with them. By then, the coaster had accelerated to twenty-seven miles per hour, and the inertia turned the cars 180 degrees and sent them crashing upside down outside of the gates, where there were several hundred people waiting in line to enter the park. To make matters worse for Sesame Place, owned by SeaWorld Parks & Entertainment, several of the individual cars' camera footage were leaked on all the social media and Internet video sites. The media outlets that ran with the tragedy showed a well-edited version of the six car cameras' leaked videos, which had captured a great deal of the carnage and raw brutality. In the end, the backlash and lawsuits proved to be too much for Sesame Place to overcome. The park shut down permanently in 2020.

Mark was pulling off the interstate onto Exit 40, and Em refocused her attention to her AR glasses. Em instructed Richards to turn left at the end of the exit ramp onto Veteran Highway. The next turn took them right onto New Falls Road.

"We stay on New Falls for just over four miles; look for Vermillion Hills on the left-hand side." Em was concentrating most of her vision on the optical display of her AR glasses. "Then, the first right is Vividleaf; it should be the third house on the left."

"Thanks," was the only response Mark offered. He continued to drive in silence to their destination, trying to shift his concentration to the interrogation that was sure to follow.

"Is it possible we no longer have clearance? It could be someone on the inside," Em speculated.

Richards thought about this for a solid minute or more.

"I think that seems unlikely. Let's get back to the here and now; we can deal with that later," he said, closing the topic of conversation.

The two agents pulled into the driveway two minutes later. By the look of the house, the neighborhood was an old one. In fact, Em had used some of the quiet time on the ride up to do a little historical research of the area and had found that the majority of houses were built between 1950 and 1969. Almost one thousand homes went up in the area during that time period, slightly less than the average of Levittown, Pennsylvania. The Levitts were no strangers to home building. After World War II, the family had built houses under government contracts along the East Coast for returning veterans. Next, the growing company had branched out to build whole communities. At that time, the Levitts were undertaking one of the most ambitious housing projects to date, producing over seventeen thousand homes in the new community of Levittown, New York. This was accomplished by perfecting the method of mass producing up to thirty homes a day. The Levitts purchased the Pennsylvania land in 1951 and began building affordable housing in the area almost immediately. The first homes could be bought with little more than one hundred dollars down, and by the end of the decade, the new Levittown was thriving.

Not that Grey Chapman knew any of this . . . or cared.

The agents rolled to a stop a block short of the home; Richards killed the hybrid engine and turned to Emily Myers.

"We've still got another block," Em said.

"Those things can do live video chats, right?" he asked, referring to the glasses.

"Sure."

Mark grabbed his tablet, turned it on, and brought the Skype app to life. He asked her to call him so they could do a test run; she obliged and made the call. He instantly received a first-person point of view video feed from Em's AR glasses.

"Can you hear me?" he inquired.

"Of course I can," she began. "How do you think video chats work?" There was a dull hiss of feedback as the sound began to loop from microphone to speaker. Mark dropped the call and ended the shriek.

"Chapman knows who I am, but he doesn't know who you are."

"So you want me to be the eyes and ears," she gathered.

"Exactly, I'm gonna stay in the car and guide your questioning. I think he'll be more likely to slip up talking to an unfamiliar face." Mark paused, staring up the street. "If I go in, he'll know this is about Alessandra; you can play it closer to the chest."

Em Myers smiled. "I'm liking this plan."

Mark pressed the "Start" button, and the engine fired up, sloshing light snow off the windshield and giving him a perfect view of the house a block away. Em was on the stoop in less than forty-five seconds. She knocked, and after a moment the door cracked open and a balding man in his early forties peeked out.

"Yes?" he asked.

"Hi, I'm Agent Emily Myers"—she smiled as she held up her credentials—"of the Central Intelligence Agency. I'm looking for Jason Chapman."

"Grey, I go by Grey," he said and opened the door a little wider. "What's this all about? If it's about—"

"I just have a few questions for you, Grey," Em said in a very casual manner. "May I come in? It's cold out here."

Grey looked over her shoulder toward the black hybrid. He saw a man in the vehicle looking down at something but couldn't make out any of his features. Em noticed his curiosity and improvised.

"My partner doesn't like these trivial Q&A sessions; he's more of the throw-'em-in-jail-and-ask-'em-later type." She let out a tiny giggle, and Grey seemed to relax a bit. Myers scanned him with her AR glasses, and his biofeedback showed no elevated heart rate or change in blood pressure.

"Yeah, please . . . come in." He opened the door and gestured for her to enter.

"Thanks."

She entered the modest home, and the door closed behind her.

"Have a seat; can I get you anything?" Grey asked.

"No, thank you. I just want to talk." Em sat in the nearest chair with a clear view of Grey.

"Sorry about the mess, I wasn't expecting anyone." Grey folded his arms sheepishly.

"No worries. Sit down; I don't want to take up a lot of your time, sir." She smiled again and, again, he relaxed.

• • •

Mark watched all of these things unfold on the tablet he held between his legs. He could hear both people quite clearly. He'd asked Em just before she got out of the car if she could also record the conversation with her glasses, to which she'd responded, "Absolutely, and it's already rolling."

Mark saw Chapman sitting in a beige armchair across the room from Em; he seemed calm.

"Tell him you need to double-check that he's Jason Chapman. Ask him for his phone number, not an ID; we need to match it to the one in the file," Mark said into his tablet.

Em did; Grey responded quickly.

"That's the one from the record," Mark said to Em.

• • •

Inside the house, Grey was spouting off the ten-digit number of his cell while Em nodded.

"How long have you been using this number, Mr. Chapman?" she asked politely.

He shook his head. "Probably ten years or more. Why?"

"Let me ask the questions, Mr. Chapman," Em responded kindly. "Do you know someone from"—she consulted her tablet to keep up the illusion while Mark spoke in her ear—"Boulder City, Nevada?"

He shook his head. "No, I don't think so."

"How about . . ."

• • •

Richards was furiously trying to remember all the places that the calls had originated from, which had been listed on the cell-phone records he had looked at only a few hours before.

"Um . . . try . . . uh"—he rubbed the center of his forehead—"Rocky Springs . . . Utah. No, no! Wyoming"—he spat at the screen—"*Rock* Springs, Wyoming."

Mark watched as Grey denied knowing anyone from that city as well.

• • •

"How about any family or friends in Omaha, Nebraska, or Des Moines, Iowa? Hell, let's go for the big one, Chicago." Grey was becoming visibly more anxious with each question that Em asked. The readings from her AR glasses showed an increased heart rate.

"My family is all in Florida; what's this all about?" he asked.

"Why don't you tell me, Grey?" Em said in a strikingly more serious tone. "Youngstown, Ohio, maybe? Obviously, you've been receiving calls from these places; phone records can't lie. Who's calling you, Grey? What do they want?"

She realized she was standing.

Grey stood too. "I think it's time for you to leave."

• • •

Mark saw that Myers was losing her grip on the situation. Her voice came booming through the tiny but powerful speakers built into the tablet as he watched the world move into a standing position.

"Obviously, you've been receiving—"

"Em, you're losing control of the situation, take a breath and relax," he said with growing frustration. "We know he's lying, but if he kicks us out, we won't get anything else."

"I think it's time for you to leave," the image of the man stated.

"Shit! Tell him we know—"

• • •

"We know Alessandra is coming to meet you, Mr. Chapman. The pattern of calls has been closing in on this location for at least six months." Em glanced at the staircase. "Is she here now?"

Grey stopped halfway between the door and Em Myers.

"Alessandra? Really?" his face darkened. "I haven't seen or spoken to her in over fifteen years. Even then, I knew her for less than six months. You people are crazy."

Grey took the last steps to the door and pulled it open. "Now, get out of my house."

Em moved toward the front door. "If you know where she is, Mr. Chapman"—she handed him a card from her pocket—"you can reach me directly at that number. We'll find her with or without you." She turned before leaving, then added one final thought, "Oh, I hope you don't have any plans on 'vacationing' soon." She stepped out of the house.

"I've moved on with my life after being harassed by your agency." He threw the card out of the door and abruptly shut it in her face.

Em reached the car door and tapped the touch pad on the edge of her AR glasses. The video call shut down and so did the recording feature.

"That went well," she said, sliding into the passenger seat of the hybrid.

"It always does," Mark countered dryly. "I'm going to call the Philly office and see if we can get a shadow on Chapman. We need to know what he is doing at all times. Something's happening soon, I can feel it."

The black hybrid backed out of the driveway and left Vividleaf Lane.

• • •

Grey Chapman went to the second floor of his home, where there were two bedrooms and a bathroom. He opened the door to the room on his far right. Lying on the bed, asleep, was a young woman; she looked no older than twenty-eight or twenty-nine, with sandy-blonde hair cut short but stylish. He sat on the edge of the bed, rubbing his face in his hands. Then he gently shook her awake, only briefly glancing into those faded blue-green eyes.

"Hey, good sleep?" he asked.

She smiled and nodded.

"We may have to act sooner than we thought," Grey said.

"Really?"

He nodded as she rolled onto her back. "They've tracked you here, Aless."

7:40 A.M.

ITALY, 1941

Breakfast had just finished for the older children who now called the underground labs their home. Most of these children had lived here for more than a third of their lives. Spirits were unusually high this morning. Many of the children were laughing and acting silly as they might have acted before with natural brothers and sisters. Now this was the only family that most of them had.

It had been more than four weeks since any of the older children had been sent home. All of the older children understood that being sent home was not really what happened. None of them discussed it, but they all knew it meant that you had died. The ages of the children ranged between three and eleven. There had been a total of fifteen young people here; that number had dropped over the past six months, but new blood would be coming in soon—it always did.

The underground lab was divided into six corridors, each extending off the main hallway; first was the main living area, where the children slept, ate, and did general activities. Across from that was the scientific living quarters, the next set of parallel doors were the research offices to the right and the kitchen/pantry to the left, and lastly, there were the labs—A and B. Lab A was also an observation zone where the doctors could watch the children for any manifestations or changes in behavior while they were dosed with increasing levels of radiation. Many children felt ill after long doses, and some of the children were "sent home" after their time in the playroom. The playroom was the largest of the rooms in the underground facility. A full playground was built in the room as well as a basketball hoop, hopscotch, and play areas for the small children too. There were large wooden dollhouses and tea sets for the girls, and many different obstacles to climb on and hide around for the boys. The children felt safe playing inside Lab A . . . most of the time.

Lab B was the opposite. The doctor had been instructed to condition the children into believing that bad behavior would result in time inside of Lab B, the yucky room. Over time the children learned to fear the room and therefore cooperate with the adults. On occasion a child would be pulled out of the group in front of everyone to instill the fear that constantly hid just behind the children's eyes. As for what went on in Lab B, the children were told to never speak of it unless they wanted to return to the lab for more of the same—or sometimes worse. The majority of the children heeded the warnings; there were some who did not, and that was the intention of the doctors, to instill more fear into the children. Fear meant, ultimately, submission to all the godless tests.

The yucky room was much smaller than the playroom, even though it contained more items. The children saw these items as torture devices. To the doctors they were medical instruments that were key figures for forwarding the species. There were various forms of fluid-removing instruments like a basic syringe, catheter tubing, and full-blown spinal-tapping needles. Each tool had seen much use in the yucky room, more often than not from poorly trained individuals. The children were given only a basic injection that fogged their sense of time but did nothing for the pain. Injections were given freely in Lab B, including all types of harmful chemicals and liquids to test the body's resilience. One child, named Herbert Blackbourn, had undiluted bleach injected into his spinal column to test the effects of the chemical as a weapon. Herbert was "sent home" after.

The doctors told the children about Herbert getting to leave, to go home to his family for good behavior. The reality was Herbert, and so many before and after, didn't leave at all. They stayed in Lab B. Sometimes only parts of them stayed, and other times whole bodies stayed for further research. More often than not, the children who held no potentially positive results were fed into the incinerator, where their tiny bodies were burned to little more than ash and bone fragments.

There were a few tables with thick leather straps that were used to restrain children as needed. There were tables for autopsies, with large drains and hoses for cleaning. There were chairs that were made of metal and connected to electrical wiring that could deliver shocks that ranged from a bee sting to something fatal. The power of the mind was also exploited through various horrors.

The mind, to most of the doctors, was the doorway to unlocking the secrets of the body. Many children were given various mental tests in things like telepathy, telekinesis, and suggestibility. There were different experiments performed on the children to see how much emotional strain could be placed on someone before they collapsed. The teen minds were especially intriguing, because of the developmental stage of puberty. Puberty, by nature, ushered children into adulthood by throwing out most inhibitions and decision-making skills instilled through family values, thus making teens the most perfect candidates for suggestibility. The pubescent mind ignored possible consequences and was influenced heavily by peer pressure. In most cases, these traits made manipulation of their minds easier than the younger children. An early experiment in manipulation saw one Geraldine Krauss, thirteen, willfully attack a younger child who was perceived as a threat to her food rations. The doctors subtly suggested that she continue to torment the child and even supplied her with small weapons that she used on the poor little one. She ultimately ended up strangling the boy to death, losing her mind in the process.

Life inside the underground compound was vicious.

Eugene Trickens missed his family, especially his sister. The siblings had been born only minutes apart outside of Corby, Northamptonshire, in England. Eugene and his sister, Eugeneia, were the first set of twins born into the Trickens bloodline in more than five generations. Gene and Nia, as the family knew them, were by all accounts happy children. The siblings made friends easily, loved being outdoors, and were all-around good children. It'd been more than a year since he had seen Nia. He was beginning to forget what she looked like.

The Trickens family decided on a holiday by train across Europe in the early fall of '39. They dipped into a hefty savings fund and purchased their tickets on the Orient Express. The family traveled to London by automobile and arrived at the train station half a day early. Gene and Nia's father had once worked in London, and the two siblings had visited the city on a special occasion once before. The little family spent time enjoying each other's company and seeing the sights that were within walking distance of the train station. They took time to marvel at the Great Clock of Westminster and enjoyed the sound of the Great Bell, better known as Big Ben, while eating lunch under the baby brother, Little Ben. When it came time to board the train that would route them to France, the twins were overwhelmed with the excitement of taking their first journey across Europe. The train moved toward the coast of England very quickly, and they soon discovered that the ride would detour onto a ferry across the English Channel. This detour didn't last more than a few hours, and then they were right back onto the Orient Express.

The train cars were painted a royal blue that gleamed with the rays of the sun. Gene could see his and his sister's reflections in the brilliant shine. When they'd entered the car, they'd seen all the great armchairs of the dining cars lavishly decorated, and each chair was wide enough for both children to sit together. The windows of all the train cars were adorned with beautiful drapery, and the woodwork throughout was amazingly detailed. To the children there had never been anything so beautiful, until they reached their sleeping car.

The sleeping cars were designed for top-of-the-line luxury, and they did not disappoint. There was a surprising amount of room in each sleeping car; the sitting area folded out into two separate comfortable beds, and the children chose to sleep on the upper while their parents took the lower. There was even a closed basin for washing. The Trickens had rented a modest section in sleeping car 3309. Ten years prior, just outside of Istanbul, the Orient Express had been trapped by snow for about a dozen days. The only car left in line after the natural disaster was 3309.

Just before dusk, dinner was served in the dining car. The children dined on exotic seafood that was extremely delicious, while their mom and dad had the best cut of filet mignon they would ever enjoy, cooked perfectly dark brown on the outside and hot pink in the center. After a brief stop in Gare du Nord in Paris, the children were tucked in for the evening, and Mr. and Mrs. Trickens went down to the bar car to enjoy cocktails and live piano music until the early hours of the morning. As the family awoke the next day, the train was passing from Strasbourg, France, to Germany. That day everything changed for the Trickens family.

On September 1, 1939, Germany invaded Poland for supposedly perpetrating attacks in German territories, successfully beginning World War II, which would eventually pull in every major country in the entire world and result in the greatest loss of life from any conflict ever on the face of the planet. September 1, 1939, also happened to be the day the Orient Express crossed the German border and most of the passengers were never heard from again.

• • •

The train raced across the tracks, leaving France for Germany as the sun rose over the horizon. The twins slept soundly while their parents dozed below them. The train swayed gently as it moved across the expansive open fields and rolling hills of southern France and Germany. In the dining car, the chef was preparing food for the passengers' breakfast, which began at seven and continued until ten, with a staggering pattern to accommodate the over two hundred passengers and crew aboard. Gene was the first to awaken to the smell of *pain perdu*—which he knew as French toast. He shook his sister to wake her, almost spilling her onto the floor of the cabin.

"Do you smell the cinnamon?" Gene asked.

"Of course I do, now let me sleep!" Nia said with her eyes still closed.

"Come on!" he exclaimed. "You're gonna sleep all day!"

She peered through one eye at her younger-by-minutes brother. "Naff off and leave me to sleep!"

She rolled to face away from Gene, which meant she was looking down the meter-and-a-half drop to the floor.

"You're out of your head, you are," he began. "Mum and Dad are not going to let you sleep through a whole new country. They are going to see that you are up as soon as I wake 'em."

Nia shot into a sitting position and in a blur smashed Gene's face with the fancy bed pillow that had made its home under her head the night before. She delivered a blow so quick and forceful that she almost tumbled off the upper bed herself; she grabbed the side of the bunk for stability just in time.

"Oy!" Gene squealed under a face stuffed with pillow.

"Leave me be, Eugene!" Nia shouted.

"Kids, please!" The twins' squabbles had woken their parents, who were now reluctantly beginning to get out of bed.

"He started it," Nia said with a shrill tone of accusation.

"What? She's a liar," he defended.

"Take a running jump, Gene!" she rebuffed dismissively.

"Knock it off unless you both want to stay here for breakfast," Mrs. Trickens advised.

"Yes, Mum," they said in that eerie unison that only twins possess.

The quartet did their usual morning rituals, brushing their teeth, combing their hair, and fighting about what to wear and who was going to lead the way to the dining car. They decided that today it would be Gene, since Nia had lead the night before. The family entered the dining car from the far end and made their way toward the middle of the car. Seating was limited due to the full passenger load traveling east. This was also the third scheduled breakfast of the morning. The family found small, comfortable seating in the middle of the car, flagged the waiter, and ordered the *pain perdu* for everyone. The meal came with orange juice, fresh strawberries, and jam. The smell of sugar and cinnamon filled the nostrils of the children, and their eyes widened with delight as the waiter placed a plate in front of each child. The family then closed their eyes, bowed their heads, and blessed the food that had been placed in front of them. As they finished their prayer of thankfulness, the train began to slow. It decreased its speed in measured increments down to the final twenty meters, where the conductor had to break hard in order to not collide with the tank that sat on the train tracks. Painted on the side of the tank was the insignia of the Baltic cross, signifying a German tank. Seeing an armored vehicle, in itself, was not odd, since the train was passing over German soil. A tank parked on the tracks, however, was a different story. A large young man opened the tank and climbed out onto the deck. His uniform bore the red armband that would become infamous in a few short weeks.

• • •

Eugene sat at the small table away from the other children. He was observing their fleeting happiness, wondering when the day would begin in earnest. This morning's breakfast was a special treat from the doctors. Today, the children were given a small portion of *pain perdu*. Eugene did not eat his. His thoughts drifted to the train and his sister and how the two children who were once so happy to be exploring the European countryside were now separated. The Germans had boarded the train immediately, claiming it as German territory. An image of the concierge standing up to protest the boarding flashed through his brain. The man did not speak two sentences before his life was cut short with a bullet between his eyes. The gore sprayed across the dining hall. Unfortunately for the Trickens, the concierge stopped a few feet past their table. Eugene clearly watched as red specks dotted his ornamented place setting.

Bringing his attention back to the present, he pushed his current *pain perdu* away from him and glared at the other children, who had clearly forgotten where they were. Were they at fault for feeling this fleeting happiness while he suffered? They all suffered at some point. Were they not entitled to have some joy? Eugene sighed, closed his eyes, and tried to imagine his life before being trapped here. Yet, somehow here was better than immediately after the train was seized. Eugene had an amazing amount of vivid nightmares during the weeks following the train incident; he was *still* having nightmares about all of this. He felt that his life was one never-ending nightmare. Early on into this horror come to life, he'd assumed he would not live to see another birthday, although he had. It was his first birthday ever being apart from his twin sister, and it was horrible. He spent the day locked in complete darkness, alone and afraid. Only the darkness kept him company—that and the memories.

The German soldiers had invaded the train like cockroaches swarming to a molded, crusty loaf of bread. It was flanked by two dozen transport vehicles of all sizes dumping out soldiers to round up the passengers of the Orient Express. Mr. and Mrs. Trickens's natural instinct was to protect their children first at all costs. When the soldiers motioned the family to rise from the table and exit the train, the children were positioned as far from the gun barrels as possible, placing mom-and-dad-size human shields between them. Gene pasted himself against his mother's body, clinging for his life. His fingers gripped the flesh of her leg with enough force to leave welted red marks. She never felt the pain. The soldier closest to Mr. Trickens hit Mrs. Trickens in the face with the butt of his gun when she turned to situate the children, crumpling her to the floor of the dining car. Her cheek was torn open, sending cascading blood down her face, neck, and blouse before spilling to the floor. Tears chased the thick red blood down her cheek, but she did not cry out. Though dazed, Mrs. Trickens found her way quickly back to her feet and pushed Gene behind her once again. Mr. Trickens stared in helpless horror, with the business end of a K98 planted firmly in his chest. Mr. Trickens would feel shame for the rest of his short life, but Mrs. Trickens never faulted her husband's choice to stand by idly.

Outside it had begun to rain.

Once off the train, all the passengers were placed into the transport vehicles and moved to Dachau concentration camp outside of Munich. Gene and Nia wept silently while their parents hovered over them during the twenty-minute drive to the camp. Once the caravan of Orient Expressers arrived, the soldiers began dividing and processing prisoners. The camp was large but not enormous. There were several small buildings and one large building all situated off the main courtyard. The transport vehicles parked inside of the rain-soaked courtyard, where there were several hundred other people already captive. Some were huddled around a fire pit for warmth. The last time that Eugene Trickens would see his family was after they were pushed from the back of the transport vehicle onto the muddy ground. German soldiers hoisted them up, dragged them apart, while screams of desperation, agony, and emotional distress flew from the lips of each member of the family. Mr. Trickens fought back with fury, biting the guard that held him and drawing blood. The soldier screamed in misery and released on instinct. Trickens sprinted toward his wife, covering the distance in a half a dozen strides. He threw his shoulder with all his force into the back of the soldier carrying away his wife, spilling them both to the mud below. Regaining his feet, he clutched Mrs. Trickens's arm and began dragging her to her feet. The mud-soaked lovers got two steps before tragedy struck. One deafening shot of a K98 reverberated across the complex. Mr. Trickens fell forward as his heart was punched out of the front of his chest by the slug. Gray smoke billowed from the barrel of the rifle as the hand that squeezed the trigger bled from the human bite inflicted moments before. Trickens's head landed in the mud, turned in the direction of his wife of fourteen years. Her eyes found his, two sets of light-brown irises locking in for the last time. His eyes filled will sorrow as he registered what was happening. She watched the life drain out of them. Mrs. Trickens reached out a muddy hand and felt the warm skin of her dead husband's face. Nia shrieked a repeating piercing tone that would leave her vocal cords raw and swollen. Gene's muscles lost all rigidity, and he dangled in the grip of his captor. Mrs. Trickens was pulled roughly to her feet, her eyes never leaving the breathless body of her husband. She was dragged one hundred meters to a small shack, where the guards were processing another woman from the train. The German soldiers picked up the dead weight of Mr. Trickens and disposed of his corpse into the fire pit that was burning on the opposite side of the compound.

The divisions in processing were by gender and age groupings. All adults were separated from their children. The remaining Trickens family members were systematically stripped of all clothing and personal belongings. Nia covered her naked body with her dirty, pale hands. She wept hysterically. Gene had lost his favorite glass marble. The soldier that processed him had taken it. Gene had placed the toy in his trouser pocket after brushing his teeth just a few short hours before. Strangely, in his shock, he felt more pain at losing his marble than his father. For Mrs. Trickens, the shock of watching her loving husband and the devoted father of her children die as he tried to rescue his family, and seeing her children carried away, manifested in a complete mental break. As she was being stripped of her clothing and personal possessions, she sat stoic, staring silently straight ahead. Her mental breakdown was in full swing when she decided that she would take as many down with her as she could.

Muddy, naked, and shivering, Mrs. Trickens bent down, picking her blouse from the floor as the guard was turned the opposite direction. She wrapped the shirt edges around each hand and rushed soundlessly toward her captor, swinging the remaining material around his neck while throwing her body onto his. This caused the man to fall forward to the ground with the blouse pulled taut against his airway. Mrs. Trickens planted one grimy knee firmly in the nape of the man's neck, pressing all of her force and body weight against the fragile bones that construct the human airway. Her eyes squeezed shut as she bared her teeth in an animal-like grimace, cracking open her scabbing wound from the butt of the K98. Warm blood trickled down her face once again. Her grimace turned into a smile as she heard the grinding, crackling sound of the bones and cartilage losing the battle. The blouse began to rip as the man let out his final breaths. Tears flowed from her closed eyes.

• • •

Felix Müller lit a cigarette, inhaled the tobacco smoke, and stared across the room at the table where the children were eating their breakfast. He was growing disillusioned with torturing children in order to test for genetic anomalies. So far the only promising child was the Sartori girl, who didn't seem to be affected by the radiation doses. She was currently being prepped for injection of radioactive material directly into her bloodstream. Müller was low in the chain of command, so he wasn't sure if the girl had had any other testing yet.

One boy sat alone, off from the other children. He had slid his untouched breakfast away and had placed his head on the table. Müller inhaled deeply, letting the smoke penetrate his lungs. As he exhaled, he studied the small boy through the white smoke. Today, young Eugene Trickens was going to have a difficult day. Müller consulted the folder that lay on the table before him, reviewing his procedures. He would let the children have their amusements for a while longer. Then, they would move to Lab A, all of them except Trickens.

After breakfast ended, Eugene was pulled aside as the rest of the children moved down the corridor toward Lab A. Müller spoke English to the boy and explained that today he was scheduled to visit Lab B. Eugene did not fight Müller, knowing that fighting would only make things worse for him. Eugene had seen the direct results of the struggle in the form of bruises and occasional broken appendages. In his personal experiences, the yucky room had not been so bad. He could barely remember most of his visits, due to the drugs that were injected before they began their work, and he mostly thought about his family during the ordeal.

Almost two years had passed since the day his father was murdered and his mother and sister were dragged away. Gene had heard stories of his mother on occasion while still in Dachau. He had heard she had killed one of the soldiers that had taken her away. The prisoners sometimes talked about how she had escaped the compound. The guards spoke of how they'd mutilated and killed her. They said she'd begged to be killed while they were torturing her; they said mutilation wasn't a strong enough word for what they did. Then the laughter came . . . always laughter. He did not know who to believe but felt if his mother had escaped, she would have come back for Nia and him. Surely she would have come back for her children. No matter who spoke of his mother, the prisoners or the guards, Gene felt the same sorrow, the same depth of anguish. His sister was absolutely contained somewhere on the compound. Several prisoners had seen her and told the boy of her physical state.

The Germans had discovered that Gene and Nia were twins early in their stay at Dachau. The two children continued to be separated from each other for this very reason. Twins were thought to carry a unique genetic coding, especially identical twins, which could be the key to unlocking the world of genetic engineering. Constructing a better class of people was a goal the Third Reich took extremely serious. They had begun experimenting in the late 1920s, ironically, following in the footsteps of the United States, which by then had been talking eugenics for the better part of forty years. California had passed laws concerning eugenics and purification of the societal dregs through sterilization and then had proceeded to forcefully sterilize more people than the rest of the states combined. Also, North Carolina had begun an extensive program that would outlast the Third Reich by more than thirty years. Selective breeding and sterilization became a common practice in Germany, with more than four hundred thousand forced sterilizations. Before the war was over, more than two hundred thousand people were exterminated by Action T4, the Germans' forced human euthanasia program. Shortly after the Trickens family was detained at Dachau, Hitler had signed documentation to construct a hidden facility where private research could be carried out on individuals who had potential for genetically improving German soldiers and future German citizens. The hidden facility began construction on the isle of Sardinia in late '39. It was completely underground in a rural mountainous section of the island. Within ten months the facility was fully operational. Gene was moved with the first wave of children soon after completion. The facility was named Laughlin Zentrum für Genforschung (Laughlin Center for Genetic Research) after the American, Harry Laughlin, who was a leading eugenicist and whose ideas were the model for Germany's eugenics program. Originally, a young German doctor who worked in eugenics named Josef Mengele had been selected to be the lead scientist at Laughlin Zentrum für Genforschung. Word had spread of his desire to study genetic heredity in human subjects, with twins being high on his list of test subject. But the Angel of Death, as he would become known, was given different orders by Hitler and wouldn't start terrorizing the children and adults of the Auschwitz camp for a few years. Long before then, Nia would be dead.

Müller extended his right hand out to the young boy, who stared at it for a long moment. Eugene then reached up and placed his hand inside of the man's large palm. The two people walked together like father and son beyond the door labeled Lab B. The room was brightly lit by many overhead bulbs, causing Eugene to squint from the change in light from the hallway to the lab. Müller led the boy to a desk, offered him a chair, then fell into the chair perpendicular to Eugene's. He placed the folder unopened on the desk. Eugene noticed it had his name written on it.

"Don't be worried, little one," Müller said, again in English for the boy. Eugene just stared at him. He had seen the man before but had never talked with him or "worked" with him in either of the labs before. Müller opened a drawer on the opposite side of the desk and removed an object.

"Would you like a sweet?" he said, handing the boy a small sugar cube. "They are very tasty." He also placed a cube into his mouth and began to suck on it.

Eugene looked down at the cube between his fingers, turning it over and over, debating what he should do. Müller pretended not to notice the indecision as he began flipping through the folder.

"You're Eugene Trickens, correct? Born 18 May 1932 in Corby, Northamptonshire, England?" Müller asked.

The boy, still looking at the sugar cube, nodded a silent response.

"Good. It says here you are one half of a pair. You have a sister?"

Eugene's head lowered and his eyes closed; at the same time his fingers opened, dropping the cube onto the floor of the lab. He slowly shook his head from left to right just once.

"Do you know what happened to her, Mr. Trickens?" Müller prodded.

A small voice came from the child seated across from Müller. "She died at Dachau. I was told starvation."

"Yes," Müller spoke with a tender compassion, "that's what our records show. She was special."

A tear rolled down Eugene's cheek as he nodded.

"Not only to you and your family, but to us as well. Were you ever told why you were brought here?"

Müller observed carefully, but the boy did not respond.

"After she passed, it was discovered that she had something unique within her. The probability that you are unique is very high, Mr. Trickens. And that is why you are here, because you, too, are special. All of the children here have some predisposition to be special." Müller smiled as he concluded, "You are the future of mankind, son."

He handed the boy another sugar cube.

◆ ◆ ◆

Dachau remained Eugene Trickens's home for almost ten months. He had heard no news about his mother in close to nine months. His sister had passed away three weeks ago, or so he had been told. The guards had said she died of starvation, and the few prisoners who had seen Nia in the previous weeks confirmed she'd looked very ill. He was alone in this hell until he would die too; he prayed for it every evening before he closed his eyes, yet every morning he would wake and weep.

He was startled out of sleep by an unfamiliar noise. Eugene shared the room with thirty other people, who usually went to bed exhausted from the day's labor. Noises in the dark were extremely uncommon in the prisoner area. He sat up and tried to stare around the black blanket of night. Eugene could sense the presence of another and knew he was not alone.

"Who's the—"

A large man's hand shot out of the dark and covered the majority of his face, choking off the words before they could fully form in his throat. The hand held a rag that smelled oily and strong with chemicals. Eugene tried to break away from the hand, but the other arm of the giant man had wrapped around him like a vine strangling shrubbery. His lungs burst into flames, struggling for oxygen. He gasped for breath between the man's fingers but only received more of the oily, chemical-filled rag. After a few moments of struggle, Eugene's eyes became heavy and his bodily protest became weaker the more he breathed the noxious rag fumes. The man stood, still gripping the small boy as he faded into unconsciousness.

Eugene awoke to complete darkness. He was slumped over with his head leaning in the corner of a wall. He reached out in the black, feeling for anything, but he didn't even straighten his arms all the way before he scraped his hand along cement bricks or mortar. That seemed impossible; his back was up against a wall also made of bricks and mortar. The room's floor plan could have been no more than two square feet, with no discernible door. Eugene felt along the corners of the tiny enclosure and followed the seam down to the floor. He felt something hard but forgiving under the pressure of his hand. He raised it to his nose and sniffed. It was bread, he was sure. He reached down and found three other chunks. How long was he going to be in here? He dropped the bread back on the floor, stood, and groped for a ceiling that didn't seem to be within reach, and then banged his hands against the bricks and mortar, yelling for help or to be let out, for what felt like hours to no avail. Finally, in despair, he dropped to the cramped floor and began to cry.

Happy birthday, Nia, he thought. *I miss you.* His tears turned to sobs; he paid little attention as the room began to shake. Fourteen hours went by.

He slept poorly most of the time in the box. Depression drained him physically and mentally. He had several nightmares ranging from his father's death to his sister falsely blaming him for their mother never returning. He wept on and off during his slumber. When he was awake, he held on to the good memories of his happy family, the ones he could still recall. He was having a hard time remembering any positive things now that his life was spiraling down a never-ending pit of hopelessness. The only memories that never failed him were the ones of lunch under Little Ben and seeing the astonishingly marvelous train for the first time. He remembered their father laughing as he and Nia danced around the clock tower while hearing the distant pealing of bells from the big brother clock. His eyes watered. He thought of how their mother looked like a queen in her best evening wear while sitting in the dining car enjoying her filet. Impossibly, he was weeping again. *How are there any tears left?* he thought. He was sure that he would dehydrate and die if this continued for much longer. Suddenly, the room tilted onto its side and Eugene was thrown into the solid wall. The roof exploded into blinding sunlight. His eyes tried to retreat into the back of his skull at the blazing inferno of rich light that poured in.

Before his eyes adjusted, he was yanked out of the box and taken to a room with twenty cots and other children. Eugene did not yet know it, but he'd arrived at Laughlin Zentrum für Genforschung.

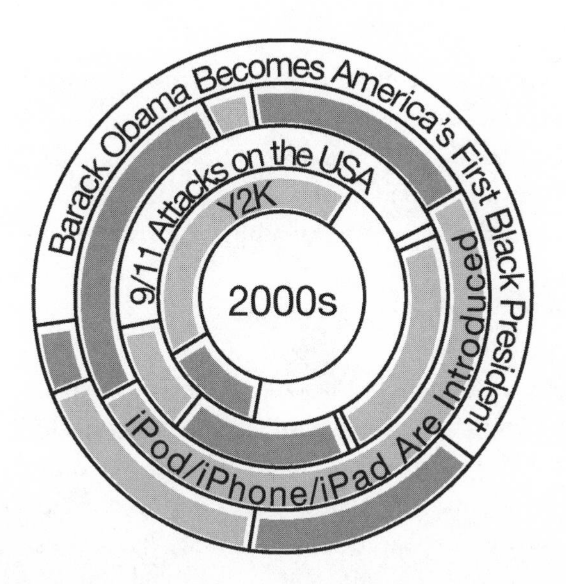

6:54 P.M.

VIRGINIA, 2006

Aless pumped her legs as hard as she could manage. Remnants of sticky blood were beginning to crust on her pants from her once-injured leg. Even healed, there was a ghost of the former pain lingering, although that could have been just her imagination. Across the field and highway she could see the combination gas station and mechanic shop where they had left the car. It was Grey's car—the man who she was leaving behind.

She ran through the thick tangle of weeds and tall dying grass in the small field. The blanket was mostly balled up under her left arm, but some dangled between her legs, causing her to stumble more than once. She pulled the flopping pieces back up into her arms and kept pushing. As she approached the highway, she heard more gunshots erupt behind her. Instead of slowing to watch for traffic, Aless ducked and went headlong into the road. Luckily, only one car had to swerve to miss her. She was stepping up the opposite sidewalk before the guy even honked at her indifference.

She ran into the open garage bay, digging into her pocket for the keys, and looked around for the old car that had been littered with fast-food bags the first time she'd gotten into it. The car was sitting off to the left; it looked like it was in working order too. Aless hadn't thought about the possibility of the car not being put together. She'd lucked out. With the keys out she moved to the driver's side and tried the handle. It popped open immediately; she jumped in, threw the bloody blanket into the backseat, and shoved the keys into the ignition, twisting the starter hard.

The engine sputtered and coughed but didn't turn over.

"Come on, dammit!" Aless growled.

She turned the key again and again, but it wasn't much more than wishful thinking. She slammed her hand down on the steering wheel.

"Hey!" a man yelled. "What the hell are you doing?" It was the same guy that they had spoken to the morning before about getting the car fixed. He was coming out of what appeared to be the office area. Aless began to feel the panic set in, so she breathed deep and closed her eyes. *Please,* she thought, *please work.*

She turned the engine over, this time pumping the gas pedal at the same time. The engine coughed again, but this time harder, before the combustion inside the cylinders kicked in, choking the engine into life.

"YES!" Aless screamed.

She threw the car into gear and punched the gas pedal so hard that the engine threatened to stall out. It didn't. She drove out of the little shop and onto the highway that she'd just crossed. The man came running out of the shop, trying to stop her, but he wasn't able to keep up with the automobile. In the rearview mirror, Aless could see the small motel shrinking along with her chances of ever seeing Grey again. Her elation at the escape quickly shifted to guilt over the abandonment.

Aless drove for more than thirty-five minutes before she decided she needed to figure out which direction she was heading. She stopped at a rest stop to check the map, but before she got out of the car, Aless grabbed a spare pair of pants from her overnight bag, took off the bloody ones, and then stuffed them into the bag. It turned out she was going west on I-64 toward Charleston, West Virginia. She went into the restroom, found a stall near the back, and locked herself inside. Once the lock clicked home, she leaned up against the metal door with her forehead rested against her forearm. She sighed and began thinking about Grey. Her face slowly pinched, and she couldn't hold back the tears any longer. Aless didn't sob, but she had a hard, silent cry. She thought about everything that was happening, and had happened during her life. She thought about Lela, her mom, the woman who'd raised her more than any other person ever had. She cared about Lela, and she really thought the woman had cared for her, even though she had betrayed her. Aless briefly thought she could just be rationalizing, but she squashed the thought before it could take over.

As she cried, she couldn't help but be reminded of a time when she first tried going to school to be normal, at least in a sense. Lela and Aless had recently relocated to the home in Oregon, and once Aless had mastered English a bit more, Lela made the suggestion that Aless try to get her education in the local school system. Aless, of course, was uncomfortable with going out into the public on a daily basis. Lela convinced her to give it a try and find out if she could adapt or not.

It was the middle of the fall semester when Lela took Aless up to the school to enroll her in junior-high courses. Aless was very street smart, but she'd never had a chance to find out if she was book smart or not. Aless discovered that she loved learning about new things more than almost anything else. She would study for long hours every day, losing herself in learning.

After a few days Lela asked, "How's it going?"

Aless was very eager to tell her everything, while her surrogate mother listened, smiling and drinking coffee.

"Have you made any friends yet?" Lela asked.

"I . . . I don't have time," Aless answered, shying away from the question.

The reality of the situation was that Aless did not get along with many of the other children. She was shunned by most of the other girls, and she found all but a few of the boys to be too immature.

One day, about a week after their conversation about school, Lela came home from work to grab a bite for lunch and heard crying from the upstairs bathroom. It was Aless, leaning against the door.

Lela knocked softly. "Hey, kiddo," she said. "Do you want me to come in?"

Aless quickly got quiet, and, after several seconds, she whispered, "I hate school. I'm not going back."

Lela placed her back on the outside of the door and slid down into a seated position.

"You're not?" she asked.

"No," Aless responded.

"I thought you loved learning," Lela lightly prodded.

"It's not the learning!" Aless said defensively.

"OK."

"It's"—she hesitated—"it's not the teacher either. I love Ms. Price! She's funny!"

"Ms. Price is a great teacher, one of the best, I'm told," Lela said.

"I hate those girls!" she said through choked tears. "I hate their stupid faces, and their bad haircuts, and their dumb boyfriends, and, and . . . and." The sobs came back.

Lela sat and listened for a long time. Finally she said, "You know, people can be mean. Sometimes they don't need a reason, but a lot of times it's because they're jealous of who you are, or what you can do. These girls might see you as something of a threat."

"But why? I didn't do anything to them."

"Sometimes that doesn't matter. Sometimes life's not fair, Aless. Maybe it's because you came in and became the teacher's pet because you love to learn. Or maybe you're just the new girl, and they've decided to push you around to see how tough you are."

"You know they can't hurt me."

"Maybe not on the outside. But it looks like you can be hurt on the inside. Understand what I mean?" Lela asked.

There was a long silence, and Lela was about to ask again, when the door opened. Aless sat down and snuggled up next to the woman.

"I love you, Lela."

"Love you too, kiddo." She wrapped her arm around Aless, squeezing her tight.

◆ ◆ ◆

Aless wiped her face and unlatched the bathroom stall at the rest stop. She stepped out and checked her reflection in the mirror. She always looked terrible after crying, and this time was no exception. She turned on the tap and waited for the water to warm—which it never did—and splashed the water across her face.

Three minutes later, she got back into the car and consulted the map one final time. As she placed the key in the ignition, she remembered that the car had had a hard time starting before, but this time she pumped the gas pedal the first time, and it sputtered back to life. She got back on the highway and drove until the gas light illuminated, then she looked for the nearest motel, finding one on the Chicago side of Lafayette.

She paid the clerk with cash for the last tiny room available. After checking in she went back to the car to get her few items from the trunk, and then she went to her room, four doors down the hall. She took the bloodstained blanket, stiff from drying in the backseat, and placed it in the bathtub. The only other items were Grey's backpack and, fortunately for Aless, her overnight bag. She dropped the two items on the bed, opened her bag, and rummaged for her toothbrush. She found it stuck deep in the bottom of the bag under her bloody pants and realized she had no toothpaste. She brushed with water and the faint taste of previous toothpaste that had somehow remained on the brush, and then she changed out of her clothes. She placed the keys and Grey's cell, which he'd given to her before she'd run off, onto the nightstand.

Aless went over to the bed and sat down. She stared at Grey's bag for a while, then reached over and opened it up to look inside. She found normal things like pens and paper lining the pockets of the bag, but it was Grey's laptop that caught her eye.

Yes, maybe I can see what's going on in the world, and if there is any mention of Virginia, she thought as she yawned. *I wonder if it has a password . . .*

Aless was lucky to find that the computer booted right up and she didn't need to enter a password. The desktop was immaculate, unlike Grey's car. It seemed he cared more about the organization of the digital world than the real world. The background of his desktop, as far as Aless could tell, was a screenshot of his gaming world. There were only about a half of a dozen folders on the left side of the screen, most of which were system folders. One near the bottom was labeled "Grey."

She clicked this folder, and a window popped up. Inside of the "Grey" folder there were many other folders for all occasions; school, pictures, website archives, music, videos, travel, gaming, taxes, and more. The one that caught her eyes was simply called "Writing."

She clicked the folder and dived deeper down into the digital rabbit hole. Buried inside of this folder were many other folders and some document files. Most of the writings seemed to be fictional in nature. One folder was all about world building and designs for some of these fictional worlds. Aless clicked the folder and found the contents were fairly extensive. There were scanned drawings as well as detailed documents about each of the ideas that Grey had created. They ranged from the mundane, almost real-world ideas to ideas that explored the extravagant deep recesses of the imagination. Grey was meticulous about each of these worlds, and he had written and compiled far more about each world than he wrote in his stories. As far as she could see, the stories were secondary to the worlds he created. In fact, she saw that most of the stories fizzled out after a few pages.

She clicked the back arrow, bringing her back to the main "Writing" folder. She scrolled down to see some of the other folders. "Digital Journal" drew her attention. She hesitated, wondering if she should be snooping through Grey's personal files, and decided to close the laptop's lid.

"This is wrong, Aless," she scolded herself out loud. "You shouldn't be looking through his stuff."

She put the laptop down on the bed, stood up, and walked over to the TV. She turned it on, grabbed the remote, and began flipping through the channels aimlessly. The lights and sounds coming from the television barely distracted her from the extreme pull of curiosity. She glanced at the laptop several times over the next ten minutes, telling herself that she just wanted to know how he felt about her. She would get up the nerve to reach for the device, then she would pull her hand back, reminding herself that it wasn't right. She flipped through the channels; click—animals dancing, click—basketball game, click—cooking show, click—monster trucks, click—game show, click—family sitcom, click—local news, click—rom-com, click—she switched the television off.

"The hell with it," she said to the emptiness, reaching over and plucking the laptop from the opposite side of the mattress. She lifted the lid, bringing the device back to life. The window was still there with the folder labeled "Digital Journal" highlighted from when she'd almost clicked it earlier. This time she did open it.

Inside the folder were other folders organized by year; she clicked "2005." Once in, she saw there were folders for each month, containing almost daily entries, especially in the early months. Of course, the first one Aless opened was the day they met. She scrolled down the page.

From the personal digital journal of Grey Chapman, October 27, 2005:

. . . and we began to think of someplace to go; however, Aless quickly reminded me that this wasn't a sightseeing adventure. She suggested that we leave quickly, even though I had assured her that she would be safe staying at least one evening at my apartment. I could see the distress on her face, so I told her to give me a few hours to get my affairs in order. Truth be told, I'm broke! I had to find some money fast, or we weren't going to make it to Orlando, much less anywhere else. As I was packing a bag, she began telling me that she didn't want to drag me into anything crazy or dangerous. I told her not to be silly, I was making a choice, and I knew I needed to do something different to get out of the crazy rut I'd been stuck in. Dead-end jobs, no money, and playing video games all night and all day; my life was directionless. Aless was the change I needed.

That's when she said to me, "I know you aren't financially stable"—that hurt BTW—"so I want you to know that I am. Any and all money that we need, I can provide." I'm paraphrasing, of course. My jaw hit the floor, and I asked if she was certain that she could support two people for an indefinite amount of time.

She nodded and asked, "Can we get out of here now?"

Who was I to say no? When a beautiful girl wants you to run away with her, and you have nothing tying you down, you run. So we did.

The first stop we made was at a car wash, and we had my little car cleaned inside and out. She didn't mind the trash, or so she said, but it was best to be comfortable when we were putting miles behind us. We left Naples and began traveling north up I-75. North was as far as we had planned in the apartment, but by the time we reached the outskirts of Tampa we'd decided on New Orleans. Aless had never been, and I've always wanted to go, so it was settled. We found a nearby Best Buy, purchased a GPS to guide us, and haven't looked back. That was a few days ago. I haven't had a lot of time to write since Aless literally bumped into me, but it has been some of the most memorable times of my life. I'll try to write more soon.

Aless closed the document and was surprised to find that she had a few tears rolling down her face. She remembered all of these things so clearly in her mind that it could have been yesterday instead of about three months ago. Grey had been so kind to help her. She felt a pang of guilt as she remembered that very early on, she had just been using Grey. Aless searched around the folder, settling on the first entry in November.

From the personal digital journal of Grey Chapman, November 1, 2005:

Happy All Saints' Day to me! Aless and I arrived in New Orleans the day before yesterday. We've crashed outside of the city in a dumpy little abandoned motel. It seems like the only thing we could find outside of the flooded zone. Katrina really devastated this place. The destruction is still evident everywhere, even more than two months later. I haven't seen any crews doing anything about it either. I feel so bad for these people. Aless asked me yesterday if I would want to go into the city and maybe volunteer with her. It's not really my style, but I am feeling really moved by the atmosphere here. I told her I would go and do my best.

Aless has told me that she has seen a lot of death and destruction in her life. I can't help but wonder what she's been through. She told me her mom died a long time ago and she really misses her. Other than that, I find she doesn't talk much about her past. I do some talking about mine, though. I have finally given some hints to my own screwed-up existence, but I think I will leave the giant info dump to when we have moved on from this little piece of hell. And to think, on the road I was hoping we might drink it up on Bourbon and do the stupid things people do in the Big Easy. Boy, was I wrong.

Aless thought back to when they'd first arrived in New Orleans; by then she had known that Grey was more than just someone to get her from point A to B. He had quickly grown to be a great friend. The two of them had one major thing in common: they were both struggling with finding a purpose. She was quickly becoming smitten with the man.

Aless yawned; she was exhausted. She looked over to the clock and was surprised to find that it was after midnight. As much as she wanted to keep reading, she knew that she would have to be on the move again in the morning; sleep was a necessity. She closed the laptop and moved it to the floor. After turning off the bedside lamp, she laid her head on the musty motel pillow and was asleep within seconds. There were no dreams, even though she fully expected them to come.

Aless slept until her internal clock woke her. It was about ten in the morning, and she was a bit disappointed to find that she'd missed breakfast, even if it was only continental. She repacked her things. The laptop seemed to call out to her again, but she fought the urge, knowing she needed to get moving. She picked up the keys and cell from the nightstand, shoved the keys in her pocket, and held the phone for a second.

He would have called if he was OK, she thought. Aless flipped the phone open and noticed it was off. She had a moment of panic, thinking the battery had died, and that the charger was back in Virginia, but after a quick check, she realized it was just turned off. As the phone powered up, she wondered if Grey had left her a message, or had sent a text, perhaps. If so, she may never know, as she hadn't used a cell phone more than a few times, and that was exclusively for calls. She definitely didn't own one, because they could trace it. Even now, turning Grey's on could be a huge mistake for her, but she had to check.

There was nothing: no voice mail, no text, no missed calls.

She shut the phone down, deciding that she would power it up only once a day to check for news from Grey.

Once packed and checked out, Aless stuffed the bloody blanket into the trunk of the car; she'd have to try to deal with that problem later. She took the car back onto the interstate. This morning the car had had no trouble starting; in fact, it felt almost perfect as it cranked right up and rolled down the highway. Her goal today was to get to Chicago, thinking it would be better to be a needle in a haystack than a needle out in the open. The good news was she was only a few hours away and she would have plenty of time to find somewhere to crash for the night.

Alessandra arrived in the heart of Chicago by 1:00 p.m. Her first need was some new clothes; it was January in the Windy City, and the air coming off Lake Michigan was devastatingly cold. Fortunately there hadn't been any major snows yet. She bought a legitimate suitcase and a few hundred dollars' worth of layers to stuff inside of it. By this point it was late afternoon, and she was ready to find a place for the night. She picked the first place she came to, an expensive, ritzy hotel off North Michigan Avenue across from Millennium Park. She'd done the usual, paid cash and given a completely fake name and history along with a fake ID. The hotel wanted a credit card on file, but the clerk took an extra tip of fifty dollars to let it slide.

In all the years that she'd lived, she'd never been to Chicago, and she very much wanted to check out the nearby park; Aless had also heard many wonderful things about the music, artwork, theater, and just all-around interesting things to behold in Chicago. Ultimately, she decided it would be safer if she just stayed at her hotel. She longingly gazed outside for a while from the window of her room before closing the curtains and unpacking her things.

Aless realized she hadn't bathed since the incident two days before, so she drew a hot bath in the extra-large tub in her suite. She soaked her body for so long that the heat left the water and her skin had shriveled in many places. During her soak, she found it extremely difficult to stop thinking about Grey. She wondered where he was and if he was OK. Would he hate her forever? Would he turn her in to the authorities if he had the chance? Had she permanently damaged the best relationship she'd had since Lela died? All of these thoughts swam around her brain, clouding her thoughts.

After her bath, Aless decided to order room service from the bistro downstairs. While she waited for the food to arrive, she took the laptop from Grey's bag and booted it up again. She hoped that reading more of his writing would make her feel closer to him. She really missed him and his goofy smile. These thoughts made her feel sadness, happiness, and guilt. The computer came back to life, and Aless opened Grey's "Digital Journal" folder. She clicked the "November" folder and noticed something she hadn't seen the night before. There were more sporadic entries in November, unlike the almost daily entries in October and other earlier months. Aless opened a random document from November.

From the personal digital journal of Grey Chapman, November 18, 2005:

Today was difficult; I saw a man eating from a garbage can. He was wiping maggots off of a half-eaten apple that was dark brown with age. It looked like he was wearing a bed sheet sort of wrapped around him in the fashion of a toga. I don't think Aless saw me, but I was sick in the bushes behind one of the houses.

We have been in New Orleans for more than three weeks trying to help these people. It's overwhelming me; I've been having dreams about these homes filled with standing water, mold, and rotten walls and furniture. The dreams amplify the rotting smell of decay and death, literal and figurative death. But the worst is the rats; I'm talking about the real rats, not the dream ones. They have been driven out of whatever their natural habitats were and have moved into these flood-destroyed homes that we have been trying to salvage. I've seen no less than two rat bites this week. The second one was on a woman not much older than I am. It was bad! She was bitten in that meaty part of your hand between the thumb and pointer; it went all the way through, leaving a bloody whole the size of a dime! I mean, she held it up and I could see the sun shining through it like some sort of grotesque kaleidoscope. I can't stay here much longer. I have really tried to help, and I feel good about some of the things, but . . . I don't know how much longer I can stand it.

Tonight, I am going to ask Aless if we can continue moving. If she wants to stay, I will stay for her . . . with reluctance. Maybe . . .

. . . She smiled at me today for no reason! :)

Aless read the last line over again and again, and found herself smiling. She remembered the reason that she'd smiled at him; she was just beginning to fall for him, and after his selflessness in New Orleans, she was definitely beginning to trust him. Aless had learned that she and Grey were a great team during that difficult time. They'd just worked well together helping those people who needed it.

She closed the doc and opened the next chronological entry, which was also the last one for November.

From the personal digital journal of Grey Chapman, November 28, 2005:

I haven't written in a while, but I think that's because I love the mountains of North Carolina! I always have. There is something about the air here that is pure and refreshing, revitalizing, even. Aless reassures me that these are not mountains; they are only hills in comparison to the Rockies out West. I don't care what she thinks, these are MY mountains! I'm glad to have known about the spare key my grandparents have hidden by their camper. As soon as we left New Orleans, I knew this was the place we should end up. We stopped in the little valley town and purchased some essentials (TP, food, shower items), then my little car climbed the cliffs—in my mind they're cliffs—to the campground. Believe it or not, the tiny camper was a large step up from the abandoned motel room. We have unbroken access to electricity, warm water, and wireless Internet! We are camping in style, and only twenty yards from a breathtaking, crystal-clear, clean river. I even cleaned and oiled up my grandpa's old .22; too bad there are no bullets. Did I mention I love the mountains!?

I know I have already said it, but I can't express enough the joy of being away from the terrible devastation of New Orleans. Aless agreed wholeheartedly that the place was slowly draining the life out of us. She, too, was longing to move on, but she didn't want to hurt my feelings because I had wanted to visit. Can you imagine that? Her hurting my feelings? It would never happen. We have spent the past few days exploring the local areas, and in the evenings we have sat under the stars looking at the cosmos. I find it genuinely romantic. I've noticed over the past month that I am becoming very infatuated with the beautiful Aless. Her eyes sparkle in ways I would've never imagined possible; the moonlight dancing in her eyes has no comparison. Last night, her hand slid into mine as we lay looking into the blanket of the night. We held hands for what felt like an eternity of happiness, although I'm sure it was less than ten minutes. My palm became extra clammy when I began to think of the implications of our touch, so I pulled away to mop it across my jeans and she sat up.

"Grey?" she asked.

"Yes?" I countered, moving into a sitting position as well.

"I think it's time you know more about who I really am," she said slowly and deliberately.

"OK," I said. It was all I could muster.

The entry abruptly ended there. Aless had begun to reread the entry, when she heard a knock at the door. She was expecting her food from the bistro, so she hopped up from the bed, tied her robe tight, and peeked through the peephole—just in case Richards had found her. It was a member of the hotel staff with a food cart, just as expected. She let him in, thanked him for the food, tipped generously, and closed the door behind him after he left.

Aless rolled the cart over to the round table in the corner of the suite and off-loaded the meal, which consisted of stuffed baked chicken, grilled Parmesan broccoli, and risotto. The food smelled delicious, but she didn't want to eat without some reading material. Before

Alessandra sat down at the table, she grabbed the laptop from the bed and brought it over. The first thing she did was close the November 28 document and open the "December" folder. Aless took a bite of the risotto and navigated the mouse to the first entry.

From the personal digital journal of Grey Chapman, December 1, 2005:

This is the first entry I have written on the subject of Alessandra Sartori since the startling revelations revealed to me over the last few days here at the campground.

In order to organize my thoughts, I will just list the things presented as I can recall.

1. Alessandra is Italian, like old-world-grandma Italian.
2. She is a fluent speaker of at least two languages.
3. Aless was born in 1934(!) but somehow still looks twenty-four.
4. Aless was alive and captured by the Germans during WWII.
5. They experimented on her for genetic reasons.
6. She has some kind of genetic . . . thing(?) that keeps her young or aging super slow.
7. She has been on the run through ten administrations.
8. She is seventy-one years old in her mind! Seventy-one!!
9. She has a vivid memory of most of those years.
10. She learned to drive in the '70s—before I was born!
11. She is a multimillionaire through inheritance.
12. She never saw her true parents after age five.
13. As far as she knows, she can't be hurt or maybe even can't be killed because everything heals quickly.

And most importantly . . .

14. I love her.

I am truly in awe. This woman has experienced things that I only learned about in school. Just that one simple fact blows my mind! It really is no wonder the government is trying to contain her. What if she could live forever? Could that even be possible? An immortal being . . . alive here and now? Maybe her blood can cure disease, or her touch, or even just understanding her genome might lead to huge leaps in the science of aging—the possibilities are endless.

Number 13 on the list has me intrigued. The way she explains it, she can heal from any wound exponentially faster than I, or the rest of the known universe can. She showed me by slicing her finger with a knife in the camper. It bled a little but healed without a scar in less than five seconds. LESS THAN FIVE SECONDS! But there are some cells in the human body that just DO NOT REGENERATE, like the human brain. If something ever happened to her brain, I am afraid that she could, and quite probably would, die.

Of course number 14 is the most important to me. I have fallen hard for her, no matter what her extremely extensive past might hold. The way she smiles makes me melt. I can feel my entire body tingle from head to toe. I have never felt this way about anyone before. I am going to stay with her and keep running for as long as it takes, even if it's forever.

She has my heart.

Aless read the bit about her brain many times. *That couldn't be correct, could it?* she wondered. *Could it be that easy, or wouldn't my brain heal like everything else?*

She pushed the thoughts aside and closed the document and the lid of the laptop. She quickly finished the rest of her meal without reading, doing her best not to think of Grey or Richards or Lela or healing or living forever. She left her scraps and turned on the television, flipped through some channels until she found a comedy. Aless fell asleep before the show finished.

She dreamed about Grey, about the adventures they'd had together. She saw his smiling, caring face. When they touched hands, her body quivered, and she smiled, and they kissed, and she cried from the joy of it all. They were happy. She dreamed of a life where Grey grew old with her. They walked on the beach and got married at sunset. They had a child and raised him to be an adult. He didn't have the curse she held inside of her genes and molecules. He went to school and graduated from college in the blink of an eye. They danced at the young man's wedding, and were at the hospital for the birth of their first grandchild, who they named Lela, after her great-grandmother. Grey and Aless persevered through the hard times; he developed cancer and she was by his side for the entire treatment. Grey fought it into submission. It came back with a vengeance; he passed away at the age of seventy-three.

Aless, however, continued to live. She watched their son die in a car accident two years after Grey; she was there when her granddaughter married, had kids, and died from heart failure like her namesake; she watched those children grow up and die and the great-great-greats come and go as well.

Still, Aless lived.

She awoke from the dream in a cold sweat, breathing heavily. This was the first time she'd ever experienced this type of dream. Aless rolled over to see the clock read 5:47 a.m. She stretched, threw the covers back, and walked to the bathroom to relieve herself. She splashed water on her face, rubbing the sleep out of her eyes. She walked over to the table and reopened the laptop, bringing the display back to life. She could hear the traffic below beginning to get crowded for the morning commute and peeked out the window. The park was so beautiful and inviting. Today she might throw caution to the wind and take an adventure. First she would do a little more reading. She clicked over until she was in the "January" folder for 2006 and opened the last entry he'd ever made.

From the personal digital journal of Grey Chapman, January 10, 2006:

Dry Falls is not dry as the name might suggest. Let me take a time out and describe this natural wonder: The falls are amazing to behold! They cascade over a beautiful natural overhanging bluff dropping seventy-five feet and reconnecting with the Cullasaja River below. What makes the falls one of the best places that we have visited is the fact that we were able to walk under the bluff and continue around to the opposite side of the falls. Technically, the walkway was closed, but we jumped the fence and ventured to the opposite side anyway. I wish I could describe the falls in a way that would do it justice. I would love to add a picture here, but the Internet seems to be down right now, and we don't take many pictures for fear of them leaking out. The only thing more beautiful is my Aless . . .

Alessandra Sartori began to cry at this unassuming last entry. She missed Grey so much, and she wondered what he was doing right then. He was probably still asleep wherever he was. She moved back to the bed and flopped down onto the comforter. Her eyes felt puffy from the continued stress of this life. She put her face into the pillow and screamed a muffled shout of frustration, anger, and guilt. She replayed the events of the last day they had spent together before she'd had to run again. She watched the memories play like a video inside her mind. Aless rolled over and saw the bluish glow from the computer, and a thought occurred to her. She sat up and let the whisper form into an idea. Aless got up and walked back over to the computer, sat down, opened a new document, and began typing.

From the personal digital journal of ~~Grey Chapman~~ Aless Sartori, January 25, 2006:

It's been three days since Grey sacrificed himself . . . for me. We had decided to move on, away from the campground—how stupid, right? I was just getting so anxious sitting around there. I felt like I was just waiting around to be caught! At least Grey had the foresight to bring the rifle. Oh, Grey, I am sorry, Grey! I'm so sorry! I have cried so much!

We left on a Thursday morning, heading north through Greensboro, North Carolina, on our way to Philadelphia. We were on US 29, a somewhat smaller road, smaller than I-95, and less populated, when Grey's car started acting up. We made it all the way to Charlottesville before we decided to stop and have the car looked at. Good thing, too; all those little towns in the hills had me feeling a little crazy about stopping. (Yes, I am stereotyping people in the Virginia hills *_*—I'm sure that EVERYONE isn't a hillbilly—right?) We took the car to the closest shop once in town. They looked it over and determined that it wouldn't be a big deal to fix—I'm not sure what was wrong, but I didn't care as long as it was repairable—but we would have to wait for a part to be shipped in from out of town. Red flags and warnings went off in my brain, but I ignored them, thinking that the car had to be fixed, even though I now know it was nothing detrimental and I've driven it for days since. It was that wait time that was the problem; if we had been able to get out of there sooner, Agent Richards would have never caught up with us . . .

She paused here, rereading what she'd just written and thought about what to put next. Aless had never really journaled much before, but she was feeling exhilarated by getting her thoughts out of her head. She continued.

. . . Grey had hidden his grandfather's rifle under his coat in the trunk but grabbed it as we were leaving the repair place, being careful not to expose the rifle. Then we checked into a small motel that was a short walk from the repair shop, on the recommendation of the mechanic. We used fake names like always, at the shop and at the motel. Grey liked to take the lead; I noticed that early on, so I didn't stop him. This fantasy of being other people seemed to make him happy. He wasn't a natural when it came to lying on the spot about his life. He would flub stories and not quite remember the tiny details he'd made up. I guess he was trying to be too intricate, or make his pretend life more believable; whatever it was, it was bound to backfire on him someday, so I stepped in at the repair shop and sort of overrode what he was telling the mechanic. The guy probably thought we were lunatics! Anyway, at the motel, Grey gave a completely different story, which is never a good idea in case someone is tracking. I would say it was either the mechanic or the desk guy at the motel that called us in. We went to our room, oblivious of everything, and, in the end, that's where it all happened.

Friday morning we woke up late, around eleven or so. Grey showered while I watched the television in the room. (I have never been so emotionally attached to another person. I am crying all over again as I rerun the day in my head. Lord, I am so selfish and guilt ridden!) Grey finished up in the bathroom, dressed, and asked if I wanted to wander around town a little bit. I said, "Sure." Then, I showered and dressed while he watched TV; it took no more than six or seven minutes (my mania about being captured spills over even into shower time). After I dressed we headed out the door.

I still have a hard time with everything that happened. It just seemed like it was in fast-forward and slow motion at the same time.

I opened the door and led the way out with Grey behind me, then there was shouting from across the parking lot. Grey pulled me down behind a car, banging my head against the bumper, although I doubt he ever knew. Next thing I knew he was telling me to stay down, and he ran back to the door of the room, which was still open. Then, he appeared in the doorway with the rifle.

"Stay back or I will shoot!" Grey screamed across the parking lot.

"You need to get in here as soon as it's safe." Those were his exact words to me.

I panicked. I panicked, I panicked, I PANICKED. I hopped into a squatted position and steadied myself to bolt for the safety of the room. I didn't even make it two steps; my right foot kicked the parking barrier, sending me sprawling onto the sun-bleached pavement, digging rocks into my palms, tearing my flesh. I popped right back up, rubbing my hands across my jacket, and then the shots rang out. Grey was screaming. I couldn't hear what he was saying; it was mental block not a physical one.

The next feeling I had was a pure fire, a white-hot whistle up my left calf. There were two ripping, stinging balls of fire searching for a path through my leg. I went down a second time, and Grey dragged me inside the room, slamming the door behind us.

I screamed in agony; I couldn't help myself. Grey reached down and dragged farther into the room. I could feel the shattered bones grinding against each other.

"Oh my God, Aless!" Grey's face distorted into crumpled skin. "You're OK, right? I mean, it's gonna heal, right? Right?" He was frantic and pacing around the room.

I moaned, "I don't know, I don't know, something doesn't feel right. It hurts! Oh God! It hurts!"

He stopped suddenly, grabbing the blanket from the bed. "Here, shove this under your leg; try not to bleed anywhere but on that blanket," he said.

I took the blanket and shoved it under my leg. I think Grey was peering through the curtains across the parking lot, looking for Richards. That's when Richards spoke again.

"Alessandra Sartori"—he knew who I was—"you're wanted for the murder of Agent Anthony Richards, and I am going to take you with me, alive or dead. The choice is yours!" Or something like that.

I remember wanting to shout, "I don't know that person! I've never killed anyone!" Maybe I did shout it; I can't remember much other than pain during that moment.

"It looks like your leg is trying to heal maybe, but it's still bleeding a lot," Grey said. I was crying, sobbing really, and I would end up being thankful for those tears. You see, my hands had mostly healed, so I mopped the tears out of my eyes, feeling something painful on my face as I did so. I looked at my palms and there, right under the newly forming skin, was a large piece of rubble. I reached out with the pointer and thumb of my opposite hand, pinched out the rock, and watched it heal over almost instantly. That's when I knew.

I pulled my tattered pants leg up above my calf gingerly. I could see the wounds on the outer side of my calf bleeding onto the motel blanket, and the skin was healing over at the same time. The upper wound was in worse shape than the lower. It was going to be bleeding internally if the skin closed up too soon. I checked the inner side of my calf, and it was just as I feared. There was only one exit wound, for the lower bullet, but it was mostly healed. The upper must be the one that shattered the bone; it was still lodged in there somewhere.

I'm going to do the best I can with this next part. It was horrific.

"Grey," I said through tears, "I have to get this bullet out or it's not going to heal right. I'm gonna bleed to death."

"OK, OK, OK, OK," he spewed, running his hand over his face. "What can I do?"

"Is there anything like tweezers here?" I asked through gritted teeth.

He grabbed a pair of scissors from his shaving kit and gave them to me, saying it was the closest thing he could think of. I took them with no hesitation. The bullet would have to come out, either from the way it went in or from some other direction. Grey looked back out the window.

"Listen, I have an idea," he began. "That window in the bathroom, it's big enough to climb through." He took his keys and cell phone out of his pocket. "You can see the repair station from here. When you get there, my spare key is on this ring. Get that bullet out and take it and the blanket with you; do not leave them any DNA if you can help it. Then, go as fast and as far as you can."

Now my sobs were from more than just the physical pain.

He stood up, and I asked, "What about you?" as I took the keys and phone.

"I'm gonna buy you some time." He leaned back over me, wiped the tears from under my eyes with a gentle touch, placing his free hand on my cheek, and then kissed me deeply. My pain temporarily vanished, and in that moment I knew love.

He stood and walked out the door, closing it behind him. I refocused on the bullet wounds, the lower of which was all but healed. There was a thin layer of skin over the upper wound. I pushed the points of the scissors through it, reopening the hole made by the bullet. The pain was intense. I pushed my index finger inside the wound to open it more. About an inch in, I felt something hard and foreign; it could only have been the bullet. Outside, I heard the shouting of Agent Richards, and then Grey's reply to the man. I felt the sweat running down my forehead, mixing with my salty tears. I kept on going, pushing through the pain as fast as

I could. I managed to get the bullet near the surface with only my index finger. The blood was coming so quickly I remember being surprised that I could lose that much and still be alive. In fact, my popliteal artery must have torn as the bullet treated my leg like a pinball machine. As the projectile reached the surface of my leg, I pinched it between my thumb and index finger and pulled it free with triumph, dropping it onto the blanket beneath me.

Now, my worry was about healing in time. The lower hole was gone, like it had never happened. Then, right before my eyes, the upper hole began closing again, now it wasn't bleeding profusely. I moved my leg slowly back and forth as the hole began to completely disappear. The grinding of bones was also almost nonexistent. My leg was healing in a fraction of the time I thought it would. I was standing within twenty seconds of freeing the bullet.

"I love you, Grey Chapman," I said under my breath to no one, gathered the blanket, then opened the window, jumped out, and went as fast and as far as I could.

Aless stopped typing for the first time in several minutes. She felt satisfied at what she'd written, and had just hit the return key to start a new paragraph, when the computer made a funny ding sound. Alessandra didn't know what it meant, but a little bubble popped up in the bottom right corner of the screen. It read: "New Message."

When she clicked the little bubble, a new window opened up, and she saw that it was some sort of messenger program. It looked like someone called TakeMeGnomeTonight was messaging. The message was short and to the point.

Don't use the phone. They can trace it. I'm fine, I was taken in and interrogated for a few days. We can communicate this way as long as you keep moving. DON'T RESPOND TO THIS IF YOU AREN'T SURE IT'S SAFE! We will only call when things cool off, if they ever do. I love you. Grey.

She began to laugh, and then she broke into tears. He was alive.

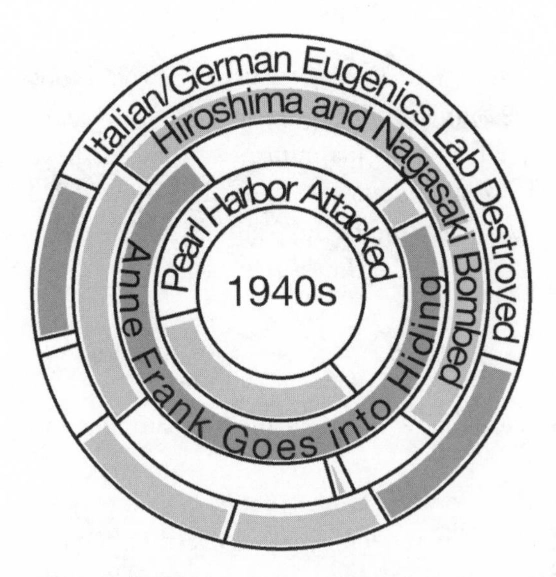

8:12 A.M.

ITALY, 1941

Eugene stuck the sugar cube into his mouth. Müller reached out and ruffled the boy's hair.

"Stay here, Mr. Trickens," Müller instructed.

The man stood and moved to a table on the opposite side of the room, where there were two more men working on things that Eugene couldn't quite see. He recognized the two men as doctors or scientist or whatever they called themselves. The names of the men did not immediately jump into his mind because he usually only saw them here in the lab, and his memories didn't stick too well in here. The three men began speaking in German about the objects on the table. Müller nodded his head and glanced back toward Trickens, who sat seemingly relaxed. Then Müller turned his attention back to the table, stretching out a stress knot in his neck. He was feeling more and more uneasy about the things he had done here at Laughlin; the things he was continuing to do. The three men continued their conversation about the procedures that the boy would be undergoing. Müller glanced again and saw that the boy's head was beginning to loll.

Eugene's eyes began to fuzz just after Müller glanced at him. His lids began to feel heavy. He refused to believe that he was sleepy; after all, they had only woken no more than an hour before. The room took on a surreal quality that made him feel oddly at peace. The horror stories of Lab B were pushed far back into his mind. He tilted his head upward and stared into the bright lights overhead. His eyes rolled back into the sockets and slipped around to the front again. The room phased out of existence, and there was darkness.

• • •

"Make sure the restraints are tight. We don't want him slipping and flailing around."

"They are tight; I have checked them twice already."

"Look, he's waking." The men had been speaking German to each other; now the fuzzy silhouettes switched to a heavily accented English. "Eugene, blink your eyes if you can hear me?"

His eyelids moved slowly as his pupils began to dilate. He tried to speak but found his mouth was like sandpaper. He wanted nothing more than to lick his lips, but his jaw was unnaturally hinged open. He moaned a groggy, openmouthed response, making eye contact with the doctor standing over him. It was Dr. Vogel, dressed in a white smock covered with an apron that appeared to be leather or some other type of thick fabric. Dr. Vogel had talked with Eugene on many occasions about his feelings toward his family. Eugene always lied about the way he was feeling to hide the fact that he was miserable. He had never expected to see Dr. Vogel in this capacity. He tried to close his mouth and realized, finally, that he could not. Sensibility began to return to Eugene, along with other emotions, most notably fear and anxiety.

Eugene tried to speak. "Eh uh ah oo ooee oo ee?!" The piece of metal jutting from his mouth turned the words into nothing but unintelligible syllables. The medical mouth gag had been ratcheted open as wide as the team could make it without shattering his temporomandibular joint. The pain Eugene would feel in the aftermath would be excruciating. He tried in vain to lift his right arm, then his left. The men had wrapped both of his wrists in leather restraints, and he felt one large strap covering both his legs below the knees. Tears began to trickle down the sides of his temple, following the grooves of his small, anxiety-ridden face. The liquid pooled in his ears. As he attempted to shake it out, he noticed that his head had also been strapped down to keep him motionless.

"Leesh! Leesh! Leht ee oh! Leht ee oh, leesh!" he begged as his tears came furiously. *Please! Please! Let me out! Let me out, please!* He was now becoming hyperaware. The boy could taste the metal bitterness inside of his mouth, he felt the beginnings of drying salt crusting around his eyes, he understood that the cold metal table was against the bare skin of his tiny body, and he could smell the ammonia used for cleaning the blood from the instruments, walls, and floors. Recognizing these harsh realities, he began to tremble uncontrollably.

Dr. Vogel motioned to Müller, who moved a microphone mounted on a rolling stand closer to the table.

"My name is Dr. Klaus Vogel," he began, switching back to German. "Today is 11 March 1941. We are in the Laughlin Center for Genetic Research under Mount Limbara on the island of Sardinia in Italy. This is subject number"—he paused, squinting to read the ink under the skin on Eugene's left forearm—"080580, a male, nine years of age, weighing approximately thirty kilos with a height of roughly one hundred thirty centimeters. The subject is a native of Great Britain but appears to be at least partially African in descent. He shows little signs of reaching puberty, and it is my professional opinion he has not yet reached this developmental stage. His hair is coarse, brown, and loosely curled; iris is light brown. There are no discernible markings or scars visible on the subject's body."

Vogel paused again, consulting the folder that Müller had set on his desk earlier. "The subject is dizygotic in nature. His twin sister is deceased. The autopsy revealed that she had genetic markers consistent with possible genetic anomalies. After initial blood work of subject 080580, the possibility of sharing these markers is extremely likely. Today's experiments will be to determine if these genetic deviations can be induced into changing from dormancy to activity."

Eugene stared horrified up at the three men hovering over his restrained, undernourished flesh and bones. He listened as Vogel spouted off paragraphs of meaningless German into a microphone next to the table. His mind raced as he thought of possible escape. His pulse beat wildly in anticipation; his hands were clammy with sweat. He had been struggling against the restraints for several minutes and could feel his stringy muscles burning, threatening to give in. His eyes darted back and forth between Dr. Vogel, Müller, and their unknown accomplice. What could he do? What? *WHAT?*

"Mr. Müller," Dr. Vogel instructed, "please, prep the subject for test number one."

Müller looked at the boy with contrition, saying, "Yes, doctor," then moved to get the instruments required for the first test.

Test one was a basic reflexive test. It investigated muscle reaction and motor reflex with minimal outside influence. Heat was the catalyst.

Müller and the unnamed assistant had left the table to get the instruments. When they returned, Eugene could smell the acridity of kerosene and glimpsed what may have been a blowlamp. His eyes were sharp. The blowlamp was filled, primed, and ready to be lit. There was a dark hue to the instrument, and the metal where the flame jet would soon be was thoroughly scorched from repeated use. Eugene's breath came in quick, shallow pants as the men came closer to the table.

"Mr. Müller, please light the blowlamp," Vogel said in a mild voice.

Müller picked up the striker from the small side table where the lamp was resting and then primed the pump a few more times for good measure. He placed a small amount of methylated spirits in the lighting reservoir, checked to see if the air valve was closed tightly, and struck the striker, lighting the spirits. Eugene knew that the lamp would need time to heat up from watching his father use one at home a few times. He was running out of time. How long would he have? A minute? Five? He had to control his breathing or he was going to pass out. Truthfully, passing out didn't seem like a terrible idea, all things considered. He closed his eyes, tried to swallow, but only succeeded in making a dry, clicking sound with his mouth forcibly agape. He struggled against his restraints with a newfound energy but was met with the same resistance, and he realized he was only struggling with his arms. He tried to move his legs up and down with no luck, but he didn't think of moving them side to side. He opened his eyes with this revelation just in time to hear the whoosh sound of the lamp coming into fiery life.

"Dr. Vogel, beginning test number one," Vogel dictated to the microphone. "Muscle reaction and reflexive response. Heat stimulus. Distance: one meter."

The doctor picked up the blowlamp, refining the flame with a slow twist of the air valve. The sound was like a minirocket in the quiet of Lab B. The yucky room was about to live up to its horrible and childish nickname. Eugene began to panic, forgetting about the slim chance of freeing his legs and pulling his arms with all his might, willing for the restraints to break, even one just one of them, so he could swat the lamp onto the ground. But they did not.

Vogel carried the lamp to the opposite side of the table near Eugene's right leg, dragging the microphone behind him. He checked the air valve one last time and unceremoniously turned the white-blue flame jet toward Eugene. The boy screamed out in terror, taking huge, gulping breaths, but his fear consumed him more than the flame hurt him. A distance of one meter was enough to feel the flame burning your skin, but it was far from melting the flesh from your bones. He had jerked his leg to the left when he felt the heat, and Vogel seemed satisfied with the result.

"Right leg; acceptable movement within range, taking into account the variable of being strapped to the table," Vogel said into the microphone. "Moving on to right side. Distance: one meter."

Müller wrote the information down in a notebook.

Dr. Vogel continued with the first test all the way around the perimeter of the boy's body as Müller, the assistant, and the recording logged all the information. Eugene was still very anxious about the blowlamp burning his skin but found he was slightly more relaxed than before. In time, the boy would regret this.

After the first test was finished, the three men reviewed the results. This took some time because the assistant's information did not match Müller's own writings. The three men had to consult the recording to review what Dr. Vogel had dictated. Vogel seemed very annoyed by this waste of time, verbally reprimanding the assistant. Eugene lay very still on the table and listened to the Germanic bickering. He used the time to rest his tired body. The amount of adrenaline that had coursed through the boy, as well as pure terror, had left him exhausted. He had no way of gauging how long he had been on the table. His jaw was sore from being held open for this unknown period of time. His mind turned toward his family once again. He wondered if his mother and sister had had to endure such grotesque punishment. He wondered if his sister had died during "tests" similar to the ones he was receiving. He tried to swallow again, but the pain shot through his parched throat.

"Aher. Leesh, aher," he said in broken vowel sounds, supplemented with throat clicks. *Water. Please, water.* The men did not hear, or they chose to ignore him.

After several minutes the men returned to the table where the boy lay naked and strapped down.

"Mr. Müller, let us begin preparing for our second test," Vogel said in English so Eugene Trickens would understand.

Müller, who had brought back a towel, began wiping the boy down as if he had just come from bathing. He toweled every reachable inch of the child's body, specifically focusing on the legs and feet. After he had done a thorough job, he placed the towel under the table. Müller then spoke to the other assistant in German, requesting that he bring a specific device over to the table. Eugene could not see what he'd requested, and, even if he could have, he would not have known what the device was.

The device was transported in a large suitcase over to the side table where earlier the men had prepped the blowlamp. Müller opened the case to reveal a machine that was no more than a few knobs attached to an unassuming black casing. The knobs had indications of being able to tune up or down. There was a large battery in the suitcase as well. The black casing had a few short wires coming out of the side that the assistant was attaching to the battery. Lastly, Müller took out a two-foot-long copper prod. One end of the prod was wrapped in rubber; there was wiring leaving this end of the prod, disappearing into the black casing. The opposite end was a small rounded ball made of copper as well.

"Dr. Klaus Vogel, beginning test number two," Vogel dictated for the microphone, once again in German. "Electrical stimuli to the feet, low voltage, dry. Mr. Müller, you may begin when ready."

Müller stared at the doctor and then looked to the boy. He partially swallowed the hard lump that had formed inside of his throat, looked toward the assistant, who was waiting beside the suitcase, and nodded his head just once. The man turned the right-hand knob, bringing the machine to life with a humming noise. He adjusted the left knob slightly, raising the voltage moving through the copper prod. The instrument thrummed in Felix Müller's palm, and he wiped away newly formed beads of sweat from his creased brow. His stomach twisted as he moved to the far end of the table.

The sound penetrated deep inside of Eugene Trickens, vibrating his entire being. His dry mouth clicked and moaned against the use of the device, low voltage or otherwise. Once again the boy uselessly tugged at his restraints. In desperation, he began to bounce his midsection up and down on the table. His breathing was on the verge of hyperventilation. He shuffled his feet in an attempt to keep them away from the copper prod as it moved closer to his uncovered flesh. It proved to be utterly fruitless; he could not move either of his feet more than a few inches from left to right. The prod came down in the arch of his left foot with coolness and searing pain simultaneously.

"ARGHRAH!" Eugene shrieked through the medical mouth gag. The electricity coursed through every atom of his being. He felt pain in places he was unaware he had pain receptors. His arch was molten lava, as the muscles contracted, forming a clawed gnarling of toes. The muscles throughout the rest of his body ripped into contorted caricatures of their normal state. His shriek was cut off almost as quickly as it had begun, due the constriction of the muscles along his vocal folds. Eugene could not breathe; his rib cage had collapsed in as the current ran its course, and he would later think that it must only compare to drowning. His body seized in ultimate loss of control, as did his bladder. Then, it was gone.

Müller had held the prod against the boy's skin for three seconds before removing it. The boy took a gasping breath in and let out an agonized moan. Müller's hands trembled slightly as he placed the prod back into the case to write down his observations.

Dr. Vogel dictated German gibberish into his microphone as tears cut pathways across Eugene's temples. Müller wrote down his findings with a still-shaking hand as the boy was panting off to his right. After he had finished, he placed his pad down next to the suitcase that contained the black casing. He leaned over the table with his head hanging low.

"Mr. Müller," Vogel said, "let us move to the legs."

"Dr. Vogel, continuing test number two," Vogel spoke to the microphone. "Electrical stimuli to the lower legs, low voltage."

Müller slowly raised his head, avoiding eye contact with everyone, especially the boy; he steadied his hands and picked up the prod once again. The assistant powered up the small machine again after Müller gave him the signal. This time the unmistakable fire began in the left calf of Eugene Trickens. The electrical impulses overloaded the boy's nervous system for a second time, causing his muscles to seize and his back to arch. His diaphragm again forced air from his lungs as it suddenly, and violently, contracted. Eugene's pain receptors lit up like a tilting pinball machine. He screamed, briefly, before his air was all gone. Again, Müller made a silent count of three seconds and removed the copper prod from the boy's calf. Then the men recorded their findings. This process continued for the next fifteen minutes until the prod had come in contact with all the appendages of the boy's body. He was in terrible pain, but he was alive. Vogel noted during this time that subject 080580 had no indication of the activation of dormant genes . . . yet.

Eugene Trickens hurt everywhere. His body had taken more than a dozen direct electrical shocks in the span of twenty minutes, each ranging from three to six seconds in duration. He couldn't see his flesh but knew there were burn marks by the unmistakable smell of singed body hair. His mouth, which had been hinged open for an insurmountable time, was so dry that his inner checks began to chap. But he was alive, and he clung to that thought, along with the memories of the train station.

Dr. Vogel came close to visually examine the boy. He saw the singe marks left on the boy's appendages, noting into his microphone that the ones on the underside of the biceps were the worst of them. He also performed a basic check of the boy's heart, lungs, and blood pressure.

He then took a syringe and drew blood from the boy's arm for later testing.

Vogel turned on his heels and began walking back toward his microphone, saying, "Mr. Müller, I believe we can move forward with the next part of the procedure."

"With all due respect, sir," Müller began, "do you think this is wise? I mean, do you think we should give the boy a rest? He has already endured more than most today."

Vogel halted, turned, and looked over his shoulder at Müller with annoyance in his eyes. "Mr. Müller, insubordination will not be tolerated; *move forward* with the procedure." The last few words were percussive and distinct, indicating Vogel's lack of patience. Müller sighed, nodded with understanding, and moved back to the table. Eugene had his eyes closed, attempting to rest his body and mind, as the men conversed in German. He had heard Müller approaching the table, and looked up, his eyes pleading with the man.

"Leesh, leesh," was all Eugene could manage with his dry, dusty voice. *Please, please.*

Müller could tell the boy was begging even through the mouth gag. *Please,* the boy begged, *please.*

Müller didn't look down; he couldn't bring himself to look at the face of the child, who lay naked and shivering on a cold table in a lab underneath the earth, being tortured by monsters. He simply could not. So, he kept his mind busy with his work. The next step, test number three, would need slightly more setup than the earlier tests.

Müller reached down under the table and produced a bucket that he needed for the third test. He carried the bucket to the far side of the room and filled it with cold water from a tap that was used for cleaning. Slowly, deliberately, he carried the bucket of water back to the area where the boy was strapped down. He put his back to the boy's eye line in hopes that he would simply not look at the man, but he knew he would always be the monster that would haunt this boy, just as these actions would haunt him. Müller lifted the bucket and poured the water all over boy's naked body. The water was extremely cold, and Eugene let out a gasping noise as the water found its way into all the crevices. He saved a small amount to pour over the boy's head and into his mouth.

"Close your eyes," Müller said over his shoulder, in English. "Do it now."

Eugene did and immediately felt the cold water washing over his upper face and head. Then, a tiny amount of the liquid found its way into the boy's mouth. The sound the boy made reminded Müller of a fish who had been out of water and was thrown back into the shallow edge of a river, gulping and gasping, struggling to breath, but refreshed by receiving a chance to live.

Müller placed the bucket back under the table and thoroughly dried his hands on the towel that was also under the table. At that point, he returned to the suitcase and asked the assistant to double-check that the machine was off. Next, the assistant looked inside the case and found a small set of prongs attached to a long section of copper wiring. He took the wiring and wrapped the middle around the copper ball at the end of the prod into a tight coil. The prongs dangled at the opposite end of the wiring, bouncing off each other like large fishhooks. Müller took the prod/prong combo from the assistant and walked the two feet over to the table where Eugene was lying soaked and shivering. The boy was looking up directly into Müller's eyes; Müller stared back for several seconds. He broke eye contact, produced the towel from under the table, and threw it over the upper part of the boy's head, covering his pleading eyes. Eugene began to pant and breathe in, gasping, moving his tongue to pronounce *please* in his openmouthed dialect. Müller did his best to ignore the noise.

He took one of the prongs and slid it between the boy's lower left cheek and mandible, securing it in place with a small hook on the end of the prong. He repeated the process on the right-hand side of the boy's mouth. Eugene tried to fish the prongs out with movement from his tongue but only found the hooks driven deep. The boy had begun to sob again.

"Leesh! Leesh! Isa oolah! Leesh lop!" the boy panted. *Please! Please! Mr. Müller! Please stop!* He began jerking the leather restraints anew, willing something to give.

Müller ignored the boy and nodded toward Vogel to let him know everything was ready. Vogel leaned toward the microphone and spoke in German.

"Dr. Vogel, beginning test number three; immersive electrical stimuli to the soft tissue, medium voltage. Mr. Müller, on your count."

During this test, the device had to be switched on with the setting already correct, so Müller asked the assistant to check that the voltage was in the middle of the dial. After some adjustment, the assistant confirmed he was fully ready.

"OK, on my mark," Müller said, closing his eyes.

"Three . . ."

Eugene Trickens knew he was going to die. He could feel the cold metal of the hooks and prongs digging into the interior of his cheeks. He could hear the men speaking in German, picking up on a few words that were similar in English—*elektrische,* for example. Eugene knew that meant "electricity" or something close to it. Even though Müller had covered his face and he couldn't see what they were doing, he knew the prongs must have something to do with electricity; plus they had soaked him with a bucket of water. Water and electricity didn't play well together, Eugene knew from school. If he were lucky, he would be dead before he knew he was being juiced. He needed some luck but doubted he would see it today.

"Two . . ."

He tried to calm the raging ocean of panic inside him to no avail. His breathing was labored, his heart raced, and his emotional state was volatile. Eugene's mind drifted from family, to capture, to train rides, to torture, and back again. How could he escape? He needed more time to think, he needed more time to work on the restraints, he need more time with his family, more time to live his life, more time with Nia, more time to be a child, a grown-up, in love, to play with the other kids, more time to breathe, more time to get past this electrocution, more time—

"One . . ."

At that exact moment there was a large flash of white light as if all the overhead bulbs had simultaneously blown. Müller instantly thought the device in the black casing had overloaded and blown up.

For Eugene, that exact moment was the first time it happened. The room began to disintegrate before his eyes, entire chunks of reality falling through one another. He saw through the once-solid towel as Müller turned into white light then shattered glasslike into trillions of speckles of Müllerlight. Dr. Vogel lit up also and immediately imploded into a perfect pinpoint of brilliant whiteness. The assistant splashed to the ground like a human water balloon and evaporated in the span of a second. The ceiling above the boy shot toward him as if he were falling up to it, then he went through it as easily as moving through air. The room around him spun violently, quickly ripping itself apart at the cellular level, leaving behind white blackness that enveloped nothingness. He heard violent ripping and tearing. He felt babies crying and old men screaming, women sobbing and children laughing. He heard machines roaring, bombs exploding, the anger of animals, the crunching of bones, and the sloshing of liquids. Eugene heard and saw these things with his mind, instantly, simultaneously.

• • •

"Where's the boy!?" Dr. Vogel shouted as his eyes readjusted to the room's light. "Where is *the boy*?" Vogel moved toward the other men as he spoke.

Müller looked around the table frantically. "I don't know, I don't know! I don't see him."

"Lock down the lab, find the boy. He has manifested!"

The assistant ran to lock the lab doors while keeping an eye out for the child. Müller began ransacking the lab, trying to feel in the empty spaces for a person. He had a strange feeling that this might be how it felt to be blind. Vogel moved quickly back to the microphone.

"Subject 080580 has manifested, I repeat, subject 080580 has manifested." He spoke with urgency. "My best description would be that he turned into pure white light and vanished. Early speculation leads me to believe the boy is bending light around himself to become invisible. Purely conjecture at this time. We have secured the lab and are trying to find him. This is hands down the biggest event since 110102's hyper-rapid cicatrization period. Bigger, even!" Vogel was breathing hard and smiling wide. "That was amazing."

Müller began rooting around under the tables and desks, looking for the boy. In desperation, he started calling out the boy's name. Vogel wandered away from the microphone and began groping around for the boy while still feeling euphoric. Müller wondered if the boy might have just bleeped out of existence, when suddenly back at the center of the room was another brilliant flash with a pop sound attached to it. The three Germans spun on their heels to see the boy lying on the table unrestrained, but in the same position and location as he was when he vanished. Then he lurched forward and vomited.

Thirty-three seconds had passed.

• • •

Eugene had almost a half a dozen vials of blood drawn as soon as they cleaned him up. The vomiting had taken a lot out of him. He needed rest, food, and fluids. Dr. Vogel was adamant about starting a new round of testing as soon as Trickens finished vomiting, but Müller stepped in to be a voice of reason. He convinced Vogel to give the boy twenty-four hours to recuperate, and then they could start with basic questions. Maybe the boy could do this at will and didn't need the pressure of the testing, but that was something they wouldn't find out immediately. Vogel was very excited about the morning's progress and wanted to duplicate the results as soon as possible, but he was content with the blood work for now.

The next day, Dr. Vogel and Felix Müller sat down with Eugene Trickens and had breakfast away from the other children. Dr. Vogel formulated a huge list of scientific questions, most of which Eugene wouldn't even be able to comprehend. Müller would do his best to translate the meanings.

"Mr. Trickens, how are you feeling today?" Vogel asked, feigning concern.

He pushed around his food with his fork and didn't look up when he responded, "I don't like it here."

Vogel glanced at Müller. "I'm sorry to hear that. Yesterday was . . ." He trailed off, not knowing where to go with his thought.

Müller jumped in. "Yesterday was difficult for you. We understand that. It was also difficult for us."

"Yes, it was," Vogel said, still feigning interest, "but it was an incredible event. You must feel that too."

Eugene stared down at his half-eaten breakfast, unresponsive.

"Dr. Vogel would like to ask you some questions so we can better understand what happened yesterday, Eugene," Müller said.

He sat for a long period of silence, pushing the food around.

"Eugene—" Vogel began.

"You hurt me; that's what happened," he interrupted.

Müller sighed. "I . . ." He was at a loss for words. Vogel jumped in impatiently.

"Yesterday, your vital readings were more or less normal for the amount of stressors under which your body was placed. The systolic and diastolic numbers were within limits and your secretions of adrenaline remained relatively low throughout the morning. Why is that?"

Now Eugene did look up, confusion plastered on his face.

"Dr. Vogel, he's nine years old; he doesn't understand you." Müller turned to Eugene. "What Dr. Vogel is trying to say is that your body seemed calm, at least in comparison to"—he rubbed his face—"other data. Where you feeling scared?"

Eugene looked back down at the plate in front of him. "Yes, more than I have ever felt."

Müller suddenly began to relive the guilt that he'd experienced during the testing the day before. He felt his face flush.

"Why doesn't your body show normal signs of being scared?" Vogel asked.

"How should I know?"

Vogel stared coldly at the boy. "Your blood before and after the event show no signs of change, can you explain this?"

"Dr. Vogel, let's just hear the story in his words. It might be easier for everyone," Müller stated.

Dr. Vogel cut his eyes at Müller but nodded in agreement. "Very well, Mr. Trickens, you may begin, and please be detailed; I am making a report of this conversation."

"OK. Well, I was on the table, scared, and Mr. Müller placed the towel over my face." The boy began to tremble slightly. "Then I could feel him putting that metal into my mouth. I started to really feel frightened for my life." Eugene looked away from the men, but went on. "I thought about my family and how I wished I could see them again, my sister most of all. I thought about dying. I just was really scared."

"Yes, yes, we understand you were afraid, move on to the event," Vogel said without empathy.

The boy looked hurt. "I closed my eyes and wished I wasn't there, and when I opened them, I was still on the table."

"You never left the table?" Vogel questioned.

"No."

"And is there more?" Vogel demanded expectantly.

"No, not that I can remember," he lied.

"You were invisible for more than thirty seconds, surely you remember something."

Eugene shook his head.

Vogel's lips thinned. "Well, your sibling was more helpful than you are."

"My sister? You saw my sister?" Eugene cried out.

Vogel said nothing, stood, and walked away. Müller looked at the boy and got to his feet to follow the doctor.

"Dr. Vogel"—Müller called after the man, reverting back to the German tongue—"what are we doing here? What I mean to say is, what is the point of continuing to—"

Vogel stopped and spun on his heel so quickly that Müller almost ran into him. "The point, Mr. Müller, is that this boy holds the key to saving lives! *German* lives! Our men are out there being killed every day while we sit in here and play teatime with children! I cannot in good conscience let more men die when I am so close to having results! Once we can isolate the catalyst—"

Müller stood his ground. "How do we know what we're doing *is* the catalyst that brings about these manifestations?"

"We are doing what has *shown results*," Vogel said. "Evolution has shown that the body will adapt to change. We want it to adapt *faster*, hence our methods!"

Eugene watched from a distance as the two men argued in the language that he couldn't understand, and he decided he'd figure out how to use this . . . whatever, to get him out of this nightmare.

• • •

Over the next three months, Eugene visited Lab B, the yucky room, an average of four times per week. During that time, there had been fourteen manifestation events, two of which were prompted without any physical stimulation. Before those, there were three times that the stimulation was very minimal. In short, Eugene was learning how to control his gift, if that's what it was.

It was manifestation number eleven that Eugene rested his hopes upon. He was in the lab with Müller and Dr. Vogel when it happened. The two men had attempted many different tests when the original three had failed to yield the same results. This particular time had started with some stress testing, as was the usual protocol, although Eugene was no longer afraid of being killed. He felt confident that the men needed him alive to test, even though his certainty was misguided. Vogel would've killed him to study his body if the boy stopped giving results, and he'd use what he'd learned on the next child, as he was undoubtedly going to do anyway. Eugene knew the man was a monster, but what could a nine-year-old do? Manifestation number eleven was about to shed some light.

After the stress test, the men repositioned the boy to lie face down.

"Just strap his arms, leave his legs, Müller," Vogel instructed.

"Yes, sir."

The men spoke in German as usual when testing the boy.

"Dr. Vogel, beginning test number two hundred sixteen," he dictated into the microphone. "Insertion of radioactive isotope number Strontium-90 into the spinal cord between the C2 and C3 vertebrae. A dose of ten ccs will be administered. Mr. Müller, if you will angle his head correctly."

Müller took the boy under his jaw and at the top of his cranium and pushed it forward to open space between the vertebrae, while Vogel prepared the syringe. The door to the lab creaked slowly open. Vogel looked over; he saw no one in the doorway. Then his eyes moved down to the ground. There stood a girl.

"What are you doing in here?" Vogel barked. "Müller, get her out of here."

"Yes, sir."

After Müller let go of the boy's head, he swung it around to connect his light-brown eyes with the wide, ocean-blue-green eyes of a young girl with sandy-blonde hair that fell into her face. She was carrying a doll with a flower on her little dress. Eugene knew her name was Alessandra, but the older kids and the younger kids didn't often share the same playtime. Müller chased the girl away, locked the lab, and returned to holding the boy's head. Vogel confirmed that he had the correct amount of the isotope in the syringe, then felt the boy's neck for the correct point of insertion. He plunged the long needle through the skin, fibrous tissue, muscle, and, cracking through the cartilage, into the spinal cord. Vogel squeezed the plunger, sending the 10 ccs directly into the boy. Eugene gasped, and brilliant white light filled the room again.

When he opened his eyes, he could hear Vogel talking.

". . . isotope number Strontium-90 into the spinal cord between the C2 and C3 vertebrae. A dose of ten ccs will be administered. Mr. Müller, if you will angle his head correctly."

Müller took the boy under his jaw, and Eugene realized he'd been here before. It had worked differently than ever before. Vogel suspected he was becoming invisible by bending light, or perhaps flipping over into an alternate dimension located beside our own. Eugene never led him to believe anything different, because he wanted to learn about his manifestation to benefit himself.

After his third manifestation, Eugene had requested that he be allowed to face the direction of his friends across the way in Lab A—not so he could see them, but so he could feel comfortable. Vogel was against it, of course, but Müller had convinced the doctor by telling him if the boy felt more comfortable, he may manifest more frequently or even with different events. Vogel's greed led him to quickly agree. Eugene's real desire was to be angled toward the clock. A week later, during his fourth manifestation event, he looked directly at the clock as the world melted into white light. It read 11:23 and forty-five seconds. When his vision cleared, the clock read 11:25 and fourteen seconds. One minute and twenty-nine seconds were gone; he had traveled forward in *time*. Every event from the first until the eleventh had been a forward jump, the longest being two minutes and ten seconds long. He couldn't see the clock, lying on his stomach, but he guessed he couldn't have gone more than forty seconds or so into the past.

The door opened, and a little girl with sandy-blonde hair and ocean-blue-green eyes entered. He smiled this time, but she didn't see it.

Müller returned and took the boy's head again.

"Dr. Vogel, I feel sick." Eugene was paler than before the girl came. "Can we stop for today? We can continue tomorrow. I know I am not scheduled for tomorrow, but I feel awful, and I don't mind coming in."

"Give him today, Dr. Vogel," Müller said in German to the man with the syringe. "He manifested yesterday. Let him recover, for better results."

Vogel nodded and put the cap back on the syringe. "You can go, boy."

Müller was already unstrapping his arms.

Back in his room, he commenced creating a plan of escape using his newfound power. Over the next few weeks he would come to call his manifestation "time displacement," because so far he couldn't do more than displace a few minutes. He decided that he needed to spend some more time learning how to use the gift before he tried anything drastic. Before Eugene Trickens's eyes closed for sleep that evening, he had a bare-bones idea growing inside of his mind.

◆ ◆ ◆

It had been four months since the first manifestation of Eugene's time displacement. He had displaced time on more than two dozen occasions. Many of the most recent events included both traveling back in time and then moving forward, too. Vogel and Müller didn't know the difference. For his scientific captors, time was linear, and they hadn't seen him go anywhere unless he went forward; for them, a backward displacement was a nonevent. He also noticed that traveling to the past had a different effect on his body than going to the future. Jumping forward usually made him feel woozy, light-headed, or nauseous. But he could shake that feeling off within a minute and be back to normal. Going back was something entirely different. It made him feel as if he were being crushed, and it usually took anywhere from a few minutes to a few days to feel right again.

As he grew to control his manifestations, Eugene also started to feign friendship with Felix Müller in order to access part of the complex where kids normally were restricted; namely, the main hall where the main doors were located. He had walked by them several times in the past two weeks with Mr. Müller. The doors were held permanently closed with a combination lock that looked impossible to crack to the now ten-year-old. However, he had a plan and was going to try to stick to the plan.

"Where does our food come from?" Eugene asked Müller one day as they walked by the doors.

"Our food comes from people who take care of us on the outside," Müller simplified.

"Oh. OK," was the only response that Eugene needed to say. He had seen what he wanted to see. Müller looked over at the doors as he responded, letting the boy know that was most likely a way out of the underground compound. Now the only other obstacle was the lock.

Müller offered more. "Wanna see the kitchen?"

Eugene smiled and nodded. The boy and the man entered the kitchen, which held more food than Eugene had ever seen in one place. There were probably fifty shelves lined mostly with canned or boxed food, but the amount was staggering to the little boy from a small town in England. His village shop didn't have half as much food. It made Eugene feel anxious.

"So, I guess the food doesn't come often?" Eugene questioned.

"Oh no, this is just the dried and canned stuff. We get fresh meat and veggies every other Tuesday."

"Really? Sounds good; I'm hungry." The two of them laughed, genuine laughs, which were hard to come by in this nightmare.

Eugene began watching for deliveries the next Tuesday. But there wasn't a delivery that week, apparently, because the cook didn't leave the kitchen all day. When the following Tuesday came around, Eugene was stationed where he could see once again. Most of the adults had come to accept Eugene hanging in places he shouldn't be because of his closeness with Felix Müller and the fact that he was currently the golden boy keeping all of them in jobs; they turned a blind eye as if he weren't doing anything wrong. Eugene was a good kid; he just wanted out, and no one knew he had a way.

The delivery took place at about 4:15 Tuesday afternoon. The plan was to observe this time and next time to see if there was a pattern. However, an opportunity presented itself. The cook was waiting by the door for the banging on the steel doors.

"OK, I hear you," the man said in Italian. "Let me get this lock." He began a tuneless whistling while he worked the combination, finally getting it on the third try.

"Hello," he said to the man breathing fresh air.

"Hey, trouble with the lock again?" Eugene understood none of the conversation, because he did not speak any Italian.

"Yes, that lock is always sticking. What do we have this week, the usual?" the cook asked.

"Oh no, I have something special for you, Moroccan white sea bream right from the ocean. Take these vegetables. I'll watch the door. Then, I'll go get the fish."

"I could make a white fish soup and feed everyone for days, fantastic!"

The cook continued to whistle his tuneless song as he pushed the cart of vegetables into the kitchen area. The delivery man stood by the door and lit a smoke. He inhaled the cigarette deeply into his lungs and began coughing. Hacking was a better description. The man bent at the waist, placing his hands on his knees to steady himself. Still he continued to whoop and bark deep guttural sounds from his blackened lungs. Eugene watched all this from a corner where he was sitting, pretending to play with a small toy ball. He saw the man fall to one knee, gasping for air and clutching his chest. Eugene slowly stood and looked around the corner for the cook. The hall was completely empty. When he looked back, the man had begun to cough up something dark and thick like blood; he'd fallen on both knees and was changing from red in the face to the color of a ripe plum.

Eugene turned to run for the cook, took a few steps, and then stopped. The door to the kitchen would open and the cook would return soon, if Eugene waited things out. He noticed the coughing had stopped and looked over and saw the man facedown in a growing pool of thick red liquid.

Probably his blood; he's dying while I watch, he thought. *Maybe I can help him.*

An idea popped into the young boy's mind as Eugene watched the man take his final breath. He looked down all the hallways that led to this point. Empty. Next, he walked over to the body of the dead man and took his keys from the pocket of the jacket he was wearing, just in case he could use them. He looked around, realizing that he had to hurry if he was going to help this man *and* escape. He ran through the doorway into the corridor that lay beyond, pausing to grab the lock from where the cook hung it on the open door. There were steps that led to the ground level, or so Eugene hoped; he'd never seen them before. The boy hid under the stairway, closed his eyes, and concentrated; in seconds he disappeared into a white flash like the sun breaking through the cloud cover on a rainy day.

When the white faded, he could hear the tuneless whistle disappearing down the hallway corridor that led to the kitchen and pantry. Through his cover of stairs he saw the delivery man reaching in his pocket for his smokes. The boy felt woozy with pains in his back but shook it off the best he could. Eugene waited until the man had his back turned, stepped out from the cover of the staircase, ran up until he was directly behind the man, and threw the lock at his head. At the close range of three feet he connected directly with his target, sending the delivery man right to the ground, and hopefully saving his life in the process, or at least postponing his death. He turned and bolted up the stairs, pumping his little legs as hard as he could. He briefly thought about how he knew the halls would be empty for the next few minutes but kept pushing himself as hard as he could.

He reached the fourth floor panting—man, they were deep underground—but the adrenaline kept him going. He saw a door, grabbed the handle, and twisted it violently back and forth to no avail. The door was locked, one last precaution to keep the prisoners captive. He smashed the door with both his tiny fists—he was so close!—and then he began to cry and slid down the door to the floor. As he fell to the ground, he landed on the keys he had taken from the driver. A revived feeling of exuberance shot the boy back to his feet. He pulled the key ring out and began trying keys in the lock. The third key slid home, and the boy turned the tumblers and the knob almost at the same time. He burst out into the afternoon sunlight, breathing fresh air for the first time in over two years. He desperately wanted a moment to take it all in but realized he couldn't stop running, not yet. He took off into the mountainous rocky landscape, leaving the large delivery truck and this nightmare behind.

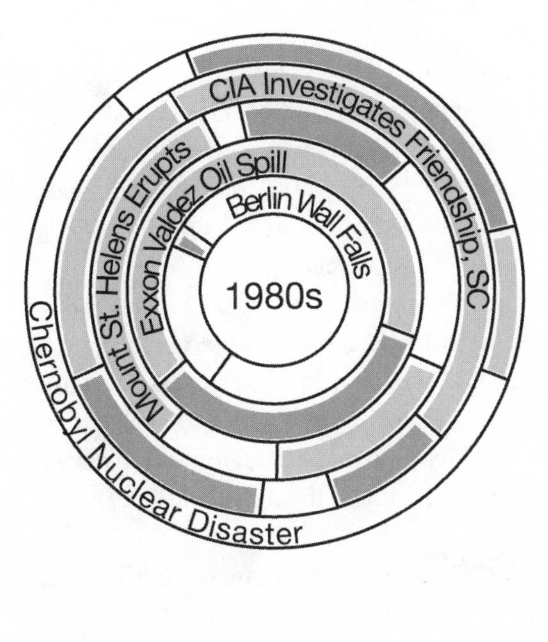

9:31 A.M.

SOUTH CAROLINA, 1986

The man in the wheelchair rolled down the aisle of Willodean's Market. He filled his little basket with fruits and vegetables that were handpicked that very morning, at least according to the signage. He wished for an electric wheelchair, but all he had was one of those human-powered ones that you could catch a ride in at every hospital on your way to the curb. He wore faded dark slacks, with a button-down light-green gingham collared shirt. On his head he wore an old beige flat cap made of cotton to cover his sensitive scalp. He wasn't much of a man anymore these days; his body was atrophied from being wheelchair bound for too long to remember, and his appetite had been tapering steadily over the last two years or so. The man knew he was dying; time was the only variable.

"This will be all for me, today," he said to the attendant behind the meat counter with a hint of an accent. He lifted his arm with a mighty grunt to raise the small but heavy basket up onto the high countertop.

"Yes, sir. Would you like to add any meat to your purchase today? Truck just came this morning," the attendant asked with a toothy smile.

"No, thank you," the old man said. "I have exactly what I need."

"OK, then, seven dollars and forty-six cents is the damage," the young man said after punching the ringing keys of the old cash register. The man in the wheelchair dug deep into the pocket of his shirt and produced a wrinkled ten, then passed it up to the man. He changed it from the drawer with the quick ease of a professional.

"All right, Mr. Tate, we'll see you next week!"

The attendant came around the counter and returned the change and a paper bag of groceries to the wheelchair-bound customer. Mr. Tate thanked the young man and wheeled himself across the faded linoleum out of the exit into the morning sunlight. He took a deep breath, filling his lungs with the rich, warm air. Breathing free air was a luxury he never took for granted; he knew the air was much sweeter aboveground.

The train was rolling into the station at the same instant Mr. Tate was rolling up to the meat counter. Over the years, the train schedule had changed significantly as Friendship grew from an unincorporated community into a full-fledged town. Deliveries were coming to Friendship more frequently in eighteen-wheelers and trucks rather than by train. This had slowed the need for stops in Friendship down to a trickle. The train only halted in the town three times a week now, with mostly passengers on board and a few dry goods. This morning's stop was the only one scheduled in Friendship for the next two days.

About twenty people exited the train. Most of them left just to stretch their legs or maybe sit down at the counter of the Gordon Diner for a late breakfast while the few supplies were offloaded and the train waited for the track to open up down the line. A young woman wearing an orange sundress and flip-flops on her feet strode off the train in the middle of the crowd. Her sandy-blonde hair was pulled into a messy bun at the back of her head. She glanced around Main Street, which included storefronts of everything you could possibly need or want. The little town was enjoying a boom during this thriving economic time, and after the depression in the late '70s, everywhere needed a little boom. Tourists headed to see the center clock of the Myrtle Square Mall and spend their days baking under the sun usually stopped for a bit of homelier goodness in Friendship. The little town with the quirky name was becoming a nice side adventure for travelers. Of course, it didn't hurt that Main Street was now part of a highway that connected Florence and Conway directly.

The young woman in the sundress was not here for a vacation. Gordon Diner was to her immediate right, and the smell of fried bacon and eggs was heavenly. To her left was the bulk of Main Street's business district, with the town hall bookending the far side. Three shops down from where she was standing, the door opened and a dark-skinned man in an old wheelchair rolled out onto the sidewalk. She watched as he breathed deeply, smelling the free air. The woman knew exactly what that feeling was like; she, too, knew freedom would always smell sweeter.

She turned toward the man in the wheelchair and began moving in his direction as he enjoyed the morning warmth. He was less than fifteen seconds of brisk walking away, but she didn't want to lose him. She watched as he turned his chair in her direction and began moving it with the power of his fragile arms. The two people's paths were clearly meant to intersect. The woman planned on finding the man in the wheelchair, and was only slightly surprised when she'd lucked into seeing him from the train station platform. She always seemed to be lucky.

If it weren't for Mr. Tate's tardiness from his normal routine, they would not have shared the street that day. Fortunately for the woman, due to some overly intense pain in his back that morning, Tate had been delayed. As she neared the man, she purposely walked in his way, causing him to stop his chair short of running her over.

"Excuse me, miss," he said kindly.

She smoothly sidestepped his chair and simultaneously bent at the waist, lowering her mouth to his ear.

She whispered, "I know who you really are, Eugene."

His head snapped to the side in an awkward angle as he tried to look the woman in the eyes. He gained his composure quickly.

"I'm afraid that I don't understand, miss," he said steadily.

She stepped back and turned her left arm over, revealing a series of light marks on her inner forearm. Tate leaned in close, where he could scarcely make out the numbers *110102*.

"My God," he said with astonishment, looking into her blue-green eyes, "Aless?"

◆ ◆ ◆

"Uncle Tony!" Mark Richards came pushing his way through the crowded office. "Uncle Tony! We got a hit!"

"Whoa, kid, slow down," Tony Richards said. "What are you talking about?"

"Alessandra Sartori is what I'm talking about." He placed a printout on his uncle's desk. The elder man bent slightly and squinted, trying to see the tiny print. He mumbled to himself as he read and reread the paper.

"When did this come in?" Tony asked his nephew.

"Early this morning; I've already called and talked to the man who gave the tip. He said he recognized her face but couldn't place it. After pulling the station's surveillance footage and seeing her again it dawned on him that he knew that face from the missing-persons posters."

"All right, kid, good work!" Tony Richards slapped his nephew hard on his upper back. "Where does that train dump out?"

"Thanks," said Mark Richards, rubbing his tingling shoulder. "A man who worked at the station in Columbia, that's where she boarded, said that the train goes all the way to the coast."

"Columbia, South Carolina?" Tony inquired, picking up the paper and looking it over again.

"Yep, he said it makes intermittent stops along its route. I'm thinking—"

"Friendship," Tony said, and looked up at his nephew. "She's going to Friendship.

"Isn't that where she wanted to surrender once?" Mark asked his uncle.

"Yeah." Tony's mind wandered off to the morning in question. Almost thirty years had passed since that night. Tony could recall it like a home video. He reached over the desk, picked up the red folder labeled It110102, and then flopped it down in the area in front of the two men. He flipped it open, finding his report from 1957, and read aloud.

"Alessandra Sartori never appeared at the dairy farm as she indicated she would in her letter directed to the CIA. She was not seen in the area before, during, or after the allocated meeting time in the same letter. Deputy Jack Wilson was on hand for the duration of the surrender period, corroborating the account present herein. Blah, blah, blah; you get it, she didn't show up," he finished, throwing the document back onto the ever-growing pile inside of the folder.

Mark smiled "So?"

"So, I guess I'll call Jack Wilson, and you get us on the next plane to Charleston. We need to leave within the hour." Tony stood from the chair, leaving Mark to work out the travel arrangements.

Something had always felt off to Tony about his time in Friendship. He constantly had a vague nagging that something was . . . odd in '57. It was the best word he could think of to describe his feelings. When he stepped back around to his side of the two connecting desks, he picked up the receiver of his phone and began turning the rotary dials. Tony knew that some of the younger guys had picked up one of those crazy-looking bag phones or cellular telephones that were becoming popular for people who could throw their money away on toys that didn't work half of the time. That brick phone was a hefty *$4,000*, and you couldn't talk to anyone longer than thirty minutes without having to recharge the battery. He even heard that one of the paper pushers had his cellular phone number stolen by some creep. The security was terrible on those things, and if they wanted to be the way of the future, then there was a lot of work to be done. He spun the dial to eight, then zero, followed by three, and suddenly realized that her couldn't recall the rest of Jack and Ginny's number. It had been a while since he'd last called—more than fifteen years, to be exact. He clicked the plunger down, disconnecting the line, thought for a second about being old, and then lifted his finger again and dialed the secretary of the building.

"Hey, Candy, this is Tony Richards . . . yeah, I'm fine . . . sure this Friday is great . . . I can't wait. Say, can you get me a number? The PD in Friendship, South Carolina . . . thanks, I'll be at my desk. Oh, and be ready for dancing Friday." He laughed as he dropped the handset into its cradle.

Tony sank into his swivel chair and then threw his feet up onto the desk. He dug a Lucky Strike out of his breast pocket and his trusty Zippo out of the front of his pants. As Richards lit up, he glanced around the small office and began to wonder where the time had gone. It seemed like he had just been undercover in Eastern Europe yesterday. He had been permanently reassigned to work stateside only ten weeks ago, requesting a desk job as he finished out his last few years before retiring. The good news was he got to mentor little Markus and be his right-hand man. He puffed in gray fire from the cigarette, cleared his scratchy throat, and was thinking seriously about cutting back on the cancer sticks, when his telephone rang.

"Richards," he said after scooping up the handset.

"Agent Richards, this is Deputy Thaddeus Bowman of the Friendship PD; your secretary called and told us to contact you, that it was an urgent matter," the man on the other end of the line stated.

"Well, Deputy Bowman, urgent might be a strong word," Richards said, "but I'm glad you contacted me so quickly. You see, I need to get in touch with Jack Wilson. I know he was once on the force there."

"Yes, sir," Bowman said. "Although now most of us call him Sheriff Wilson. If you'll hold a second, I'll patch you through to his office."

"Thank you, Deputy."

Tony heard the click of the line as he was put on hold. A short amount of time passed, and then he heard a very familiar voice on the other end of the line.

"Tony Richards, how are ya?" the sheriff inquired. Tony noticed that his voice was much older than he remembered, but the same old Jack Wilson was buried in there somewhere.

"Jackie, I'm doing great! How's Ginny?" Tony responded.

"Oh." Wilson's voice instantly lost all its jovial qualities. Tony could hear the smile melt off the man's face. "Ginny"—he hesitated—"she died, Tony, back in '84."

"Oh my God, Jack, I'm sorry." Tony sat up at his desk and leaned his head into his free hand. "What happened?"

"She got real sick"—Tony heard him swallow hard—"and the doctors couldn't lock it down. They tried really hard, but in the end it was just too much for her. She was just bad off, you know, real sick."

"Jesus, Jack. I'm sorry, buddy. Is there anything I can do?"

"No, Tony, but thanks." Wilson tried to move the conversation forward. "What can we do for the CIA down here in Friendship?"

Tony was still shaken at his foundation, but he was a seasoned professional, and he switched gears with the best of 'em. "We think we've tracked down a fugitive coming into your area."

"Well, you know you can count on having the full cooperation of the Friendship PD. Just out of curiosity," Wilson added, "this wouldn't happen to have anything to do with the case back in '57, would it?"

Tony smiled. "You know I can't discuss details over the phone, Jack."

"I know," Jack said, also smiling.

"My nephew and I are on the next plane to Charleston; can you send someone to pick us up?"

"Yep, can do. I'll send Bowman; he'll be in a squad car." Wilson jotted down the information as he spoke.

"We should see you this afternoon, Jack." He paused. "I'm looking forward to it."

"Hey, Tony, is your nephew tagging along for fun and games?"

Tony laughed. "No, he's an agent too."

"Oh great," Jack said, pouring the sarcasm on thick, "two spooks, just what we need!"

The two men laughed; it felt good to laugh. "See ya soon." Tony hung up the phone.

• • •

After the initial shock wore off, "Gene Tate" insisted that they get back to his home as quickly as possible. Alessandra pushed the man in the wheelchair down the block, turning up Fifth Avenue, the nearest street. The two passed the sheriff station on their right, where Sheriff Jack Wilson would soon receive a phone call from his long-time friend, Tony Richards. Tate asked her to push him up to Hibiscus Street, where his small home sat on the corner. Once inside, he began with the questions.

"Help me close the curtains," Tate asked as he wheeled himself over to the bay window that looked out to the street. She followed suit until all the curtains were drawn, giving them privacy. Then she sat on the couch in the living area, and he stared at her in awe, apparently still in a bit of shock.

"What is going on?" Gene said, mostly to himself. "I would offer you a spot of tea, but I am afraid my curiosity has gotten the better of me."

Aless smiled but said nothing.

"Well, I guess I'll start with the obvious: Why are you so young? You were always younger than me, but"—he waved his hand—"this . . . I don't even know."

"You knew me?" Aless asked with a look of confusion on her face.

"Yes, I knew you." He reminisced. "You had a tangled mess of hair, and always had a ragged doll with you. They kept the older kids and younger kids separate most of the time. So it's understandable that you don't remember me. Besides, the years haven't been as kind to me. You must be at least fifty, correct? It's incredible."

"I'm fifty-two this year," she said with some hesitation.

"You don't look a day over twenty." Gene smiled, letting his wrinkles crease his face.

"It's weird, you know? I haven't told many people my real age, not for a long time."

"I found out that you were alive in 1957. I looked for you on and off for many years; now I see why I couldn't find you. So, this is how you manifested?" Tate wondered aloud. "Amazing."

"Manifested? I don't understand," Aless said, confused again. "And how did you know I was alive?"

"Your gift;" he said, ignoring the second part of the question, "the reason you were in the underground labs in the first place."

"This 'gift' is a curse!" she spat. "You can keep it."

Tate chuckled at the woman sitting on his upholstered pea-green couch. "My dear girl"—he shook his head, still smiling—"my gift has been useful throughout my years, and"—he sighed—"it has also left me paralyzed." He nodded and continued. "That's right, I wasn't in some terrible auto accident or born this way; my spinal column has steadily degraded since manifesting long ago in those rotten underground labs."

Aless's empathy was written on her face. "Was it the testing?"

He shook his head. "I don't think so, no."

"I'm sorry," Aless said. "How do we differ? I mean, what's your gift?"

"In time, but let us remain focused on our current subject. Now, tell me what led you here to me."

"I had been living with a woman for many years, and as she was dying"—Aless hesitated as a lump began to rise in her throat—"she told me of a man who knew all about me."

"A man?" Gene asked. "To whom was she referring?"

"A German man, by the name of Felix Müller."

Aless watched as Gene Tate's face contorted with surprise, fear, and concern. He composed himself rather quickly and motioned for her to continue.

"He had been living under an alias in America for a long time. He's dying now, or perhaps dead already. Apparently he had been keeping tabs on my whereabouts through the woman that I had grown to love and trust. It hurt to learn that she had been accepting money to keep him informed. But, she was divorced and raising me alone, so she definitely needed the money."

Aless had turned her head toward the window, lost in memories of Lela Jenkins. Tears slowly began to roll down her cheeks as her mind returned to the hospital room where she had watched the only mother figure in her life stop breathing. She cried silently in anguish for several long seconds. Gene Tate did not interrupt her tears, and finally, Aless spoke again.

"Müller told me about the labs and what was going on with me, as well as he could anyway. I guess my real gift is that I am a healer. He compared it to when you scrape your hand, it takes time but it will heal eventually, and I guess for me it is near instantaneous. Somehow that also affects my aging too."

"Incredible," Tate said, almost in a whisper.

"He told me about another person like me; a boy who was 'special' named Eugene, but he didn't know if you were still alive," she continued. "He told me about how you'd escaped the facility long ago. Although, he didn't have many details on what really happened." Aless paused and looked at the man in the wheelchair. "He also thought you were the person who was going to change the world with your ability, at least in the eyes of the Nazis."

Aless noticed that Tate was now consumed with memories. She looked away from him when she noticed he was staring at the floor, blinking back his own tears.

After a moment's hesitation she went on. "Müller wouldn't tell me what your gift was, but he said it was an incredible thing and that it would be best for me to learn about it from you." She looked in his direction again and noticed the man rubbing his weary eyes. His hands dropped, and she could see his wrinkled lids closed tightly.

He sighed quietly and spoke softly. "That is because he did not know what it was, not truly. I was but a boy when I left that place. I threw a lock at a man's face and knocked him out while I was escaping. As far as I know, it saved his life. He had choked, or something, before, but I gave him another chance." Aless looked at him with some confusion.

His eyes opened; they were lined with candy-red swollen blood vessels, no doubt irritated by the rubbing and the slight tearing.

"I climbed the stairs that led to freedom and ran into the woods when I escaped. The beauty of the world, of freedom, did not go unnoticed." He looked at Aless. "Did you know we were on an island?"

"Yes, I found out after the lab was taken over by the Americans; Sardinia, right?"

Tate nodded slowly. "Well, I came out in a mountainous region and headed north, although at the time I did not know it. The terrain was rough in spots, and I had a difficult time getting food and water, but after a few days I found my way to a little town where I stole some supplies. The most important thing I picked up was not the food or water but a map of the island. It showed the northern part of Sardinia, and with it I could identify my location." He reached up and rubbed his head in thought. "I can't remember the name at this point; it was so long ago."

Aless smiled and nodded slightly.

"Most importantly, the map showed another island adjacent to Sardinia, the island of Corsica. And with some rudimentary calculations I discovered that I was near enough to the coast that I could walk there within a day or so, and that Corsica was no more than eleven kilometers away from Sardinia through the Strait of Bonifacio. The map also showed that Corsica was French territory, and therefore part of the Allied forces. I later found out that the Americans had stationed themselves there and were using the island as a base of operations for the tactical bombing of Italy during the war."

Aless was intrigued with the story and asked, "How did you cross the strait?"

"I did what I had to do. I stole a canoe from a small port once I reached the strait. I stole more food and water and headed out to sea in what I thought was the right direction. It was very beautiful, very dangerous, and in hindsight probably very stupid. The first day I went from the main land to an archipelago that was still part of Sardinia. It took me several hours of hard rowing against a fairly flat, calm sea, and luckily there was some sort of civilization there because I had severely underestimated my water consumption. I was only still a small boy; how was I to know? So, I stole twice as much water and even more food for my improbable journey to freedom. My gift, or curse, as you put it, helped me immensely during that time. You see, Müller, Dr. Vogel, and everyone else thought I could become invisible, but that was not true. Believe it or not, it is actually stranger."

Tate stared at the young woman sitting on his couch and debated how to tell her about his manifestation. Here he was, sitting with a woman who looked not a day older than twenty but was almost the same age as he was, and he was worrying about her thinking that he was cuckoo. He swallowed with a soft click of his throat and spat the words pointedly from his lips, "I can travel in time. But only short distances, that is, short *times*, I mean to say."

Alessandra Sartori turned her head to the side as if she were trying to hear him better, and her mouth dropped open slightly. It was clear to Gene that she was trying to process this profound information. Her eyes were squinted in thought or perhaps disbelief. Gene watched intensely for what felt like minutes as the idea of time travel bounced around her brain.

When she did speak, she spoke slowly. "What's it like? I mean, is it like that movie with the car?"

"I'm afraid I don't make it out to many movies, Aless, so I wouldn't know. It's been a long time since I have done it, but for me, it's like the first time I filled my lungs with free air after years of being trapped in that hell. It's exhilarating," he said, then added, "and anxiety ridden."

Gene absently rubbed his right thigh with his hand. There was no sensation in the leg anymore; the sense of touch had packed up its belongings and left town long ago. Aless tried to pull her gaze away from the hand as it skated across the worn pants covering the lifeless lower limbs of Gene Tate, originally Eugene Trickens.

"I'm sorry for you," she lamented, just above a whisper.

Gene looked up from his lap and smiled. "Young lady, don't be ridiculous. I have lived my life as a free man, in a free country. I used my gift for many nefarious and adventurous things before this wheelchair caught up with me. I have lived a full and rewarding life, and I have no regrets, except perhaps that I did not meet the adult you sooner."

Aless smiled a crooked smile at this compliment.

"Besides," Tate continued, "I have not displaced time in quite a while; I fear that this paralysis is only the beginning. Death shan't be far behind."

Aless considered this. These must be the types of side effects that Müller had talked about. What would hers be like? Would she wake up one day suddenly unable to move, like the wheelchair-bound man sitting across from her? She felt an interior shudder and hoped that it didn't come all the way up to the surface.

"What happened next?" Aless asked, pushing back the negative feelings and emotions fighting their way up.

"Ah, after I stole the food and water, I rested for the evening to gather my strength for the longest leg of the trip. When I awoke the next morning I pulled my little stolen canoe back into the Mediterranean and paddled in the direction I hoped was Corsica. After several hours I began to get discouraged and extremely tired."

Mr. Tate paused here and rubbed his mouth absently before continuing. "The water was not as calm in the strait as it had been on the way to the archipelago. It was tossing the little canoe with some vigor. Regardless, I needed a rest, so I decided to lie down in the bottom of the canoe for no more than ten minutes to rest my weary back and arms. Lady Luck was smiling on me that day, for as soon as my head touched the canoe, I saw an American plane flying low overhead in the direction perpendicular to mine. As I sat up to watch the plane, I noticed it was lowering its landing gear, which could only mean one thing: it was headed for Corsica. I grabbed my oars and turned my canoe in the direction the plane was headed and paddled like a madman. Within twenty-five minutes I saw the plane land, and by the end of the hour I was touching the surf."

"That's truly amazing," Aless said.

"It definitely is a story to tell the grandkids, although it's tough to have grandkids without any children." He smiled wanly and decided to change the subject. "Well, my dear, I believe I am feeling a bit thirsty and hungry after all that. I'll just grab us a snack. I purchased some lovely vegetables from the market earlier." Tate rolled gracefully away from the couch and entered his kitchen.

"Would you like a hand?" Aless called.

"Nonsense, you just stay put, I have managed alone for forty years. I think I will be fine for a few moments."

Tate made some rattling noises as he went through what must have been the lower cupboards looking for whatever dishes he needed. Aless sat where she was and gazed around the room. The walls were bare of any personal pictures, which was strange to Aless, even though she instantly understood why. He had been alone his whole life. However, there were several pictures of exotic locations. To Aless they looked like professional pictures from magazines. Gene Tate's wheelchair creaked slightly as he came from the hardwood kitchen onto the living area's carpet.

"He we are, some fresh cucumber and ripe tomatoes," he said, smiling. He'd balanced the plates in his lap. Aless realized it must have been a skill he'd honed since becoming confined to the chair. She thanked him as he handed her a plate filled with sliced vegetables, and then she proceeded to take a large bite out of a ripe red tomato slice on her plate.

"So, Müller lead you to me, eh?" Tate asked right before filling his mouth with cucumber.

"Sort of, indirectly, I guess."

"He kept tabs on you. Do you think he knows my whereabouts?" He paused. "If he's even still alive?"

"No, he didn't seem to know where you were, and I don't think he would still be alive; he was in bad shape. It's been more than ten years since he told me about you," she said and finished off her slice of tomato.

"Ah. You decided to take your time and think about if you really wanted to see me, hmm?" Tate teased.

"No," Aless responded seriously. "I don't know if I believed him at first. Besides, I was looking for my family, my real family, I mean. After my foster mother, Lela, passed away I was really down, so I went to Europe to search for anyone related to me. Lela left me money when she died, and I needed to find out for myself."

"Good news?"

She shook her head. "I found one distant cousin; I never talked to him, just watched him from afar. He would have never known my immediate family; he's too young and they're dead. I researched through archives in several different libraries in Europe. I found out they were killed in 1938, the same year they were forced to give me up to the Third Reich. At least I hoped they were forced and didn't do it freely." She paused, and a look of sadness crossed her beautiful, soft features. "Anyway, I decided I would travel across my native land. It's beautiful. I never went back to the island, though."

"I am sorry for your loss," Tate said gravely. "I know all too well how difficult it can be."

She waved away his concern. "I didn't know them. I was taken away when I was so young; I never knew them even as well as I know you." She placed her plate next to his empty one on the end table.

"So, Aless, why have you really come to see me? Not just for my amazing vegetables I hope," Tate asked.

Alessandra smiled. "Well, I wasn't really sure I ever wanted to find you, actually." Her smiled faded away. "I'm alone in this world. There is no one else like me. I wanted to see if we were the same; I guess I wanted to know if there were really others out there."

"Well it's—" he began but was cut off by the sound of the doorbell.

• • •

Deputy Bowman stood beside his cruiser just outside the concourse at the airport, where the agents would be picking up their luggage from the nonstop flight from DC to Charleston. Bowman was chewing on a stick of gum and listening to planes touch down on the runway on the opposite side of the building. He slid his sleeve up and glanced at his watch. According to the itinerary Mark Richards had faxed over, the plane carrying both agents should have landed twenty minutes ago. He popped a small bubble that had grown between his teeth and swiftly sucked the air that smelled of sour jet fuel deep into his lungs. He wanted a cigarette but had been moderately successful with switching the cancer sticks to sticks of gum. It'd been more than a month since he had last smoked. Now the problem was all the sticky sugar on his teeth from the gum.

I'm gonna have to switch to sugar-free, and that shit sucks, he thought with some disdain. He spit the spent gum out onto the side-walk and pulled in a large breath, checking his watch again. Thirty-four seconds had passed since he had last looked. He rubbed his hands across his face, scratching absently at his five o'clock shadow. Another day on the job.

He had parked the cruiser in an unloading zone with the hopes that the plane would actually be on time. It seemed like it rarely worked that way. Bowman leaned his rear on the hood and stared across the four-lane loading/unloading zone toward the glass doors of the terminal. The building itself was relatively new, and Bowman observed that some sections still might have ongoing construction. Although, he hadn't been here since the city had decided to move the terminal to this location, and, he realized, he also hadn't been to Charleston at all in more than five years. His mind began swimming through the memories of his last trip, when a voice pulled him back to the surface.

"Officer," Tony Richards said. "How are ya?"

Bowman turned his head in the direction of the voice, which happened to be almost on top of him. His daydreaming seemed to have gotten a little out of hand.

"I'm well," Bowman said, extending his hand. "You must be Agent Richards." He shook Tony Richards's hand. "And you must also be Agent Richards." He smiled at his quip while shaking Mark Richards's hand.

"You got us," Tony said, throwing his hands up in mocking surrender, "Deputy . . ."

"Bowman, Deputy Thaddeus Bowman. Thad, if you'd like."

Thad Bowman moved around the cruiser to open the trunk for the men to deposit their small carry-on luggage. Mark let Tony do the talking while he stowed their bags.

"I'm Tony, and he's Mark. Glad to know ya, son." Tony gave a friendly clap to the man's shoulder. "How long is the drive to Friendship?"

"An hour and a half or so, maybe less if we don't hit bad traffic."

"Great!" Tony opened the passenger door. "Let's get movin'; I want to be there before the Q-tips call it a day."

"Q-tips?" Bowman asked.

"Yeah," Tony replied. "You know—the old people. White hair, white shoes, skinny in the middle—Q-tips." Tony winked as he fell into the passenger seat.

Mark rolled his eyes and followed suit by getting into the backseat of the cruiser, leaving Bowman standing alone by the rear of the car. He felt the sharp craving of nicotine bite him once again. He popped a fresh stick of gum in his mouth and climbed into the driver's seat.

"Huh, Q-tips . . ."

Twenty minutes later, the Friendship police-issue cruiser was well outside of Charleston and the surrounding suburbs. Bowman and the two agents had time for plenty of small talk about their flight and how things were going in DC, the whole Chernobyl disaster and what it might mean for nuclear power, even what they might be having for supper. The men were laughing, trying to remember the last time they'd had a home-cooked meal. It was the talk of supper that pushed Tony Richards's mind to the inevitable.

Tony asked, "What happened to Mrs. Wilson, Thad? Jack wouldn't give me any details, and I suppose that's OK, but my curiosity has gotten the better of me."

Bowman stared forward at the road speeding past. His face slowly changed from good-natured into a solemn look that was almost too painful for Tony. After several seconds he took a deep breath and sighed.

"Hell, I don't even know all the details; the sheriff doesn't talk about it much. No, he doesn't talk about it at all. But I can tell you this much, she was like a mother to all of the guys and gals on the force."

Tony nodded gravely.

"OK, so here's what I know," Bowman said after another long pause. "Mrs. Wilson was part of the church, and they do mission trips to parts of the world that need a saving grace, you understand, right?" Bowman looked into the backseat for approval from Mark Richards, who nodded slightly in agreement.

"So anyway, she volunteered for a mission trip to somewhere in Africa. West Africa maybe, Cameroon or something, I can't remember. That was in early 1984. Things were crazy in the neighboring country with civil unrest and political uprisings; you know how it can be over there, always some apartheid holding people down."

Mark Richards smiled slightly at the ignorance of that statement and thought it must exemplify the opinions of most people who lived in the Deep South, and then he was slightly ashamed of his own judgments.

"Somehow the fight turned ugly, and there were unexpected bombings," Bowman was saying. "Mrs. Wilson and the missioners were caught in the wrong place at the wrong time."

"Oh my God," Tony interjected suddenly. "She was killed in a bombing?"

Bowman shook his head. "No, sir, she was only injured; others were killed, though, missionaries from other parts of the US. You probably heard about it."

Bowman eyed Tony Richards. He couldn't have known that Tony had been deep undercover in Eastern Europe during the end of the '70s and into the early '80s. Most of the happenings in the world passed him by unless they were important to his mission. Uprisings on the African continent were definitely not.

"Possibly," was all Tony could manage. "What happened next?"

"They were in a remote area of the country near the border, I think, so the injured had to be housed in the middle of the jungle or desert or whatever they have. The point is, the medical was shit, and people were dying. Her physical injuries weren't life threatening, but she had lost a lot of blood and was in critical condition because of it. So the decision was made to give her an emergency transfusion."

Realization spread across Tony Richards's face like a cancer stretching its tentacles from one cell to the next. He closed his eyes and leaned his head back onto the headrest. Bowman either didn't see this or figured that he had made it this far and he was going to finish.

"The sheriff hopped on the first plane across the drink to be by her side. By the time he got there, the locals had moved her to the nearest actual decent hospital. Mrs. Wilson's recovery started well, but the blood was bad, real bad. At the time, no one knew what was going on, but she began getting real sick. It started out with flu-like symptoms and developed into these weird rare forms of infections that ran rampant in her system.

"HIV," Tony spat out like it burned the roof of his mouth.

Bowman nodded once. "She died before the new year came. After she was flown back for the funeral, the sheriff took an extended sabbatical and never really spoke to any of us about it before, during, or after."

Tony Richards stared out of the window and blindly watched the trees roll by. He thought back to the game night so many years ago and how he'd wished for the happiness that the couple shared. He blinked back his emotions rapidly and sat in silence. Bowman understood and quietly turned on the radio. Soft country crooning filled the interior of the sedan.

Ten minutes later, the three men were driving across Friendship's town limits.

Tony Richards continued to stare out the window, lost in thought. He subconsciously took notice of the world around him as they rolled through Friendship. There were clear signs of urban decay on buildings Tony remembered being new thirty years ago. Thirty years, it seemed, could make a monumental difference. He scarcely recognized the houses that littered the streets perpendicular to Main. There were even several fast-food chains that had popped up all over the town. Convenience and simplicity seemed to be infecting all parts of the world, even this sleepy place.

The cruiser drove past the storefronts on Main Street, stopping at the several lights that had been installed. Tony casually wondered which light was the lone solitary one that had been there when he'd last visited. Then the storefront that was once Gina's Consignment came into view. Richards came briefly out of his daze and looked into the store only to find emptiness and a sign that read "For Lease" in the entryway. He craned his neck, looking up toward the second-floor apartment he had called home for about a week. He recalled standing in the window and looking out at the fledgling town. The small room had held only a bed, a table, and an old writing desk where he'd combed through the tattered red file folder containing everything known about Alessandra Sartori. Tony remembered that it was only a short walk to the station and, assuming it hadn't been moved, they would be stopping any second. He composed himself and peered back toward Mark. He gave his nephew a wink and then flashed a brilliant but brief smile as the car pulled into the parking space outside of the Friendship Police Department.

"Well, well, well, look at what the cat dragged in," Wilson said good-naturedly as he opened Tony Richards's passenger door. The sheriff had stepped out onto the curb just after Bowman radioed the station with an ETA of under five minutes. He'd waited for them on a little bench outside the modest station that was situated right off Main Street, right next to the small post office. During his short downtime, he'd thought of his wife, Virginia, and had wondered if Tony would ask about her. What would he tell him? He was barely keeping things together as it was.

Tony Richards pumped the man's hand while throwing his other arm around Wilson's back. After their embrace, he said, "Jack, this is my nephew, Mark, he's like a son to me."

"Mark, it's a pleasure." Jack Wilson gave and received a firm grip while shaking the younger Richards's hand. "Let's get inside to my office, and you can fill me in," Wilson continued.

Once inside the office the three men sat; the elder and younger Richardses sat in front of the large maple desk while Wilson sat opposite. He reached into a large desk drawer and produced a half-full bottle of Jack Daniel's Black Label and three glasses.

"Nothing like a little ninety proof when you want to get some talking done. Gentlemen?" Wilson asked, tipping the bottle in their direction.

"Sure, we'll have a nip," Tony replied. Wilson removed the cap and poured generously into each glass. Mark watched the bottle disappear as quickly as it had appeared. Tony picked up his glass and raised a brief toast.

"To better luck this time," he said and knocked back a large swallow of the half-full glass. Wilson and the younger Richards followed suit. Hot pain shot down Mark's throat, and he grimaced.

"So, fill me in, boys. Does this have anything to do with whatever the hell happened last time you were here?"

"We think so," Tony said and passed the conversation off with a quick glance toward Mark.

"We had a call come in about a possible sighting of an age-progressed missing-persons drawing that is hanging up in the train station in Columbia," Mark said. "The person in question is the same one who Uncle Tony was searching for here about thirty years ago. According to the train schedule, a stop was made right here in Friendship earlier today. We think our missing person may have gotten off here."

Wilson leaned over and pressed a button on his phone to start a conference call. Deputy Bowman picked up.

"Thad, connect me with Nick over at the train station."

"Yes, Sheriff." There was a click as the deputy put the men on hold.

"What's this person look like?" Wilson asked. The two CIA agents glanced at each other.

"Listen," Wilson began, addressing the elder Richards, "if I am to be of any use to you, this time I need to know what I'm dealing with. My men and women can only follow blindly so far. We need information."

"Of course," Tony said. "I have been chasing this girl on and off my entire life, and I'm ready for some help." The phone between the men made a clicking noise as Thad came back on the line.

"OK, Sheriff, it should be ringing," he broke in. There was a brief pause, then the buzzing of a ring tone. It only rang twice before it was answered.

"Friendship Railway Transportation and Shipping, how may I help you?" The voice was friendly.

"Nick, this is Sheriff Wilson. I've got a couple of quick questions for you. Do you have a minute?"

"Sure thing, Sheriff," Nick responded.

"A few hours ago some people got off the train, right?"

"Yes, sir, pretty much the same people every day."

"Oh, good, then you might remember anyone who doesn't usually get off." Wilson gave a thumbs-up to Tony and Mark.

"Yes, sir. In fact, now that you mention it, there was a pretty young woman that got off with the usuals today. Light-colored hair and wearing a dress; I don't remember the color, though."

"That's all right, Nick. Do you know if she got back on the train?" Wilson asked.

Tony sat forward in anticipation. He'd hoped his gut feeling would pay off.

"I watched her leave the platform and walk across Main Street. Then she stopped outside of the Willodean's Market, where she talked to a man in a wheelchair. Then the two people left together heading away from Main."

Wilson's brow furrowed, and he rubbed his forehead in deep thought. "A man in wheelchair . . ." he mumbled.

"Thanks a lot, Nick." Wilson ended the call. He leaned back in his chair, looked up at the ceiling, and rolled what was left of the whiskey around his glass. Mark and Tony Richards waited as Wilson worked out the puzzle in his mind. Finally, he spoke.

"There is an old school teacher who is wheelchair bound, Bates or Gates maybe is his name. But he's been here forever; I don't know what she would want with him. Maybe it was an out-of-towner and she was meeting him here."

"Possibly, but it won't hurt to start with this teacher guy," Tony said. Then he started from the beginning, telling Sheriff Jack Wilson the story of case It110102—the story of Alessandra Sartori.

• • •

The bell rang again. Gene Tate looked at the door with horror.

"Who knows you're here?" he hissed toward Aless.

"No one knows," she countered.

"Someone does; go to the room down the hall, the first one on the right. Get in the closet. There are some guns there; get one and stay hidden." Tate began rolling toward the door as Aless sat shocked. "Move, girl!" he hissed again.

She got to her feet and seemingly floated down the hallway as quickly as she could. She spared one last glance at Eugene Trickens and disappeared into the bedroom.

The doorbell rang for a third time, and the sound was shortly followed by a muffled voice.

"Mr. Tate, this is the sheriff, open up, please." Sheriff Jack Wilson sounded friendly but impatient, and, as he tried to peer through the curtains of the window to the left of the door, he heard the chain begin to rattle.

He started to repeat his sentence, when the door popped open. Jack saw a smiling wheelchair-bound man, whose face was slightly pale.

"Sheriff, I'm sorry for the delay, but I was lounging on the sofa, and it took me a moment to position myself into my chair. What can I do for you today?"

"Well, Mr. Tate, I have a few quick questions for you," he said in his southern drawl. "Were you out and about earlier today?"

"Yes, sir, I went to the Willodean's Market to get some food for my supper."

"Uh-huh. You didn't happen to come across anyone unfamiliar or unusual today, did you?" Wilson asked while making mental notes about the section of the house he could see.

Gene Tate hesitated slightly. "Well, yes, yes, I did. It was a young woman. We talked for a moment, she actually helped by pushing my chair for a bit, then she and I parted ways."

"Uh-huh, then what?" Wilson asked.

"She walked, I rolled, and then we separated."

Wilson studied Tate's face. He looked hard and deep into the man's eyes, willing him to give a tell, to look away or just change his story altogether. After a few seconds, Wilson said, "OK. Now if you're sure that's all . . ."

"Oh, that's all, Sheriff, I assure you. Feel free to come in if you'd like to look around," Tate said, even though he really didn't mean it. He hoped the sheriff would just go.

"No, no. I don't need to come in," Jack Wilson said. He hesitated and then added, "I don't need to come in, but I think I will anyway, just in case."

Tate, agitated by his own mistake, rolled his chair back out of the doorway and motioned for the sheriff to enter. He angled himself in a certain way to prevent Wilson from roaming down the hallway into the bedroom where Aless was hiding. Wilson scanned the room slowly. His detective skills were not what they had been before he'd moved behind the desk, but they were better than average. The first thing he noticed was that there were two plates sitting on the end table, and they had been used very recently.

"Mr. Tate"—Jack Wilson slowly began to spin around, still scanning the room—"have you had any guests today?" When he finished his turn, he saw a bright-white light were Gene Tate was, and then there was an audible pop.

• • •

"Holy shit!" Aless exclaimed. Eugene "Gene Tate" Trickens didn't register the words, only the emotion that went with them.

"What's wrong?" he said in a groggy, pained voice. He felt numbness crawl through his abdomen where it hadn't been before.

"You just vanished and reappeared on the other side of the room. Can you teleport?"

"What?" Trickens's head was splitting as reality was reforming in spinning slowness. He could see Aless starting to get up from the couch and realized he was sitting in his wheelchair near the entryway of the house.

"You were sitting here and you had just handed me my plate when, *boom*, big white light, and then you were over there." Adrenaline was pumping through her veins, causing her to be overly enthusiastic.

"I don't know." He struggled with the words.

Things were sharpening for Eugene. His head was a cantaloupe being severed by a samurai sword, but he was functional. "I haven't ever witnessed it. No one really has, except the doctors on the island and . . . it's not important, we have got to get out of here, the police know you are here and they're coming."

"What? How do you know that?" Aless was asking while she crossed the room to meet him by the entry.

"Because when it looked like I teleported, I actually came from the future, if you can believe that. I guess I can't occupy the same space . . . or maybe it's time, who knows. I think I physically stay where I am and everything around me changes, so it looks to you like I moved, but I was there when I—we don't have time for this, we have to go; we might have ninety seconds if we are lucky."

"So, you can control when you want to time shift or whatever?" she asked.

"Yes"—he was growing impatient—"time is of the essence, Aless!"

She gasped, then covered her mouth. "Your ears are bleeding!"

Gene reached up and touched the warm, sticky liquid that had spilled from his lobe. "It doesn't matter. We have to go; every second counts."

He rolled his wheelchair swiftly toward the bedroom down the main hall, cutting the corner sharply as if he had done it a million times.

He headed right for the closet where a random scattering of weapons was stored. Gene threw open the accordion doors, pulled down a bag that was on a hanger, and began to put ammunition into it. He grabbed two small handguns with extra clips and stuffed them into the small bag. He began to roll his chair back, hesitating when he saw a brick of three sticks of dynamite taped together propped up in the corner next to a long rifle.

"What's wrong?" Aless asked.

He stared at the dynamite with childlike wonder.

"I thought we had to go," Aless said impatiently.

Gene blinked twice. "Right, we'll head out the back." He reached down and grabbed the dynamite, stuffing it directly on top of the other weapons, then slung the bag across his empty lap. "Let's roll."

• • •

The police cruiser slowed down a block away from the house.

"Here's how we work this," Jack Wilson was saying. "I am going to just talk with him first. There is no reason to alarm the man, especially if he has no idea what I'm even here for."

"I'm good with that," Tony said. Mark nodded from the backseat.

"I was thinking that I'd just ring the bell," Jack said.

"I'm gonna head around back, just in case he runs." Tony shook his head. "I mean, I know he's in a wheelchair."

Jack gave Tony a sideways look, then turned to Mark. "Right . . . son, you come with me and watch my back."

"Yes, sir," Mark said, nodding in agreement.

Three of the cruiser's doors swung open, spilling the men out into the street across from the Tate house. They silently moved into position, Jack Wilson taking point. As he went up the small ramp onto the porch, he noticed that curtains and blinds fully covered the windows. Wilson gestured to Mark, silently showing him that he should hold his position several feet back from the house. Wilson walked slowly toward the windows and tried to see into the small home, with no luck. He moved back to the large oak door and rang the bell that hung loosely in the frame. Wilson heard a muffled bing bong as the bell rang inside. He waited, listening with a furious intensity that he hadn't felt since long before Ginny had died.

Dammit, he thought, *she found a way in again!* He shook the brief distracting thought of his dead wife out of his mind with a literal shake of his head, sighed, and pushed the bell again. Jack threw a glance over his shoulder toward Mark, who was waiting at the ready in the shade of a small tree.

Tony had made his way quickly around the back of the house, where he found another ramp that led to the back entrance of the home. He cautiously made his way to the door, which he could see had a glass window. As he reached the window, he heard the second bing bong of the doorbell. Unlike Jack Wilson, Tony had an unobstructed view into the interior of the house. Richards carefully peeked through a small window, momentarily catching the reflection of the sunlight. He was looking for any movement, but he saw an empty kitchen that led to an equally empty sitting room. He walked around to the other windows that weren't covered by curtains, peered in, and drew the same conclusion for each one. The last window he came to belonged to Tate's bedroom. Tony Richards cupped his hands on the window to cut the glare and had just begun scanning the room when his eyes fell upon a cane leaning up against the wall by the closet. He stared, transfixed, at the old, battered cane. It was auburn in color, with decades' worth of use that showed across its splintered body. Tony felt something stir inside of his mind, a light breeze that threatened to turn into a cyclone, a strange déjà vu. He found it nearly impossible to turn away from the empty room that held this treasure from a different time. He jerked almost violently away from the window and searched his brain for the meaning of his stupor, but found nothing, nothing except . . . milk.

The bell rang a third time.

"Mr. Tate, this is the sheriff, open up, please," Sheriff Jack Wilson said with increasing impatience as he tried once again to peer through the curtains of the window on the left of the door.

"It's no use, Jack," Tony Richards said as he popped around the corner of the house. "The house is empty. I could see almost the entire place from the windows around back. There are also tracks in the grass back there; they look like they could belong to a wheelchair."

"Damn," Jack said, dismayed. "Well, let's head to the schoolhouse; maybe he is over there."

"I don't know," Tony said slowly. "I saw . . . something . . . in the house."

Mark listened as his uncle spoke in an unsure way; it was completely out of his character.

"Send a unit over there, but I think we should look somewhere different."

"Where?" Jack asked.

Milk . . . Milk . . . Milk . . .

"The . . . dairy farm," he said after some internal struggle raged behind his eyes.

"That old place? The man is in a wheelchair; hell, you can hardly get around on foot over there," Wilson protested.

"Call it a hunch," Tony said as the three men made their way back to the cruiser. A voice crackled from the dashboard CB radio.

"Sheriff, are you there? Over," the voice squeaked from the little speaker.

Wilson reached into the window, grabbed the handset, depressed the button, and said, "Yeah, Bowman, I'm here, go ahead."

"Sheriff, are you still at the Tate place? Riley called in and said that he thinks he may have seen Tate with some woman. They were rolling down the side of the road heading toward the old dairy farm."

Jack shot a look at Tony only to find the man staring right back at him with no surprise.

"Bowman, send 7635 to the schoolhouse in case Tate went there and get Riley over here in case he comes back in the meantime. Then, I want you to get to the old farm ASAP. We'll meet you there. And get me all that information we were digging up on Tate. We may have a hostage situation on our hands here. Out."

• • •

The wheelchair wasn't made for traveling on any surface that was less smooth than glass. Eugene felt every pebble that he rolled over deep in his guts—or he would have, if he were able to feel anything from his chest down. The realization that he was moving ever closer to "not being" stayed in the back of his mind, for now. In the front of his mind were matters of more immediate attention. He knew that Aless must escape this town before the authorities could catch up to her. He also knew of one place that had worked for him in the past.

"Where are we going?" Aless asked after several minutes.

"We are going to an old dairy farm, called Livin' the Cream."

"Like the milk in the supermarkets?" she asked, smirking.

"The same; the company had humble beginnings here in Friendship. The old facility has been shut down for a number of years since moving production elsewhere. They wanted to make it a Livin' the Cream museum of sorts, but I don't think that ever made it past the planning stages. It's not much farther."

"That's neat and all, but how is it going to benefit us exactly?"

"There is a back way out of this town . . . or at least there used to be," he said, throwing a worried look over his shoulder toward the woman.

Aless pushed the chair for a moment in silence. "Your gift is incredible. I see why you think I should treasure mine."

Gene drew in a large breath, noticing the empty numbness that was now covering 70 percent of his body. "It has its drawbacks, I assure you, child."

"I watched you vanish and reappear, from the future, no less; it was incredible. What do you think happens?"

"I truly do not know. I have conjured many theories over the years. Am I creating alternate timelines, or perhaps tearing through our own original timeline? Turn right here." She did as he instructed.

He continued, "Does time not exist like we perceive it? What I mean to say is, instead of a straight line chronologically, does time exist all around itself? Is everything that *is* happening, *has* ever happened, or ever *will* happen, all going on at the same time, and maybe I can hop around from one thing to the next like a child playing hopscotch on some quantum sidewalk?"

Behind the wheelchair Aless looked lost but interested.

"I guess lately I have been thinking that instead of creating hundreds of alternate timelines through my life, I immediately destroy the one that I left when I travel back in time, if time has direction, that is.

Think of it this way, a floppy disk, yes?" He looked over his shoulder and saw that she was still following his line of thinking.

"Yes, a floppy can only hold a finite amount of information, but when you want to add new information to the disk, you simply write over the old information. I think that's what is happening; time is writing over itself, destroying the old, unwanted time. Of course it's just a hypothesis; who really knows. There"—Eugene pointed at the gate one hundred yards ahead of them—"that's where we're going."

Pushing the wheelchair through the rough foliage that surrounded the gate proved to be a large challenge for Aless, who was small in stature and not overly strong. The gate, once a yellow A-frame in perfect working order, was now rusted and pitted as time undid it like it undoes everything. Aless worked the chair, helping the man through the thick growth in small chunks. Tate helped as much as he could with his arms, but they both tired quickly. The lost time at the gate was what Aless would always remember as the turning point in their run from her would-be captors.

The pair had finally crested the overgrowth, putting the wheels into the compressed earth that made the entryway, when the police cruiser came into view.

"Oh God, no!" Hopelessness poured from Aless's mouth.

"Quick," Eugene said, grabbing the wheels. "Come on, push!"

She didn't hesitate, grabbing the handholds on the back of the wheelchair; she began pumping her legs with everything she had. The once-and-always Eugene Trickens used his hands to guide the chair in the direction of the barn, which was located near the back of the farm. A lot of the farmland had changed as the business had grown during the '60s and '70s, but the main hay storage barn had not been moved or replaced. Repainted? Yes. It now stood in all of its faded lime-green glory seventy-five yards away from the scrambling woman, who was pushing the chair like some sort of wild, out-of-control lawn mower.

The car labeled "Friendship PD Sheriff" skidded to a halt just short of smashing into the rusted A-frame gate. Mark Richards, having younger legs, was out of the cruiser and hopping the gate before his uncle and the sheriff could even slam their doors.

"Mark, they went left!" Tony shouted to his nephew as he was stepping over the gate. Mark was only eight to ten steps ahead of Tony and Jack, but that distance grew with each stride. Mark cut to the left, looking on the ground at the tracks that the wheelchair couldn't hide in its attempt to flee. By then Tony was in a full sprint and was pleasantly surprised to see that somehow he was closing the distance on his nephew, but then he realized that Mark had slowed.

"Uncle Tony, what do we do?" Mark had stopped completely when he had realized that this was the first time he'd ever been in a situation like this. He felt insecure and wanted his uncle to take the lead.

"We keep up the pace and don't let them get away, kid!" Tony exclaimed as he ran by his nephew. Jack Wilson, who was starting to catch up, was thinking about all those free breakfasts from the diner combined with skipping the gym and cursing himself for his laziness.

Mark ran after his uncle. Wilson followed close behind them, yelling into his radio for Bowman to "hurry his ass up."

Aless and Eugene came hustling closer to the barn.

"Aless, the door, you have to open it!" Eugene shouted.

"That seems like a bad choice, a dead end."

"There's a back exit; get the door!"

She put all her weight onto the back of the wheelchair and slammed her feet into the ground, skidding to an ungraceful halt and almost tipping Eugene out onto the dusty ground. He instinctively cursed and grabbed for the wheels to steady himself. By then she had already left him and was trying to pull the large barn door open. Her body was running on pure adrenaline, and her muscles were all but putty. She yanked and pulled the door with all her might, tears beginning to pool in her blue-green eyes as panic settled its hand across her chest. She screamed a primal yell as she put every last ounce of her being into one final wrench, releasing the rusted hinge bolts and opening the door. She laughed under her breath, and Eugene rolled in between the large doorway. The opening was barely enough for the chair to fit through.

Just as Eugene rolled into the shadows, he heard Tony Richards's voice.

"Alessandra Sartori, get down on the ground! NOW! DOWN!" A gunshot exploded the air, sending echoes rippling across the woods and all around the dairy farm.

Eugene gasped at the sound. In the split second between the gunshot and the report's echoing response, Eugene was a child again. He saw his father pulling away from the men at the camp. He screamed out in muted silence for his father not to run toward his mother. Then he watched once again as his father knocked the guard down, trying to save his family. Eugene placed his hands over his ears where dry blood was beginning to crust and chip away. His lids reflexively squeezed closed, spilling tears down the crevices of his unduly old face. His heart raced inside his chest; it burned with the agony of having to relive the day he watched his happy family splinter, fracture, and break. He cowered in his wheelchair, waiting for the panic to subside, unsure of how to proceed, and reliving the moment his father's heart had pushed from the front of his chest as the bullet shredded his shirt, skin, bone, organs . . . everything. He shook with fear. Outside, he could hear the other men coming up, as well as quiet sobs from an extraordinary woman.

"Hands on your head!" Tony shouted. "Mark, cover me."

Eugene heard the sound of metal jangling around, knowing it could only be handcuffs. He heard a man talking on a radio to someone, explaining that they had caught her. Eugene still could not bear to open his eyes. Then he heard Aless sobbing and begging to be let go, asking for mercy and help; Eugene opened his eyes and made a decision that would cost him his life.

Just a little bit, just a bit, he thought as he closed his eyes again. Outside the barn, Tony, Mark, and Jack had lifted Aless to her feet and were walking her back toward the entrance of the farm, when there was a brilliant white-hot glow that shot through the boards of the barn, lighting up the world in a whiteness so pure that it could only be described as awe-inspiring. Too bad no one would ever remember it.

• • •

Darkness surrounded a distant pinpoint of white light. The only sound was muffled to the point of unregistered decibels. Searing pain ran through Eugene Trickens's brain as he began to reemerge from the displacement. There was a distant feeling of thick wetness running from his ears, nose, and mouth. The pinpoint widened to the tip of a knife while the sound of the world around him started to break through the thick padded wall of time. Eugene's brain felt as if it were being shredded in some industrial paper shredder where the pieces were gathered and shredded over and over again into nothingness. The light jumped again, filling his strained retinas with a blurred sense of familiarity. He felt the clammy sweat rolling off his arms and face, and was shaking from sheer exhaustion. The sound of creaking broke through the blanket covering his eardrums. He tried to reach up and rub his eyes with his dominant left hand and discovered he couldn't move it as well as he would have liked. His head screamed with agony, and he would have cried out if he had been more with it. Eugene gathered enough wherewithal to squeeze his eyes closed. He felt thick warmness slide down his face. Against every natural instinct, Eugene tried to shake his head, to clear it out, which instantly brought on nausea and indescribable pain. Through the fog of pain, he heard the grunting. Aless trying to open the door; he had jumped back; there was still time to fix things.

"Aghh," Eugene tried to speak but found there was something thick blocking his throat. He coughed and spit warm blood out across his chin and chest.

"Aless," he continued in a low, gravelly voice.

Outside, Aless spun to see emptiness where she had left the wheelchair, turned back toward the barn door, and said, "Eugene?" as she grabbed the door and tried to force it open.

Eugene had rolled himself a little closer to the door. "Don't worry about the door," he said in an airy croak. "Get to the woods behind the barn—"

"What?"

"Quiet!" he managed to scream in a broken voice. "Behind the barn you will hit an overgrown path about three-quarters of a mile in; stay on it going away from town. Eventually you will run into the train tracks; follow them any direction. Don't come back for any reason. Keep running!"

"I—"

"Go! Time's up, go!"

She could hear that the man in the wheelchair was struggling to speak and remembered the blood coming from his ears the last time he had displaced time. Aless took one hesitant step, "Eugene—"

"GO!" he managed with a thick choke.

She turned on her heel, hearing the oncoming footfalls of the three men who would be within sight of the barn in less than five seconds. Aless disappeared around the back of the barn just before Tony broke into view.

Inside the barn, Eugene had managed to open the bag that he had lying in his lap. He'd just vomited over his right shoulder; it was mostly blood, so he knew it was bad. He removed the brick of dynamite, untaped the single match stuck to the side, and held it at the ready. His head was a spinning, aching mess; while his vision had doubled and blurred, his hearing was still as good as it gets.

God, he thought, *forgive me.*

◆ ◆ ◆

"Uncle Tony, what do we do?" Mark had stopped completely when he had realized that this was the first time he'd ever been in a situation like this. He felt insecure and wanted his uncle to take the lead.

"We keep up the pace and don't let them get away, kid!" Tony exclaimed as he ran by his nephew.

Tony Richards had a good idea that he was heading to the same barn that he waited by all day in 1957. He took the lead, rushing down the little dirt road, following the tracks of the wheelchair. He reached the end of the milking stations and swung a right, catching his first view of the barn in almost thirty years. His first reaction was to the "new" color; it was lime green like someone's sofa from the late '60s. He finally pulled his weapon from the shoulder holster, pointing it toward the ground as he ran. Tony Richards pushed his legs to the limit, trying to catch Sartori and her wheelchair-bound hostage, Gene Tate.

As he approached the building, he saw the tracks of the chair led all the way to the closed large double doors of the barn. He was still several feet away when he began shouting, "CIA! GIVE UP THE HOSTAGE AND COME OUT OF THE BARN, NOW!" He slowed just enough to stop himself from slamming into the barn doors, turning at the last second to prop his back against the door.

"YOU HAVE UNTIL THE COUNT OF THREE TO COME OUT WITH YOUR HANDS UP!" he shouted, holding his weapon to the sky. "ONE—"

• • •

Boom! The barn exploded outward in a fiery shower of wooden debris. Bales of burning hay flew through the air along with lumber flipping and smoldering across the void. The percussive shock wave of the explosion halted Mark Richards's and Jack Wilson's forward momentum, driving them backward onto their backs. Tony Richards was thrown forward through the air with the heavy barn door flying right behind him. He smashed the ground hard face-first with the large heavy wooden door coming down on top of his body and crushing his rib cage. Wooden and metal shrapnel pierced his body in more than half a dozen places.

Jack Wilson sat up, dazed, his hat ten feet behind him, his eyes watering, and his ears ringing. To his left was an unconscious, seemingly unhurt Mark Richards. Jack's old body creaked as he made his way to his feet. The remnants of the hay barn lay scattered in all directions, with some fires growing larger. Jack scanned the rubble from right to left, searching for Tony. He spotted the man crumpled under the leftover pieces of the large pine door. At that moment, he heard Mark waking up.

Mark's eyes were watering like Jack's; his left eardrum had ruptured and was dripping a small amount of blood down his face and onto his black suit jacket. He got up onto his knees and surveyed the damage, looking for his uncle. The tinny ringing in his good eardrum was all he could hear. Jack Wilson tried to shout to the young man, but his screams went unnoticed. Mark continued to scan the debris. Like

Jack, he spotted Tony under the barn door about ten yards away. He stumbled to his feet and drunkenly ran over to where his uncle lay.

"Uncle Tony, UNCLE TONY!" Mark yelled. He felt the sound rumble through his chest and throat but still heard nothing except the squeaky buzz. He shouted again as he dropped to his knees, quickly pushing the remnants of the door off the man's broken body. He carefully rolled his uncle's limp body over, instantly seeing a large, rusty hinge bolt protruding from the left side of his uncle's chest. His uncle was sipping shallow, gargled breaths.

"Just hang in there, Uncle Tony; help's on the way," Mark said through tears. "Hold on, hold on."

Mark looked desperately toward Wilson, who understood the pained looked all too well. He turned and scanned the ground for his radio, which had blown away like his hat during the blast. He retraced his steps. There, not a foot from his hat, was the two-way. He picked it up and began frantically calling out to anyone listening.

"Man down, I repeat, man down! We need immediate ambulance dispatch to Livin' the Cream dairy farm at the dead end of Rose Road. Repeat, we have a man down."

While Wilson was calling the ambulance, Mark placed Tony's head on his lap. Tony Richards's head had been the first part of his body to connect with the ground after his one-man flight across the barnyard. The right temple region, all the way to the crown, was smashed, giving his head an awkward flat-tire look. Mark stroked the hair on the side of his head that was still normal. Tony's breathing was becoming increasingly slower and shallower.

"Hold on, Uncle Tony, just hold on," Mark sobbed as he heard his own voice coming back into focus. "We're gonna make this, we're gonna do it. We can do it, me and you. We're . . . we're"—he choked back a giant lump in his throat—"we're gonna go back to that sandwich shop that you love and get that great Rueben and say hello to the pretty girl. Just stay with me, God, stay with me!"

Tony's eyes moved up to Mark's; he managed a thin, weak smile and slurred a whispered, "Get her, kid, get her," in a tiny, frail voice. His eyes unfocused, glazed over, and then rolled back, his eyelids half-closed. His broken body exhaled one final breath as he gave up the ghost. Mark Richards's face crumpled under the strain and stress into turbulent despair while tears rolled down his cheeks, matching the blood running from his ear. He held his uncle's dented head gingerly against his chest and rocked the limp body back and forth while he wept. The agony of losing the man who was his only father figure engulfed his brain. He moaned one word over and over until his throat betrayed him: "No!"

◆ ◆ ◆

Aless ran through the woods as fast as her legs would carry her. She looked around frantically, searching for the path that Eugene told her about. It must have been several years since Eugene had made it into this part of the woods; everything had grown over. Behind her there was a massive explosion that caused her to drop to the ground in surprise, cutting her arm on a branch as she fell; it healed instantly. She saw the orange glow of a fireball through the pine trees south of her. Her mind went to Eugene and she cried out, but then she decided to honor him by following his instructions. She pushed her tired body up off the forest floor and looked around intensely, searching for anything that looked like a path. She was about to give up when she saw something less than twenty yards from where she was standing. The path was almost completely overgrown with weeds, foliage, fallen pine needles, and leaves. Aless wouldn't have seen it if she had kept blindly running.

She made her way down the path as quickly as she could manage through the thick overgrowth, crying as she went, not only for Eugene but also for herself because she knew now, if there were ever any doubt, that she would never be able to stop running. Her lungs were burning, her muscles were tight, and she was developing a stitch deep in the left side of her body. Occasionally, Aless looked back over her shoulder searching for her inevitable pursuers, but she saw no one and only heard her own feet connecting with the ground. She had just slowed her run down to a jog, trying to give her overworked body a break, when she saw an opening in the pines. She returned to a full run, despite needing rest, as she headed for the opening.

The warm sun shone down on her face as she came through into a clearing where the old train tracks moved perpendicular to the trail. Aless looked to her left, then right, seeing endless tracks in both directions, surrounded by woods the whole way. She bent at the waist, placing her hands on her knees, and tried to slow her breathing. Within the first breath her face distorted as she broke into tears again. She dropped to the ground, physically and emotionally drained, letting hopelessness in for the first time in many years. She hadn't been careful enough, and now she was alone, again, with another death to weigh on her soul. Alessandra let the emotions take control for a while; against her better judgment, she closed her eyes and sleep took hold. Life around Aless continued as she reset. When she awoke, she got to her feet, picked a direction, and began to follow the tracks into the unknown.

◆ ◆ ◆

The crime scene that was once the hay barn of Livin' the Cream dairy farm was buzzing with activity within an hour. The South Carolina State Police had arrived in Friendship less than thirty minutes after the explosion. They had marked off the entire area around the barn and closed Livin' the Cream to all reporters and any unnecessary personnel. Deputy Thad Bowman of the Friendship PD, along with the EMTs, had been the first responders. Bowman had pulled Jack Wilson to the side and tried to get his story straightened out before the state troopers arrived. When he'd arrived, Mark had been sitting motionless next to the body of his recently deceased uncle, Tony Richards. The deputy had surmised that the young man was in shock.

Now, the sun was setting in the west while Tony Richards's lifeless body lay on an ambulance gurney with a sheet covering his fractured skull and hollowed eyes. Firefighters had stamped out all the small spreading fires that the explosion had ignited. The men were currently digging through the charred debris, looking for the place of origin and the ignition source. The state police rigorously questioned Sheriff Jack Wilson and Agent Mark Richards about the events that had taken place earlier that day. Mark, still an emotional mess, was less helpful than Jack. Jack relayed all the information as he understood it. They had been tracking the man in the wheelchair, Gene Tate, and had cornered him here at Livin' the Cream dairy farm. The three of them had chased him into this barn, and as Tony Richards was trying to coax him out, it had exploded. Jack was careful to leave out any mention of the woman who didn't age, for fear of sounding like a lunatic. He'd decided that telling anyone about Alessandra Sartori was not a good idea. Mark could at least refuse to disclose her existence, due to national security; Jack on the other hand could blab, but he didn't because Tony, his friend, was dead and he would respect that. Jack pulled Mark to the side.

"Son"—he pointed across the farm to a large light pole—"that is a closed-circuit camera. Jefferson Fillmore, the owner of the land, installed them across the farm when he wanted to make a museum out of this place. I suggest that the CIA get those before the state police see them."

Mark looked at the camera on the pole, still in a brain fog. "Thanks, Sheriff. I will make it happen." He began to walk away.

"Hell, I don't even know if they work," Wilson called to the young man.

"Does it matter?"

"It's not your fault, kid!" Wilson said.

Mark turned around and stared at the man with haunted eyes. "I hesitated," he faltered, "because . . . because I was scared. He would still be alive if I hadn't." The young man slumped, turned slowly, and walked away.

The body of Eugene "Gene Tate" Trickens was charred and disfigured. There were several large pieces scattered in a five-foot radius. The crime-scene investigators were taking pictures, bagging and tagging as they went. The charred remnants of his wheelchair were bent at strange angles. Bowman brought along all the information that Sheriff Wilson had asked for about Gene Tate. It wasn't a monumental task; there was next to nothing about Mr. Tate. Bowman told Wilson that it seemed like Tate didn't exist before coming to Friendship. In truth he didn't, something Mark Richards would learn within two days of the incident at Livin' the Cream.

Gene Tate was a figment of Eugene Trickens's imagination, an invention of necessity. In the early '70s, the paralysis had slowly confined him to the wheelchair, forcing Trickens to make a choice. His choice was Friendship, where he could have a "normal" life after traveling the world and traveling in time. He created Gene Tate, the paraplegic schoolteacher who was relocating from the dreariness of the English countryside to the sleepy town of Friendship for a change of pace and atmosphere. The lie became his life until a young woman with sandy-blonde hair stopped him outside of Willodean's Market. Less than twelve hours later, burned chunks of his body were being placed in labeled plastic bags.

Mark Richards stopped and sat on the ground beside the gurney where his uncle lay dead, covered by a cheap sheet. In his daze, he accidentally leaned a little too hard against the small bed, pushing it off balance, but he shot up right away to keep it from toppling over. It only leaned slightly, quickly settling itself back on four wheels once Mark moved. He heard something thud on the hard-packed ground behind him. He turned and saw his uncle's lighter lying in the dirt. Mark picked it up, studying the fire starter like it was something from another world. He squeezed it in the palm of his hand, trying desperately to transfer his emotional pain to the object.

I'm sorry. I'm so sorry, he thought as he fumbled with the lighter, and let the tears come. *I will find her, Uncle Tony. I promise.*

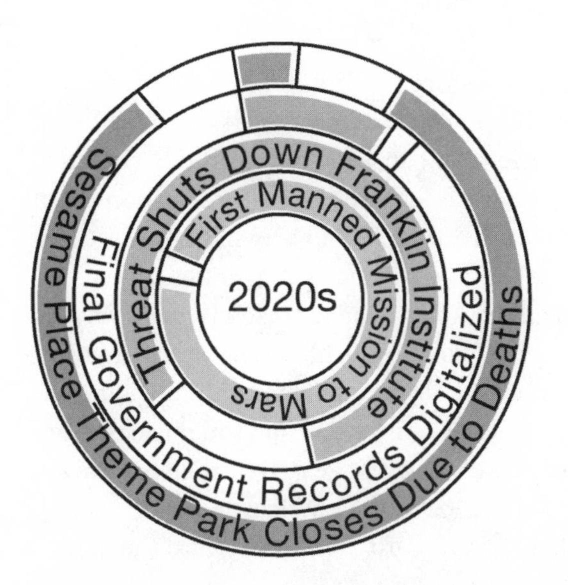

1:23 P.M.

PENNSYLVANIA, 2024

"Aless," Grey said as he came into the house. "Aless, we gotta go, come on." He peered upstairs. "Aless, it's time," he called again from the bottom of the stairs, not wanting to pull off his shoes. He waited for a response and grew concerned after not hearing anything from the second floor of his home.

Two weeks had passed since Agent Emily Myers and her mysterious friend had visited the home of Grey Chapman—two weeks since Grey had urged Aless to act sooner rather than later. Aless had kept a low profile since her arrival in Philadelphia, extremely low. She had ventured downstairs to the kitchen in Grey's home on Vividleaf Lane less than a handful of times for food, but only when Grey wasn't around. Grey kept up a more or less normal appearance; he went to work every day, came home every evening, cooked dinner, watched TV, did all the things he would normally do. He even went out for a New Year's Eve party. The only major difference was that Aless was shut in upstairs.

In the evenings, Grey would retire as usual, except, at the top of the stairs, he would make a right into Aless's room. Once in there, the two of them would solidify the plan, bringing it into focus with each passing day. Aless was extremely tired of running, which made their options limited. However, planning and doing were two very different beasts of burden. The plan originally consisted of going to Washington, DC, to find the physical archives and destroy all the information about the experimentation on children during World War II. Grey was quick to point out that destroying the original files was pointless due to the legislation that digitalized all records during the last ten years. Anyone with the proper clearance could pull up the file at any time. Grey said that their only hope would be to infiltrate the digital archives *and* the physical archives in DC. He went on to say that he could use the network at his job in Philadelphia to possibly get to the digital archives, but they would have to travel to DC for the physical ones.

Grey slid his shoes off and started up the stairs toward the second floor of his aged Levittown home.

"Aless?" he questioned. "Are you there?" *Where else could she be?* he thought.

Grey looked around the corner as he crested the steps, seeing only an open door that led into an empty room where Aless should have been. He hurried into the room, desperately searching for the woman with the strange gift of seemingly everlasting life. He saw no one. Grey began scurrying through the room as if he were playing a game of hide-and-seek. She had left him while he was at work; after a month of living in this room, she had exited, stage left, leaving Grey clueless and confused. He opened the closet to an emptiness that cut him to his core. She had really left; after all the planning and working together, she had left. Grey had a hard time grasping the concept. *Where did she go; why did she go; how, even?* Sulking, Grey flopped himself face-first onto the bed and heard a strange crinkling noise that at first he didn't register. Aless and Grey had been together again, and now she was out of his life just as abruptly as the first time they'd split. Admittedly, the circumstances were completely different. He rolled his head to get some air, when the crinkle sound happened again; this time he heard it.

Grey lifted his body off the bed and pulled back the covers, which unveiled a short handwritten note.

G,
It's a risk for me to leave this note, but I didn't want to just vanish on you again. They are watching the house, most likely following you too. I saw the woman from the window. I have to leave, even though I don't want to. I'll see you in the stars.
-AS
It's you; it's always been you!
222 20

Grey stared at the note for a long time, not really reading it but seeing it. Myers was watching him and had scared Aless away. The CIA must be closer than she would have liked.

I'll see you in the stars.

What was that all about? he pondered. *She's never said anything even remotely close to that to me. It's always been me.* Grey smiled a goofy sideways grin. He stuffed the note into his pocket and headed down the stairs with the intention of going to try to find Aless.

Grey came out of his house in a hurry, digging in his pocket for the car keys.

"Mr. Chapman," a voice said from behind the old car Chapman drove.

"Oh, come on, get the hell out of here," he said to Agent Emily Myers. "I don't have to talk to you, and I feel like you are starting to harass me."

She smiled slightly at his agitation. "I assure you, Mr. Chapman, I have no intention of harassing you, just like you have no intention of harboring a fugitive inside your home."

"Really? I mean, really! Come in," he said, gesturing toward the house. "Come on, I won't even ask for a warrant. You can dig through every inch until your hands bleed and your eyes pop out. Let's go."

Em Myers stood there looking at the man in amusement. "I think I'll pass. I'd want a warrant so anything found would be admissible in court; mostly because I think you'd lie about having given me your consent. I'm sure you understand. Home early, aren't we?"

"I'm outta here. Get off of my property," Grey said, unlocking his automobile, but before he could get in, Em grabbed his shoulder.

"Mr. Chapman, help us out. She's dangerous; she's going to hurt you, if not physically, then definitely emotionally."

"Take your hand off of me"—he glared at Agent Myers—"now!"

She removed her hand. "Enjoy the rest of your workday, Mr. Chapman."

He slammed the door to the vehicle. Em stepped back as he tore out of the driveway and speed off down Vividleaf Lane, leaving Myers staring up at the window where Aless had spent the last month.

Grey could feel the heat radiating from his face as he drove. One glance in the rearview confirmed his ears and cheeks were red from anger. He took a few calming breaths, trying to control his emotions, and he told himself that Myers was just trying to get under his skin.

He huffed and mockingly spat, "Enjoy the rest of your workday, Mr.—" Something in the dark depths of his brain stepped forward, and Grey's mouth hung open as the pieces fell into place. He quickly changed lanes, looking to pull off Route 1 into the breakdown lane, and almost getting sideswiped in the process. His old car skidded to a halt, and he almost fell down on the road trying to get out. Grey dug deep into his pocket, grabbing the note Aless had left him. He reread it quickly, laughed a barking "Ha!", and then got back into the car and spun out of the breakdown lane. He turned left onto Woodhaven Road, which led him to I-95.

A short while later, Grey took Exit 22 to Philadelphia. He was pushing his little economy car to the max; it got great gas mileage for an old 2014 hybrid. He turned down the radio, looked at the clock, then tapped the icon on his steering wheel, bringing to life his Bluetooth connection to the car.

"Call . . ." He hesitated. Who could he call and trust with this sort of information? He tapped the "End Call" button and glanced down at the clock again; he was still at least six or seven minutes out.

• • •

Em tapped the side of her AR glasses, pulling up a map of the world. She slid her finger along the arm of the glasses and watched the display zoom in to a pinpoint moving down Interstate 95.

"Mr. Chapman, where could you be headed?" she spoke aloud to the emptiness inside her automobile.

Em touched the side of her glasses again. "Call Mark Richards."

He answered on the second ring. "This is Richards."

"It's Myers. Are you in Philly yet?" she asked.

"Sort of, I am stuck in traffic just outside of the city," he responded.

"According to the live feed," she said, tapping the side of her AR glasses, "the traffic is moving slow but steady."

Richards grumbled, "Yeah, thanks for the update. Why don't you give me some good news?"

"OK, how's this, I put an undetectable GPS tracker on Chapman's car," Em explained. "You can see where he's going with your tablet." Another swipe and tap combo to the side of the AR glasses. "I just sent you a link."

Mark Richards leaned over slightly, picked up his tablet, and used the voice activation feature to power up the machine. He clicked the notification for a new message and opened the link inside. It showed an extremely detailed real-time map of a dot moving off Interstate 95 near Philadelphia.

"It seems like traffic was good for you today; he's heading into the city now," Em continued.

"I see that," Richards said, signaling to be let over so he could exit at the nearest Philly exit. "I am going to try to get out of this gridlock and follow him; you continue to track him, and get over here ASAP."

"I am already on I-95 coming toward the city. The Philly tail was a good idea, Mark. I have a good feeling about this. Call you when I get close," she said.

"OK, or I'll call if anything changes. Bye." Richards tapped the button on the earpiece that disconnected the call. He finally was able to merge into the far right lane, and saw an exit coming up in less than a mile. He looked at the tablet display and watched the little dot merge onto I-676, known as Vine Street to the locals. The dot slowed around North Broad Street, due to central Philadelphia traffic, no doubt.

The driver in the car behind Richards impatiently honked his digitized horn, trying to get Richards to move along with an unfriendly gesture of his hand. Richards thought about pulling his gun from his shoulder holster and waving it in mock salute toward the man in the expensive SUV but thought better of it, being in the City of Brotherly Love and all. Mark began moving his black hybrid forward to catch up with traffic, then decided that he needed another look at the tablet. He shifted his eyes back and forth between it and the road ahead of him. Even traveling at fifteen miles an hour, dividing your attention felt dangerous to Richards; he didn't know how the hell Em could wear those AR glasses *and* drive. He noticed that Grey Chapman had turned his car down North Twenty-Second. It was beginning to rain, and Chapman was turning around.

Richards tapped his earpiece. "Call Emily Myers." The phone rang only once before he heard her cheerful young voice.

"Hey, Richards. What's up?"

"He's going to work."

"OK, yeah, looks like it. But isn't that where he goes every day? Why is that so urgent?" she asked.

"Yeah, I don't know, something feels wrong . . . I can't explain it. Contact the Franklin Institute and let them know that we have a potential situation."

"Will do. I have an ETA of nine minutes. Mark, I doubt you will, but if you get there before me, wait for me before you go in," she pleaded.

"We'll see," Richards said, smiling. He couldn't help but like the young agent. After working together on It110102 for the past two weeks, Mark was feeling good about having a partner again.

Em tapped the side of her AR glasses twice, and the virtual screen floating in front of her eyes changed from the map tracking Grey Chapman to a blank display.

"Call the Franklin Institute."

• • •

The Franklin Institute, established in 1824, began in the original building at Fifteenth South and Seventh Street in Philadelphia. This was the location for more than one hundred years before moving to its current location on Benjamin Franklin Parkway and Twentieth Street. The Franklin Institute was Pennsylvania's most visited museum, and it was a renowned and innovative leader in the field of science and technological learning. In 2006 plans were set into motion to expand the Franklin Institute by adding a new wing, called the Nicholas and Athena Karabots Pavilion, providing an additional fifty-three thousand square feet to the facility. This new area included a first-floor educational center for young people to explore science in unique ways and a second-floor exhibit on the human brain and its functions, while the third floor was reserved as a revolving door for less permanent exhibitions. The original areas of the institute had also been set up with a three-floor system. Many different types of exhibits had come and gone over the years, including fun things like Spy: The Secret World of Espionage, the incredible rotating IMAX films, the Giant Heart exhibit, and the Benjamin Franklin National Memorial. The first floor of the Franklin Institute had housed the Fels Planetarium since 1933, the year before Alessandra Sartori took her first breath.

Grey Chapman pulled into the parking garage, took his ticket from the automated machine, and parked in the first spot he could find. He jumped out of the car and had taken five quick steps before he realized he had left his key card and badge in the car; he spun around and went back to retrieve the items. He needed his badge for clearance and his card for entry. Grey grabbed the items lying in the console, closed the door, and clicked the lock as he hurriedly walked away. Two minutes later Grey was swiping his key card at the employee entrance to the Franklin Institute.

Grey again used his key card to access the rear of the Fels Planetarium. He scanned slowly from right to left but couldn't see anything discernible other than humanoid silhouettes in the near blackness of the vast room. Overhead was the brilliant vastness of space that always sucked Grey's attention away from whatever he was doing. Even now, with the urgency he felt, Grey sacrificed a few seconds to gaze upon the greatness of the universe. Grey noted that Mars was off in the distance and wondered in the back of his mind if the loved ones of the astronauts currently being hurled along at thousands of miles per hour were worried about ever seeing them again.

Then the vast planetarium lit up as the sixty-foot dome was overtaken by video of Earth's sun. The narrator was saying something about the age of our solar system and the planets, dwarf planets, and belts that it contains. Grey took advantage of this light to scan the room again; he saw a hooded sweatshirt from his almost alma mater, Coastal Carolina University. It looked exactly like the one he had loaned Aless the other day when she was cold. He moved toward the person.

"We will be landing on the Red Planet in 2025," the accompanying narration was saying, "almost a decade after discovering flowing water on the planet's surface."

"Aless." He spoke just above a whisper. A woman with the faded blue-green eyes lifted her head, peered from under the hood, and smiled. Strands of sandy-blonde hair hung loosely in her face. Grey reached up, instinctively brushing it aside as he sat down in the empty seat next to her.

"You understood the note," she said with relief.

"Yes"—he gestured into the openness of the solar system surrounding their vision—"I'll see you in the stars. It didn't hurt that you wrote the address on the bottom."

"I didn't know what to do; when I saw that agent outside your house, I panicked. I thought the best place to come would be to your work, but I wanted to leave some sort of clue in case you weren't here."

"It was perfect." He embraced her. "I thought you'd run again."

"No," she whispered, looking away while shaking her head. "No more running." After a moment, she turned back toward Grey. "This place is so cool. What do you do here?"

She looked up as the projection of the solar system widened into the great expanse of the known universe. The narrator was now positing life outside of our galaxy or even our reality.

"Well, it's pretty neat," Grey whispered with visible excitement. "I've always loved falling into imaginary worlds, not unlike video games or reading and writing. Basically, they let me create these awesome different worlds and stories. You know, so it's interesting to the kids—"

Grey stopped short, distracted by some commotion coming from the side of the room. A radio crackled loudly and was abruptly turned way down. The lights came up in the planetarium midnarration. A young man of perhaps twenty-five who had been running the projector stepped out in front of the now-confused moderate-size crowd in the Fels Planetarium.

"Ladies and Gentlemen, I'm sorry for the interruption; however, we have been notified that there is a small issue here at the institute. We will be closing today as soon as possible. There is not an immediate emergency, but we will need everyone to gather their belongings and head to the nearest exit. Thank you."

Aless threw a concerned look toward Grey.

"What about my money?" a man shouted from the middle of the room.

The young man looked flustered, grabbed his radio, and posed the question to his superior. After a moment of silence, the young man, who had inserted the earpiece, keeping his conversation a little more private, received an answer.

"You will all be able to go online and type in your entry ticket number and be given a free voucher to return," the projectionist said. "Now if we could please all move toward the nearest exit."

The complaining man grumbled a half-hearted protest, going along only because his wife was looking mortified.

"Come on," Grey said to Aless. They used the mass exodus to slip back through the employee entrance that Grey used to enter the planetarium.

After going through the door, Grey said, "Someone might know we're here."

"It's them, you know it is," Aless said. "Why else would they be shutting this place down today?"

The building-wide intercom system then squealed into life. "Attention, please, could I have your attention, please. This is Larry Dubinski, president of the Franklin Institute. Due to unforeseen circumstances, the institute will immediately be shutting down for the rest of the day. Arrangements are being made to issue free vouchers to everyone who is being inconvenienced today. In the meantime, we ask you to please move safely to the nearest exit; this is not an emergency, I repeat, this is *not* an emergency. However, we ask you to cooperate by leaving in a quick and orderly manner. Thank you for visiting us at the Franklin Institute, and we look forward to seeing again you very soon."

"Stay right here," Grey said, looking directly into the eyes that he had fallen into so long ago. "I'll be right back."

Aless nodded, pulled the hood back up over her head, and leaned on the wall closest to her. Grey went up the corridor, trying to find the nearest window. The patrons of the institute were beginning to make their way out of the exhibit areas into the halls and moving toward the exits. Grey reached the nearest window before it became too congested. He could only see one entrance from this window, and what he saw made his stomach drop. His first instinct was to pound the windowsill and swear. He turned back and fought his way through the thickening crowd back to where Aless was still leaning on the wall.

"It looks like they have agents covering the exits," Grey said. "I don't doubt they have our pictures and are ready to grab us once they've smoked us out."

Aless looked instantly panicked. "I can't get caught, Grey!"

"OK, OK." He looked around. "This way!" Grey grabbed her hand and turned back toward Fels. He stopped abruptly, pulling Aless back toward him. The short hallway was no longer than twenty-five feet. At the end was a door that led to a hallway that was the behind-the-scenes work zone of the institute. Grey wanted nothing more than to get out of the public area and off the normal grid. But standing fifteen feet in front of them was Agent Emily Myers.

Grey positioned himself between the two women. "Move, Myers!" he yelled.

"This isn't going to end well for you, Chapman! Just give us the girl!"

"Go to hell!"

"Have it your way, then," Em said and leapt into a blistering sprint that closed the fifteen-foot gap almost before Grey knew she was moving.

The next several actions seemed to move in slow motion for Grey Chapman and Em Myers. Em was obviously quicker and younger, but

Grey's biggest mistake was to underestimate her because she was a relatively small female. She threw her knee upward in a blur of motion as she reached Grey. The knee connected with a crack against Grey's right side, instantly fracturing the seventh and eighth ribs; the inertia threw them both to the ground. Before he could even make an agony-filled sound, Em had established a dominant position by straddling the man. She planted a right cross to his temple, rocking his head back to the left and smashing it into the carpet-covered concrete. Grey raised both arms defensively, deflecting blows that Em was attempting to rain down on him. When he saw an opening, he hammered her with a laced-fingered sweep of his large hands that landed squarely against her right shoulder, sending her sprawling to the carpet. A raw, powerful instinct took over inside of Grey, and he got back to his feet almost as fast as he went down. It was apparent that Myers was trained in hand-to-hand combat; Grey was not, but he made up for that in size and intelligence. Em smiled, getting to her feet, a vicious grin forming on her face.

She lunged at Grey with a speed that he couldn't match. The two people once again became a tangle of limbs on the dark carpet. They rolled back and forth, exchanging close-quarter blows. Em continued to work the man's ribs, gaining the advantage. She rolled over the top of the man and squeezed her legs together, crushing his chest. Em dug her right thumb into his left lower ribs, pushing down with all her force. He grunted in agony, trying to hold back a scream. Grey grabbed at the woman's legs and tried to pry the death grip apart, but he found he couldn't get enough traction. Sweat was dripping into his eyes when he saw it. Em Myers had a standard-issue firearm holstered under her jacket. He quickly assessed the situation, knowing that she would shatter his ribs soon enough, and he would pass out from the extreme amount of pain.

Desperate times, he thought.

As quickly and as powerfully as he could, Grey reached up with his right hand and snagged the butt of the firearm, yanking it from the holster. At the same instant, he positioned his left arm with all his might against the woman's chest, with the hopes that she would go flailing off him. Her knees, with their vise grip, were slowly collapsing his chest, and they kept her from being pushed more than a foot or two, but he now had her gun.

Sort of.

She grabbed the wrist of the hand that was holding the gun as she was falling, pulling it awkwardly downward. He felt his arm twisting in an unnatural way, so he tried to counter the twist by sitting up. This gave the advantage to Myers again, and she swung her elbow with all her might directly into his rib cage. Grey let out a full shriek this time, dropping the gun and pulling away.

Em picked up the gun with lighting speed. She also looked around for her AR glasses, which had come off during the struggle.

"I can tell by the way you're favoring your side, Mr. Chapman," she said, picking up the glasses, "that I hurt you." Em panted, watching as Grey reached up to his broken side. "Poor baby. This could all have been avoided—"

"SHUT UP!" Grey broke in, grimacing with pain as the muscles tightened in his chest and abdomen, grinding the broken ribs together. He slowly got to his feet.

Em chuckled. "Have it your way." She lifted the gun, aiming it in Grey's general direction. "I will shoot you if I have to; either way she is coming with me."

"She will NEVER go with you, not while I'm still breathing," he shouted through the pain. Then he did something no one expected; he charged the agent.

Startled, Em said, "Stop, I *will* shoot you!" Then she began to backpedal. A split second later, the first shot rang out.

• • •

Aless didn't think; she just reacted.

As Em was telling Grey to stop, Aless stepped up in three short moves, putting a hard shoulder into Grey's back, not all that different from their first meeting almost twenty years prior, shoving him just far enough out of the way that the bullet that ejected from the barrel of the sidearm missed him and sunk into her right shoulder. Aless then took four quick steps forward, closing the gap between herself and Agent Em Myers.

Myers unloaded a second round into Alessandra Sartori before she lost her advantage. Aless reached out with both of her hands, landing them, just after the third shot sunk into her body, on the much younger woman's neck, and squeezed as hard as she could manage. Em instinctively dropped her gun, clawing at the death grip that had snaked its way around her neck. She gurgled and gasped for life-sustaining air.

"Shh . . . hush," Aless said in a barely audible tone, wheezing for breath. Something inside of her mind had snapped.

I am done with this! I'm sick of you people chasing me! she thought. *I'm so tired of running!*

Grey had regained his feet. He hustled over and snatched the gun off the floor, pointing it at Em Myers.

"OK, you can let her go," he said to Aless.

She either didn't hear, or chose not to; somehow her hands tightened more. Agent Myers's face was changing from a pasty white to a dirty purple.

"Aless, let go," Grey pleaded. "Doing this isn't going to make things better for you."

The calmness written on Aless's face and behind her blue-green eyes terrified Em.

"Nothing can make it better," Aless said in her ghostly whisper. "Nothing."

"This will make things far worse," Grey said. He switched the gun to his opposite hand and reached out, placed his warm palm softly on the nape of her neck, and rubbed slightly. "We can do this, but it starts with letting go."

Aless slowly closed her faded blue-green eyes, feeling the warmth on her neck; his hands melted her deep-seated anger, and she loosened her vise grip, letting air flood back into Em Myers's lungs.

Myers took a gasping breath as she dropped to her knees and began violently coughing as her lungs spasmed. Grey continued to point the gun at her.

"Take off the ARs," he said. "Do it now!" He touched the barrel of the gun briefly to her head.

Em had both of her hands around her own neck, eerily mirroring Aless's own hands seconds before, but instead of trying to take life she was trying to restore life. The bruises would be deep and dark for several weeks afterward. As soon as the cold steel touched the flesh of her temple, Em shivered and then slowly moved a hand up, removing the glasses and then throwing them to the ground. Grey didn't hesitate at all. He put the heel of his shoe through the hard plastic and electronic components that had augmented Em's reality for so long.

"Cell phone and any other electronics that you use, get 'em out NOW!" he demanded. "Hurry up!"

She reached slowly into her pants pocket, throwing down an expensive 5G touch screen with voice activation and 3-D virtual keyboard. Again, Grey's heel put an end to the artificial life embedded in the device.

"That's all I have," she said in a gravelly, damaged voice.

"Shut up! Turn around and face the wall. Don't talk or I'll be forced to shoot you," Grey said, hoping that he wouldn't have to shoot the agent. Em stayed on her knees and turned to face the wall, then leaned her head up against it.

"Aless, are you OK?" Grey asked when he saw the bloodstains on her clothes. There was a lot of blood running down her right arm and one large burgundy spot blotting out the CCU Fighting Chanticleer centered on Grey's borrowed sweatshirt.

Aless looked down. "Oh my God," she said, turning around and putting her back to him. "Can you tell if they went all the way through?" The surge of adrenaline had dulled the pain of the gunshot wounds.

He kept the gun leveled on Agent Em Myers and took a few steps over to check for exit wounds. There were two holes on the backside of the right sleeve, so that meant that two shots had gone through clean and not gotten hung up on anything internally. Grey began to feel panic when he didn't immediately see the critical chest wound's exit hole. He glanced at Em, who was still leaning against the wall, rubbing her throat, then back to the sweatshirt, using his free hand to pull the baggy fabric taut. Grey sighed with relief as he saw the third hole unroll itself from the fabric.

"All three shots were clean," he said gratefully. Aless slid her hand under the sweater and her own shirt, feeling for any sort of wound. Her skin felt smooth underneath the thick, sticky blood. She sighed as well, reflexively wiping the blood from her hands onto her sweatshirt.

He pointed toward the entrance to the work area, signaling to her that it was time to go. Then he gingerly bent and grabbed his key card off the floor where it had fallen in his struggle with Em Myers, headed to the door, and swiped it. The door opened with a green indicator. The two, now armed and dangerous, disappeared into the work zone, leaving Em Myers leaning against the wall, trying desperately to swallow with her swollen throat.

◆ ◆ ◆

Em Myers was getting to her feet when Agent Mark Richards came pushing his way into the little side corridor where the showdown had taken place only moments earlier. He quickly scanned the area, noticing bloodstains, bullet holes, and the crushed electronics.

"Em," he began, but she interrupted.

"What the hell," her scratchy voice asked. "I video called you even before they saw me; what took you so long?"

"These damned people." Richards gestured to the large group of people still filing out of the museum. "I had to fight my way through. I heard and saw the beginnings of what happened through your AR," he explained, "but I hung up after I pinpointed your location."

"I shot her; apparently she can't die either. Add that to your damned file." She pointed to the work-zone access door. "They went in there."

Richards ran down the short corridor to the door at the end. He produced the all-access key card that Dubinski had given him and swiped it, turning the light green.

Em called out the best she could, "Be careful! They took my gun."

Richards reached inside of his black suit jacket and produced his own agency-issued firearm, checked the clip and safety, then disappeared into the lighted hallway beyond the doorway.

• • •

Aless and Grey ran down the hallway, passing many doors that led to office spaces and the archives of the Franklin Institute. The two of them ran, turning seemingly random rights and lefts. Grey dragged Aless along without telling her where they were going. He held the gun in one hand and Aless's hand in the other. They stopped only when there were intersections that someone could hide behind. Grey would check for clearance, and then the couple would run on. The halls were completely empty, due to the evacuation that had occurred; Grey was heading toward the Karabots Pavilion.

As they approached the four-way intersection that led to the door of the Karabots Pavilion, Grey stopped, embraced Aless, and said, "Are you OK?"

She stared at him for a second before answering. A million different answers came to her lips but stopped short of falling out. She wanted to scream, to tell him that nothing is ever OK, not for her. She wanted him to know that this was only a small taste of the things that she had endured in her long life. She wanted to tell him she was tired—exhausted, really. She wanted him to know that she was alone; even though she was with him now, she could never stay with him. She wanted to tell him that there was nothing else for her here in this ridiculous world.

"I'm fine" was what actually came out of her mouth. "Let's go."

He smiled at her, held up the gun, and leaned slowly around the corner, making sure it was clear. He could see that the short hallway across from their current position was an emergency exit, which he knew led into a small back alleyway between sections of the building. He rounded the corner with the gun pointed out in front of him into another short hallway that led into the employee entrance of the educational center in the Karabots Pavilion. Both perpendicular halls were clear. Grey had just relaxed the gun and turned to tell Aless that everything was OK when the Sheetrock exploded near his head, dropping him to the floor and reigniting the pain in his rib cage.

"Aless," he breathlessly yelled, but she had already hit the ground and shuffled into the short hall where the exit door was located.

"SARTORI," Richards roared as he came quickly down the hallway, "that was a warning shot! There is nowhere to go! Give up and live!"

Grey slid his shaking hand around the corner and fired a blind shot down the main hall. Richards saw the gun and sidestepped into a small crevice that held the emergency extinguisher and fire hose, even though the shot was wild. Richards was too old and too close to take a stray bullet.

"Chapman, the game is over; throw out the weapon now and you can still walk away from this," Richards bellowed.

Grey looked at Aless, who was sitting with her back against the emergency exit with her eyes squeezed closed.

"What do you want her for? Government experimentation, just like the Germans did," Grey shouted back.

"She's wanted for murder," Richards said from his crevice, "of a federal agent and an unidentified hostage. But you already know that, don't you? Alessandra, don't pretend like you don't remember the farm in Friendship, where you blew up the man in the wheelchair and my uncle in cold blood!"

Across the intersection, Aless opened her eyes and stood; she took two steps into the open area of the main hallway. Grey watched, horrified.

Aless screamed, "I HAVE NEVER KILLED ANYONE! NEVER, EVER!"

Mark Richards heard Aless and clearly recognized that she was no longer under cover. He raised his firearm and spun into the hallway. Grey leapt across the intersection firing wildly, tackling Aless as he did so. She was still screaming as he pushed her through the emergency exit, spilling them both to the wet ground in the narrow back alley. Grey jumped to his feet as quickly as his broken ribs would let him and pushed the door closed as fast as he could. Surprisingly, the alley was empty. He frantically searched for some way to block the door from opening. His eyes widened when he saw a large Dumpster on wheels not far from the door. He ran over and heaved it with all his might. It didn't move.

"Do you know why I stayed with you, Grey?" Aless asked distantly.

"What? What are you talking about?" He was still trying to push the Dumpster. He grimaced in pain. "Help me out here."

She ignored him. "I stayed with you because you and I were alike. We both had very little going for us, and I found that endearing."

He rocked the Dumpster back and forth, breaking gravity's hold, and started rolling it in front of the door.

"Now, you have a life, and I am ruining it; you've already given yourself up to me once. Don't do it again." Somehow she seemed more distant, calm, even.

Grey stepped hard on the locking wheels, firmly planting the Dumpster in front of the emergency exit door.

• • •

Inside, Richards had dropped to the ground, covering himself before he could get off a shot as Chapman flailed across the hall firing Em Myers's gun wildly. Richards rolled and crawled back to his crevice as quickly as he could, not quite placing the buzzing sound of the emergency exit opening until it had stopped as the door closed. He waited. There was no sound.

• • •

"Come on," Grey said to Aless. "We can get to my car if we run."

He turned and saw that she had the gun in her hand. Grey surmised he must have dropped it when they'd fallen into the alleyway.

"I can't run anymore." She was calm but crying. "I just can't."

"What?"

"I read your journal entries; you said my brain can't regenerate. Let's test it out."

"Aless . . ."

"Separate my brain from my body, Grey."

She placed the gun just above her larynx.

"NO! WAIT!"

In an instant the top of her head opened up, spouting out blood and gore. Her body fell limp and lifeless onto the ground. The gun, still smoking, clanged on the pockmarked pavement. Aless landed on her back, facing the clouds. The last images that her severed mind registered were the colors in the sky. She pieced together one last thought: *I have never seen a rainbow like that.*

What she saw was almost as unique as Aless herself—a fire rainbow.

Grey heard pounding on the exit door that led to the alley. He fell to his knees, not hearing his own cries of agony.

"ALESS, NO, GOD, NO!" he cried.

He crawled to her body, clutched her exploded head in his hands, and wept, his tears mixing with the light rain falling over Philadelphia.

Separate my brain from my body, Grey.

Grey slowly reached up and ran his hand through her wet sandy-blonde hair, feeling the gore tangled in. He found the opening in the top of her head where the bullet ripped its way out.

"I can't, I can't," he sobbed as he fished his fingers into the three-inch opening in her skull.

Grey Chapman felt his mind slipping into oblivion, but he would give Aless her final wish, even if it drove him completely mad. He gripped a spongy, warm piece of the brain, a brain that he had fallen in love with, and pulled. His stomach twisted and convulsed under the emotional strain his body had to endure. The piece of brain tissue came free with a wet rip. Grey was sobbing uncontrollably and saw everything double in his moistened vision. He dropped the chunk onto the ground and reached his fingers in again to see if he could get more, and felt relief when he found that he could not reach anything else. He leaned down and kissed her cooling lips, eyes, and forehead, leaving a trail of tears in place of his departing lips.

Grey gently placed her head on the ground, then stood up beside the body that had once been Alessandra Sartori of Italy. He reached into his pocket and produced a cheap plastic lighter. *They won't get you,* he thought. He shielded his lighter from the rain, bent down, and held it to the small chunk of brain he'd removed from Aless's head. It didn't blaze, but it did smolder, destroying that section of Aless forever. After that, he tried to light her body, but gave up after the first two attempts were unsuccessful.

Grey stepped on the smoking chunk of brain, squashing it under his shoe. He then lay beside Aless in the growing puddle of water, wrapped his arms around her cooling body, and waited for Mark Richards to come.

◆ ◆ ◆

"And then she shot herself," Grey said. He sat in an interrogation room very similar to the one he'd found himself in a long time ago. It was empty save for a small table, a digital recorder, Agent Em Myers, and Agent Mark Richards.

Richards nodded, looking down at his tablet in his left hand.

"Check the gun. I know it's encoded; you can see that she was the last to fire it. I didn't kill her; I loved her."

Agent Richards tapped the tablet and turned it around so Grey could see it. The image shown on the screen was from a security camera at the Franklin Institute. The time stamp showed it was from three days prior; it showed Aless, still alive, standing with Grey. He had her in a half embrace and was looking longingly into her eyes, lost in their faded blue-green depths. He touched the screen, setting a security protocol into motion that suddenly shut the machine down, leaving Grey looking into blackness. He collapsed into in own his hands and began to sob in grief.

"Em, arrange a ride back to Philly and get him out of here," Richards said, then got up and walked out of the interrogation room.

After the door closed, Em sat at the table, wringing her hands nervously as Grey wept. She swallowed hard, feeling the pain deep in her throat and the dryness of her mouth.

"Mr. Chapman, I wanted to say something," she began. Grey lifted his wet, reddened face and looked across at Agent Myers, seeing the dark handprints around her neck left by Aless during their struggle—Aless, who was now nothing more than a ghost. She saw him looking and felt embarrassed.

"I"—she hesitated, trying to continue—"I wanted to say thank you for stopping her from killing me. I'm sorry about your injuries." She wiped a solitary tear from one eye, rose, and left the room with Grey still crying.

Em walked down the hall toward the office area, talking to a cab company on her brand-new pair of AR glasses. She walked across the room to the adjoining desk that held the nameplates of Emily Myers and Markus Richards. Mark was bent over, rummaging through one of the lower drawers of his desk; Em took a seat at hers, ended her call, and began to do a final review of the report of the Franklin Institute fiasco.

"Spary wants us to get this to him today if we can. I've been doing some hard thinking about who's tampering with the case file over at the records department. I don't yet have any proof, but I think there is someone blocking you from the inside. Think about it; you wouldn't try to sync because you think you're the only one adding to the file. I messed up the plan when I came on board. What are you doing down there?"

Richards sat up and lifted a box up onto the desk.

"What's up, Richards?" Em said, noticing the box.

"I talked to Spary after I left the interrogation room," he began slowly. "Em, I'm finished. I'm retiring as of right now. There is nothing else for me here."

"What about the file?"

"What *about* the file? So, there's a chance someone else is puppet-mastering, so what? Alessandra is dead. There's nothing else I care about."

"There's me." She was slightly hurt.

He sighed and smiled. "I'm old, kid. I have finally gotten some resolution from the case that has haunted me my whole life. I'm ready to let go." His smile faltered and brow furrowed. "This job has ruined me. I'm tired, exhausted."

"I'm going to miss you." Em stood, rushed over to Richards, and fell into his old, strong arms. Richards reluctantly put his arms around her.

"I'm going to miss you too, Emily," he said. "But I'm not dying, we can still Skype." He smiled.

• • •

The thunder tore through the wet air of the bleak night. Grey stood, again, at the mausoleum, staring at the cenotaph for Aless. He'd purchased it himself to honor his fallen love. Grey had fallen into a strange routine in the months and years following the incident at the Franklin Institute. He didn't sleep well, and when he did, he dreamed of Aless pushing the gun under her chin, and he awoke in a scream as he heard the roar of the weapon. He had been seeing a psychiatrist to deal with the stress of the whole ordeal. Against his better judgment (and his shrink's advice), he'd spent many evenings alone in the dark of his Levittown home lying in the bed where Aless had spent the month before she killed herself. And he always ended up here at the mausoleum touching her nameplate made of cold stone. The empty slot behind the marker was the empty spot in Grey Chapman's heart.

ALESSANDRA SARTORI

B. 1934–D. 2024

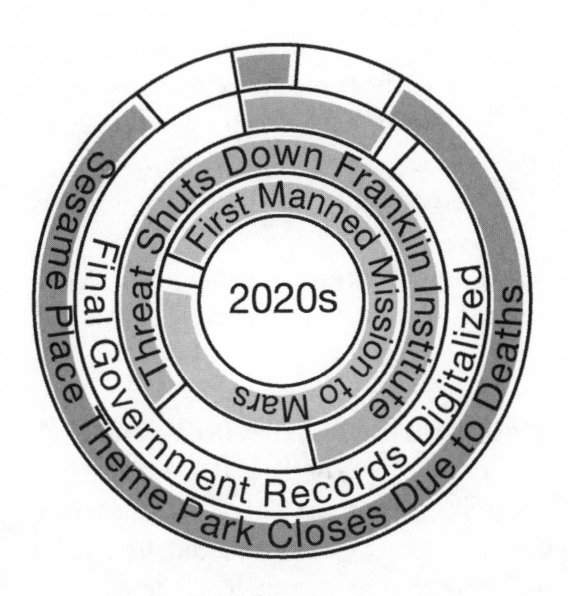

2:37 P.M.

CANADA, 2028

EPILOGUE

The remodeling of the parietal bones is basically flawless," the doctor commented to the nurse standing to his left. He was bent over the head of the patient. The skin was pealed back so he could see the changes to the skull.

"Nurse," he continued, "how are the vitals? Has our patient been stable since my last visit?"

"Yes, sir, there has been no change; only limited brain functions have returned, but neurogenesis seems to be taking place. As you know, the patient has been breathing unassisted for several years with light neural activity. An induced REM-like sleep state has continued since her arrival."

<*Flashes of light*>

<*Beeping*>

"Yes, I'm aware, nurse. How has harvesting been? Any progress with the Augmented Life-Extension Systems?" the doctor asked as he circled around the bed.

"Harvesting is going very well; we have recently cloned the DNA with marginal results; although, initial test subjects have not survived the rejection period. Not like—"

"Please, keep the gory stuff to yourself, Nurse," he interrupted.

"Sorry," she said.

"No worries." He flashed a crooked but endearing smile at the woman. "My imagination can run wild sometimes. Better to not give it any fuel."

<Aneeee feul>

She returned his smile, picked up the hypodermic needle, and stuck it into the permanent IV line, drawing some of the patient's blood.

"Have a seat, please, and roll up your left sleeve, sir," the nurse politely requested. The doctor did as she asked. She placed the syringe on the table beside the small chair and helped undress the bandage that was in the crook of the doctor's arm. The exposed skin showed the track marks and bruises of repeated entry.

"That looks bad, but I see no signs of infection. That's good," she said as she inspected his arm.

"Give it a minute," he said.

The nurse retrieved the syringe with the blood of the young woman, stuck it into one of the marks on the doctor's arm, and depressed the plunger until the barrel was empty. He inhaled sharply, sucking the air between his clenched teeth.

"Ah," he sighed. The marks along his arm began to fade away, and the wounds began to close. The nurse noticed that the gray hair around his temples regained its color and the lines in the man's face smoothed out a bit.

"Better?" she asked.

"I can't even begin to describe the feeling."

There was a knock on the door. A woman stuck her head in. "There is a video call for you, Dr. Miller."

"Eva"—he rolled down his sleeve as he walked to the young lady standing in the doorway—"how many times have I asked you to call me Felix?"

ACKNOWLEDGMENTS

This book would not have been possible without the support and encouragement of my wife, Kim, my daughter, Parker, my brother Bryan (Amanda, too), and my parents, Tim and Vicky. I love you all very much!

It takes an army of people to see a book through to completion. Without the talents of the following individuals, *Ageless*, may have not made it to your bookshelf: the amazing staff at Girl Friday Productions, including the skilled production editor, Devon Frederickson, the dexterous developmental editor, Lindsay Robinson, and the exhaustive efforts of copy editor Michelle Hope Anderson, all of whose time and effort in the drafting stages proved invaluable; the team of wonderful people at Inkshares Inc., including the amazing Avalon Radys, Jeremy Thomas, Matt Kaye, Thad Woodman, Larry Levitsky, and Adam Gomolin, who made this book into a reality beginning with the Sword & Laser Collection Contest all the way through publication; many thanks. Also, thanks to Marc Cohen, of MJC Designs, for the beautiful cover design and freelance artist Melissa Berg for the unique timeline. The book wouldn't be the same without your talents.

I would also like to recognize the wonderful people who helped with the foreign languages; mother and daughter Annette and Yana Tatgenhorst, whose German is impeccable. Your expertise made this fictional world a more believable place.

A special thanks goes to Jason (Pete) Frye for tipping me off to the great possibilities of the Sword & Laser Collection Contest on Inkshares.com, and for being my first true critic. You got the job, buddy!

Thanks to Jean-François Dubeau of *The Life Engineered,* G. Derek Adams of *Asteroid Made of Dragons,* Jim McDoniel of *An Unattractive Vampire,* Joseph Terzieva of *Lost Generation,* Nick Scott and Noa Gavin of *Practical Applications for Multiverse Theory* for sharing the first official Sword & Laser Collection Contest winners circle. I couldn't be in better company.

Finally, to all my family, friends, loved ones, colleagues, and students, without your support and encouragement none of this would have been possible, and I say thank you. I am forever grateful.

ABOUT THE AUTHOR

Photo © 2015 Kim Inman

Paul Inman has a passion for storytelling across many platforms, including all styles of music, short films, podcasts, and different genres of writing. As a graduate of Coastal Carolina University, he holds a BA in music performance and an MA in teaching.

His debut novel, *Ageless*, is one of the winning entries in the Sword & Laser Collection Contest from Inkshares. He currently teaches chorus at Myrtle Beach Middle School and lives in Myrtle Beach, South Carolina, with his amazing wife, Kim, and wonderful daughter, Parker.

Follow Paul Inman on:

www.paulinmansc.com

YOU ARE AGELESS

LIST OF PATRONS

Ageless was largely made possible by the following individuals' selfless patronage. These people were critical in getting the book funded and into production by helping *Ageless* become a winner of the Sword & Laser Collection Contest. I am indebted to you all.

Aaron Holt
Al Benninghoff
Alana Bedenbaugh
Alexis Newberry
Amanda Bobak
Amanda Watson Price
Anarra Whitcher
André Martins
Angela Stevens Huggins
Ann Mclemore
Anna Grace Benton
Anthony Constantino
Arielis Martienez
Bethany Peterson
Bettie Olivieri
Betty A Holt Turner
Bob Price
Brian Tisdale
Bruce Crocker
Cale Pritchett
Carissa Page
Casey Cook-Fair
Connie Johnson
David Graham
Deborah Bulei
Destiny Franklin

Elisa Diaz
Emily Gray
Frank Bulei
Felipe Martins
Galaxy Lawing
Gizel Barrios
Jackilyn M Stavrakis
Jaime Vanderlip
James Markey
Janae Gillispie
Jared Smith
Jen Senn
Jerrod Paige
Joey Bellamy
John Gooding
John Price
Joseph Foster
Kaylee Petty
Kiera Cass
Kim Inman
Kimberly M Price
Kristin Bates
Krystal Karlish
Louise Price
Madison White
Makayla Zilonka
Matthew McCarty
Matt Sellers
Patrick Ryerson
Robbie Taylor
Ryan Carter
Samone Simmons
Scott Baun
Sebastian Porter
Serinity Wood
Sierra Walls
Tim Inman
Trever Blum
Tyler Gamba
Valeria Taube
Vicky Inman
Wendy Dossey

INKSHARES

Inkshares is a crowdfunded book publisher. We democratize publishing by having readers select the books we publish—we edit, design, print, distribute, and market any book that meets a preorder threshold.

Interested in making a book idea come to life? Visit Inkshares.com to find new book projects or to start your own.